LORD
OF THE
ROYAL UMBRELLA

Reader Reviews

- 300 Brave Men, *based on the early life of the iconic figure of Chhatrapati Shivaji of Maharashtra, is most engaging. Written in lucid language, it recreates the sequence of events in an easy conversational style that compels the reader to become part of the narrative. It maintains a good balance between historical fact and fiction. A book in English on this subject was long overdue. However, the author's idolation of Shivaji is very evident and the narrative eulogizes the icon. A more critical evaluation would have made the novel more contemporary. Notwithstanding this, the book makes very interesting reading and is certainly un-put-downable.* Dr Prof. Sonali Pednekar, Head, Department of History, V G Vaze College Mumbai

- 300 Brave Men *takes you back into 17th century India. This truly captivating story, written in a simple yet appealing manner which makes it hard to imagine it is the work of a debutant author. This book should be read by everyone so more people know Shivaji's story. I am waiting for volume II to be released soon.* Rohit Raut, Goodreads

- 300 Brave Men starts *slowly and grows upon you. The palaces, the forts, the large cannons, the pomp and splendour, all come alive as one is transported to that era. The undercurrent of tension between Shahaji and Jijabai regarding Shivaji's future and their dream of Swarajya is beautifully captured. Midway through, the book gains speed and becomes un-put-downable. Even when you know what is going to happen, every page makes you want to read on in anticipation.* Meghdoot Karnik, Author, Blogger and Corporate Executive

- 300 Brave Men *is nail-biting to say the least and succeeds in instilling a great sense of pride in this Maratha king. It makes you feel you are watching the action unfold live! For me, the best parts of the book were Shivaji's victory over Afzal Khan, and the battle of Gajapur Pass (for which the book is named). One of the best books I've read this year.* Neeti, Goodreads

- *Part of the Shivaji trilogy,* 300 Brave Men *is an extraordinary novel. The overall message is what makes it a worthy read even if its delivery is pedantic at times. The historical context it provides is tremendous.* Bhuvaneswari Padmanabhan, Goodreads

- *An exceptionally well written and captivating recount of Maratha history. Such a rush reading this book! Gautam's captivating and action-packed writing helped me visualize the details of Shivaji's life and the events of Maratha history. The details of the hold-off by the 300 is breathtaking and heart wrenching at the same time. I am dying to read the next one!* Chetna, Goodreads

- *The author gave a Time machine, though we couldn't participate, we could feel as if a live match and the places mentioned, can be googled to get a glimpse.* Arun Kumar, Goodreads

- *'Another book on Chhatrapati Shivaji?' I thought when I saw the Cover on Kindle. A great admirer of the Greatest King of India, I have read the story of his life by many an author, including translations from Marathi masterpieces. But I was mesmerised by* 300 Brave Men. *As Mr Pradhan wove his masterly tapestry, scene after scene kept playing in my mind's eye. Now I am like a man thirsting for more water on a hot day, having drunk the first glass in a great hurry, waiting for the next volume, and the next.* G Raghavan, Amazon

- *Great confluence of research and imagination. A highly engrossing novel which is difficult to put down.* Ajay Tendolkar, Amazon

- *Despite the many historical books I have read, I have a special mention for Sri Gautama Pradhan. The narrative is so real and authentic that it is difficult to see where history meets imagination, until described in his own words at the end. The language and style are flawless and the flow of events gripping and dramatic. I appeal to Sri Pradhan to complete life history on Shivaji.* S. Gopalakrishnan, Amazon

LORD OF THE ROYAL UMBRELLA

Epic Story of Shivaji Maharaj,
India's Greatest Warrior-King,
And Birth of the Maratha Empire

Book II: 1661—1674

Gautam Pradhan

Platinum Press
Premium Fiction

ISBN 978-93-88942-76-8

Maps & Sketches: Recreated by Gautam Pradhan
Layout: Hitanshi Shah
Printing: Nutech Print Services - India

Published in India 2020 by
PLATINUM PRESS
An imprint of LEADSTART PUBLISHING PVT LTD
Office 119-123, Building J2, Shram Seva Premises
Wadala Truck Terminus, Wadala (East),
Mumbai 400 022, Maharashtra, INDIA
T + 91 96 99933000 **E** info@leadstartcorp.com
W www.leadstartcorp.com

DISCLAIMER: Though based on real events and individuals, this is a work of fiction and should not be taken as an accurate historical account. The author does not claim that all incidents and descriptions in the book are historically exact or documented; they should not be used as references by scholars and students. Some incidents have been taken from traditional folklore and cannot be proven. Clarifications appear in Author's Notes at the end of the book. All maps have been hand-drawn by the author from available sources with the sole objective of aiding the reader's understanding of the places described. They are not to scale nor are claims made as to the accuracy of boundaries, territories, provinces and places depicted; they should not be used as reference material for scholarly purposes. At no time has the author intended to hurt the religious sentiments of individuals or groups. References to religion or caste have been made solely in the context of 17th century Indian society, and the characters involved. The opinions expressed in this book do not purport to reflect the views of the Publisher.

In memory of the greatest warrior-king
this country has ever produced;
a true inspiration for every Indian;
a thinker far ahead of his times:
Chhatrapati Shivaji Raje Bhosale.

About the Author

GAUTAM PRADHAN is a Radiologist by profession. Educated in Mumbai, he has been in private medical practice for nearly two decades. He lives in Thane, Maharashtra, with his wife Dipali, son Aditya and daughter Aryaa.

Passionate about history, Gautam reads voraciously on the subject and enjoys visiting places of historical interest. Possessed of an imaginitive mind, he felt caged within the restrictive confines of the medical profession and took to writing as a hobby. It seemed a natural choice to base his first book on historical events and the life and times of a man he has always revered. He devoted eight years to the research and writing of this book, receiving valuable inputs through extensive discussions with eminent historians. The project on Shivaji's life, in three dramatized volumes, has been an emotional but intensely fulfilling journey. *300 Brave Men* (Book I), was published in 2017, to critical acclaim. His other interests include wildlife photography, music and movies.

He can be reached at: gautammpradhan@rediffmail.com

Contents

Preface ... 11

Cast of Primary Characters ... 14

Prologue ... 21

Chapter 1 Muzzle of a Gun ... 24

Chapter 2 War of Attrition ... 59

Chapter 3 Shivaji the Sorcerer ... 75

Chapter 4 Payback ... 111

Chapter 5 Old Foe Punished ... 141

Chapter 6 Defeat and Humiliation ... 158

Chapter 7 A Veteran Humbled ... 202

Chapter 8 A Tiger Roars in Agra ... 216

Chapter 9 The Eagle has Flown ... 248

Chapter 10 Lifelong Regret ... 274

Chapter 11 Interlude ... 288

Chapter 12 Reconquest ... 295

Chapter 13 War on all Fronts ... 332

Chapter 14 Lord of the Royal Umbrella ... 346

Epilogue ... 360

Author's Note ... 363

Glossary ... 379

Bibliography ... 390

Acknowledgements ... 393

निश्चयाचा महामेरू । बहुत जनांस आधारू ।

अखंड स्थितीचा निर्धारू। श्रीमंत योगी ।।

The epitome of determination, a protector of his people,
firmly resolute in intent...

Wealthy, yet detached from his opulence; an ascetic...

या भूमंडळाचे ठायीं । धर्म रक्षी ऐसा नाहीं ।

महाराष्ट्रधर्म राहिला कांहीं । तुम्हां करितां ।।

Nowhere on this earth was there ever, a greater protector
of his people, culture and righteousness...

It is because of you, that the culture of Maharashtra has survived...

~ SAMARTH RAMDAS SWAMI

Preface

It gives me great pleasure to present the second in this series of books on the life of *Chhatrapati* Shivaji. In the past months, I have received a lot of feedback on the first book, from friends, family, and readers unknown to me. Their comments have spurred me on to complete this second book in record time. The idea of presenting the story of this remarkable man to English readers seems to have been a success. My initial aim behind the books has been fulfilled, for non-Marathi speaking Indians, Maharashtrians of my generation, and more importantly, the younger generations, who have seldom read about the *Chhatrapati* in Marathi, seem to have unanimously welcomed the first book of the trilogy, *300 Brave Men*.

In this volume, I continue to narrate *Chhatrapati* Shivaji's story, beginning in the year 1661, and carrying it through to his coronation in 1674. These fourteen years of his life saw almost unceasing action for the Marathas, on all fronts. We find Shivaji and his troops, no longer a band of mavericks, having swelled into a very real and disciplined army, battling enemies on all sides of their tiny fiefdom called *Swarajya*. They clash with the Adilshah in the South, with the Abyssinians and Europeans along the coast, and with the mighty Mughal Aurangzeb in the North. Incredibly, they hold out against all three, till the end.

These years are full of some of the famous Shivaji stories traditionally told to Indians, including his daring night raid on Shaista Khan, and his almost unbelievable escape from Agra. While I have narrated these incidents in great detail, I have also tried to bring forth some lesser known incidents and battles from this period. I have also tried to portray the politics around the main events. To know the real person that Shivaji was, one needs to understand the immense 'behind-the-scenes' action as well, and it has been my constant endeavor in these books to describe in detail Shivaji's immaculate planning of each expedition, as well as his ingenious political moves.

During this period, Shivaji also tasted his first major reverse, at the hands of the Rajput Jai Singh, followed by the humiliation of having to bow before Aurangzeb. Again, we would fail to understand the man if we did not make an attempt to feel the pain he experienced in this period. Added to his deep mortification, was the grief of seeing the devastation of his lands and people. Historians often fail to go beyond the mere 'signing of the Purandar treaty' and 'the fiasco of his Agra visit'. They get so lost in the clauses of the treaty and what actually transpired in Aurangzeb's court, that they conveniently forget the central character of Shivaji himself, a real man with real emotions. But my book, being literature and not historical biography, I have had the unique opportunity to explore and at least try to understand what Shivaji the person went through during this very difficult period. Undoubtedly, my portrayal of events and emotions come from my own mind, but they attempt to give the reader a glimpse into what *could have been* Shivaji's own thoughts.

With the expansion of Shivaji's army and ministry, as well as the scope of action, the number of people around him multiplied. But, to keep things simple, I have stuck to portraying only a chosen few of his men and family members. I have tried to limit my characters to those who played an important role in these fourteen years. Shivaji had a large family and it would be difficult and confusing to include everyone in the story. Not to mention that very little is known about his family beyond his sons Sambhaji and Rajaram. He had eight wives and six daughters, about whom we know precious little, and hence I have chosen to limit the depiction of Shivaji's family and focus on the man himself.

The book culminates in the grand event of Shivaji's coronation. Readers should try and understand that this was not merely another event in 17th century India, but an occurrence with far reaching consequences on Indian history as a whole. It was the beginning of nationalistic thought. It was the first instance in centuries that the people of this ancient land had declared with one voice that *they no longer wanted foreigners to rule them*. For the first time, they lifted their heads and said with pride, *we want our own ruler!*

Too often has Shivaji and his remarkable rebellion against the Mughals in particular, been relegted to a regional event in Indian history. Foreign historians are largely to blame for this depiction. These Western scholars, who are generally regarded as neutral observers, have, to my mind, failed to see beyond the 'great Mughals' in India's illustrious past. For them, only the Mughal Emperors were 'great', while people like King Porus, Chhatrapati Shivaji, Maharana Pratap Singh, Prithviraj Chauhan and Rani Laxmi, were mere 'rebels'. I reject such portrayals, where foreign, barbaric invaders of an ancient land are portrayed as the heroes, and the indigenious bravehearts who tried to stop them, as mere sideshows.

Shivaji's coronation was thus an event of tremendous significance, not only in the context of our history, but more importantly, for us as a people. It was the beginning of our freedom struggle, which culminated in our independence two hundred and seventy-three years later.

Once again, as in the Book I, I would request my readers not to take my narrative as a scholarly historical account, but rather as a drama based on history, for that is what it is meant to be. If I can make my readers experience the emotions of these eventful years of *Chhatrapati* Shivaji's life, my hard work would have been worthwhile.

Cast of Primary Characters

Shivaji's Family

Shivaji Bhosale/ Shivaji Raje/ Raje/ Seevaji/ Seeva: Founder of the Maratha Empire. Born 19 February 1630; Died 3 April 1680. Formally crowned himself King on 6 June 1674, assuming the title *Chhatrapati* or 'Lord of the Royal Umbrella'.

Jijabai: Shivaji's mother and first wife of Shivaji's father, Shahaji Bhosale; daughter of Lakhuji Jadhavrao of Sindkhed, a nobleman in the Nizamshah's service.

Soyara (Soyarabai): Shivaji's second wife (according to most sources), hailed from the Mohite family and became Shivaji's chief consort following the death of his first wife, Saee.

Sambhaji Bhosale (Shambhuji, Shambhu): Shivaji's eldest son, born of Saeebai, on 14 May 1657.

Note: Shivaji had several children, but just two sons. Of Saibai: Sambhaji [son], Sakhubai, Ranubai, Ambikabai [daughters]; of Soyarabai, Rajaram [son], Deepabai [daughter]; of Sagunabai: Rajkunvarbai [daughter]; of Sakwarbai: Kamlabai [daughter].

Putalabai, Sakvarbai, Sagunabai, Kashibai, Lakshmibai & Gunwantabai: Shivaji's other wives.

Note: In all, Shivaji had eight wives. Polygamy was an accepted custom of the time, especially among royal families. It is also noteworthy that Shivaji did not have unwedded consorts or concubines, a then widespread practice.

Shivaji's Men (The Marathas)

Moro Trimal Pingale (Moro Punt): Shivaji's *Peshwa* or Prime Minister.

TRYAMBAK PUNT: Shivaji's *Dabir* or Minister for External Affairs.

RAGHUNATH PUNT: Shivaji's diplomat.

NILO PUNT SONDEO: Shivaji's *Muzumdar* or Finance Minister.

ANAJI PUNT DATTO: Shivaji's *Surnis* or Minister for Land Revenue

NIRAJI RAOJI (NIRAJI PUNT): Shivaji's diplomat, later appointed as his *Nyayadheesh* or Chief Justice.

RAMCHANDRA PUNT: Shivaji's *Muzumdar* (later *Amatya*).

SONO VISHWANATH DABIR (SONO PUNT): Shivaji's (retired) *Dabir* or External Affairs Minister; father of Tryambak *Punt*.

NETOJI PALKAR: Shivaji's most celebrated *Sirnaubat* or Commander-in-Chief of his armed forces.

KUDTOJI (PRATAPRAO) GUJAR: Shivaji's Captain, appointed as *Sirnaubat* or Commander-in-Chief of his armed forces after the sacking of Netoji Palkar.

HANSAJI (HAMBIRRAO) MOHITE: Shivaji's Captain, appointed as *Sirnaubat* or Commander-in-Chief of his armed forces upon the death of *Prataprao* Gujar.

TANHAJI MALUSARE, SURYAJI MALUSARE, SURYAJI KAKADE & YESAJI KANK: Shivaji's Captains and earliest adherents; faithful followers to the end. Tanhaji is remembered for his attack on Fort Kondhana in 1670, in which he perished.

BABAJI DESHPANDE, CHIMNAJI DESHPANDE: Shivaji's earliest and faithful adherents, who accompanied him on his raid on Lal Mahal. They were the sons of Bapuji Mudgal Deshpande, a former employee at Lal Mahal.

MURARBAJI DESHPANDE: Shivaji's Captain, who joined him after the Jawli campaign of 1656, and served as Commander of Fort Purandar. Famous for his suicidal attack on Diler Khan's Pathans during the Mughal-Maratha War of 1665.

FIRANGOJI NARSALA: Commander of Fort Chakan, he is famous for his stoic defence of the fort against Shaista Khan for nearly three months.

GODAJI JAGTAP, SAMBHAJI KAVJI KONDHALKAR, CHANDJI JEDHE, HIROJI FARZAND, KOYAJI BANDAL, RAGHO MITRA, KONDAJI FARZAND, HAIBATRAO SILIMBKAR & PILAJIRAO: Shivaji's trusted Captains.

JIVA MAHALA SAKPAL: One of Shivaji's most trusted men; presumably one of his bodyguards.

KANHOJI JEDHE: *Deshmukh* of Bhor, a Maval district on the eastern face of the Sahyadris; a faithful adherent till his death. All his sons were in Shivaji's employ.

BAJI (SARJERAO) JEDHE: Kanhoji Jedhe's son and Shivaji's trusted Captain.

BAHIRJI NAIK: Shivaji's most celebrated spy and Chief of Intelligence; was involved in the intricate planning of several of Shivaji's famous battles and missions.

RAMAJI PANGERA: Commander of Kaner Fort; remembered for his suicidal attack on Diler Khan's forces in 1671.

DARYA SARANG, MAYNAK BHANDARI: Naval officers.

BALAJI AVJI CHITRE: Shivaji's *Chitins,* Secretary for Correspondence.

MADARI MEHTAR: Shivaji's personal attendant during the Agra visit; designated *Takhta Firosh* before his coronation.

THE MUGHALS

AURANGZEB: Sixth Mughal Emperor of Hindustan, son of Shah Jahan and Mumtaz Mahal.

PRINCE MUAZZAM: Aurangzeb's son.

JAHANARA BEGUM & ROSHANARA BEGUM: Aurangzeb's sisters.

SHAISTA KHAN: A pre-eminent noble at the Mughal court and Aurangzeb's uncle.

JAFAR KHAN: Aurangzeb's *Wazir.*

MOHAMMED AMIN: The *Mir Bakshi* of the Mughal Empire.

DILER KHAN: Mughal *Mansabdar* and military Captain; presumably one of Aurangzeb's trusted men.

JANI BEG: Mughal officer. *Mir Bakshi* of Jai Singh's army

KARTALAB KHAN: Mughal Captain in Shaista Khan's army, famous for his collosal defeat at Shivaji's hands at the Battle of Umbarkhind.

SHAMSHUDDIN KHAN, ALAYAR BUKHARI, MAHABAT KHAN, HABSH KHAN, UZBEK KHAN, NAMDAR KHAN, KAMDAR KHAN, BULAKHI KHAN, SAR-AFRAZ KHAN & QUTUBUDDIN KHAN: Mughal Captains.

Ikhlas Khan: Mughal Commander-in-Charge of the siege of Fort Salher; was defeated by the Marathas in the famous battle of Salher, in 1672.

Inayat Khan: Mughal Governor of Surat.

Fulad Khan: *Kotwal* of Agra.

Rad-Andaz Khan: Commander of Agra Fort.

Bahadur Khan: *Subadar* of Gujarat.

Mukhlis Khan: Low ranking Mughal *Mansabdar*. Received Shivaji in Agra, along with Ram Singh.

Gazi Beg: A Mughal officer who accompanied Shivaji on his journey to Agra.

Akil Khan: Mughal court attendant.

Mir Abdul Mabud: Shaista Khan's Artillery Commander.

Abul Fath: Shaista Khan's son.

The Rajputs

Mirza Raja Jai Singh: King of Amer, a principality in Rajputana, and high ranking Mughal *Mansabdar*.

Kirat Singh & Ram Singh: Jai Singh's sons.

Jaswant Singh: King of Jodhpur, a principality in Rajputana, and high ranking Mughal *Mansabdar*.

Udairaj Munshi: Jai Singh's secretary.

Ugrasen Kachchwah & Tej Singh: Jai Singh's office bearers.

Girdhar Lal Munshi: Ram Singh's secretary.

Ballu Sah & Mah Singh Shekawat: Ram Singh's men.

Rao Bhao Singh, Amar Singh & Mitrasen: Rajput Mughal Captains.

Udaybhan Rathore: Rajput Mughal Commander of Fort Kondhana; famous for his battle against Tanhaji Malusare in 1670.

Marathas in Mughal Service

Rai Baghan (Savitribai Deshmukh): *Jagirdar* of Vasind, Usad, Malegaon and Mahur districts; an officer in Aurangzeb's service.

JADHAVRAO: Maratha Mughal Captain.

HOUSE OF BIJAPUR

ALI ADILSHAH: 8th Sultan of Bijapur. Some claim he was Muhammad Adilshah's son by a concubine/slave, others say he was merely adopted by *Badi Begum*.

BADI BEGUM/TAJ-UL-MUKHADIRRAT: Ali's mother.

SIKANDER: Ali Adilshah's son.

ABDUL MOHAMMED: Ali Adilshah's *Vizier*.

KHAWAS KHAN: Abyssinian noble at the Bijapur court; chief of the Deccani nobles faction.

BAHLOL KHAN: Bijapuri noble; chief of the Pathani nobles faction.

SHARZA KHAN: Abyssinian noble at the Bijapur court.

MARATHAS IN BIJAPUR SERVICE

BAJI GHORPADE: *Jagirdar* (hereditary chieftain) of Mudhol; sworn enemy of the Bhosales.

SURYARAO SURVE: *Jagirdar* of Shringarpur.

JASVANTRAO DALVI: *Jagirdar* of Palavni.

LAKHAM SAVANT: *Desai* (Chief) of Kudal

MISCELLANEOUS CHARACTERS

KHANDOJI KHOPADE: *Deshmukh* of Utravali, who defected from the Maratha camp to Afzal Khan's in 1659. Was severely punished by Shivaji for his treachery.

ADNYANDAS: A poet and composer of the famous ballad commemorating the Battle of Pratapgad.

PILAJIRAO SHIRKE: *Diwan* of Shringarpur's Suryarao Surve, who joined Shivaji after the fall of the fief; his daughter married Shivaji's son, Sambhaji.

GAGABHATT: The eminent, learned Brahman who officiated at Shivaji's coronation.

KASHI PUNT: Brother-in-law to Moro *Punt*, the *Peshwa*.

Sadashiv: Gardener at Lal Mahal.

Shah Abbas: Emperor of Persia.

Invented Characters

Raghav, Gondaji & Ganaji: Maratha soldiers.

Mahadev: Maratha spy.

Saoji: Tanhaji's rock climber.

Hussain: Aurangzeb's spy.

Mahadu: Khandoji Khopade's attendant.

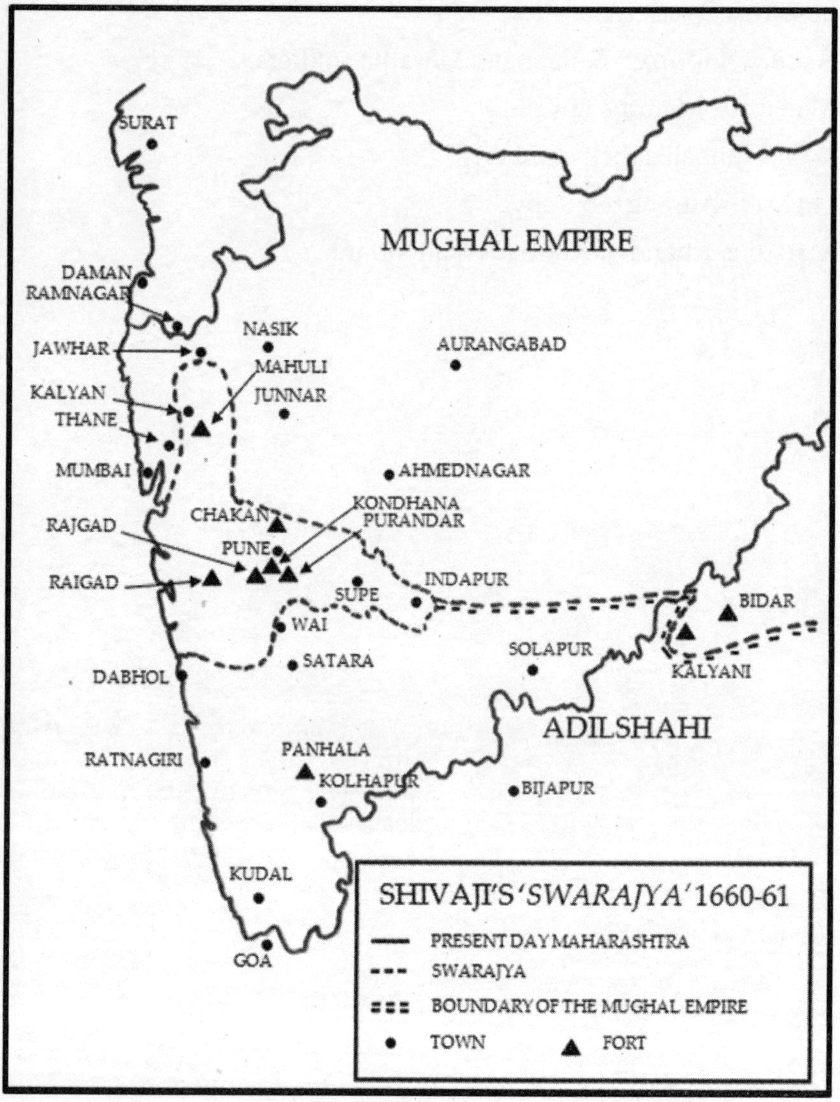
SURAT
MUGHAL EMPIRE
DAMAN
RAMNAGAR
NASIK
AURANGABAD
JAWHAR
MAHULI
KALYAN
JUNNAR
THANE
MUMBAI
AHMEDNAGAR
KONDHANA
CHAKAN
PURANDAR
RAJGAD
PUNE
RAIGAD
INDAPUR
SUPE
BIDAR
WAI
SOLAPUR
SATARA
KALYANI
DABHOL
ADILSHAHI
RATNAGIRI
PANHALA
KOLHAPUR
BIJAPUR
KUDAL
GOA
SHIVAJI'S 'SWARAJYA' 1660-61
PRESENT DAY MAHARASHTRA
SWARAJYA
BOUNDARY OF THE MUGHAL EMPIRE
TOWN
FORT

Prologue

Maharashtra, Mid-17th Century

The Maratha homeland has experienced centuries of subjugation under foreign rule. Generations have suffered injustice and bigotry. The Marathi populace has long forgotten what freedom felt like, having resigned themselves to their fate and to their rulers.

At long last there rises a man who has a radically different mindset from those around him. He realises that his fate lies in inspiring and leading his people to rebel against foreign rule and free their homeland. The journey is long and perilious, yet he embarks upon it, followed by thousands who believe in him. He is Shivaji Bhosale, son of Shahaji Bhosale, a nobleman in the service of Sultan Adilshah of the Deccan.

Circa 1646

At the age of sixteen, Shivaji declares rebellion against the Adilshahi by usurping Torna Fort, inviting the Sultan's ire. The infuriated sovereign first arrests his father, and then sends an army against him. But, as fate would have it, the Adilshah underestimates Shivaji's military and political skills, and thus not only suffers an ignonimous defeat, but must release Shahaji from prison, under Mughal pressure. A lull ensues in which the Adilshahi government is loath to initiate further action and Shivaji is quiet as well.

Circa 1656-58

Ten years after initiating his struggle, Shivaji commits his first brazen act of defiance against the Adilshah by killing Chandrarao More, a powerful chieftain of Jawali, in the Maval district of the Sahyadri Hills, annexing More's entire fief to his own. Shivaji's gains from this campaign are tremendous, as besides the fief itself, he gains control over several forts, key routes and mountain passes. He is now periliously close to Adilshah's coastal territory in the Konkan. The Adilshahi administration is rudely jolted from slumber, but can do precious little against him as Sultan Muhammad Adilshah himself is terminally ill. The Sultan's demise later that year sees power pass into the hands of his widow, Badi Begum. No sooner has she placed her young son on the throne and stabilized her government, than the ambitious Mughal Prince Aurangzeb arrives at their doorstep with a large army, ready to swallow the Sultanate.

Shivaji takes full advantage of Bijapur's helplessness and usurps as much territory as he can, rising in stature and power. Aurangzeb's plan to annex the Adilshahi receives a setback however, as he receives news of Emperor Shah Jahan's illness and has to rush back to the Mughal capital to claim his throne. A bloody war of succession ensues between him and his brothers. Aurangzeb eliminates all challengers, imprisons his father and ascends the throne as the sixth Mughal Emperor, assuming the title *Alamgir*.

CIRCA 1659-60

Having received a reprieve in Aurangzeb's departure from the Deccan, Badi Begum turns her attention to Shivaji, and appoints her faithful noble, Afzal Khan, to lead the campaign against the Maratha rebel. The giant Khan, feared across the land, vows to bring back Shivaji dead or alive. In the wake of Afzal Khan's march into his *Swarajya* with a large army, Shivaji shifts base to Pratapgad, and invites the Khan to a personal meeting in the Jawali valley. Blinded by ego and overconfidence, Afzal Khan misreads Shivaji's tactics and demeanor and lands his army in the dense forests of the Koyna Valley. What ensues is the stuff of legend. Quite spectacularly, Shivaji manages to kill the massive Khan during their meeting and flees to the safety of the fort, while his men attack the Khan's army from all sides, annihilating it. The Marathas then follow up their victory with a whirlwind invasion of the Adilshahi territory, swallowing large tracts of land and annexing forts.

The Adilshahi is shaken by this collosal defeat. The young Sultan Ali decides to sideline his mother and assume full control of the government. Hastily, he puts together a massive force and appoints the able Abyssinian officer, Jauhar, to head it. Jauhar follows Shivaji's movements, finally besieging him in Fort Panhala. The siege continues for four months, driving Shivaji to his wit's end. Finally, he makes a desperate escape from the fort on a stormy night, with six hundred chosen men, and his Captains, Baji Prabhu and Fulaji Prabhu, two brothers who vow to take their King to the safety of Fort Vishalgad. Their nocturnal adventure is discovered by Jauhar's spies, however, and Jauhar sends a force of three thousand in hot pursuit. The Bijapuris accost the Marathas in a mountain pass near Gajapur. Realising they can no longer outrun the enemy, Baji and Fulaji stay back at the pass and block the enemy's advance with three hundred men, while Shivaji makes good his escape. A bloody battle is fought for over twelve hours in the Gajapur Pass, in which Baji and Fulaji perish.

CIRCA 1660

Mughal Emperor Aurangzeb has sent his uncle, the renowned noble Shaista Khan, to the Deccan to subdue Shivaji. Shaista Khan marches almost unchallenged into the heart of Shivaji's fief – Pune, and stations himself in Shivaji's childhood home. The Maratha land and its people buckle under the impact of Mughal depredation.

Shaista Khan's first military mission is to capture Fort Chakan, to the north of his own position in Pune. He expects it to be a simple affair, but is surprised by the stoic resistance put up by the fort's small garrison. For well over two months, the small Maratha garrison resolutely fights Khan's large army. Faced with hunger and fatigue, they refuse to surrender. *Lord of the Royal Umbrella* begins with this battle.

1
MUZZLE OF A GUN

THE FORT OF CHAKAN, NORTH OF PUNE,
NIGHT OF 14 AUGUST 1660

It was an unusually dark and still night. The rain had finally let up that morning, so had the Mughals, in the sprawling enemy camp besieging the fort of Chakan, which stood in the plains, some ten *kos* north of Pune. Firangoji Narsala, the fort Commander, carefully scanned the enemy camp for any suspicious movements. There were none. For the past two months, he and his Maratha garrison of three hundred and fifty men, had held the vast Mughal army of over seventeen thousand, at bay. They had successfully beaten back several determined attempts by the Mughals to storm the fort. The fort cannons had thundered and his men had used their muskets and fire tipped arrows to telling effect, forcing the Mughals to keep a safe distance from the fort. Firangoji's men had held their guns in readiness, pointed at the enemy, while he hoped for some respite and help from his King.

But help would never arrive, for unknown to him, his King had been walled off in Fort Panhala, on the southern boundary of their *Swarajya*.

Firangoji finished his inspection of the night guard and barked stiff orders to the Captain on duty. "Keep your eyes and ears open," he said. "It is not like the Mughals to remain quiet for so long. I am sure they are planning something!" The Captain nodded his head in agreement. With one final glance at the Mughals, Firangoji turned around and headed to his own chamber for some well earned rest.

Amir-ul-umrao Mirza Abu Taleeb Shaista Khan, General of the imperial Mughal army, and maternal uncle of Emperor Aurangzeb, sat in his command tent on the northern side of the siege camp, awaiting word on the final progress of the tunnel his men had been digging for the past two weeks. Attendants fanned him tirelessly, attempting to counter the humid heat left behind by the lull in the rain. Shaista Khan tried to analyse his Deccan campaign. His vast army had marched right to Pune, the center of Seeva's fief, almost unopposed. Seeva's Marathas had launched several brief raids, slaughtering his men, but these had hardly caused a dent in his armour. Once in Pune, he had occupied Seeva's home, Lal Mahal, and his army had sprawled out across the plains. He had then begun his campaign by leading a detachment of over seventeen thousand equipped horse and foot soldiers to Chakan, the northern boundary of Seeva's lands. The lone fort which stood guard there was a relatively small affair; a squarish construction with a bastion at each corner, and more bastions in between. He had expected his vast army to engulf the fort and capture it in a matter of hours, but Seeva's Maratha garrison in the fort had quashed his plans and had obstinately defended the fort for the past fifty-five days! Though he had maintained a calm demeanour, inwardly the Khan was frustrated and exasperated with his Captains, who had failed in their many attempts to take this small fort. The large hearted Khan also silently admired the resilience of his enemy. The fort was so small that it could house no more than a few hundred men at the most, yet they had managed to resist his army and cannons.

Two months to take a small fort on open ground! So how long would it take him to reduce the rest of Seeva's fief, his hill-forts, Khan wondered. Probably years! Shaista Khan was getting a taste of things to come.

There was a rustle of the tent awning as his *quorchi* entered and said, "My Lord, the Captain wishes to see you."

Shaista Khan nodded, and within moments a hefty man entered the tent and bowed curtly. His tight trousers and footwear were soiled with mud and slush, and it was evident he had been in the thick of things, commanding operations at the tunnel. Despite a full day of hard labour, he stood erect before his General, his tough face showing no fatigue.

"Well Habsh Khan, how progresses the tunnel?"

"We are ready, My Lord!" Habsh Khan replied with a slight smile. "The tunnel has been carried forward to the bastion and packed with explosives, ready to be blown on your command."

"Excellent!" Shaista Khan smiled. "Order Shamshuddin Khan and Uzbek Khan to get their contingents ready. I want one thousand fresh, well-rested men ready for the assault!"

"My Lord!" Habsh Khan bowed and left to carry out the orders.

Raghav peered over the rampart of the north-eastern bastion into the darkness. He had detected some movement in the Mughal camp, but had not been sure what they were up to. After watching intently for some time, he thought he saw ranks of soldiers getting into attack formations. Good Lord! Raghav signalled to his fellow guards on the bastion and then rushed off to summon his Captain.

Captain Gondaji arrived and strained his eyes in the dark for some time before he too was convinced the Mughals were up to something. "Keep watching," he said to Raghav. "I'll go fetch the Commander."

Gondaji returned shortly with Firangoji. The Commander joined the men in intently watching the Mughal camp.

"They seem to be planning another *Sultan-dhawa,*" Firangoji said finally. "I want every man on the fort ready with weapons in hand. Muskets to the northern ramparts! Gondaji, rush to the South to see if there is any enemy movement on that side. And keep those torches burning bright!"

Firangoji frantically gesticulated to his men as he shouted out his orders. This wasn't unusual. The Mughals had attempted to take his fort several times by launching massive attacks. He and his men had succeeded in foiling their plans every time. But two months into the siege, he was drawing on his last reserves of ammunition... of food...and energy. Firangoji gritted his teeth and descended the stairs of the north-east bastion. If the Mughals charged, they would get it back from him and his men. Arrow for arrow! Shot for shot! They may have been short on ammunition and food, but they certainly weren't short on determination.

As he rushed to the western side of the fort, Firangoji glanced at the saffron pennant which fluttered in the night breeze, high on top of the central citadel. His thoughts veered to his King. "Fear not," he murmured,"I will not let them have the fort that easily!"

There was a mad scramble as Firangoji's men rushed to get ready for battle. Every man in the fort was wide awake and alert. Within minutes they had stationed themselves on the ramparts and behind the gates, waiting for the enemy to attack. Firangoji had, meanwhile, ascended to the north-western bastion to watch for enemy movements and to inspect his own troops. There was not much happening here, he thought. Whatever they were planning seemed to be on the other side. Firangoji barked orders to move more men to the north-eastern bastion.

One thousand Mughal *hashams* stood in attack formation, swords, shields, muskets and bows in hand. Shamshuddin Khan had been appointed Captain for this charge on the fort. He inspected the formation and then said to the men, "As soon as the tunnel blows, we charge toward the breach in the ramparts. Remember, we cannot allow them time to recover! They have held the fort for too long, but tonight, we take it from them! *Allaho Akbar*!"

Allaho Akbar! A thousand men echoed the war cry.

Shamshuddin nodded to Uzbeg, his second-in-command, who rushed off to inform the General. Shaista Khan was seated in his tent, waiting for an update on the progress of the attack.

Uzbeg entered. "The men are ready, My Lord," he announced.

Khan nodded, rising. "Blow the tunnel!" he ordered.

MIDNIGHT, 14/15 AUGUST 1660

Glancing around the fort, Firangoji saw his men at their stations at the gate and on every bastion, awaiting the enemy charge. Torches burned everywhere, illuminating the fort ramparts and interiors. Let them come, he thought, gripping his own sword. We will drench them in their own blood! The fort was now silent, as the Marathas waited for the Mughals to make the first move.

The silence was shattered by an ear-splitting blast from the north-eastern side. Firangoji was so shaken that he dropped his sword. For a brief moment, the blast lit up the dark night and Firangoji saw the north-eastern bastion blown sky high. Stones and debris flew in all directions, as did the shattered and mangled bodies of the men who had been stationed on that bastion. Firangoji's heart sank as he realized what had happened. The damned Mughals had somehow managed to dig a tunnel from their camp, right to the fort ramparts! Lord Mahadev! This might be the end for him and his men. Thousands of Mughal troops would pour into the fort through the breach. They were three hundred and fifty, and many of those now lay dead.

As the dust and debris settled and the men recovered from the shock, there was chaos in the fort. Firangoji picked up his sword and rushed from the north-western bastion to inspect the damage. He was joined en route by Gondaji, who looked shaken.

"They blew a tunnel!" Firangoji exclaimed, his voice trembling. "How did they get past the ditch?"

Gondaji shook his head. "They must have dug deep, going underneath the ditch."

"Under the ditch...." Firangoji was momentarily amazed. "How many men have we lost?" he asked, fearing the worst.

"Don't know, Commander. But there were at least seventy to eighty men on the bastion when it blew up."

Firangoji grimaced. The two men soon reached the site of the blast. There was a gaping breach where once the north-eastern bastion had stood. Dislodged stone and debris had formed a high mound. The dead and dying lay everywhere and the air was filled with the agonized screams of the wounded. Strewn around carelessly were limbs and chunks of burnt flesh. The stench of gunpowder hung about them like a miasma.

Sword in hand, Firangoji ascended the mound of debris and looked across at the enemy. Rank upon rank of Mughal *hashams* were marching toward him. "All men to the blast site!" Firangoji shouted. Gondaji echoed the order.

"Muskets! Archers! Take positions to cover the approach to the breach!" Firangoji knew in his heart that all was lost. There was no way he and his small garrison could stem the Mughal tide. But he was far from done and resolved to fight to the death. If the Mughals wanted the fort, they would have to take it from him. He would give them a taste of the Maratha sword!

Firangoji's men assembled behind him at the mound. Those with guns and bows stationed themselves at vantage points to get clear shots at the enemy. The Mughals charged at the breach screaming *Deen Deen!* Their front ranks were pounded by arrow and shot, but they kept coming and falling upon Firangoji's defence formation. The night was filled with the sound of clashing weapons, screaming men and gun shots. A terrible battle had begun at the breach in the ramparts of Fort Chakan.

DAWN, 15 AUGUST 1660

The eastern skies over the fort of Chakan brightened as dawn approached. Shaista Khan sat in the *howdah* of his towering war elephant and looked across at it. He could see the tired and injured Maratha soldiers taking a breather on the mound in the breach. He could also see his own *hashams* stationed some distance from the fort, just out of range of the Maratha guns. After much bloody fighting through the night, the Mughals had withdrawn and camped away from the fort. Two *prahars* after the Mughals had blown up part of the ramparts, the fort still remained unconquered.

What kind of men are these, Shaista Khan wondered. He could not help but admire the stubborn resilience of the Marathas. More than two hundred and fifty of his men had perished and over six hundred had fallen back, wounded. The Marathas too, would have lost scores of their own. Yet they refused to stand down and surrender. How could one man ignite such passion and devotion in his people?

The elephant swayed gently, shaking the *howdah* and pulling Shaista Khan out of his trance. Shaking his head, he glanced around for his *quorchi*. "Send for Shamshuddin!" he shouted.

Shamshuddin Khan, Captain of the assault forces, arrived.

"Your *hashams* seem unable to get past the breach, Shamshuddin Khan," Shaista Khan derided his Captain. "It is quite curious that you cannot defeat a handful of fort defenders."

"My Lord, the Marathas fight like possessed men! Try as we might, we cannot dislodge them." Shamshuddin lowered his gaze, burning with humiliation.

"You and your men are dismissed! Summon Alayar Bukhari."

Shamshuddin bowed and departed, leaving Shaista Khan deep in thought. He knew he would take the fort sooner or later, but having breached the rampart, the loss of so many men was unacceptable. Ever since he had begun the siege of the fort, two months ago, the Marathas had harassed him with night raids, slaughtering his men. They appeared out of the dark night, and disappeared just as quickly. Khan was amazed by their war tactics. If the Mughals were to win in the Deccan, they would have to understand the Maratha brand of warfare and counter it effectively. They would also need to understand their psyche...and their mad devotion to Seeva.

"You sent for me, My Lord?" It was Bukhari.

"Assemble a thousand fresh men and assault the breach at once. Let us see how the Marathas withstand a fresh attack!"

"Yes, My Lord!" Bukhari banged his fist to his heart and left.

From his position on top of the mound of debris, an injured and exhausted Firangoji could see a fresh Mughals force amassing on the plain in front of the fort. He had received a deep gash across his chest and dried blood caked most of his torso. He had lost his turban, his hair was dishevelled and *angarkha* torn. But he still gripped his sword firmly and stood obstinately in the breach, determined to stop the enemy. As the Mughals began marching toward him, he tore off the tattered *angarkha*, baring his muscular, bloodied torso. His eyes bloodshot, he shouted, "Enemy approaching! On your feet men!"

His weary men struggled to their feet and stood behind their Commander. The fresh Mughal *hashams* fell upon them and the battle restarted with a vengeance. The plains of Chakan were once again filled with the sounds of clashing weapons and the screams of men as their flesh was slashed and limbs torn by hungry blades. Firangoji fought like a tiger, but finally this fresh assault was too much for the tired Marathas to endure. Slowly but surely, the defenders were pushed back, and the Mughal forces entered the fort. In desperation, Firangoji ordered his men to fall back to the central citadel.

In dire peril, Firangoji and his remaining men managed to get to the citadel and close its doors. They continued to fight from the ramparts of the citadel. Though the fort was occupied by the Mughals, Maratha musketeers and archers continued to pick off Mughal targets and harass them.

Bukhari, who had entered the fort with his assault troops, stood behind a barricade, directing operations. He could clearly see there was no hope for the Marathas, yet they refused to stand down. It was pure madness.

Shaista Khan had seen his troops enter the fort. 'At last!' he thought, 'the battle would finally end'.

But half a *prahar* later, Bukhari's *hasham* returned with more frustrating news. "The Marathas will not surrender, My Lord!" the man said.

"What the...?" Shaista Khan angrily banged his fist on the railing of the *howdah*. "Do they think they can eliminate our entire army? What kind of crazy men does Seeva employ?" Khan sought in vain for a solution. On an impulse, he said, "Summon Rao Bhao Singh immediately."

The Rajput Captain, camped on the south side of the fort, arrived and bowed to his General.

"Bhao Singh, approach the Maratha *killedar* and drill some sense into his head. Appeal to him in the name of your Hindu Gods and make him surrender, or else I will order our cannons to be moved inside the fort to blow his citadel to smithereens!" Khan said viciously.

The Rajput left on the peace mission. In his heyday, he had known many a bloody battle and many stubborn soldiers, but none like these Marathas. They seemed to prefer to fight on even in the face of assured death. He entered the fort and located Bukhari, stationed behind a barricade. "What's the situation?" he asked the Mughal Captain.

"There can be no more than a hundred and fifty men in the citadel. We have repeatedly asked them to surrender, but they refuse to budge. They continue to fire muskets and arrows if we try to move near. If the General orders it, my men can blast the citadel to hell!"

"Let me try to convince them to surrender," Bhao Singh said. He was loathe to kill so many brave soldiers for seemingly no reason. "If they still refuse, we will blast them out."

Bhao Singh moved out from behind the barricade, untied his *dushela,* and moved closer to the citadel, waving the waistband to signal he wished parley. When he had advanced sufficiently close to the citadel wall, he shouted, "Let me speak to the *killedar*. I come to offer you a choice between safe passage and death."

A begrimed face peered down at him from the ramparts. With his thick moustache flowing into an unkempt beard and broad sideburns, his set jaw and bloodshot eyes, Firangoji looked like anything but a man about to beg for his or his mens' lives. "What is it, Mughal?" he called down to Bhao Singh.

As their eyes met, Bhao Singh looked at the Maratha with respect and admiration. For a brief moment, he felt humiliated that a brave son of the soil had chosen to fight the Mughal outsiders and die for his King, while he himself had chosen to side with the foreign rulers. The Maratha Commander had referred to him as 'Mughal'. In that moment, as he stood below the barricaded citadel of Fort Chakan, Bhao Singh realized that as long as he remained with the Emperor's forces, the world would see him as a Mughal, not a Rajput.

Shaking off such thoughts, he called to his adversary, "Brave *killedar*, we have already taken the fort. Look, even the main gate is in our custody and wide open. Thousands of our troops stand outside in readiness to move in. You and your men will be slaughtered. Surrender now and we will let you go unharmed. Refuse and we will blow you, your men, and this entire citadel to the skies. Do not be a fool! By Lord Mahadev, you have proven your courage. Shaista Khan *Sahib* admires your bravery and has agreed to spare your lives."

Firangoji felt his heart fill with despair at these words. He had lost the battle and his fort. What was he fighting on for? Over half his garrison had already perished. Those that still lived and were with him in the citadel, were exhausted beyond imagination, some half-dead. They had insufficient food and water. Even if they held out, they would not survive for long. Yet, not one man would stand down unless he commanded them to do so.

Firangoji turned and looked at his men. Each seemed to silently request him to take the Mughal assurance of safe passage and surrender. Yet he knew that at a signal from him, every man would rise, weapon in hand, and continue the fight. He turned back to the Mughal officer and said, "I have two conditions."

"Tell me what it is you want, *killedar*," Bhao Singh said graciously.

"Many of my men are seriously injured. Allow us to take some provisions with us, else these men will die."

Bhao Singh nodded. "Agreed! What else?"

"We will take our King's saffron standard with us."

Bhao Singh nodded again, in silence.

The Mughals watched the defeated Marathas leave the fort. Firangoji Narsala lowered the saffron pennant from its mast atop the citadel, with his own hands and took it with him. As the garrison passed Shaista Khan's elephant, Firangoji looked up defiantly at the Mughal General. Some day, he thought, some day we will get back at you! Shaista Khan looked down at the Maratha Commander and nodded in acknowledgement of their bravery.

With heavy hearts the Marathas began their long journey south, to face their King, Shivaji *Raje*.

Rajgad, a few days later

Firangoji Narsala and his Captains stood with heads lowered in front of their Lord and Master, waiting for him to pronounce their fate. Firangoji was all too familiar with the customs of the time. Officers returning defeated from war faced the King's ire. As if the humiliation of defeat was not enough, they would receive punishment, demotions, sometimes even banishment from the King's service. Traitors would, of course, be put to death if caught. From the time he had renounced Mughal service and joined the man he now called his Lord, this was the first time Firangoji had returned, defeated.

Shivaji *Raje* sat at the head of his assembly on his customary *baithak,* upholstered with plush silk covered cushions. He was flanked by his *Peshwa,* Moro *Punt* Pingale, and *Sirnaubat* Netoji Palkar, while the other ministers and officers sat further away. Shivaji *Raje's* face was calm as he heard Firangoji narrate the entire ordeal of the war at Fort Chakan. His rugged face with its neatly cropped beard, that met on either side of his face with his thick sideburns; his pearl earrings and the crescent shaped tilak on his forehead, showed no anger.

Firangoji said finally, "This unfortunate soldier has lost his fort, Your Highness. I accept whatever punishment you pronounce."

Shivaji *Raje* turned to his *Peshwa*. "What punishment should we give to these men, Moro *Punt*, for losing the fort?"

Moro *Punt* smiled, knowing his master's mind. "As you deem fit, *Maharaj*."

"How does one punish brave souls who defend a fort against an enemy fifty times their own strength, for two months?" mused Shivaji *Raje*. "How does one punish soldiers who refused to back down, even in the face of death, and stood at the breach in the ramparts, taking on a massive army head on, with only a handful of their own?"

Firangoji raised his eyes and looked up. The King was smiling, pride writ large on his face. Shivaji *Raje* rose from his *baithak* and immediately, the entire assembly did as well. *Raje* walked up to Firangoji and looked up at the man who was considerably taller than himself, but stood with drooped shoulders and hung head.

"Firangoji," Shivaji *Raje* addressed his Commander, "victory and defeat are two faces of life. We have to face both as we strive day and night to achieve freedom from these opressive Sultanates. When I send you, my men, on missions, I know that not all of you will succeed. But what I demand is complete dedication and devotion to our cause, and above all, loyalty. And that, my friend, you have shown in full measure. I applaud you and your men for your acts of extreme bravery, which will be remembered by our people for ages to come."

Firangoji's face lightened on hearing these words of praise from the King. Lowered heads were once again held high and drooping shoulders straightened.

Shivaji *Raje* removed a gold bracelet from his own wrist and clasped it around Firangoji's. "I am proud of you, my men. Now go and rest. Soon you shall receive your new appointments."

Firangoji's eyes glistened with unshed tears as he moved back and bowed to offer obeisance to his King.

Somewhere in the Maval forests, September 1660

A middle-aged man, dressed in a ragged *dhoti*, a crude cotton jacket, with a dirty cloth tied around his head as a turban, stepped cautiously along the foot track that led through the sparse woods of the Jambhul Khore, one of the Maval regions on the eastern side of the Sahyadri range. As he walked, he kept an alert eye to see if he was being followed. After a tiring trek that had taken him nearly all day, he had finally reached the village where his master was eagerly awaiting the news he brought. The sun had set before he could reach his destination and it was now dark.

The village was quiet. The man easily slipped past the huts, which numbered fewer than fifty, and reached the far side of the village, where a small mud house with a thatched roof stood, separated from the rest of the village. He gently knocked on the door. A man in his late fifties, his face half shrouded with a head covering, opened the door. Recognising the man outside, he let him in. The door was promptly locked from within.

"You took a long time to return, Mahadu," the man who had opened the door, said to the visitor. "What news have you brought?"

"Forgive me, Master, the way was long and difficult to negotiate on foot. I had to make sure I was not followed," Mahadu replied, picking up a *lota* and drinking thirstily.

Having drunk his fill, he continued, "Shivaji *Raje* has sent out an alert for you. If you go into the open, his men will kill you!"

Khandoji Khopade pushed back the cloth that covered most of his face and let out a long resigned sigh. "I joined Afzal Khan during the Pratapgad war. Shivaji *Raje* is sure to take revenge."

"You are safe here, Master," Mahadu assured him.

"How long can I remain hidden in this hut?"

"For as long as required," Mahadu replied bluntly. "I met Shilimkar *Deshmukh*. He said he will try to help."

Khandoji felt somehwhat reassured on hearing the name of his son-in-law, Haibatrao Shilimkar, mentioned. "Haibatrao serves *Raje* faithfully. He might be able to secure a pardon for me." Khandoji did not sound too hopeful.

"I have heard Shivaji *Raje* pronounces severe punishments on those who displease him, especially those he considers traitors."

"You are being most encouraging." Khandoji walked to the window and stared out at the darkness. The thought crossed his mind that his future was as dark as the night.

Gunjan Maval, about the same time

Haibatrao Shilimkar sat brooding in his bedchamber, thinking about the particularly sticky problem at hand. The man who had met him a couple of days ago had informed him that his father-in-law, Khandoji Khopade, was hiding in the Maval forest, and now sought a pardon from their King. Khopade had sent him a message, requesting him to speak to Shivaji *Raje* about it. Now how was he supposed to do that? He had served *Raje* for years, and knew how strictly he enforced discipline. A traitor would never be forgiven. *Raje* was certainly not going to accept any pleas from him.

Haibatrao thought hard and finally a name popped into his mind. If anyone could help procure a pardon from Shivaji *Raje*, it was Kanhoji Jedhe. *Raje* would never turn him down.

Haibatrao left for Kari village the very next day.

Kari village, Rohid Khore, the next day

"Help Khopade get a pardon, Jedhe *Naik*," Haibatrao pleaded. "He is repentant and will never betray us again."

Kanhoji was silent. He knew what the man was asking him to do was impossible – to get a traitor pardoned by Shivaji *Raje*. He also knew that Haibatrao himself was a genuine loyalist. He had faithfully served *Raje* and the *Swarajya* for years now. But he was unsure of Khopade. Men like Khandoji Khopade were perennial chameleons, ever ready to change colour with the skies. He had no inclination to intervene on his behalf. But Khandoji's *Deshmukhi* was located right next to his own, in Rohid Khore. Ultimately, Kanhoji realized, it was in the best interests of the *Swarajya* that all Maval *Deshmukhs* stood together, aligned to Shivaji *Raje*.

After giving it long thought, Kanhoji finally said, "I will try, Shilimkar *Naik*. But you know that this is a very difficult task."

Fort Pratapgad, a few days later

"Shaista Khan has returned to Lal Mahal, Highness. My man informs me that he is likely to reopen his campaign against our *Swarajya* soon," Bahirji Naik, the Head of Intelligence, informed Shivaji *Raje*, as they sat in conference in the citadel.

"After his experience at Chakan, Khan is unlikely to try and take another fort any time soon. He might change his strategy," Shivaji *Raje* mused.

"I think he might try and enter the Konkan, Highness," Moro *Punt* Pingale said.

Shivaji *Raje* nodded. "I think so too. He may try to annex our Konkan territories and open negotiations with the Siddi of Janjira."

"That would be dangerous for us. We have invested too much time and money, and lost too many lives, in acquiring the Konkan. Even the Adilshah has left us alone now. If the Mughals move in, we may find it difficult to dislodge them." Moro *Punt* voiced his opinion.

"We must stop Khan's forces from entering the Konkan," Shivaji *Raje* agreed. "Bahirji, keep your best men on the job. We must have information of the Khan's plans and his troop movements on a day-to-day basis."

"Certainly, Sire!" Bahirji assured him.

The men dispersed after more discussions on the current political situation. Once they had left, Shivaji *Raje* sat alone in the conference chamber, deep in thought. He needed to work out a strategy to deal with the Mughals. Shaista Khan currently occupied the Pune–Chakan region, and he could not leave those areas under Mughal control for long. But open conflict with the Khan's massive juggernaut would be foolhardy, at least for now. How then could he deal with the Mughal incursion?

An attendant entered to announce the arrival of Kanhoji Jedhe. Kanhoji came in and bowed to his master. Shivaji *Raje* smiled at his senior comrade and offered him a seat. He knew Kanhoji had not been keeping good health of late.

"How is your health, *Naik*?" Shivaji *Raje* asked him.

"I am better now, Your Highness."

Shivaji *Raje* could see the awkward stiffness on Kanhoji's face and realized instantly that he had come to see him for some special reason. "You seem disturbed, *Naik*. Tell me what's on your mind," he said.

"Highness..." Kanhoji hesitated. He knew the mere mention of Khandoji Khopade's name would be enough to send the King into a rage. Yet he had promised Shilimkar he would try and intervene. He had travelled all the way to Pratapgad for that very reason. He could not back out now. He, like most men, feared Shivaji *Raje's* legendary temper, and hoped the King would at least hear him out.

"Highness," Kanhoji began again, "Khandoji Khopade has sent me a feeler through his son-in-law, Haibatrao Shilimkar."

Shivaji *Raje*'s smile vanished. His face hardened and eyes became cold with anger. "*Naik,* do not mention that traitor again!"

"Highness, he repents his actions. Please give him a second chance. I will stand surety for him. If you do not forgive him, the entire Khopade clan will be destroyed."

"He does not deserve forgiveness! No traitor deserves forgiveness, *Naik,*" Shivaji *Raje* said firmly. "He had lost his *Deshmukhi* to his kin. We helped to re-establish him in his *watan*, remember? You and me. Yet, that rascal had the guts to join Afzal Khan and raise his sword against us!" Shivaji *Raje* rose angrily from his seat.

Kanhoji was promptly on his feet as well. "I know he has wronged us, Highness," he pleaded. "But I beg you to forgive him."

"*Naik,* men like Khandoji Khopade should be chopped to pieces and fed to the dogs. Do not intervene on his behalf!"

"My King, after generations, there has been some peace amongst the Maval *Deshmukhs*. We must hold the peace and keep the *Deshmukhs* aligned to us. Haibatrao has been a faithful adherent. Khopade is, after all, his father-in-law. Pray give the matter your consideration, Highness."

His back toward Kanhoji, Shivaji *Raje* walked to the window and looked out. He was fuming within, but forced himself to remain calm. He was disinclined to slight Kanhoji. The man had been a father figure to him; an advisor, friend and loyal supporter. His *Swarajya* existed because of men like Kanhoji. There was nothing he would have denied him. But how could he forgive a traitor?

Kanhoji stood patiently with folded hands, waiting his master's decision. Finally, Shivaji *Raje* turned and walked up to him. His face was grim and his usual smile was missing. Kanhoji knew he had put his King in a major dilemma.

"Kanhoji," Shivaji Raje said, adressing him, "it is only on your insistence that I have decided to spare Khandoji Khopade's life. Ask him to appear for an audience."

Raje abruptly walked off without looking back.

Pratapgad, a few days later

Shivaji *Raje* sat in his conference chamber, at the head of the assembly of his chief council members. The immediate problem before them was, of course, the Mughal occupation of their fief, and it formed the topic of heated discussion. As the men deliberated on the best course of action, Kanhoji Jedhe entered the chamber. The conversation hushed and then stopped as the assembled men looked at the person following Kanhoji. It was Khandoji Khopade, *Deshmukh* of Utravali, the man who had betrayed them in the last battle with Bijapur.

The new entrants bowed in obeisance to Shivaji *Raje*.

Shivaji *Raje* nodded at Kanhoji, but chose to ignore Khandoji Khopade. He had checked his anger due to his promise to Kanhoji, but in no way was he ready to speak to the traitor in his own court. *Raje* exchanged a few formal words with Kanhoji and then gave the men leave to depart.

For the next two days, this drama was repeated. Kanhoji would come to court with Khandoji in tow, *Raje* would ignore Khandoji, and then give them leave to go. On the third day, however, Kanhoji had to leave the fort on a matter that needed his attention in Jawli village, so Khandoji came to the court alone. This was the opportunity *Raje* had been waiting for, to catch the traitor alone.

Khandoji Khopade stood before his Lord, downcast and fearful. He had erred in judging the man and his capabilities. He had expected Shivaji Bhosale's rebellion to be blown away by Afzal Khan's massive invasion, rather, by the Khan himself. But, quite spectacularly, the man who sat before him now, had inflicted on the imperial army its worst defeat ever. Those men, like himself, who had deserted to join the Khan's forces, now faced *Raje's* ire.

Shivaji *Raje* looked at Khandoji, his eyes blazing with rage. Khandoji saw his own death in them. He sank to his knees and bowed his head to the ground, begging, "Highness, spare me! Please forgive me!"

"I never forgive traitors, Khopade!" Shivaji *Raje*'s voice was cold and menacing enough to freeze the blood of the man grovelling on the floor. "I have said before, and I say it now: Those with me will prosper; those against me will perish!"

Khopade was trembling with fear. "*Maharaj*, you promised to spare my life! You gave your word to Kanhoji Jedhe!"

"I did. But I never said I would not punish you." Shivaji *Raje* was on his feet. Immediately, the entire assembly stood up, and so did Khandoji. "Arrest this man!" *Raje* ordered his guards.

Armed men rushed forth from all directions and held Khandoji by his arms and neck.

"*Maharaj*, please forgive me! Spare me! Have mercy!" Khandoji begged, struggling with his captors.

"Take him outside!"

The man was dragged into the courtyard outside the conference chamber. Shivaji *Raje* stood facing the courtyard and pronounced the punishment: "Chop off this man's right arm and left leg."

Khandoji's eyes widened in horror and he began screaming and begging for mercy. His captors kicked him to the ground and then, as some of the guards held him down, another pulled out his sword and hacked off Khandoji's right arm, and then his left leg.

Shivaji *Raje's* menacing gaze was locked on Khandoji as his screams echoed all over the fort, sending shivers down the spines of all those who heard him. The screams died only when Khandoji collapsed into unconsciousness.

"Keep him alive," Shivaji *Raje* said coldly. "I have promised to spare his life." He turned and left the conference chamber.

Silence filled the chamber as the most powerful men in the kingdom stood in trembling fear and awe.

Late that evening, Shivaji *Raje* sat in his own chambers. He knew Kanhoji would visit him to demand an explanation. And he did. Visibly disturbed and angry, Kanhoji Jedhe was ushered into his presence.

"Highness! Just a few days ago you promised to forgive Khopade, yet today you hack off his limbs! I convinced him to come out of hiding on the assurance of safety. Now I have been made to look like a double-crosser! No *Deshmukh* will ever trust my word again!"

"Calm down, *Naik*." Shivaji *Raje* knew he had to somehow convince Kanhoji to see reason in what he had done. "Do you recall my words, *Naik*?"

Kanhoji stuttered. "Er...Highness, you promised to spare his life."

"He *is* alive, *Naik*. I have not killed him."

Kanhoji was confused. The man had been brutally punished.

"I never said I would not punish him, *Naik*. I merely promised to spare his life, which I have." Shivaji *Raje* walked up to his elderly comrade and placed a hand gently on his shoulder. "*Naik*, Khandoji was a traitor. If I had let him go unpunished, it would have encouraged others to do the same. People would have thought that in Shivaji's *Swarajya,* one can get away with anything, if one knows the right people. That would not be good for our state. We must have the same laws for all, *Naik,* and a corruption-free leadership."

Kanhoji hung his head, ashamed. He had attempted to get a traitor pardoned. His Master had cleverly foiled his attempt. He looked up at the King. "Forgive me, Highness. You are right. I used my influence to get Khandoji pardoned. I erred."

"*Naik,* your place in my life is next only to my father's. You are close to my heart. Our *Swarajya* exists because of men like you and your sons. Even my mother has said this. Forgive me if I have caused you hurt, but as King, I must look at the larger good, even if I have to hurt those closest to me."

"Sire, nothing can come between us. My sons and I will remain by your side till death."

Rajgad, last quarter, 1660

It was late evening. Jijabai reclined on a *divan* in her chamber. Winter had set in and the evenings were particularly chilly. Jijabai pulled her shawl closely around herself and looked at the handsome young man who squatted on the floor, giving her a foot massage. "That's enough, Shivba," she said. "Come and sit beside me now."

Shivaji *Raje* smiled at her and raised himself to sit on the couch by her side. He cherished these quiet evenings spent with his mother.

Ever since he could remember, he had experienced real peace only in her presence. Besides, her understanding of politics and matters of state was far beyond that of most of *Raje's* diplomats, and she had advice for him whenever he needed it.

"The Mughals are unshakeable, mother," he said to her. "The Mughal army is like an ocean, while we only have a small rivulet at our disposal. Netoji and his men are raiding and skirmishing regularly, yet we have been unable to even ruffle their feathers."

"The Mughals are the leeches that sap the blood from our veins, Shivba. We must get them out of our *Swarajya.* But you are right, mere brawn is unlikely to work. We will have to do it with a combination of guerrilla warfare and wise diplomacy."

"It may take us a long time to deal with this menace, mother, and till then, our people will continue to suffer."

"Do not despair, Shivba. You have just defeated that monster Afzal Khan. In comparison, this Mughal General seems a lesser problem to me."

"Open battle with his massive army is impossible. We have to wait till they get into the hills."

"Plot a counter move to his every move. Foil his plans. Do not leave him anything to write to Aurangzeb about. Frustrate him, checkmate him."

Shivaji *Raje* thought about what his mother had just said. "After his victory at Chakan, Shaista Khan has not made too many moves. But we expect him to, soon."

The door opened and a toddler, clad in a *dhoti* and a smart silk *angarkha,* ran toward them, instantly lighting up their faces with smiles. Three-year-old Shambu giggled as his father picked him up and planted a kiss on his cheek.

"So what mischief have you been up to, little one?" he asked.

"I wath fightin' the enemy... I kill them all!" Shambhu babbled with a heavy lisp, making his father and grandmother laugh.

Soyarabai entered and walked up to them. She bent down to touch Jijabai's feet and then threw a quick glance at Shambhu. The boy hid his face in his father's chest and hugged him tightly.

"There is no point hiding now after all the ruckus you created in the kitchen," Soyarabai said in a sharp tone.

"What did he do, Soyara?" Jijabai asked calmly.

"He and his friends were enacting battle scenes and barged into the kitchen, dislodging every pot and pan in sight."

Shivaji *Raje* smiled at his son indulgently. Jijabai was reminded of similar acts by her Shivba, long ago.

"And where are your sisters, Shambhu? Don't they look after you?" *Raje* asked.

Shambhu shook his head vigorously. "They play doll... Shambhu no like doll."

Jijabai and Shivaji *Raje* laughed again, while Soyara fumed.

"He is only a child, Soyara. Shivba was a bigger monster at this age," Jijabai said, laughing.

The door opened again and Putalabai walked in. Smiling, she said, "Don't worry sister, the kitchen mess has been cleared."

Shambhu turned around and smiled at Putala. "You must be more careful, Shambu *Raje*," Putala said to him.

Soyarabai walked off in a huff. Jijabai and Shivaji *Raje* momentarily exchanged a glance as Putala gently extricated Shambhu from his father's embrace.

"Come now," she said, planting a kiss on his cheek. "Look, your clothes are all messed up. You need a change."

Shivaji *Raje* smiled affectionately at his younger wife. Thank God for Putala, he thought. Saee's absence was bound to have an effect on Shambu's upbringing, but he could see that Shambhu had taken to Putala very well. Jijabai was there, of course, but she was ageing now, and could not be the presence in Shambhu's life Saee could have been. Saee... Shivaji *Raje* felt a pang of loneliness remembering the one woman he had loved truly.

"Shivba," Jijabai said as Putala left the chamber with Shambhu in her arms, "do not worry about the children. They are well taken care of. You must focus on being a King to your people."

Shivaji *Raje* got up and paced the chamber, his hands clasped behind his back. With a great effort he pushed Saee's memory from his mind and forced himself to think.

"I have invited the poet Adnyandas, to Rajgad," Jijabai said, changing the subject. "I have asked him to compose a *powada* on the Pratapgad war. I intend to hold a special *durbar* in which Adnyandas will perform. The *powada* can then be sung by *gondhalis* in the far reaches of the Marathi lands, so everyone can hear the exploits of their sons."

"That is a very good thought, mother. I too, have been thinking of summoning a special *durbar* to honour and reward our war heroes. Adnyandas can regale the assembly on the same day."

The special *durbar* was held in the Rajgad palace. The top officers of the kingdom were invited to the event, especially those who had taken part in the Pratapgad war. The *durbar* hall was lavishly decked with expensive silks, curtains, and gold and silver ware, to emphasize the prosperity of the Maratha leadership.

The assembled dignitaries bowed as Shivaji *Raje* walked in, dressed in an orange silk *angarkha,* decorated with gold embroidery, fitted cream silk trousers, and his customary turban adorned with pearls and rubies. Strings of pearl hung around his neck, as did a string of *cowrie* shells. Diamond and ruby studded rings adorned his fingers and he held his Bhavani sword gripped in his right hand. A *katyaar,* sparkling with diamonds, was stuck into his red *dushela*. Though he chose to dress simply on regular work days, Shivaji *Raje* appeared in royal finery on such special occasions.

Raje first bent to touch Jijabai's feet, and then took his place on the plushly cushioned seat at the head of the assembly. The senior officers and prominent diplomats seated themselves on either side. Moro *Punt,* the *Peshwa,* was to Shivaji *Raje's* right, while the *Sirnaubat,* Netoji Palkar, sat beside Jijabai. Also seated were Sono *Punt,* the senior statesman, Raghunath *Punt,* the *Sabnis,* Tanhaji and Yesaji, the Infantry Commanders, Kanhoji Jedhe *Deshmukh* and Bandal *Deshmukh.* The others stood in rows behind them. Baji *Sarjerao* Jedhe was there, as was his brother, Chandji Jedhe. Suryaji Malusare proudly stood behind his brother, Tanhaji. Haibatrao Shilimkar *Deshmukh* and Pasalkar *Deshmukh* too, joined the ranks.

Tryambak Bhaskar, Babaji Bhosale and numerous other Captains stood in the rows behind these seniors.

Moro *Punt* began the proceedings by announcing the reason for the *durbar*. One by one, the war heroes and officers were called forth, honoured and rewarded. Some received, besides cash, gold bracelets, bejewelled swords and daggers from Shivaji *Raje* himself, while others were conferred the honour of a palanquin or trumpet. Each officer felt pride fill his heart as he stood before the King, who personally praised them for their brave deeds.

The question in everyone's mind, however, was who would get the prime honour at the *durbar,* the highest awarded by the King. It was the simple presentation of betel leaves on a gold plate, with a sword of honour. A court attendant brought the offerings and placed them in front of Shivaji *Raje,* on an ornamental stool.

Raje smiled and declared, "Kanhoji Jedhe *Deshmukh*! For your selfless service to this *Swarajya;* for keeping the entire Maval country united in the face of disaster; for being a father figure to me, I award you the *durbar's* highest honour!"

Speechless, Kanhoji walked to where his Master stood. *Raje* handed him the sword of honour and then offered him the plate of betel leaves. Kanhoji accepted them, bowing to his King. Over a decade ago he had been sent by Shahaji *Raje* to serve the *Swarajya*. This moment signified the fulfilment of that duty. Those assembled smiled and nodded in agreement of this ultimate recognition of Kanhoji Jedhe's service.

The poet Adnyandas was then summoned. A short and stocky man of late middle-age, he was simply clad in a cotton *dhoti, kurta* and turban. Three other men entered the *durbar* behind him, holding musical instruments. Adnyandas himself held a tambourine. The men bowed to *Raje* and Jijabai, and then Adnyandas smacked his tambourine to begin his *powada*.

"Listen all ye assembled heroes, as I pray first to Lord Ganesha," Adnyandas sang in a firm, confident voice, "and recite the battle of King Shivaji, the brave one."

As Adnyandas continued, every man in the assembly was hooked to his words, as they relived the battle! Each man recognized the particular part he had played. Jijabai closed her eyes and let the poet's words fall on her ears, as she visualized the momentous battle in her mind.

Raje himself listened calmly to Adnyandas' beautiful words. The *powada* had numerous couplets and it was nearly a third of a *prahar* before Adnyandas neared the end, reciting, "As Angad and Hanumanta stood behind Lord Ram, so did Jedhe and Bandal stand behind Shivaji *Raja*."

Adnyandas had ended his epic poem with special recognition of the Jedhe and Bandal *Deshmukhs*. The two men beamed as the entire *durbar* looked at them in admiration.

PUNE, LAST QUARTER, 1660

Meanwhile, Shaista Khan, who had camped at Chakan through the rains, had returned to his base camp at Pune. Relaxing in the luxury of the renovated Lal Mahal, he planned his next move.

Kartalab Khan, one of Shaista Khan's Captains, had succeeded in bribing the Adilshahi Commander of Fort Paranda. Ghalib, the defector, had willingly crossed over to the Mughals and handed over the fort to them. Kartalab had thus handed Shaista Khan his biggest gain of the campaign, without shedding a drop of blood. Kartalab returned jubiliant to the Pune's base camp and bowed before his General.

"Kartalab Khan!" the Mughal General said. "I applaud you on your victory at Paranda. Well done!"

"Thank you, My Lord!"

"Our campaign progresses well," Shaista Khan continued. "Only a few days ago I wrote to the Emperor, informing him of our victory at Chakan. Now I shall write to tell him of your success at Paranda."

Khan's assembled Captains nodded and smiled. Keeping the Emperor informed about the progress of a military campaign was of paramount importance. This war council in Lal Mahal had Khan's prominent Captains in attendance. Besides Kartalab, there was Namdar Khan, Kamdar Khan, Shamshuddin Khan and Alayar Bukhari. Seated on the far side was *Rai Baghan,* the senior and only lady officer in his camp.

"However," Shaista Khan said, "we cannot rest. We must take our campaign forward. The battle at Fort Chakan has made one thing quite clear – taking Seeva's forts can consume too much time. I have decided to change our strategy."

"Order us, Khan *Sahib*!" Kartalab responded enthusiastically. "Your Captains are ever ready to take to the battlefield!"

Khan nodded. "I have decided to invade Seeva's territories in the North Konkan. Kalyan, Bhiwandi, Panvel, Nagothane and Chaul are the chief towns under his control. Kartalab, you will command this campaign. Descend into the Konkan and capture Seeva's coastal territories!"

Kartalab's gaunt face lit up at the General's words. Being appointed Head of such an important campaign meant that his services were highly valued by the Mughal General.

"Take whatever you need. Cavalry, infantry, camels, elephants, cannons...name it and you shall have it. Just bring me news of success."

"Khan *Sahib*, I promise you that I will prove worthy of your trust."

"May I say something, Khan *Sahib*?" the ever cautious *Rai Baghan* asked, stemming the euphoria.

Khan gestured towards her, nodding.

"The Konkan is treacherous country. A campaign in such territory must be planned meticulously. I have said this before and I say it again, our troops are inexperienced in fighting in the hills, while Shivaji's *Mavale* troops have been bred in these mountains. It could prove an uneven match if we are not careful."

Khan looked at Kartalab and the two shared dismissive smiles. "Your suggestions are wise, as always, *Pundita*, but I too will repeat what I have said before – that our armies are vast like the ocean and will engulf Seeva's lands like this!" He snapped his fingers to indicate it would take only a moment to defeat the Maratha King.

Rai Baghan fell silent. She was one of the few Captains in the Mughal camp who, being a Maratha herself, had some experience of Maratha war tactics. She knew Kartalab was a pompous and overconfident fool who had never been in the Sahyadri Hills before. She wished that Shaista Khan had entrusted this important campaign to some other sensible officer. But the Khan was not about to take advice from a woman; she could sense that.

"Kartalab," Khan continued to his man of the moment, "I will appoint our best Captains to your command for the Konkan campaign." He stroked his beard, glancing at *Rai Baghan*. "*Pundita Rai Baghan* will go with you as well," he decided. "She has knowledge and experience of the Sahyadris."

Rai Baghan nodded, inwardly cursing her luck. A Konkan campaign led by Kartalab Khan? There was no way in hell the Mughals would achieve success against Shivaji *Raje*'s *ganimikawa*!

RAJGAD, LATE 1660

In a somber mood, Shivaji *Raje* and Jijabai sat in his chamber. It was late evening and they could feel the winter chill in the gentle draft from the windows. Jijabai looked at her son, who was deep in thought. The letter that had arrived a short while ago from Kari village in the Maval, was the cause of worry for both mother and son. It had been written by *Sarjerao* Jedhe, informing *Raje* and Jijabai that *Sarjerao*'s father, Kanhoji Jedhe, was seriously ill and might not recover.

"Shivba, I fear for Kanhoji *Naik*'s life," Jijabai said. "It would be a great loss for the *Swarajya*.

Shivaji *Raje* let out a long sigh and nodded. "*Swarajya* will certainly be poorer without him. I will be too..."

"Your father sent some invaluable men from his fief, didn't he?"

"Yes mother, he did. And Kanhoji *Naik* was the best of them. He has devoted his life to this work, as much as I have." After a brief pause, he added, "I will write to him right away."

An attendant entered to say, "Bahirji *Naik* wishes to speak to His Highness."

Shivaji *Raje* nodded. "Shaista Khan is busy planning some new advances from his base camp. I was expecting Bahirji with some news today," he told his mother.

Bahirji entered and bowed to them both. "Highness," he began, "as expected, Shaista Khan has finalized a massive campaign to invade the Konkan. Over ten thousand cavalry and almost as many infantry are being readied."

"Who is in command?"

"Kartalab Khan."

"The Uzbek Captain?" Shivaji *Raje* smiled. "What does he know of the Sahyadris? I would have thought Shaista Khan would entrust such a campaign to one of his Maratha Captains."

Bahirji nodded. "Suits us, Highness. *Rai Baghan* is his second-in-command."

"Savitribai *Deshmukh*!" Jijabai gave a bitter laugh. "She has the heart of a tigress, but what use is that to our motherland if she fights for the *Yavanas*?"

"What is Kartalab Khan planning?"

"To cross the Sahyadris through the Bor Pass."

Raje pondered briefly and then looked at Bahirji. "Assemble the war council immediately."

The Maratha war council assembled late that night in Shivaji *Raje*'s personal chamber. The men huddled around a single lamp that cast a golden glow over the map spread out on a small table.

Shivaji *Raje* placed his pointer on the map at a place that said 'Bor Ghat'. "Kartalab Khan is planning to traverse the Sahyadri Hills via this pass," he said. "We must divert him from there."

"Where do you want him to cross, Highness?" Bahirji asked.

"I think the Kuruwande Pass is better suited for the Mughal troops, isn't it?" *Raje* said with a smile, stroking his beard.

"Better suited for them, or for us?" Netoji Palkar asked, his eyes lighting up at the prospect of battle.

The men chuckled as they realized what their Lord was planning.

"Netoji, assemble five thousand troops in the Pen region and block access to the Bor Pass. Bahirji, leak the news of the movements to Kartalab's camp."

The two men nodded. These actions would definitely push the Khan to take the Kuruwande Pass, a *kos* south of the Bor Pass.

"Tanhaji and Pilaji will deploy five thousand infantrymen in the Tungar forest, around the path the Mughals are expected to take.

This deployment must be completed before the Mughals enter the forest. Our men must be well concealed, out of the enemy's sight."

Tanhaji and Pilaji had their work cut out. Their task was crucial as their men would launch the attack.

"Once the entire Mughal army has entered the hills, Netoji will move his troops to block the eastern end of the pass. At the same time, I will personally march with another five thousand men and block the western exit of the pass into the Konkan."

Netoji smiled. "Ingenious! The Mughals will get trapped in the forest with Marathas all around them!"

"Exactly!" Shivaji *Raje* clenched his fist. "Now look..." He picked up the pointer and placed it on the map where it said 'Umbarkhind'. "Umbare village lies some three *kos* west of the Kuruwande Pass. Here, the path, blocked by hills in front, turns south, with steep cliffs on either side. This is the infamous Umbarkhind, which is nearly four to five *kos* long. The Mughals will have a tough time negotiating the route."

The men nodded. Shivaji *Raje* looked at Tanhaji. "Tanhya, designate pickets to monitor the progress of the Mughal vanguard. As soon as the vanguard reaches the middle of the Umbarkhind path, sound the war drums and attack."

"Yes, Sire!"

The Maratha King had set a deadly trap and Kartalab Khan could do little but walk straight into it.

Shivaji *Raje*'s move worked perfectly. As soon as Kartalab Khan received the news of Netoji Palkar's movements in Pen region, he decided to change his plan and ordered his troops to march to the Kuruwande Pass, south of the Bor Pass, which was now blocked by Netoji and his men.

Rai Baghan was alarmed by this move and tried to convince Kartalab to avoid the dangerous route. "Khan *Sahib*, the Kuruwande Pass leads to a most arduous path across Umbarkhind. It will be extremely difficult for our troops to negotiate that route."

Kartalab smirked. Why the hell had Shaista Khan tagged this woman to his tail? He firmly believed that women should be banned from military camps. "*Pundita,*" he replied, his voice heavy with contempt, "nothing is impossible for me and my men. Seevaji must have received news of our intent to cross the Bor Pass and hence has moved Netoji Palkar to that region. If he has spies, so do we. We will counter his move and change our course to take a different route across the hills and so outflank them. Our objective is to reach the Konkan coast. I do not wish to engage Seeva's troops before crossing the hills."

"Khan *Saheb*, let us choose an easier way through the hills."

"We will waste too much time moving to another entry point into the hills. The Kuruwande Pass is the closest. We must move our troops across the pass quickly."

"But Khan *Saheb*, that way..."

Kartalab raised his hand, silencing her objections. He wanted her to know he was in command. *Rai Baghan* realized her opinion would not be heeded and fell silent.

"Order our troops to change course at once," Khan said.

"Yes Sir!" *Rai Baghan* left, thinking of the hardships they were about to encounter in the Sahyadris. Another thought crossed her mind. Was the wily Shivaji forcing them to divert to Kuruwande Pass? Shivaji's tactics were far too ingenious for the thick-skulled Kartalab to comprehend, she knew. She sensed danger, but who would listen to her?

Umbarkhind Pass, mid-January 1661

Kartalab Khan panted heavily as he lowered himself onto a rock in the mountainside, to take a breather. Damn these Sahyadris, he thought. These western hills had proved far more strenuous to climb than he had imagined. Removing his turban, he wiped the sweat from his forehead as he signalled to his attendant to fetch water. All around him, men had flopped down to rest their exhausted limbs.

The massive Mughal army had reached the environs of Fort Lohgad the previous day and camped for the night. Much against his men's wishes, Kartalab had given the order to march early the next morning. His Captains complained the men had not had sufficient rest, but Kartalab pushed them on, not wishing to waste time and allow the Marathas to make any further deployments. Another day or two, he had thought, and they would be through the hills. Once out, the Konkan was his for the taking.

But that was easier said than done. His reconnoiterance platoon warned him the route was fraught with difficulty. And then there was that Maratha woman, *Rai Baghan*, who kept insisting they change their plans to avoid the route. Despite these deterrents, he had persisted with his plan. How difficult could it be? It was a mountain after all. Soldiers were required to surmount all difficulties, including those posed by the terrain.

The Mughal army had entered the hills via the Kuruwande Pass and traversed three *kos* of foot tracks in the gorge, between steep hills. They had, wisely as it turned out, left behind their heavy guns, elephants and camels at their base camp on the plains. It would have been impossible to move those through the forest.

The men had trudged *kos* upon *kos* of punishing mountainous track. The going was slow and tougher than tough. The sun scorched their bodies, draining them of fluids. The forest was untenable, with no provision for food or water in the hostile territory. Now, as he sat panting on the rock, Kartalab began doubting his own decision.

The Mughal vanguard, under the command of Rajput Captains Amar Singh and Mitrasen, had advanced quite a fair distance

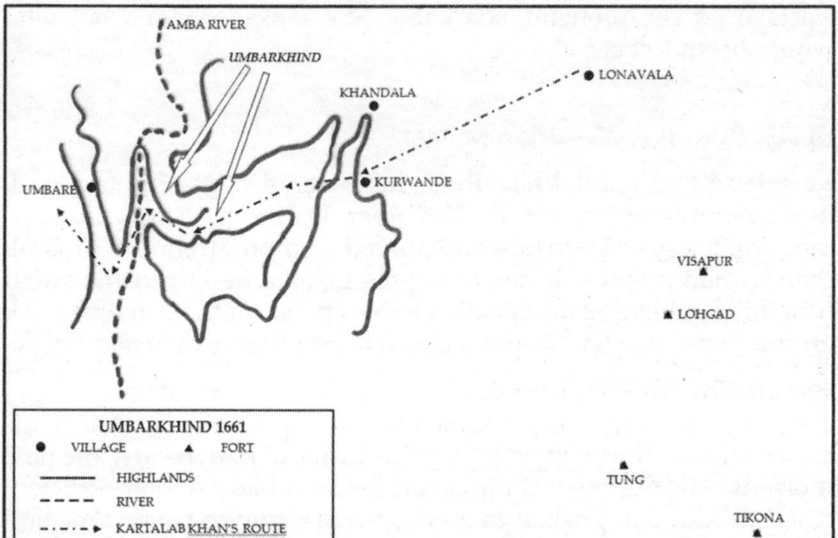

over the Umbarkhind trail, the most treacherous part of the entire route. As the men struggled on, to their right was a steep cliff, rising to the skies, and to their left was a precipitous fall into the valley. The incline, the slippery path and the ever present fear of falling into the gorge, sapped the men's resolve. Kartalab's own contingent, towards the rear of the Mughal army had just entered Umbarkhind.

Rai Baghan marched right behind the great Khan. "Getting a taste of the Sahyadris, Khan *Saheb*?" the Maratha lady taunted.

Khan sneered at her as he took a swig from the leather water bag. "It will soon be over, *Pundita*," he said optimistically.

"We have just started the Umbarkhind trail, Khan *Saheb*," *Rai Baghan* replied, reminding him of the hardships in store.

A Mughal *hasham* struggled up to them, panting. "My Lord," he gasped, "there is definite news the Maratha *Sirnaubat* has marched to the mouth of the Kuruwande Pass and blocked that exit."

Kartalab and *Rai Baghan* both stood up. *Rai Baghan* was unusually alarmed. Were her worst fears about to come true? Kartalab cursed under his breath. Netoji Palkar stationed right behind them? That was not good news under any circumstance, and certainly not under the present one, when they were so compromised by the geography of the place.

"On your feet! Get moving! March!" Kartalab yelled to his men.

Rai Baghan thought that for the first time, she sensed fear in the Khan's demeanour. Then they heard it... the drums. They were beating a slow rhythmic beat in the distance. Who the hell was beating drums in this godforsaken forest?

"What's that?" Khan asked, his right hand involuntarily shifting to the hilt of his sword.

Rai Baghan had already unsheathed her's. "Maratha war drums," she replied curtly and began rallying her men.

Maratha war drums? *Ya Allah*! Where had the Marathas come from in this cursed valley?

Amar Singh heard the drums at the same time. He was marching with his Mughal-Rajput platoon in the vanguard. For a brief moment he and his men stood transfixed, trying to guage the implication of the beating drums. Then they drew their swords.

Amar Singh felt a gush of air brush his ear. His soldier's instinct made him jerk his head away in an instant, but in the very next he heard a guttural sound behind him. He turned around to see one of his men choking on his own blood, an arrow stuck in his throat. The arrow had missed Amar Singh by a hairsbreadth. His eyes widened in horror at the realization that they were being attacked.

Within moments, more men fell, arrows piercing Rajput and Mughal necks and chests alike. For some time, all they could hear was the swish of arrows cutting across thin air, followed by the screams of the men who were hit. Then came the gun shots...like sharp distant claps, echoing through the valley. The Mughal ranks were panic stricken as men fell like dried leaves. Where the hell were the arrows and shot coming from? No one had a clue. Shouts of warning and screams of the dying echoed through the gorge. There was a mad scramble for cover. The Mughal vanguard was in utter chaos.

Amar Singh and Mitrasen rallied their men as best they could and took cover behind some trees. But the projectiles seemed to come from all around them, from the slope to their right and the valley to their left. After being pounded for some time, the firing stopped and silence returned. The rattled Mughal army looked all around in fear of another onslaught.

Amar Singh summoned a foot soldier. "Hurry back and inform Kartalab Khan *Sahib* of the attack. Tell him to be careful."

The *hasham* left, fearing more for his own life than the safety of his Commander. No sooner had he left, the Marathas poured out from everywhere and fell upon Amar Singh and his platoon, slashing, cutting and killing like demons. The Mughals stepped out from cover and crossed swords, but they were hopelessly outclassed. Pre-occupied with maintaining their foothold on the narrow path, the Marathas danced a deadly dance around them. Swords slashed and lances speared the Mughals from all sides. Death ruled. And then, almost in an instant, as suddenly as the attack had commenced, the mayhem ended as the Maratha ghosts disappeared into the forest.

Amar Singh and Mitrasen just stood there, stunned by the swiftness of the attack and the death sprewn around them.

The Mughal *hasham* dispatched by Amar Singh rushed back to reach the rearguard and get the message to the Commander. He warned all the platoons along the way. Some had already been attacked by the Marathas and were in a devastated state similar to the vanguard. Nearly three fourths of a *prahar* later, the *hasham* reached Kartalab Khan's platoon and winced as he saw the death and destruction in front of him. Hundreds lay dead, more lay wounded and screaming.

The *hasham* ran around till he found the Commander. Bowing, he said in gasps, "My Lord...I come from the vanguard...to inform you that we have been attacked. But it appears I am too late."

Kartalab Khan was stupefied, unable to comprehend what had happened. Less than half a *prahar* earlier, the Marathas had attacked, first shooting at them from behind cover, and later with a sudden assault. In a short time he had lost over a third of his platoon, before the Marathas disappeared into the valley.

Rai Baghan stood next to him, dazed by the Maratha attack and worried about the utter hopelessness of their situation. They had absolutely no defence at the moment. Her intuition had proved correct. Shivaji had lured them into this death trap.

Kartalab stared at the *hasham* and managed to nod his head. An injured *hasham* appeared behind them and bowed. He was bleeding from a deep gash to his left arm, which he clutched in an attempt to stem the flow of blood.

"Sir, our scouts have returned with the news that Shivaji himself blocks the western exit of the Umbarkhind Pass, with thousands of horsemen!" The *hasham* struggled to get the words out.

Kartalab's blood froze. The full reality of his position dawned upon him. He was trapped in this forest between two large Maratha cavalry units. Netoji Palkar blocked the eastern exit of this deadly pass, while the Maratha King himself blocked its western exit. And while they could neither move forward nor back, they were being attacked by Maratha infantry from all sides. Kartalab, a veteran of war on the plains, was dumbfounded by Shivaji's war tactics. His brain felt numb. He had no answers.

Rai Baghan stepped forward purposefully. "Khan *Saheb,* have you finally realized what you are dealing with here? Shivaji is no ordinary man. He has completely fooled you and trapped us in these hills. Look around...the enemy has such strength! I tried to warn you, but you would not listen to me."

Kartalab stared at her. He had no argument. She was right. His overconfidence had done them in.

"Shivaji is a tiger in the Sahyadris. You have brought our massive army into this damned forest, into his jaws!"

Rai Baghan's strong words stung the proud Mughal warrior, but he had nothing to retaliate with.

"How could you even think that a campaign in the Western Ghats would be a simple affair? You have ruined the Mughal army's reputation with your disastrous decisions. If you wish to save the rest of our men, you must surrender to Shivaji at once."

Kartalab's anger flared. "Surrender?" he shouted, outraged. "I will never surrender! We will fight on and move forward!"

"Fight on?" *Rai Baghan* was aghast at the senselessness of this. "Fight whom, Khan *Saheb*? We cannot even see the enemy! Our men are struggling to walk this route. How can they fight? If you persist with this insanity, we will all be dead in a short while."

Jadhavrao, another Maratha Captain in Khan's army, stepped forward. "Khan *Saheb, Pandita Rai Baghan* speaks the truth. Our position is untenable. More than a third of our men are dead and the rest are simply too exhausted. Our water reserves are low and we cannot find the enemy in this forest. We must surrender, My Lord. The soldiers are unwilling to fight where there is no hope."

Kartalab sat down and cradled his head in his hands. His proud nature refused to stand down, but he realized his demoralized army could stand no more. Reluctantly, he took the decision to parley.

A young Captain was summoned and asked to play the role of envoy. He had the difficult task of approaching Shivaji and suing for peace. But where was Shivaji? The news they had received was that Shivaji was stationed at the western exit of Umbarkhind...that was miles away! He would have to trudge all that distance to find the Maratha King, hoping he wouldn't get hit by an arrow or shot, or speared by a lance while he walked.

The reluctant diplomat managed to find a white *dushela* and tied it to a wooden staff, converting it into a white flag of truce. Thus armed, he began his journey, hoping that some Maratha soldiers would see him and approach as he walked.

Much later, he heard a voice say, "What are you up to, Mughal?"

The Captain looked around, but saw no one. "I come as a peace envoy from the Mughal Commander, Kartalab Khan *sahib*," he said. "I wish to see the Maratha King, Shivaji *Maharaj*."

"What for?" the voice asked.

"Kartalab Khan *Sahib* wishes to sue for peace. The Mughal army will surrender to Shivaji *Maharaj*."

Two Maratha soldiers walked out from the forest with naked blades. Two more followed with muskets at the ready. The diplomat was searched for weapons and then led in a westerly direction toward the exit to Umbarkhind Pass. As they walked, they passed scenes of destruction, as nearly every Mughal platoon had been devastated by Maratha attacks.

On a small hill west of Umbarkhind, Shivaji *Raje* sat on a majestic, armoured white stallion. *Raje* himself wore metal armour with breast and back plates, arm and leg guards, and chain-mail covering his arms, thighs and neck. On his head he wore a helmet with a thick nose guard. His Bhavani sword hung at his side and a large shield was slung over his back. Holding the reins of his horse in his right hand, he gently nudged the stallion forward.

The Maratha King was surrounded by mounted, armoured officers and foot soldiers. Tanhaji Malusare and Pilaji flanked him on either side. Their infantrymen had done their job impeccably, attacking the Mughals in short powerful bursts at lightning speed, leaving the enemy bleeding and breathless.

The Mughal diplomat knelt on the ground, and clasped his hands in front of his face. "Your Highness, we are completely at your mercy. We surrender unconditionally. Pray spare our lives and grant us safe passage."

Shivaji *Raje* raised his eyebrows and asked tersely, "How did Kartalab Khan think he could beat us in the Sahyadris? This land is extremely difficult for any outsiders. You Mughals are not used to the mountains. Has Kartalab Khan even seen hills before?"

"Forgive this transgression, Highness. We came here on orders of the Imperial General, Shaista Khan *Sahib*, and have suffered this ignonimity. We will go back and never return."

"I will spare your lives, but on my terms. Surrender will be unconditional. You will leave behind all weapons, ammunition, animals and treasury, and return empty handed!"

"Agreed, Your Highness. We will surrender all we have." The diplomat did not baulk at the stiff terms for he had no choice.

"Then you may go back. Your lives are spared." Shivaji *Raje* waved him away.

Maratha soldiers sounded drums and trumpets as a signal to the Maratha army spread across the valley and forest, to halt the attacks. The battle ended. Silence descended upon the valley. Peace returned. The Mughals sighed in relief. Their bemused Commander gave orders to hand over everything to the Marathas. Defeated and demoralised, Kartalab Khan and his surviving army turned back towards Pune, empty handed.

Emerging from the Kuruwande Pass onto the plains, Kartalab turned to look back at the Sahyadri Hills, a solemn and silent presence behind him. Foolishly, he had set foot in this dangerous country and paid a heavy price. Never again, he vowed, would he return to Seeva's lands.

2
WAR OF ATTRITION

Having humiliated Kartalab Khan and his vast army, Shivaji *Raje* decided to descend into the South Konkan. He wished not only to reconquer the territories he had lost in the aftermath of the Pratapgad battle, but also to capture new ones in order to expand the boundaries of his *Swarajya*. From Umbarkhind, he marched west and burst forth into the Konkan with nearly twenty thousand infantry and a detachment of cavalry. Netoji was ordered to march north with the cavalry and remain in the northern Konkan, to defend it from Mughal depredations.

Raje himself marched south with his infantry and reached the coastal town of Dabhol. Seeing the massive Maratha army at his doorstep, Pilaji, the *Deshmukh* of Dabhol, promptly capitulated and accepted Shivaji *Raje*'s suzerainty. *Raje* graciously accepted and agreed to continue his *watan*. Pilaji left no stone unturned to please his new Lord.

While at Dabhol, Shivaji *Raje* visited the Dalbhyeshwar temple, consecrated to Lord Mahadev, his family diety. With deep devotion, he worshipped his God, offering prayers and alms. Sitting on the stone ledge bordering the temple courtyard, *Raje* reflected on the political situation. His man-strength had increased considerably in the past years and so had the men's confidence in facing imperial armies. Yet, in his heart, he knew they still lacked the might to take on Shaista Khan's massive army head on. He had successfully repulsed the latest Mughal advance, but as long as Shaista Khan was stationed in Pune, he would continue to send armies into the *Swarajya*. He had to somehow get Shaista Khan out of Pune.

The third *prahar* of the day was almost over. A gentle afternoon breeze offered some relief as the sun's might gradually diminished. The temple courtyard, embowered in trees, offered a peaceful sanctum and Shivaji *Raje* enjoyed this moment of sanity in a life that had been an almost unending cascade of battles and politics. He knew it would only get worse as he locked horns with the Mughals.

"My Lord!" Tanhaji Malusare appeared, breaking the peaceful interlude. "Bahirji's man is here with news."

Immediately, Shivaji *Raje* snapped out of his reverie and nodded.

The spy came forth, bowed and said, "Highness, Jaswantrao Dalvi has fled from Palavni."

"That rascal!" Tanhaji growled. "He realized he stood no chance against us and bolted. If I ever lay my hands on him..." Tanhaji gripped the hilt of his sword.

Shivaji *Raje* laughed. "Where will he go? We will find him sooner or later. He must have fled south to join his comrade-in-arms."

"You mean Surve?"

"Yes. He probably feels that joining hands with Shringarpur's Surve will make him powerful enough to face us."

Jaswantrao Dalvi and Suryarao Surve had, a few months earlier, blocked Shivaji *Raje*'s path at the foothills of Fort Vishalgad, as *Raje* fled from Siddi Jauhar's siege of Panhala. *Raje* had fought them to get to Vishalgad.

"Bloody coward!" Tanhaji snarled under his breath. "So what do we do now? Do we march to Palavni?"

Raje shook his head. "Let us ignore Dalvi and Surve for a while. That should take them off guard. Send an envoy to Shringarpur and offer peace terms to Surve. Invite him to join us."

"Do you think he will?" Tanhaji felt certain that men like Surve and Dalvi would never be inclined to join them.

"No, he wont," *Raje* concurred. "We can finish both Surve and Dalvi any time now; they do not have the forces to beat us. But our objective is not simply to avenge past incidents. We must accomplish this campaign swiftly before Adilshah decides to send imperial troops against us."

"Let him!" Tanhaji said simply. "We'll be ready when he does."

Raje looked at his comrade and laughed. Getting up from the ledge he had been sitting on, he patted Tanhaji on his shoulder. "Order our troops to break camp first thing tomorrow."

Leaving behind two thousand men and an Officer at Dabhol, Shivaji *Raje* marched, first east to Chiplun, and then south to Sangameshwar, annexing both towns. Shringarpur, which was the seat of Surve's *jagir*, lay east of his path, but he chose to bypass this Adilshahi vassal fief for the time being. He would hit back at Surve and Dalvi, but later.

Shivaji *Raje* ordered his Infantry Commander, Tanhaji, to stay back at Sangameshwar with a detachment. Pilajirao, an infantry Captain, stayed to support Tanhaji.

The victorious Maratha march continued southward, swallowing Adilshahi territory. Devrukh was soon annexed and the Marathas next landed in Rajapur, a rich business town.

Outskirts of Rajapur town, Mid-March 1661

Shivaji *Raje* arrived at the outskirts of Rajapur with four thousand infantry and camped there. The officers he sent into the town compelled the prominent businessmen and traders of the town to come and meet their Master. The rich men of Rajapur arrived and bowed to the Maratha King. A ransom amount was fixed for each, and later paid in full, as demanded.

Meanwhile, the Adilshahi officers and garrison at Rajapur, unable to face the Marathas, fled the town. Shivaji *Raje* did not have to raise his sword to annex it.

The English factory at Rajapur was thrown into turmoil when news of Shivaji's raid reached it. Henry Revington, the chief officer at the factory, who had earlier helped Adilshahi General Siddi Jauhar against Shivaji *Raje* at Panhala, feared his end was near. He had been on tenterhooks these past months, expecting a backlash from Shivaji. Now, in a desperate attempt to broker peace, he went to Shivaji *Raje*'s camp outside the town. With him went his subordinate officer, Philip Gifford.

The meddlesome Englishmen bowed to Shivaji *Raje* and sued for pardon, offering to pay some ransom. Shivaji *Raje*'s blazing eyes locked onto Revington's and the latter's limbs went numb. *Raje* was in no mood to forgive these foreigners who had so blatantly gone back on their own assurances.

"These Englishmen came here as merchants, but they have a habit of poking their noses in our political affairs. They must be taught a lesson," Shivaji *Raje* said angrily. "Arrest them!"

Revington and Gifford were chained immediately. A platoon of soldiers was dispatched to the English factory and five more officers arrested. The factory itself was sacked and dug up to reveal any concealed valuables. The Marathas carried away cash and goods worth nearly ninety thousand rupees.

Shivaji *Raje*'s Marathas took charge of Rajapur, which was annexed to their *Swarajya*. The Adilshahi administrators were dismissed and sent away, and *Raje* appointed his own men. One Adilshahi clerk, however, stuck around, refusing to leave. He begged the newcomers to take him to their King.

"Why do you want to meet *Raje*?" he was asked.

"I wish to offer him my services!" the man replied matter-of-factly.

The diminutive man, clad in a simple white *angarkha* and *dhoti*, with a cloth turban on his head, stood in front of Shivaji *Raje*. His fair, clean shaven face sported a thin moustache. He was slimly built but stood erect, with a taut chest. His eyes betrayed the admiration he felt for the man seated before him.

"Who are you, young man?" *Raje* asked him curiously.

"My name is Balaji Avji Chitre, Your Highness," he replied. "I have worked as a servant of the Adilshah for many years."

"Why did you wish to see me?"

"Highness, I have heard much about Shivaji *Raje* Bhosale. For years I have longed to see him. This is a fortunate day, for I have cast my eyes upon one so brave and noble!"

Raje smiled. He was used to adulation, real and feigned. "What have you heard about Shivaji?" he asked.

"That he is a fierce soldier, a great military General and King, and above all, that he has vowed to free the Maratha homeland from the tyranny of the Sultans."

This man certainly had a way with words, Shivaji *Raje* thought. "I have taken over Rajapur from the Adilshah," *Raje* said. "You are free to leave."

"*Raje*, I would feel blessed to work for you. Pray accept me into your service," Balaji Chitre said, hands folded in supplication.

Raje considered for a while and then asked, "What are your talents?"

"I have experience in administrative work and accounting."

Raje stroked his beard. He was always on the lookout for capable young men to enroll into his offices. Something about Balaji Avji Chitre impressed him.

"Balaji, our *Swarajya* needs enthusiastic and devoted men like you. Join us by all means. You shall be a *chitnis* in my government."

Shivaji *Raje* marched on from Rajapur and annexed territory as far south as Kharepatan. Having garrisoned the newly aquired towns and put in an administrative framework, he marched north once again. En route he received news that Suryarao Surve had agreed to be his vassal. But could he be relied upon? *Raje* was disinclined to trust Surve, but willing to give him a chance. He dispatched a letter to Surve: *I am going north with my force to Palavni. Ride north with your men and join me there...*

When Surve received this letter, he told Shivaji *Raje's* messenger, "I am but a humble servant who follows his master. I will meet *Raje* at Palavni. Take this message to him."

No sooner had the messenger left, than Surve changed his mind. In fact, he had never planned to submit to Shivaji.

"Shivaji is going north," he said to Jaswantrao Dalvi, holed up in his Shringarpur fief. "He will not return anytime soon. Let us launch a surprise attack on his force at Sangameshwar. We will attack in the night and destroy their camp."

THE MARATHA CAMP, OUTSKIRTS OF SANGAMESHWAR,
A FEW DAYS LATER

Peace reigned in Sangameshwar. Tanhaji Malusare, Pilaji and their garrison rested in their camp. Tanhaji, sleeping in the open, smiled as he looked up at the clear starry sky above him. He felt blessed to be part of this incredible *Swarajya* movement that had swept the Deccan in the past decade and a half. He felt honoured to be a soldier in Shivaji *Raje's* liberating army; to be his comrade. Shivaji *Raje*, the name meant more to him than any God he had worshipped. Shivaji *Raje was* his God. Blessed was this land to have given birth to Shivaji! Tanhaji was convinced that one day he would see his childhood friend, and now his Master and King, destroy all the Sultans in the land, even the Mughal Emperor.

Sangameshwar had been annexed, along with most of South Konkan. The people of the Konkan had welcomed the Marathas. Old neglected temples had been re-established. For the first time in centuries, people could visit temples without fear.

Jaswantrao Dalvi, the *Jagirdar* of Palavni, had fled south. Palavni, which was north of Sangameshwar, was deserted and Shivaji *Raje* had himself marched to annex it. Shringarpur, south of Sangameshwar, was no threat either as its *Jagirdar,* Surve, had submitted. The other Adilshahi Governors, officers and garrisons in South Konkan, had fled to Bijapur. There was no danger now. Tanhaji closed his eyes as sleep lulled his thoughts.

The second *prahar* of the night had just begun when the peace was rudely shattered by the sound of a horn being blown on the southern side of the camp. Tanhaji woke with a start. Who the hell was blowing a horn at this time? He did not have to wait long for an answer. Messages were relayed by blowing horns and the shouts from their pickets. A large body of soldiers was closing in on them. Who could it be? *Raje* had already gone to Palavni with his force and there had been no intelligence reports on movements by the Bijapuri army.

Tanhaji sprang up, calling to Pilaji as he put on his turban and armour. Quickly tying his *dushela* around his waist, he picked up his sword and shield and rushed to the south side of the camp, followed closely by Pilaji. By then, it was clear they had been attacked by someone. It had to be some Adilshahi army or *jagirdar* with his own force, but who?

Clashes had already broken out between Tanhaji's Marathas and the raiders. The Marathas had been taken off-guard and that had hampered their defence. But Tanhaji's arrival sparked new vigour and new purpose. The experienced Infantry Commander that he was, Tanhaji rallied his men quickly, barking orders to his subordinates. Then he jumped headlong into the melée. Tanhaji's sword began felling enemy soldiers like flies. Despite being surprised and rudely awakened, the Marathas recovered well and pushed back the enemy.

Pilaji was fighting too, separated from Tanhaji. Full of energy intially, he quickly tired. Overcome by the enemy and fearing death, Pilaji began to withdraw. Tanhaji sensed this change in the battle dynamics. Pilaji was his second-in-command here. If he fled the field, a sizeable chunk of his garrison would go with him and all could be lost. And Tanhaji hated to lose.

Making a valiant effort, Tanhaji made it to Pilaji, shouting above the clamour, "Pilaji! Be brave! Do not withdraw now!"

Pilaji looked across at his Commander. Tanhaji could see fear writ large on his face. "The enemy is too strong, Tanhaji!" Pilaji exclaimed. "We must flee, or we will be cut down!"

"Then so be it!" Tanhaji yelled, his face contorted with anger. "Who the hell is scared of death? Tanhaji and his men never withdraw from battle! They fight to win...or die!"

He grabbed the scared Captain by the arm and dragged him to the rear of the action. A few of Tanhaji's personal guard accompanied them. "Tie him up!" Tanhaji ordered. The men promptly tied Pilaji to a tent pole.

"Release me, Tanhaji!" Pilaji begged. "I will be killed here!"

"No you won't," Tanhaji promised him. "My men will stand guard here to protect you. Now watch carefully as we battle the enemy. Learn *how* to fight!"

Tanhaji gripped his sword and shield, gritted his teeth and turned back towards the battle scene. *"Har Har Mahadev!"* he screamed as he fell upon the enemy with vengeance. His fierce onslaught rejuvenated his men and rattled the enemy. It was a strange battle. There were Marathas on both sides, but those with Tanhaji were the defenders of a new order called *Swarajya,* and a new King, Shivaji, while those with Surve belonged to the old order that served the foreign Sultans. Tanhaji's relentless blade sliced through the attackers with incredible speed and deftness. In a short while he had reached Surve's own contingent at the rear. Tanhaji caught sight of Surve, who stood clad in armour behind his men and realized the rascal had first accepted Shivaji *Raje*'s peace offer, and then double-crossed him. "Surve *haraamjadyaa!*" Tanhaji screamed, rushing toward the chieftain.

Surve took one look at Tanhaji and a chill ran down his spine. He had never seen such rage on a man's face. "Stop him!" Surve's voice trembled as he ordered his men to tackle Shivaji's Commander.

Surve's men rushed forward. Screaming murder, Tanhaji struck the first of the attackers in the face. The man's left eye ruptured and jaw split open as Tanhaji's sword sliced across. The man behind was quick enough to land a blow to Tanhaji's left. Tanhaji blocked his sword with his shield and the very next moment buried his own sword into the man's chest. The man collapsed, choking on his own blood. Tanhaji yanked his sword out and, with lightning speed, whirled around, slashing the third attacker across the neck. His blow was so strong that the man's head came off clean and rolled over the ground. A fountain of blood erupted from the man's neck as his body crashed down.

Tanhaji's men had by now killed several more of Surve's bodyguards and Surve himself stood dangerously exposed. Suryarao Surve panicked. He had received news that Shivaji's contingent at Sangameshwar was relatively small and had thus expected this raid to be an easy affair. He had also received a *firmaan* from Adilshah, ordering him to stop Shivaji's raids, and he had to do something to showcase his efforts. Now he rued his decision. He had not accounted for Tanhaji Malusare.

Surve ordered his men to withdraw. "Get out of here!" he screamed. "Withdraw!"

As his men began pulling back, Surve himself mounted his horse and fled back toward Shringarpur. It was yet another reverse for an Adilshahi vassal and another victory for Shivaji *Raje*. Tanhaji's valour had saved the day.

Shivaji *Raje* received the news of the Sangameshwar attack at Palavni, the former seat of Jaswantrao Dalvi, who had fled south to join Suryarao Surve. *Raje* had annexed Palavni, and Dalvi had lost his *jagir* forever.

Now, *Raje*'s eyes blazed with anger as he listened to Bahirji's spy describe the sudden night raid. Surve had double-crossed him, but he had half expected that, had he not? In these past fifteen years, the most difficult task had been to convince the Maratha *jagirdars* to quit the Sultan's service and join him. Most had refused. 'Why join Shivaji?' had been the most common reaction. 'If we have to serve someone, why not the Adilshah?' had said Chandrarao More of Jawli, the Maval *Deshmukhs,* and now the *jagirdars* of the Konkan.

All had opposed his dream of *Swarajya*. He had been compelled to resort to force to either make them change their minds or summarily remove them from their *jagirs*.

"Pilaji was scared and nearly ran from the battlefield," the spy narrated. "All seemed lost for our garrison, but Tanhaji *Subedar* stopped Pilaji and tied him to a tent pole to prevent him from leaving and said to him, 'Watch how we battle the enemy and learn how to fight'. He then went ahead and won the battle."

Raje smiled. "Our Tanhaji does not know how to lose a battle. Is he alright?"

"He was injured, Your Highness, but all is well."

Dismissing the man, Shivaji *Raje* turned to the young Captain who stood behind him. "Get our men ready. We march south at first light. It is time to put an end to Suryarao Surve's *jagirdari* in Shringarpur."

SHRINGARPUR, SOUTH KONKAN, 29 APRIL 1661

Suryarao Surve and Jaswantrao Dalvi sat together in the former's palatial home in Shringarpur. Surve gently puffed on a hookah, while Dalvi sipped wine from a silver tumbler. Both were smarting from the reverse at Sangameshwar, but they also believed the Shivaji threat was behind them for the present.

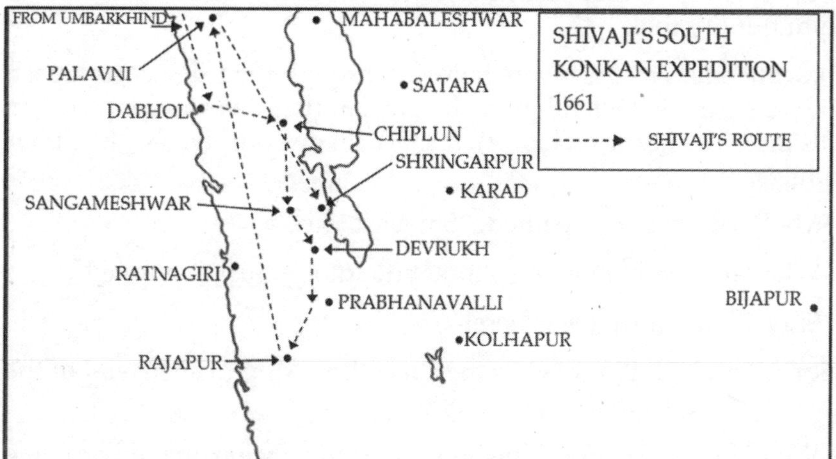

"Shivaji is bound to get angry when he hears of our attack on Sangameshwar," Dalvi said worriedly.

"Yes," Surve agreed, blowing smoke, "but he won't return now. He has already gone north with his troops."

"You should not have let your troops leave. What if he comes back?"

"He will not!" Surve said emphatically, making a brave attempt to calm their mutual nerves. "I had to let my troops go as many were injured anyway."

"I cannot fathom why the Adilshah has not sent imperial troops after Shivaji this time. He should have been blockaded in the Konkan and finished off. The Sultan has left us *jagirdars* to fend for ourselves."

Surve laughed. "You scare much too easily, Jaswantrao," he said, mocking his friend.

Dalvi shifted uneasily. "I am the one who has lost his *jagir*, Suryarao!" he replied, pained by his pitiful condition. "Look!" he said, spreading his arms dramatically, "I am living like a refugee in your house."

Attendants walked in with a selection of choice dishes to engage their masters. The aroma made Jaswantrao temporarily forget his worries. Surve smiled and offered him the food. Dalvi dug in purposefully. Worry had no doubt made him sick, but it had made him hungry too!

A while later, as they were halfway through their delicious repast, Surve's personal attendant rushed in, panting, sweat running down his face. The horrified look on his face made both *jagirdars* lose their smiles.

"My Lord," the man panted, "Shivaji... Shivaji..."

"What are you blabbering about, you idiot?" Surve snapped.

"Shivaji, My Lord. He is here!"

Surve and Dalvi jumped to their feet, knocking over several of the plates of food spread in front of them.

"What! Shivaji is here? How in Lord Mahadev's name did he come back here?" Surve was both perplexed and worried.

Dalvi was petrified. "Now what?" He looked at Surve, expecting him to have a ready answer.

"How far away is he?" Surve asked

"Our outposts last saw him about two *kos* away. He is marching toward us at great speed with a sea of troops, My Lord!"

"How many?"

"Twelve thousand...maybe fifteen…" The attendant was close to tears. "We must leave, now!"

"I told you, he would come back!" Dalvi wailed. He could see his end clearly. "You should never have let your troops go! In fact, we should never have attacked Sangameshwar! What the hell do we do now?"

Surve shot an angry look at Dalvi, but could say nothing. There was no way they could withstand such a large army. "We have no choice but to leave immediately," he said finally.

The two *jagirdars* evacuated the palace in a hurry, with as much as they could take away, and fled east towards Bijapur. The only safe place, they felt, was the Adilshahi capital.

Shivaji *Raje* marched into Shringarpur and annexed the town unopposed. He personally stormed Surve's palace and took charge of the ex-*jagirdar*'s home. As his men ransacked the building, *Raje* stood in the grand audience hall, where Surve had once held meetings with his staff and visiting dignitaries. Rows of comfortable, ornately carved chairs stood on either side of the hall, which was decorated with brocade draperies. At the far end stood a grand *baithak* covered in expensive, embroidered upholstery. It was obviously the seat of power, the seat of the King of Shringarpur.

Fuming within, Shivaji *Raje* walked up to Surve's seat. He wore body armour and a helmet. In his right hand he held his Bhavani sword and in his left, a shield. Tanhaji Malusare stood behind him, like a wall guarding his back. "These *jagirdars* are the real hurdles in our path, Tanhaji," *Raje* said, his eyes narrow slits. "How many of these petty chieftains can we convince to join our cause? Our lifespan will be exhausted, but there will still be some left who will come back to fight us. We must put an end to the *jagirdari* system itself."

With that, *Raje* raised his booted right foot and kicked the *baithak*, overturning it. Suryarao Surve had been summarily removed from his fief, just as Chandrarao More had been removed from Jawli many years ago.

"Why have you tied Pilajirao's hands, Tanhaji?" Shivaji *Raje* asked his comrade as he looked at the the young man standing before him, a blank expression on his face. The man stood erect, yet his eyes were focussed on the ground. His anger, directed against this man who called himself 'King', was countered by the humiliation of having failed to prevent his own master's annihilation. Yet, he felt irreristibly drawn to Shivaji *Raje,* unable to resist his charm.

"Release him!" *Raje* commanded. Pilajirao's hands were freed. "Pilajirao, forgive my man Tanhaji. He is obsessed with my security. He will not allow anyone within ten arm's length of my body without tying his hands." *Raje* laughed, looking affectionately at Tanhaji. Pilajirao continued to stare at the ground in silence.

They were sitting in Suryarao Surve's grand audience chamber, in the annexed fief. Tanhaji and his men had accosted Pilajirao Shirke, the ex-*jagirdar*'s *Diwan*.

"Pilajirao, do not grieve over your master's defeat. Surve had it coming. He promised to join us in our fight for *Swarajya,* and then back-stabbed us. I never forgive such men. You, however, are a sensible man. Join us now and be part of our movement."

Pilajirao raised his eyes to look at the man he had heard so much about; the man who had felled Afzal Khan and stood up against the Sultan, and survived. "You ask your enemy's *Diwan* to join you?" he asked, surprised.

Shivaji *Raje* rose from his seat and slowly walked toward Pilajirao. Gently placing his hands on Pilajirao's shoulders, he said, "I have a god given gift, Pilajirao. In an instant I can gauge a man's character. Yours is pure. You will never betray your Master...you never have. I need faithful men like you beside me. Join me now and lend your hand in creating something for future generations."

Tanhaji shifted uneasily. He had never understood his Master's ways. *Raje* had ordered Surve's stronghold to be completely destroyed and his men chased away. Yet, he spent time in trying to convince the *Diwan* to join them.

"Join us, Pilajirao! The days of Sultanate rule are numbered. The people are awakening to our own govenrment. The Gods shall see our mission fulfilled. Do not get left out."

Pilajirao sank to his knees and touched Shivaji *Raje*'s feet. "From this day, *Raje*, I accept you as my Lord," he said. "I shall remain faithful to you as long as I live. My family is at your mercy."

Shivaji *Raje* pulled him up by the shoulders. "I accept wholeheartedly the responsibility for the families of all my men, Pilajirao. That is why they never flinch in battle. Welcome to our *Swarajya*."

"Welcome Sire, to my humble abode." Pilajirao had invited his new Lord to honour his house. He ushered *Raje* to a specially made *baithak* and proceeded to ceremoniously wash his feet with his own hands. Shivaji *Raje* smiled.

He noticed two young children, standing away from the assembly of men. "Pilajirao, whose children are those?" he asked his host.

"Sire, they are my children," Pilajirao replied, beckoning the young boy and girl forward. The boy was older; he came forth and touched *Raje*'s feet. The girl tagged along behind her brother and did the same. *Raje*'s face lit up with a broad smile as he placed his hands on their heads and murmured: *Ayushyamaan bhava*...

"The boy's name is Ganaji, and the girl is Rajasbai." Pilaji beamed proudly at his children.

"Pilaji, your daughter reminds me of my own daughters," *Raje* said. Momentarily his eyes betrayed a sense of forlornness at being away from his family most of the time. Even when he was home, he had little time for his own children. That was the curse of being King.

Shivaji *Raje* appointed Pilajirao to his old office in Shringarpur, as an assistant to Tryambak Bhaskar, the newly appointed Head of the *Suba*. A few days later, *Raje* left Shringarpur.

RAJGAD, END 1661

It had been several months since Shivaji *Raje* had returned from his south Konkan campaign. While he tried to make diplomatic moves and shift his forces around, Shaista Khan and his massive Mughal juggernaut sat firmly in the Pune region, the epicenter of the

Swarajya. Try as he might, he could not figure out a way to shake up the Mughals. Kartalab Khan's defeat in Umbarkhind had hurt them, no doubt, but *Raje* knew that it would have been one small wound on their monstrous body. In retaliation for that reverse, Shaista Khan had created several mobile units of a few thousand horsemen each, under capable officers. Their only job was to spread out from their Pune camp and devastate Shivaji's lands and kill his people.

Raje paced his private audience chamber with clenched fists. His men stood silently, awaiting his orders. Bahirji Naik had arrived the previous day with news that Bulakhi Khan, a Mughal officer, had laid siege to Fort Dieri in north Konkan, about six *kos* east of Vasai town.

"Forgive me, Your Highness, but should we not plan a major strike on the Mughals?" Netoji Palkar asked impatiently.

Shivaji gave his Commander-in-Chief a frustrated look. Netoji's words were, at times, quite unbecoming of his post. "*Sirnaubat*, we do not yet have the firepower to take on the Mughals in an open war. Some day we certainly will, but this is not that day. We have to try our best to wear them down."

"I agree with His Highness," Moro *Punt* said. "Our success against Kartalab Khan was due to our strategic superiority and Khan's inferior intellect. We cannot expect similar results in an open war on the plains of Pune."

"Create swift cavalry units and spread them around the Mughal bases," *Raje* said, expounding his plans. "Find out where they get their grain and fodder supplies and cut them off. Conduct lightning raids on Mughal camps at night; slaughter as many as possible, but do not engage decisively. As soon as the enemy begins to retaliate, withdraw and flee. I do not want to lose too many of our soldiers in these raids. The Mughals may feel their men are expendable, but my men are not. Preserve our numbers."

"Understood, Highness!" Netoji nodded curtly. "I will begin spreading our forces immediately."

"But Highness," Moro *Punt* interjected, his face grave, "a war like that could go on for months...maybe years. Our people will have to suffer for that long."

Shivaji *Raje* sat down and sighed. Moro *Punt* had touched a raw nerve...his people... Did they not live in his *Swarajya* in the hope that their King would protect them from depredation by the imperial troops? And all he could do was sit in his palace and order his troops to wear down the enemy over months or years while they continued to suffer...

"Spread the word to the Maval *Deshmukhs,* that on the slightest hint of approaching Mughal troops, they are to move the people to safe hiding places in the hills."

"And what do we do about Bulakhi Khan, Sire?"

Raje turned to look at the burly man standing to his right. Sambhaji Kavji Kondhalkar had been with him like a shadow these past years. "Someone will have to go after him," *Raje* replied, smiling.

Kondhalkar's left hand shifted to the hilt of his sword. "Just give the order, Sire, and I will go," he said simply.

Raje laughed. "Go after him, Sambhaji. Send him back to Pune like we sent back Kartalab Khan!"

Sambhaji Kavji Kondhalkar left Rajgad with a detachment of Maratha forces and fell upon Bulakhi Khan's besieging Mughal troops, a few days later. In the ensuing battle, Kondhalkar and his men managed to slay over four hundred Mughals and scatter the rest of the Mughal army. Bulakhi Khan had to return to Pune, humiliated while Kondhalkar returned to his Master.

Netoji Palkar, meanwhile, conducted several raids upon the Mughal troops, harassing them. He cut off their supply chains and in many instances, their water as well, forcing them to shift their camps and withdraw from several incursions of their own. What frustrated Shaista Khan the most was that the Marathas never seemed to lose any men! The moment his troops turned on them, they fled!

In one such attack on Namdar Khan and Sar-afraz Khan, Netoji was seriously injured, and had to withdraw in a hurry, leaving behind some supplies, petty cash and some animals. These items fell to the Mughal officers, who trumpeted the incident. They declared to their General, Shaista Khan, that it was great victory over Seevaji's *Sirnaubat*. Sweets were distributed, not only in the Mughal camp at Pune, but also in Delhi, as the news of this 'victory' was conveyed to the Emperor.

Namdar Khan continued to ravage *Swarajya* lands in north Konkan. While in the vicinity of Fort Lohgad, he and his troops razed nearly eighty villages in one day. He then camped in the vicinity of Fort Tikona and continued to burn down villages for another two days. Shivaji *Raje* fumed with rage when he heard these reports from his spy network.

A few months later, *Raje* received news that Namdar Khan was in the vicinity of Mira Hill, near the town of Pen, in north Konkan. He left from Rajgad with his troops and, at great speed, rode west across the Sahyadris and emerged into the Konkan. He launched a sudden attack on Namdar Khan near Pen, defeating him. Namdar Khan fled back to the Pune camp.

Such skirmishes went on and the Mughals continued to be singed by Maratha attacks. In the nearly three years since he had marched to the Deccan at the head of a massive Mughal army, Shaista Khan's success had been limited to Pune and Fort Chakan. Shivaji *Raje* and his Marathas had managed to frustrate him everywhere else. It was time to strike the fatal blow.

3
SHIVAJI, THE SORCERER

THE ROYAL PALACE, DELHI FORT, LATE 1662

"The Pune camp is quiet, Your Majesty. Nothing much is being planned right now."

Aurangzeb's eyes blazed with anger as he heard these words from Hussain, his chief spy. The Deccan campaign had gone on for over two years and the Mughal General, his uncle Shaista Khan, had failed to achieve much against the infidel Seevaji. The imperial treasury was being emptied to support the massive army, yet Shaista Khan had little to show for it.

"Namdar Khan and Bulakhi Khan have both suffered defeats at the hands of Seeva's Marathas. Our army has won no fort of consequence since our victory at Chakan."

"Kartalab Khan, Namdar Khan, Bulakhi... aren't they supposed to be our best warriors?" Aurangzeb asked spitefully. "Seeva has defeated them all? What has our great Mughal army come to?"

"Sire, Seeva's *Sirnaubat,* Netoji Palkar, was injured in a skirmish with Namdar Khan and Sar-afroz Khan."

"Yes, I received the news. But our officers are blowing it out of proportion. It was a minor reverse for Seeva's troops. Do our officers think they can deceive me with such bloated news?"

"I agree, Your Majesty. It took eighteen of our officers, including *Rai Baghan,* to subdue Netoji."

"*Allah!* Eighteen of our *surma bahaddars* to subdue Seeva's *Sirnaubat*?"

"Sire, these past few weeks..." Hussain hesitated, knowing the Emperor would be enraged on hearing what he had to say next. He glanced up momentarily to find Aurangzeb's eyebrows raised questioningly. "...these past few weeks, the *Amir-ul-umrao* has been busy in feasts and celebrations... dancing and singing."

"Celebrations! What the hell for?"

"His daughter's marriage, Your Majesty. He married off his daughter to one of his officers."

"*Amir-ul-umrao!*" Aurangzeb swore under his breath as he banged his fists on the sidearms of his seat. "He is busy enjoying himself at my expense? Seeva, meanwhile, must be planning his next attack! I think I expected too much from my uncle."

Aurangzeb dismissed Hussain and summoned his scribe. He dictated a strongly worded letter to his Deccan *Subadar* and General Shaista Khan, ordering him to expedite matters against Seeva. He would give his uncle some more time, he decided. If he did not achieve any major success by then, he would recall him. The Deccan campaign could not drag on much longer.

RAJGAD PALACE, MARCH 1663

The first *prahar* of the night had begun. Despite the time of year, it was reasonably cool on top of the mountain. Shivaji *Raje* stood by the window of his bedchamber, gazing at the dark skies. The silence of the night was broken from time to time by the scratching of night insects and the distant hooting of an owl. *Raje* admired these night creatures, feeling that in many ways he was like them. The dark night was the best time to launch an attack on the enemy, was it not? Like an owl swooping down on a mouse with unerring precision in the dark...

A night raid! That was it! He would conduct a surprise night attack on Lal Mahal and cut down Shaista Khan himself! The idea struck him like a bolt of lightning.

There was a rustle behind him. *Raje* turned to see Soyara placing a glass of milk on a table by the side of his bed. "His Highness looks disturbed," she said, walking to him. "Is something the matter?"

"The King is bound to be disturbed when his people are not safe, Soyara."

Soyara became pensive. "The Mughals have proved pretty resilient," she remarked. "They continue to occupy Pune despite all our efforts to dislodge them."

"And I have to suffer the ignominy of sitting here in my palace, doing nothing," said *Raje*.

"Doing nothing? *Raje*, who knows better than me what you are going through?"

Raje shook his head in frustration. "Sometimes I wish I could think like my *Sirnaubat*."

"The *Sirnaubat*?" Soyara wrinkled her brow. "And what does he think we should do in this situation?"

"He thinks we should pick up our swords and attack Khan's Pune camp with all our strength."

"But is that likely to work?"

Raje gave a little laugh. "No. We will lose for sure, unless..."

"Unless?"

"Unless if we surprise them...at night."

"A night raid! But isn't their camp too large for a raid to be decisive?"

Shivaji *Raje* smiled at his queen. She certainly had a sharp brain. "Not their camp...Lal Mahal itself."

"You are planning to attack Lal Mahal!"

Raje nodded gravely. "We have to do something the Mughals would not dream we would do."

"A night raid on Lal Mahal!" Jijabai repeated as she and Shivaji *Raje*, sat in audience with their chief men the next morning. Netoji Palkar, Moro *Punt* Pingale, Tanhaji Malusare, Babaji *Deshpande* and Chimnaji *Deshpande* were all there.

"Yes, mother. We have managed to frustrate the Mughals in the past three years but these are pinpricks. It's time to dislodge them. I am convinced we can do that by taking out Shaista Khan himself."

Jijabai considered the bold strategem and then said, "A good idea if it works, *Raje*! But to conduct such a raid, we need people who are familiar with Lal Mahal's interiors. Do we have such people?"

"We know Lal Mahal inside out, Your Highness!" Chimnaji *Deshpande* said. "Babaji and I spent our childhood there."

He was right. Their father, Bapuji Mudgal *Deshpande,* was an old servitor of the Bhosales and had been one of the administrators of Lal Mahal. Chimnaji and Babaji had been Shivaji *Raje's* playmates.

Jijabai nodded. "Anyone else?" she asked.

"There is a third person," Shivaji *Raje* told her, "who knows Lal Mahal like the palm of his own hand."

"Who is that, *Raje*?" Jijabai asked, completely unprepared for what he was about to say.

"You are looking at him, mother."

"*Raje!*" Jijabai exclaimed, alarmed. "You are thinking of going yourself? This is too dangerous a mission."

The other men sat in silence. By now they were used to hearing such daring plans from their King. But, that he would go himself on such a dangerous raid was not prudent.

"Your Highness," Netoji was the first to speak, "let your men go to battle for you. The King must remain safe. It is the *Sirnaubat*'s job to carry out your orders."

"I agree with the *Sirnaubat*, Your Highness!" Moro *Punt* joined in. "It is not wise for the King to endanger his life. This mission could prove fatal if things go wrong."

"Look at the Sultans," Chimnaji said. "They never venture out of their citadels."

Shivaji *Raje* smiled. "Perhaps I am different from them. If my men can endanger their lives for *Swarajya,* I cannot be an exception. Besides, this raid is my idea. If I do not have the courage to carry it off, then I cannot expect my men to do so."

"Sire," Tanhaji, Shivaji *Raje's* closest friend, said, "meeting Afzal Khan in person was a grave enough risk. Though we advised you against it, you persisted. You have no idea what we went through, when you left Pratapgad to meet the Khan. By the grace of Goddess Bhavani, you returned victorious. But this plan is simply suicidal! Lal Mahal is guarded by over hundred thousand Mughal troops. It is simply too risky for you to go in person."

"Tanhya," *Raje* replied, smiling at his friend, "you know I don't scare easily. Our entire mission of liberating our homeland is fraught with danger. If we are not prepared to risk our lives…if I am not prepared to risk my life...we can never achieve our objective. The Mughals will never expect us to do anything like this, and that in itself will be our biggest advantage. But to pull it off, we need people who are familiar with Pune and Lal Mahal itself. I can find my way around that building in complete darkness. I must go in person for us to have any chance of finding Shaista Khan in the dark."

"But, Your Highness..." Netoji continued to argue.

Raje raised a hand, indicating the issue had been settled. He had resolved to go. Jijabai sighed in resignation. She knew it would be futile to try and make him change his mind. She felt a knot in her stomach; she knew it wouldn't go away till the mission had been concluded safely.

"Mother?" Shivaji *Raje* looked to her for final approval.

Jijabai looked up at him admiringly. Her son had turned out to be a very different King from other rulers, someone who had the courage to carry out his plans himself. Which other ruler would even dream of going on a mission like this in person? "Go Shivba," she said. "My blessings are with you. May the Goddess protect all of you."

Raje got up and his men realized the meeting was over. "Ask Bahirji Naik to speak to me in private," he said to Moro *Punt* as the men prepared to leave.

Bahirji Naik looked solemnly at *Raje* as he listened to his plan. He and his men had, on several occasions in the past two years, infiltrated Shaista Khan's Pune camp, in disguise, to gather valuable intelligence. But what *Raje* was planning now would require him to work at a whole new level. "Your Highness, this will be very difficult," he said grimly.

"I know." The two men sat alone in *Raje*'s personal chamber. "That is why your job is crucial. I need to have detailed information of Khan's camp... the placements of his various officers, especially the Maratha officers and their troops, the guards in and around Lal Mahal itself, change of duties... everything! The information you bring will help me plan the raid. And planning, my friend, is critical to our success."

"I will begin work immediately," Bahirji replied. "But Highness, what about Lal Mahal itself? How do we get our men acquainted with its interiors?"

"Do not worry about the inside of Lal Mahal, Bahirji. I know it well. It is *my* home, after all."

Bahirji nodded. "Our men will need detailed instructions from you. But..." Bahirji still had some doubts. "However well you train them, finding their way in the dark will be difficult."

"That is why I will go in person," *Raje* told him bluntly.

Bahirji's eyes widened in horror. "Sire! That is too..."

"Risky? I know," *Raje* interjected. "We have had this discussion, Bahirji, and the decision has been taken. Begin your work."

Bahirji left, deep in thought. He knew this would be the ultimate test of his intelligence skills, and of the King's, in guerilla warfare.

RAJGAD, FIFTEEN DAYS LATER

Shivaji *Raje*'s war council met in his private chambers to finalize plans for the daring raid on Lal Mahal. Chief of Intelligence, Bahirji Naik, had returned with the requisite information. Present were *Sirnaubat* Netoji Palkar, *Peshwa* Moro *Punt*, Infantry Commanders Tanhaji Malusare and Yesaji Kank, Officers *Sarjerao* Jedhe, Chandji Jedhe, Koyaji Bandal and *Raje's* close comrades, Babaji and Chimnaji *Deshpande*. A large map of the Pune region lay spread out on the table in front of them.

Bahirji began his report. "Your Highness, though Khan's total man-strength is close to a lakh, his troops are spread at several places. Some are campaigning in the surrounding territory, some are in Konkan, and some at Chakan. Recently, Jaswant Singh has camped near Fort Kondhana with some ten thousand troopers."

"That would still leave a sizeable number in the Pune region," Netoji opined.

"Yes," Bahirji concurred. "Nearly seventy to seventy-five thousand men are in various camps. Most of the camps are located to the north, northeast and southeast of Lal Mahal. There are relatively fewer directly to the south." Bahirji leaned forward and made a mark on the map, south of Lal Mahal. "That is a reasonably good place to enter the camp."

"Any news of Godaji?" *Raje* asked.

Bahirji gave a rare smile. "Godaji has settled down in Khan's camp like a true Mughal officer."

Shivaji *Raje* laughed while the others looked puzzled. None but Bahirji was aware that one of their own, *Raje's* faithful Captain, Godaji Jagtap, had already 'defected' to Shaista Khan on the pretence that he was dissatisfied with the Maratha army pay, and that no one listened to his suggestions. Khan had swallowed the story and appointed him a junior officer. To further convince him, Godaji had even 'raided' some of their own villages and presented the Khan with 'loot!'

"Godaji has been placed on the south side of the camp," Bahirji informed the gathering.

"Excellent!" *Raje* approved. "Our move has worked well. Godaji and his men will be crucial when we enter the Mughal camp."

"Any camps on the other side of the Mutha river?" *Raje* asked.

"None, Highness. However, Shaista Khan has placed several platoons on outpost duties and these platoons march for distances up to a few *kos* around the main camp, some on the other side of the river."

"Night patrols?" *Raje* stroked his beard, thinking hard.

"Sire, some of the Maratha officers like Jadhavrao, Bhosale, and *Rai Baghan* herself, are also stationed on the south side. Most of the platoons on outpost duty at night are Marathas."

Raje nodded. "The Mughals have given the toughest duties to their Maratha troopers. It may have saved them some hard work, but will prove to be a boon for us."

"The night patrols return around midnight, when most of the main camp is asleep. We could try to infiltrate into the camp around the same time." Bahirji had done a thorough job.

"*Raje,* this is the month of *Ramzan,*" Netoji pitched in. "Most of the Mughal soldiers and officers will be fasting through the day and eating heavily after sunset. That will definitely lull them to sleep by the time we get there."

The men nodded. This would certainly play to their advantage.

"But there is another side to that," Bahirji warned. "Everyone wakes early for their pre-sunrise meal, and to get this meal ready, the Lal Mahal kitchens are active pretty early...by the end of the second *prahar*.

"That could be a problem," *Raje* agreed. "Any inside information on Lal Mahal?"

"Yes, Highness. I have made contact with Sadashiv, the old gardener in Lal Mahal."

"But I thought Shaista Khan had dismissed all our old servants?"

"Sadashiv was retained. Perhaps they did not consider him a threat. But he has provided some invaluable information from within Lal Mahal."

"When do the main gates close?" asked *Raje*.

"Around midnight. There is a strict watch kept on all posts, as well as around Lal Mahal."

"There is a small door at the rear of the building," *Raje* suggested.

"That door has been closed up with mud and stones. There are hardly ever any guards on that side."

"Any modifications inside Lal Mahal?"

"They seem to have created a *zenana* on the upper storey by erecting temporary curtained partitions. The doorway leading from the kitchens to the upper level has been closed for privacy, again with only mud and stones."

"Where does the Khan sleep?"

"In one of the bedrooms on the upper storey, near the *zenana*."

Shivaji *Raje* was quiet for a long time, thinking and planning the raid in his mind. The entire operation was difficult, fraught with danger at every step. If even one of them faltered, the result would be death for everyone. But having once resolved to carry it out, he would do just that.

"Comrades," *Raje* said finally, "the mission is risky no doubt, but I am confident that we can accomplish it successfully if we stick to a plan, and if each person carries out his orders flawlessly. Listen carefully..."

The men leaned forward to take in every word.

"We will strike four days from now – the sixth night of *Ramzan*. We will leave from Rajgad in small platoons, to avoid being conspicuous." *Raje* picked up a pointer and began tracing the route on the map, for all to see. "We will circumvent Kondhana and go north, up to Donaje. From there, we go straight north, up to the Mutha river, and cross it there."

"*Raje*," Netoji interrupted, "Jaswant Singh is camped close to Kondhana."

Raje nodded. "We will have to put him off guard. I have heard that Jaswant and Shaista Khan do not see eye to eye. We can use this to our advantage. Moro *Punt*, visit Jaswant Singh tomorrow with gifts of gems and cash. Sweet talk him into removing the pickets from the eastern side of his camp. That should give us the opportunity we need to slip past their camp."

Moro *Punt* nodded. He had his first task cut out for him. He had heard Jaswant Singh was a proud and boastful Rajput, who could be flattered easily. That should not be too difficult.

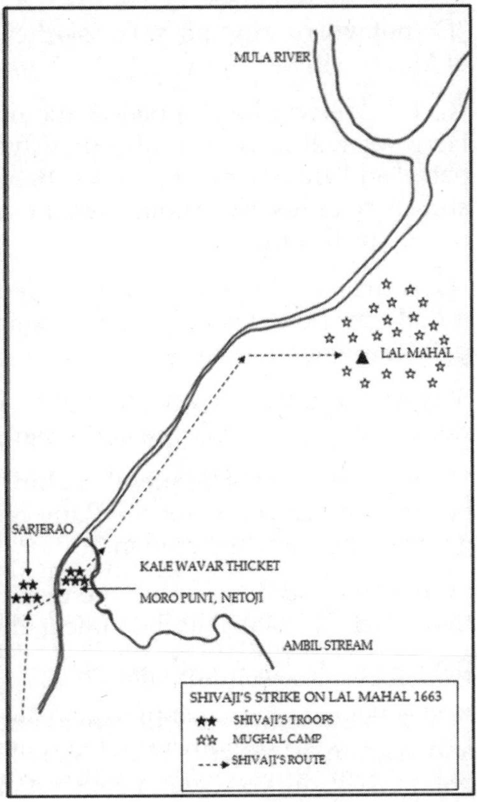

"Once we have crossed the Mutha, we will follow its northwest bank to the point where the Ambil stream joins the river. Since there are no camps on that side of the river, our progress should be unhindered. Netoji, we will leave platoons of a hundred riders at regular intervals along the path from Kondhana, up to the Ambil stream. Designate units accordingly."

"Yes, Sire," Netoji said, nodding.

"We shall leave our mounts at the Ambil stream. *Sarjerao* Jedhe will stay back with a platoon and our mounts, while we cross the river again, on foot. Once we have crossed, Netoji and Moro *Punt* will stay concealed in the Kale Wavar thickets with a thousand men, while the last platoon, the one that will actually carry out the raid, will march on foot towards Khan's camp. I will lead this last platoon in person."

The men's faces hardened. Tanhaji spoke up impatiently. "Sire, you left me behind at Pratapgad when you went to meet Afzal Khan. There is no way I am staying back this time. I go with you."

Raje looked at his best man, who refused to leave his side. "Tanhya," he said, "you will be with me till the end...and so will Chimnaji, Babaji, Chandji Jedhe, Koyaji Bandal and Yesaji Kank. We will keep four hundred men with us. Tanhya, be sure to pick out your best men for the assault team. I want the very best swordsmen, do you understand?"

"Do not worry, Highness. The swiftest and strongest warriors in all of Maval will be with you."

"Good. We will be stopped at the outposts of the Mughal camp. Here we will have to bluff our way in saying we were on night patrol and are returning to camp. Bahirji, get word to Godaji that he and some of his men should remain alert near the Mughal guards, to help us through."

"Of course, Highness," Bahirji nodded. "But Sire, it may be difficult for all four hundred to enter the camp at the same time. The night patrols are not that large."

Shivaji *Raje* gave this some thought. "What option do we have?" he asked. "We need everyone in the camp just after midnight.

"Leave that to me, Highness!" Bahirji said. "Let two hundred men be with you as you enter the Pune camp. It is my responsibility to get the other two hundred in."

"Whatever you do, see that the men are properly briefed and that they reach Lal Mahal at the indicated time."

Bahirji nodded his understanding.

"Once in the camp, we will spread out to avoid arousing suspicion, and regroup at the rear of Lal Mahal, halfway through the second *prahar*. Bahirji, you will be there at the opportune time, with

Sadashiv, to point out the exact spot where the small doorway has been closed up. In the dead of night, we will dislodge the mud and stones to create a hole large enough for us to slip through, into the Lal Mahal courtyard. Any doubts, so far?"

The men considered the plan and then shook their heads. Each man had a specific job to do. This was characteristic of Shivaji *Raje*'s planning. Each had to perform only his own task perfectly, and the plan was sure to succeed.

"Once inside," *Raje* continued, "our first task will be to tackle the kitchens. If the cooks are up already, they will have to be sacrificed. It will be unfortunate to kill those innocent souls, but we have no choice. We simply cannot risk them creating a commotion and alerting the guards. We will then have to clear the second closed doorway between the kitchen and the stairway to the upper level. Once that is done, I will go through with Tanhaji, Chimnaji, Yesaji and half our men, into the palace itself. The other half will stay back with Babaji, Chandji and Koyaji."

The six Captains who were slated to enter Lal Mahal with Shivaji *Raje*, sat upright, their attention focussed on every word he spoke. Each was elated at having been picked to lead the assault teams.

"Babaji, your team must silence any guards who see us as we break through. Once inside, our will attack begin. Chandji, your job is to cut down the guards at the main gate and take charge of the gate itself. Pre-designate your men for the job. Koyaji, you will direct a team to take charge of the *nagarkhana*. As soon as we go past the kitchen, your men must rouse the musicians and force them to beat the kettledrums. Continue the drumming as long as we are in the palace. The camp outside the palace will mistake it for the regular sounding of kettledrums to mark the anniversary of Aurangzeb's coronation. It will also help to drown out the commotion inside the palace."

Chandji and Koyaji nodded. They knew what they had to do.

"Bahirji, you will accompany our team into the palace, with Sadashiv. He will have to lead us to the Khan's bedchamber."

"Yes, Highness."

"Apprise Sadashiv of this. He will be your responsibility. Get him out of Lal Mahal safely once his job is done."

"What happens once we are inside, Sire?" Tanhaji asked.

Shivaji *Raje* looked at him and said grimly, "That is for the Goddess to decide. Our objective is to find Shaista Khan and kill him, but in the darkness that may not be easy. Tanhaji and Yesaji, you will be with me, guarding my rear as I look for the Khan. Designate a unit of ten of the very best *dharkaris* to be with me at all times during the operation as my personal bodyguard. Chimnaji and the others, meanwhile, will slaughter anyone who awakens in Lal Mahal and creates a commotion. That should divert attention away from us as we go after the Khan."

Tanhaji, Yesaji and Chimnaji would have to handle the toughest part of the operation. They accepted the responsibility willingly.

"Once our objective is achieved, we retrace our steps. The two hundred odd men who are in the palace, will return to the courtyard through the kitchen doorway. Chandji's team will then open the main gates. If the troops outside have been alerted, they will pour into the courtyard and we can easily mingle with them. We leave Lal Mahal as soon as possible, some through the main gate and some through the doorway at the rear. Remember, by then it will be every man for himself. No one waits for anyone.

Getting out of the camp itself should not be difficult. Our first halt will be at Kale Wavar, where Netoji and Moro *Punt* will await our return. We then cross the river, join *Sarjerao* on the other side, mount up and return to Kondhana by the same route. Remember, each platoon stationed along the way must wait for some time, to conduct a rear-guard action in the event that we are pursued. Then each unit returns to Kondhana."

Shivaji *Raje* finished laying out the plan. The assembled men were silent for some time, each man lost in deep thought. There was no doubt they would all be in great danger throughout the mission and their very lives would be at stake. What if something went wrong? What if they were stopped at the camp outposts? What if they were discovered and arrested? What if they couldn't get out of Lal Mahal on time? What if....? A thousand doubts and a million worries... If any of those things happened, death would be a certainty. Yet, not one of them backed out. They were ready to join the King, no matter how risky and dangerous the mission, how difficult the task. They would have given their lives for the man who led them. The thought of their own safety did not even cross their minds. It was their Lord's safety they were worried about. They simply wanted their King back safely at Fort Kondhana after this crazy raid. Whether they themselves returned alive, was of secondary importance.

"What do you think?" *Raje* prodded.

"It will be hard, Sire, the toughest mission we have planned yet. Please reconsider going in person," Tanhaji said earnestly, knowing it was futile.

"I have decided to go, Tanhya. That cannot change now. No one knows the inside of that building better than me."

The men sighed, knowing it was true. The rest could only follow where he led.

"Any doubts?" *Raje* asked.

The men looked at each other and then shook their heads.

"Good. Then let's do it! We strike on the night of *Chaitra shuddha ashtami*, four days from now."

JASWANT SINGH'S CAMP AT THE FOOTHILLS OF FORT KONDHANA, 3 APRIL 1663

The Maratha diplomat stood courteously, head slightly bowed, his hands folded in front of his body. "His Highness, Shivaji *Raje* Bhosale sends his greetings and respects, *Maharaja* Jaswant Singh," he said, smiling pleasantly and extending a hand to indicate the gifts layed out before the Rajput King of Jodhpur. On silver plates were presented precious stones, strings of pearls and bejewelled daggers and two velvet pouches containing gold coins.

Jaswant Singh was privately amazed. Where did this Seevaji *Raja* get so much wealth? He wondered. Outwardly, he smiled at the diplomat and said, "Beautiful presents, I am sure. What does Seevaji *Raja* want from me?"

"*Maharaja*, my King wishes you to befriend the Marathas. He too, is of Rajput lineage, and has asked me to remind you of it."

"I know it well. But do not forget that I am here as a Mughal officer, not a Rajput King."

"Of course, Your Highness. Shivaji *Raje* has only a small request."

"Do not expect me to betray the Emperor. What does your *Raja* want?"

Moro *Punt* smiled at Jaswant Singh. The Rajput is likely to wilt, he thought. "*Maharaja*, Shaista Khan's vast army is camped within our fief and that has made movement difficult. Shivaji *Raje* wishes to send a small force, maybe two to three thousand, east towards Jejuri. They will pass east of your camp, at a distance, of course. *Raje* has requested they be allowed to pass. They mean no harm to you or to your main camp in Pune."

Jaswant Singh's face became serious. What was the Maratha King planning? He considered the matter. He could see no harm in allowing such a small Maratha force to pass eastward.

"I will allow them to go in peace," he finally said to the *Brahman* diplomat. "But tell your *Raja* not to try something underhand. If he does, the result will not be pleasant."

"Your Highness, it is a routine errand for our men, I assure you. Please have your outposts removed from the eastern side."

Jaswant nodded. After some more formal talk, Moro *Punt* left, having accomplished the job he had been entrusted with.

OFFICE OF THE KOTWAL OF PUNE, 4 APRIL 1663

"Why do you need so many permits?" the irritated *Kotwal* asked the man squatting on the floor in front of him.

The man was a middle-aged farmer, clad in simple, cotton clothes. He gave the officer a pleading smile. "Sir, my daughter is to be married tomorrow. The groom's party will arrive in Pune tomorrow evening. Please allow them to enter the town. If the groom cannot reach my house, how will the marriage take place?"

"But you have asked for a hundred and fifty permits!" The *Kotwal*, already harassed by the constant movement of troops in and out of Pune, did not need the added hassle of a marriage party.

"The groom's father is a man of status, Sir. It is the minimum number of people he has agreed to bring. We mean no harm to the Mughals. We are simple farmers. The entire party will return the next day."

The *Kotwal* thought briefly. A marriage party; it seemed innocuous enough. He really needed the man to leave so he could get back to work. Impatiently, he waved at the man and said, "Okay, okay! Leave now. You will get your permits by evening."

"Thank you, Sir!" The farmer touched his head to the floor.

Rajgad, 5 April 1663

The final preparations for the raid were complete. The mission had been kept completely secret. Besides the chief officers scheduled to take part in it, only Jijabai, the Queens, and some senior officials were aware of it. Even the two thousand foot soldiers who were to go with Shivaji *Raje,* were kept in the dark till the last moment. Secrecy was integral to the plan.

Shivaji *Raje* bowed before his mother and touched her feet to seek her blessing. Jijabai extended a trembling hand and placed it on his head, fighting back tears as she did so. How many more times would she have to bid him farewell, knowing she might never see him alive again? When would her Shivba stop planning such deadly missions? When would their *Swarajya* be safe? Jijabai's hand lingered on her son's head as she closed her eyes and pictured the Goddess. 'Mother,' she prayed silently, 'protect my son through this, as you have done before'.

Raje straightened up and said, "I will be back, mother, I promise." He wiped a tear from her cheek.

Jijabai nodded and glanced at the Queens, waiting patiently with *pooja thalis* in their hands.

Soyara moved forward and applied a vermillion *tilak* to her husband's forehead. Their eyes met as she waved the lamp before him. "Return victorious, Your Highness!" Soyara said and smiled. Her heart filled with pride as she looked at her husband, ready for battle. She knew him only too well and knew he did not wish to see tears. Tears were for shedding in the privacy of her chambers, after he had left. Now, as he prepared to depart, he needed his wife to be strong and confident of his success. She was, after all, the wife of a *Kshatriya* warrior, the eldest Queen of the Maratha King. She could not show weakness.

Raje smiled at Soyara. "Do not worry. I will return safely...after I have killed Shaista Khan!"

Putala moved forward next. *Raje*'s soft hearted younger wife had a harder time holding back her tears. "May the Goddess protect you, Your Highness," she said in a trembling voice. "Be safe."

Shivaji *Raje* gave her a reassuring nod. "Take care of mother."

Sakwarbai, Gunwantabai and the other Queens moved forward in turn to offer their husband the sacred lamp.

With one last look at his tense mother, Shivaji *Raje* left the chamber. His men, who had been waiting in silence, quickly followed him out.

"Tanha!" Jijabai's voice made Tanhaji Malusare halt and turn around. Yesaji Kank stopped as well. The two Infantry Commanders, who had been Shivaji *Raje's* childhood friends, rushed to the Queen Mother and touched her feet.

Jijabai placed a hand on Tanhaji's shoulder, saying, "Tanha, remain with him at all times."

Tanhaji nodded. "Do not worry, mother. Shivaji *Raje* will be safe as long as Tanhaji and Yesaji stand behind him. *Raje* will return unhurt and victorious."

Outside, in the courtyard, Shivaji *Raje* mounted his horse. With defeaning cries of *Har Har Mahadev*! the Maratha party rode off into the sunset. Shivaji *Raje* had embarked upon the most audacious mission he had ever conceived.

MUGHAL MILITARY CAMP, PUNE, ABOUT THE SAME TIME

The guards on evening duty at the southern outpost of the Mughal camp watched the noisy marriage procession approach with ill concealed irritation. Two hundred men and women danced and clapped as a band of musicians belted out loud music to the rhythmic beating of drums. In the centre, mounted on a well caparisoned horse, was a little boy, presumably the groom. The wildly celebrating party attempted to go past as if the outpost did not exist at all, but the guards stopped them.

"Halt!" shouted one, tying to make himself heard above the cacophony. "Who goes there? Show your permits!"

A young man, dressed in ceremonial finery, came forward and showed him a scroll.

"Where are you from?" the guard asked curtly, examining the scroll.

"Pathargaon," the man replied. "Not too far from here."

The guard showed the scroll to his comrade. It was a permit for a marriage party of a hundred and fifty, issued by the *Kotwal* himself.

"Seems alright," the second guard murmured.

"Everything is in order I assure you," the man said exuberantly. "I got the permit only yesterday from the *Kotwal sahib*!"

The guards viewed the party. They looked genuine enough. There was no reason to doubt any foul play. With a wave of their hands, they let them through. The drums began beating again and the rest of the band joined in.

"Thank you, my good man! Do come to the feast tomorrow. It is my only son's wedding after all." The man joined in the dancing and singing as the party moved into Pune.

A third of a *prahar* later, they reached the bride's home. The women and children settled down in the temporary accommodations that had been put up for them. The men, however, silently recovered the weapons concealed in the festive bundles that had been loaded onto the bullock carts. As night fell, these hundred and fifty men melted away into the darkness in groups of four or five. Each knew when and where they were expected to regroup.

The Maratha party of over two thousand, that had left Rajgad just before sunset, reached the environs of Fort Kondhana in the darkness of the first night *prahar*. They went east, circumventing the mountain, and then continued north in the direction of Pune. They knew that Jaswant Singh's Rajput-Mughal camp was to their west, not too far away. Thus far they had not encountered any pickets or outposts. Moro *Punt's* diplomacy had done its job.

Much later, the party reached Donaje, far from Jaswant Singh's camp. The first danger had been averted. They continued to ride north till they reached the banks of the Mutha River and dismounted. On foot, leading their mounts, they forded the river at a pre-selected spot to reach the opposite, and much safer, bank. They rode on north-east, along the river bank, till they reached a spot where the Ambil stream joined the river. Here, they abandoned their horses and, while *Sarjerao* Jedhe stayed back with a platoon to guard the animals and ready them for their return journey, Shivaji *Raje* and the rest recrossed the river, to reach a thicket on the other side, at a place called Kale Wavar.

It was the ideal place to conceal a relatively large body of troops from enemy pickets. Netoji Palkar and Moro *Punt* Pingale stayed back here with a thousand men while Shivaji *Raje* marched north towards Pune with the remaining two hundred and his five dare-devil Captains Tanhaji, Yesaji, Chimnaji, Chandji and Koyaji.

All along their route, from the foothills of Kondhana to the place where *Sarjerao* himself awaited them, platoons of a hundred mounted soldiers had been stationed at regular intervals, to cover their escape.

The first *prahar* of the night had ended. The Mughal military camp, sprawled across the plains of Pune, was quiet. Most of the soldiers and officers were fast asleep in their tents and shelters. This was the month of fasting for the Muslims and, having had a heavy meal after sunset, most of the soldiers were enjoying their well earned rest. The soldiers on night watches and patrol duties were mostly Marathas and Rajputs, who did not fast like their Muslim comrades.

At the southern boundary of the camp, the guards on duty were rather relaxed. It was just another night watch for them and they awaited the sunrise, when their relievers would take over and they could return to their own tents. Nothing much happened during these night watches. There was no real danger. After all, who would dare to mess with the Mughals? Seevaji? He was safely ensconsed in one of his forts.

A body of armed men approached them from the far side. The guards were immediately on their feet, ever alert to possible danger. But the approaching party seemed harmless. The soldiers walked at a leisurely pace, chatting and laughing amongst themselves.

"Halt!" one of the guards shouted, stopping the approaching party. "Who are you and where are you going?"

The man in the lead appeared irritated by the question.

"Who are we? The night patrol, of course! We march out of the camp every evening and return after midnight. Why have you stopped us today?"

"We have never let any platoon through since we came here." The guard looked at his comrade.

"They must have crossed here before we came on watch," the other guard said.

"Whose camp do you belong to?" the first guard asked. The men were Marathas, that much was obvious to him.

The man in the lead snapped, "Whose camp? Jadhavrao *saheb's* camp, of course! We have been entrusted with the night patrols... don't you know that?" He looked at his comrades, who had begun to murmer angrily like a hive of bees.

"Where are your permits?" The first guard was persistent.

"Permits?" The Maratha's voice rose. "Who the hell carries permits on night patrol? Look man, we are tired and need to get back to camp to rest. Besides, we have been burdened with morning duty as well, tomorrow. Do not mess with our few hours of sleep!"

Some of the others from the night patrol now joined in the argument. A Maratha officer, presumably one of Shaista Khan's men, walked toward the guards. "What is the matter here?" he asked the guards in an authoritative tone.

"Sir, these people say they were on night patrol, but they do not have any permits." The guard had mellowed on seeing the officer.

"I know these men," said the officer. "They are from Jadhavrao's camp. They have been out patrolling since evening. Let them through."

The guards nodded reluctantly and stepped aside.

"You will have to answer for this!" the man in the lead shouted indignantly as he walked past.

The party of two hundred men soon split into small groups and disappeared into the darkness. Shivaji *Raje* exchanged a look with the Maratha officer who had come to their rescue. It was Godaji Jagtap, who had infiltrated the Mughal camp as a spy.

The second *prahar* of the night had begun. The deathly calm in the Mughal camp was broken only by the screeching of bats and the occasional hoot of an owl. Silent shadows moved amongst the tents and shelters, seemingly going west toward the river. These were the men who had entered the camp as part of the marriage party, the previous evening. They assembled behind Lal Mahal.

Babaji *Deshpande* arrived at the designated meeting place to find two men shrouded in crude jute blankets, crouching in a corner. On seeing Babaji, they got up and approached him.

"All well?" one of the men asked Babaji quietly.

"Yes, Bahirji," Babaji replied. "Our marriage party made it past the guard posts easily. Our men will assemble here shortly. Where is the closed doorway?"

"This is Sadavshiv, the gardener," Bahirji Naik said, nodding at the man who stood behind him.

Sadashiv guided them to where a previously existing entrance into the outer courtyard of Lal Mahal had been blocked with mud and stones.

Babaji summoned some of his men. "Break through at this spot," he ordered.

The men went to work, dislodging the mud and stones. Slowly, as time ticked by, they managed to create a hole in the wall for a man to pass through.

Halfway through the second *prahar*, most of the Maratha raiders had assembled at the rear of Lal Mahal. Shivaji *Raje* inspected the hole in the outer wall and nodded to his Captains. Chimnaji and Babaji Deshpande were the first to crouch, pass through the breach, and set foot in the outer courtyard, checking for danger. The courtyard was quiet. Nothing stirred. Chimnaji signalled to his master to follow. Shivaji *Raje* set foot in the courtyard, followed by Tanhaji, Yesaji, Chandji and Koyaji. The rest of the men silently followed their Captains inside.

Babaji's platoon quickly spread out, assaulting guards at various posts. Most were half asleep and never knew what hit them as their throats were slit in the darkness by invisible blades.

Chandji Jedhe and Koyaji Bandal moved north in the courtyard, with their platoons. Chandji's unit sneaked up to the main gate in the darkness and swiftly struck down the *hashams* guarding it. The Mughal *hashams* were replaced with their own men. The main gate of Lal Mahal was now in Maratha control.

Koyaji's unit ascended the stairs leading to the *nagarkhana,* right above the main gate. Here, they roused the sleeping musicians and ordered them to get ready to play. Naked blades were held at their throats to discourage them from making any sounds.

Shivaji *Raje* and his men had, meanwhile, moved towards the kitchen. Standing behind the doorway leading from the courtyard into the kitchen, they heard sounds. Presumably, the cooks had begun to prepare the early morning meals. Shivaji *Raje* cursed his luck. He would now have to sacrifice these innocent souls, something which always pained him. But he had no choice. If the cooks spotted them, they would certainly alert the others in the building, jeopardizing the entire mission. Reluctantly, he signalled to his men to enter the kitchen. Tanhaji, Yesaji and two other foot soldiers crept into the kitchen and launched a sudden attack on the hapless cooks, who were mowed down in mere moments. But during the scuffle, some pots and pans were dislodged, creating a minor commotion.

Shivaji *Raje* and some more men entered the kitchen and gathered at the sealed doorway between the kitchen and the stairs leading to the upper level. The men began dislodging the mud and stones barricading the doorway.

At the top of the stairs on the upper level, a couple of eunuchs, guarding the entrance to the *zenana,* were fast asleep on the floor. One of them woke with a start, hearing sounds from the kitchen below. He listened intently for a few moments and thought he heard some guttural choking sounds. His drowsy brain was unable to figure out what was happening. In panic, he rushed toward Shaista Khan's personal bedchamber, further down the corridor from the *zenana.*

The eunuch, trembling as much from fear of the danger lurking in the kitchen as the prospect of arousing his Master in the middle of the night, knocked on the door crying out, "My Lord! My Lord! We are in danger!"

Shaista Khan awoke on hearing the knocking and the eunuch's panic stricken voice. Irritated, he rose to open the door himself, without bothering to summon his attendant.

"What's the matter?" he barked at the eunuch. "How dare you wake me thus?"

"Forgive me, My Lord, but there is something happening in the kitchen."

"Kitchen!" Shaista Khan rubbed his eyes. "What's wrong there?"

"There are strange sounds coming from the kitchen, Sir. I think we should go down and find out."

"Strange sounds from the kitchen!" Shaista Khan was so infuriated he slapped the eunuch. "Imbecile! Do you not know the cooks wake early to prepare the morning meal? Why the hell did you disturb me for such a stupid reason? Go rouse the Captain of the Guard. Now get lost!"

The eunuch withdrew in an instant, bowing repeatedly as he apologized to his Master. He hurried back to his post. His companion was still fast asleep. He thought about rousing the Captain of the Guard, but decided against it. He didn't want another tirade directed at him, this time from the Captain.

He listened intently...the kitchen was quiet again. Some time later, he sat down and dozed off.

The Marathas broke through the barricaded doorway and began pouring through it into the main Lal Mahal building. The two eunuchs guarding the head of the stairs were cut down in moments, but one managed to scream before his throat was slit. In the scuffle, a large decorative brass pot fell with a loud clatter.

The ladies, attendants and other guards in the *zenana* woke up, startled by the alarming sounds. The previously quiet *zenana* erupted into hysterical screaming and shouting. Chimnaji *Deshpande* and his platoons quickly spread out, slashing at anyone who crossed their path. Fights broke out at several places as Mughal guards rushed to defend Lal Mahal.

Shivaji *Raje* summoned Sadashiv, who led them to one of the bedrooms at the far end. *Raje* entered, followed by Tanhaji, Yesaji and ten bodyguards. In the darkness, they were confronted by two individuals. One was a lady, who began screaming as soon as she saw strangers entering the chamber. The other was a man who charged at *Raje,* a weapon in his hand. But *Raje* was too quick for him and in an instant had slashed his neck. The man choked on his own blood and fell to the floor.

Pointing his Bhavani sword at the woman, he asked, "Is this Shaista Khan?"

The terrified woman shook her head. "That is…Ab…Abul Fath, his son," she stammered

Raje cursed under his breath and hurried out, leaving the woman unharmed, sobbing on the bed.

Meanwhile, Koyaji Bandal's men had forced the musicians in the *nagarkhana* to beat their kettle drums and blow their horns. The beating of the drums drowned out the commotion within Lal Mahal. The garrison outside were not unduly alarmed by the drum-beating, mistaking it to be part of the ritual commemoration of the Emperor's coronation. The military camp outside Lal Mahal remained quiet and lethargic.

Inside, however, there was complete pandemonium. Nearly all the raiding Marathas were engaged in scrimmages with the Mughal guards, slaughtering them mercilessly. The entire palace resonated with the screams of the wounded and dying.

In the *zenana,* Shivaji *Raje* had exited Abul Fazal's chamber. As he looked up and down the passage between the bedchambers, he saw someone rushing into the ladies' section. Instinctively, *Raje* bolted after him with drawn sword. Something told him it had to be Shaista Khan. The ladies of the *zenana* had extinguished all the night lamps and darkness shrouded the *zenana*.

Shaista Khan woke for the second time that night as soon as the screaming began. He rushed out of his chamber. When he realized that unknown persons had entered the palace and launched an attack, he rushed back to fetch his weapons. He grabbed a sword and desperately looked around for his shield. At that moment he heard screaming from the adjoining chamber. The Khan froze for a moment. *Ya Allah!* That was Abul Fath's chamber. His son was being attacked.

As he emerged into the passageway with his sword in hand, he saw several men exiting his son's chamber. The Khan decided against going to his son's rescue and ran in the other direction, and entered his wife's chamber. The ladies inside were in a state of panic, but even in the dark, the Khan's wife recognized him and quickly covered him in a *burqa*. The Khan sat down amongst the ladies and hid his sword. Within moments several armed men entered the chamber, staring at them intently.

Shivaji *Raje* followed the man he had seen entering the ladies' chamber. With one stroke of his sword, he tore the curtains open and entered, to find a group of trembling women huddled together. Raje instinctively knew he had cornered the Khan, but picking him out from a group of women in the dark, would be difficult. He could, of course, slaughter them all, but that was not how Shivaji *Raje* fought. He was never unscrupulous.

Tanhaji and Yesaji had followed their Master into the chamber. *Raje* pointed to the women, whispering, "The Khan has hid himself amongst them."

Tanhaji and Yesaji advanced menacingly toward the women. Shaista Khan feared for his life as he sat shrouded in the *burqa*, squatting on the floor, surrounded by his women. By now he was convinced the attack had been launched to kill him. He was the target. But who were these men? Were they Seeva's Marathas? How the hell did they get this far? The Khan cursed his Mughal garrison for being so careless.

In a few moments he sensed two of the attackers moving towards them. The Khan stirred. Reaching out his right hand from beneath his burqa, he slowly extended it toward his sword.

As Tanhaji and Yesaji advanced toward the crouching women, Shivaji *Raje* saw one of them, seated right behind the others, move. He sensed the person was reaching for something. *Raje* moved to his right and peered into the darkness. The moving person had gripped something…a sword. That was no woman. It was Shaista Khan himself. "Tanhya!" Shivaji *Raje* hissed, pointing with his sword, "Khan... Khan..."

Shaista Khan gripped his sword, ready to defend himself if discovered. He saw one of the men move in his direction, sword in hand. He had been spotted! There was no time to lose. The doorway was nearer to him than to the attackers; he could make it out if he was quick enough.

Khan threw off the *burqa* and stood up, still holding his sword, and bolted towards the doorway.

Shivaji *Raje* saw him cast off the shroud and get up, sword in hand. Even in the darkness, *Raje* clearly saw the clean shaven head. It *was* Shaista Khan!

The Khan ran out before Tanhaji and Yesaji could move. *Raje* ran after him and in a moment he stood in the doorway. He looked to his right, then to his left. He saw the Khan running towards one of the fenestrated windows at the far end of the passage. *Raje* raced after him with sword raised, ready to strike.

The Khan reached the window and looked out. He would have to jump one storey to the lower level. It was a long way down, but he had no choice. He tried to raise himself on the window ledge, but found it difficult. Momentarily, he glanced over his shoulder. The men were almost upon him...there wasn't a moment to lose. He dropped the sword he held and gripped the window sill, attempting to haul himself up.

Shivaji *Raje* was almost upon the Khan, who was sprawled on the ledge, trying to slip down. With a blood-curdling roar, *Raje* brought his Bhavani down on the scrambling figure with all his might. The Khan screamed, lost his grip and fell out of the window. He landed heavily on the ground below and groaned. For a few moments he could not move at all. Then he saw some men running towards him with lamps. *Allah!* He was done for! He had let go of his sword in his desperation to climb onto the window ledge, and now had nothing to defend himself with. The men reached his side and in the lamplight, recognized him.

"Huzoor... huzoor..." One of the men knelt down beside the Khan and attempted to raise him.

Allah meherbaan… they were his own men! They carried him to a dark corner.

Shivaji *Raje* leaned over the window ledge and stared into the darkness below. He could barely make out the Khan's form, sprawled on the ground. Tanhaji and Yesaji reached the spot and looked out as well.

"I think I got him!" *Raje* exulted.

The men exchanged victorious grins. "Sire, we must make haste and leave. Once the garrison outside is alerted, it will be difficult for us to escape," Tanhaji said.

Raje nodded. With one last look at the Khan's figure on the ground below, he turned to retrace his steps.

While Shivaji *Raje's* group had located the Mughal General and attacked him, the other Maratha platoons had literally gone berserk. Lal Mahal's Mughal inhabitants and guards had been caught unawares in a desperate situation and were being decimated. Despite the drum beating, the screams and shouts from Lal Mahal had finally alerted the garrison outside. Mughal soldiers congregated in large numbers and began hammering at the main gate. Attempts were made to scale the outer rampart, but those who managed to make it to the top were promptly cut down by the Marathas. Babaji, Chandji, Koyaji and their men resolutely held their position, awaiting word from their Master.

Shivaji *Raje,* his Captains and bodyguards, quickly made their way to the stairs that led to the level below and thence into the kitchen. Chimnaji had joined them by now with some of his men. They formed a protective ring around their Lord as they emerged into the outer courtyard, to find their men in a pitched battle with the Mughal guards. In the dim light of the torches on the outer walls, they could see numerous corpses strewn about while others were wounded and groaning in pain. The courtyard echoed with the sounds of battle.

Raje's group made it to the hole in the wall through which they had entered. Chimnaji stepped out first and checked for danger. There was not a soul in sight at the rear of the building. He signalled to his Master to follow him. *Raje* stepped out, followed by Tanhaji, Yesaji and the others. The group of twenty men made haste, running along the river bank toward Kale Wavar, where Netoji and Moro *Punt* awaited them.

The majority of the Marathas were still inside Lal Mahal. Before leaving the building, Shivaji *Raje* had despatched men to Babaji, Chandji, Koyaji and the others, with instructions to wind up and leave. Quickly, most of the men hid themselves in the dark corners of the courtyard and along the walls. Chandji's men then opened the main gate and let in the hundreds of camp soldiers who were attempting to enter the building. As the Mughals entered the courtyard, the Marathas mingled with them, shouting *Ganeem... ganeem...*

By now there were over a thousand soldiers inside Lal Mahal, with the raiders concealed amongst them. There was commotion and shouting as the Marathas screamed betrayal and the Mughals desperately searched for the enemy in the dark. But all they found were their own men, some killed and some injured. In the confusion, the raiding Marathas slipped out of the main gate.

It had been decided that no Maratha would wait for anyone else. Once the attack had been concluded, each was on his own. In small groups, they made it back to Kale Wavar to join the rest of their comrades.

In the thicket at Kale Wavar, Netoji and Moro *Punt* waited impatiently for their king to return. Each desperately wished that he had accompanied Shivaji *Raje* to Lal Mahal. But *Raje* had opted to take other Captains with him and they had no choice but to respect his decision. They both knew their master always considered every aspect before taking his decisions.

More than a *prahar* had elapsed since *Raje*'s platoon had left for Lal Mahal. They should now be on their way back.

"*Punt,*" Netoji said to Moro *Punt*, "it's been too long. I hope His Highness is safe."

"He will be. He has the blessings of the Goddess," replied Moro *Punt*, wishing he could be as certain as he sounded."

"That is true..." murmured Netoji. "But I still think *Raje* should not have taken the risk of going himself."

"I agree, *Sirnaubat*, but who can change his mind once it is made up?" Moro *Punt* sighed. He usually concurred with his King's decisions, but this time he had not. It had been a difficult *prahar*, hoping fervently that things would go right for Shivaji *Raje* and their comrades.

"*Raje* has entrusted us with the most difficult task...waiting!" Netoji said, frustrated. "It's so much better to plunge into battle."

"Do not forget, *Sirnaubat*, we have to wait here even after *Raje* has crossed the river, in case he is pursued and we must fight a rearguard action. If the Mughals do follow him, you will have your battle."

Netoji stroked his moustache. "I *do* hope they come after him,"he said simply.

A Maratha lookout announced an approaching party of men. Both Commanders were promptly on their feet with swords in hand. Soon enough, the party joined them in the thicket. Netoji and Moro *Punt* heaved sighs of relief when they saw Shivaji *Raje* in the group, a broad smile on his face.

"Mission accomplished, Netoji!" *Raje* declared triumphantly. "We got him!"

The men exulted briefly, while Shivaji *Raje* took a short breather. A foot soldier fetched him some water and *Raje* drank thirstily. Moments later, he was on his way with his platoon and Captains. They crossed the river and emerged onto the north-west bank, where *Sarjerao* Jedhe waited with their mounts.

Soon, they were riding hard, concealed by the trees along the river bank. There was no time to lose. They had to get *Raje* to the safety of Fort Kondhana.

Meanwhile, the rest of the Maratha party, save the unfortunate souls killed, had left the building and dispersed in the camp in small groups. Taking care not to arouse suspicion, they hurried south in small groups. While crossing the southern outposts, they warned the guards that the camp was under attack, saying they were going after Shivaji's Marathas, who had presumably fled in a south-easterly direction toward the hills. In this way they cleared their own exit while planting mis-information to confuse any pursuing Mughal troops.

When they had gone a sufficient distance, they blew a horn. This signal was relayed toward the Katraj Hill pass, which lay south-east of Pune and the Mughal camp. There, hidden in the trees, were more of Shivaji *Raje*'s Marathas, who had tied numerous torches to trees as well as to the horns of some hundred bulls. As soon as they heard the signal, the men lighted the torches, and then fled toward Kondhana.

The commotion inside Lal Mahal continued unabated. As torches were lit and the interior of the palace became illuminated, the horrifying scenes chilled the blood of the hardiest of Mughal warriors. Shamshuddin Khan, an experienced Mughal Captain, strode through the courtyard, inspecting the carnage. He had been alerted as soon as the soldiers from the camp had gathered at the main gate trying to force it open. He had even ordered some of his men to scale the ramparts, but in vain; the men had been slain immediately. Then, someone had opened the gate from inside and the Mughals had finally been able to get in.

One thing was immediately apparent to Shamshuddin – Lal Mahal had been attacked and the target had been the General himself. As he made his way across the courtyard into the palace, the veteran Captain was stunned by the scenes around him. Throughout the outer courtyard, the kitchen, and the *zenana* at the upper level, lay sprawled dead bodies of numerous Mughal guards and servants. A few women too, lay dead in the *zenana*. The kitchen was a complete mess. Where previously there had been barricaded doorways, there were now two gaping holes. Shamshuddin guessed the attackers had entered and exited through these. But who could they have been?

Shamshuddin stood in the passageway outside the *zenana* in a daze, not knowing what he should do next. The General! He had to find Shaista Khan first. Summoning some of his men, he ordered them to search the palace and grounds for their Commander-in-Chief. He himself picked up a flaming torch and began systematically searching the *zenana*. Wherever he went, he found dead bodies and wailing women. One of the chambers was in complete disarray. As he raised the torch, he was shocked to see the chamber floor, its walls, even the draperies, were red with blood. Savagely hacked body parts lay strewn about. In a corner lay the severed head of a woman. He was told by the attendants that it was one of Shaista Khan's *begums*.

At the far end of the *zenana*, in another bedchamber he found a young man lying dead in a pool of blood. A trembling soldier stood guard in a corner.

"The General's son," the guard murmured.

Shamshuddin exited the chamber and walked down the stairs to the lower level. He began barking orders to the men to collect the dead bodies and pile them up on one side. "I want a head count of the dead," he said. "And find out if there are any dead outsiders."

A foot soldier approached him. "Captain, we have located the General," he said.

Shaista Khan opened his eyes and stared at the featureless ceiling of a poorly lit chamber. Two Mughal guards stood beside him. For a few moments Khan didn't know where he was.

"*Huzoor*," one of the soldiers said, "are you alright, My Lord?"

The Khan stared at him, trying to think why the man was in his chamber. He tried to get up and the guards helped him to a sitting position. He looked around. This wasn't his chamber. Where the hell was he? His throat felt parched. He asked for water. One of the guards poured him a tumblerful from a pitcher.

The Khan drank thirstily, then asked, "What happened?"

"We were attacked, My Lord!" one of the guards replied. "You fell from the window of the *zenana*. We found you sprawled on the ground and brought you here to keep you safe from the enemy."

Everything came rushing back. The screaming, the commotion, the attackers pursuing him... He recalled the assailant who had slashed his sword at him before he fell off the ledge. He could vaguely remember a bearded face and cold vengeful eyes. Khan felt a stinging pain in his right hand. He looked at the blood soaked cloth tied around it. Wincing, he removed the cloth and saw three fingers were missing. The raw wound was still oozing blood. The Khan looked up at the heavens and cursed.

They heard hurried footsteps and moments later, a group of men approached with torches. Khan recognized his Captain, Shamshuddin, in the lead.

Shamshuddin bowed to his General and then knelt down beside him. The man was in a terrible state. He was sweating from the heat and from fear. The bleeding wound on his right hand had soiled his dishevelled night clothes. His eyes held pure terror. For a moment, Shamshuddin felt ashamed to see the General of the great imperial Mughal army in such a state.

"My Lord, you are injured," he said.

"Who were they, Shamshuddin?"

"Can't say for sure, My Lord, but we did find some dead Maratha foot soldiers. They must have been Seeva's men."

"Seeva! That rat! He dared attack me in my own bedchamber?"

"*Huzoor*, our people are in the palace. You are safe now," Shamshuddin said, attempting to pacify him. He knew the news he had about the *zenana* would shake the General.

The Khan suddenly remembered seeing the assailants exit from his son's chamber. "Abul Fath?" he asked. "Is he safe?"

"My Lord, Abul Fath is in Paradise. The attackers killed him in his chamber."

"*Ya Allah*!" Shaista Khan wailed, clutching his aching heart. "That *kameena* will rot in hell for this!"

"*Huzoor*..." Shamshuddin hesitated.

Finally the great Khan looked up. "What is it Shamshuddin?"

"*Huzoor*...the *zenana*...there was indiscriminate slaughter. *Chhoti Begum Sahiba*..."

"My *begum? Allah*..." Shaista Khan closed his eyes.

Shamshuddin saw tears roll down his General's cheeks. He felt sorry for the man. On top of his personal losses, he would have to face the ignominy of this defeat, and then, the Emperor's wrath.

A while later, Shamshuddin escorted Shaista Khan to a more comfortable place in the palace. He could not take him to the upper level. And he had not dared tell him how he had found his dead wife beheaded.

The *hakim* was summoned to take care of the General's wounds. As he bandaged the Khan's right hand, a foot soldier entered and bowed. "*Huzoor*, we have definite news the attackers were Seevaji's men. They have fled south-east toward the Katraj Hills."

"The swines!" Khan swore. "Go after them Shamshuddin. Go and get them!"

Shamshuddin bowed and left immediately.

With two thousand mounted soldiers, he exited the Mughal camp at its south-eastern boundary and rode towards the Katraj Hill Pass. As they neared the pass, they could see several hundred torches in the distance.

"There they are!" Shamshuddin shouted to his Captain and raised his sword in the direction of the Marathas. "Let us get them and avenge the humiliation of this attack!"

The two thousand Mughal cavalry picked up speed and rode hard toward the torches.

Meanwhile, Shivaji *Raje,* his six Captains, and his platoon of two hundred Mavale soldiers, had re-crossed the river and reached Donaje, far from Shamshuddin's pursuing Mughals. As the Maratha party rode towards Fort Kondhana, they met up with the platoons stationed at regular intervals along their path. These soldiers joined *Raje's* core platoon, thus swelling their number to over two thousand by the time they passed Jaswant Singh's camp.

As the news of the raid had not yet reached Jaswant Singh, his camp was quiet. *Raje* and his men had no trouble by-passing the Rajput-Mughals and reaching Fort Kondhana. Over the next *prahar,* all the Marathas who had taken part in the operation and survived, reached the fort. Moro *Punt* and Netoji also arrived with their men.

As Shamshuddin rode toward the torches in the Katraj Hill Pass, he became increasingly suspicious. The Marathas must surely have seen them coming. So why were they not fleeing?

The Mughal Captain rode on, but as he neared the torches, he realized he had been made a fool of. The wily Marathas had tied torches to tree trunks and the horns of numerous bulls! There was no enemy here. It had been a wild goose chase.

Shamshuddin swore vengeance even as he ordered his men to turn back.

FORT KONDHANA, MORNING OF 6 APRIL 1663

Bahirji Naik, Shivaji *Raje's* chief spy, had returned from the Mughal camp with news of the aftermath of the raid.

"The camp is in complete disarray, Your Highness," Bahirji said with a wry smile. "I would say our raid has been a success."

Shivaji *Raje* laughed. "But did we get the Khan?" He asked the question everyone was curious to know the answer to.

"No, Your Highness. The Khan is alive. You only managed to cut off his fingers."

Raje was dismayed. He had hoped to kill the Khan. But that was not to be.

"*Raje*, in all, about sixty people were killed in Lal Mahal. We got the Khan's son, Abul Fath, one of his sons-in-law, and his Captain of the Guard. The others were mostly palace guards and servants." Bahirji hesitated, knowing the news he had would sadden his King. "Twelve women were killed; one was Shaista Khan's youngest wife."

Raje's face froze into a hard mask. Killing women and children had never been his way. Given a choice, he would have spared those in the *zenana*. Most of the raid had been conducted in complete darkness and his men would have attacked anything in their path.

"The death of the women was accidental," he finally said. "Unfortunately, it will always be held against us. I would have saved those poor souls in the kitchen too, if I could have."

"Many more were injured," Bahirji continued. "Two other sons of the Khan, and several women."

"How many did we lose, Tanhaji?" *Raje* asked his Captain.

"Six men, Sire, and some forty were injured," Tanhaji replied.

Raje closed his eyes and said a silent prayer for his dead soldiers. Losing comrades hit him the hardest. Turning to Bahirji, he asked, "What is the inside information on Lal Mahal? Is Sadashiv safe?"

"He is, Highness. He is not under suspicion yet. Inside the palace, everyone is still in a state of shock and terror. Even, it is said, Shaista Khan himself. His women are pressurizing him to leave Pune immediately."

"I hope he realizes the person who attacked him was Shivaji himself," *Raje* said, grinning.

LAL MAHAL, PUNE, AFTERNOON OF 6 APRIL 1663

All signs of the previous night's attack had been hastily removed and the palace had once again been made habitable for Shaista Khan and his entourage. The guard in and around the palace had been tripled. Special forces, both infantry and musketeers, were stationed and ordered, on pain of death, to remain alert round the clock. The Khan realized he had been careless and complacent. He could not take any more chances.

The wailing and lamenting in the Khan's private quarters had not ceased. The death of his young son, and one of his *begums*, was cause of great personal grief. The Khan tried in vain to pacify his eldest wife, the mother of their dead son, Abul. "Be calm *begum*," Shaista Khan pleaded yet again. "Abul was a soldier and he died in battle. This attack was part of the war with Seeva. Abul's death will be avenged!"

"How can you ask me to be quiet when I have seen what they did to my son! There are rumours that this Seevaji is a sorcerer who can magically appear at any place, out of thin air! None of us are safe."

"Rubbish!" Shaista Khan snapped, silencing her. "Do not heed such ridiculous rumours."

"It must be true!" his *begum* insisted. "How else could he have got past a Mughal camp of over a lakh of soldiers and reached us? This place is home to demons, not people like us! I wish to leave immediately! Let us return to Delhi."

The Khan sighed wearily. He could not suddenly order his massive army to evacuate. But he could send his family back to Delhi. He resolved to do so as soon as possible. Once he was relieved of that responsibility, he could focus on Seeva.

"Do not worry *begum*. I will arrange to send the women back."

The Khan left the *zenana* and descended to the lower level, where his Captains awaited him. As soon as he was seated on a *baithak*, Shamshuddin Khan informed him that *Maharaja* Jaswant Singh had arrived for audience.

Jaswant Singh entered, bowed courteously, and said, "Khan *sahib*, accept my deepest condolences for your loss."

"*Maharaja* Jaswant Singh!" Khan addressed him indignantly. "I am truly surprised to see you alive. I thought Seeva would have reached me only over your dead body!"

Jaswant Singh swallowed this insulting jibe at his integrity. Mughal spies had brought news that Seevaji was in Rajgad, even the previous day. If he had ridden to Pune, it could only have been by traversing around Fort Kondhana. His military camp lay between Fort Kondhana and the Pune camp. Hence accusations of carelessness and incompetence on his part were to be expected. Worse, he could be accused of treachery.

"We know that Seeva's *Peshwa* visited your camp two days ago," Mir Abdul Mabud, Commander of the Mughal Artillery, said.

"Is that true, Jaswant?" Shaista Khan asked. He had heard about the visit and had made a note to ask the Rajput Commander for an explanation when they met.

"Yes, he did," Jaswant repled confidently. "But it was for a trivial matter – permission to move some of his men to Jejuri. Khan *sahib*, do not accuse me of treachery. Rajputs never betray their masters, and my Master is the Emperor. I could never betray the trust placed in me."

The Khan jerked his head in annoyance. He needed a scapegoat. Jaswant was a suitable target. "The Emperor says that *kafirs* will always gang together," Khan said, taunting Jaswant Singh.

"Khan *sahib*!" Jaswant's voice rose and his eyes flashed with anger. "I plead with you again, do not accuse me of treachery! Look within first. How seriously have you conducted this campaign? Your military camp has been lost in marriage revelry. Why blame your Captains for your failures?"

"Jaswant Singh!" The Khan stood up, trembling with rage. "Mind your tongue! You are speaking to the General of the Mughal army!"

"General? *Amir-ul-umrao* Shaista Khan, a General leads by example. If he is lost in food, wine and women, what can he expect from the soldiers guarding his camp?" Enflamed by the slights on his honour and religion, Jaswant forgot the deference due from a subordinate.

"Jaswant you have crossed the line!" The Khan tried to reach for his sword but realized he could no longer grip a weapon. Confound Seeva!

Shamshuddin intervened to control the escalating tension. "Khan *sahib*, *huzoor*, pray be calm." He physically restrained the General, forcing him to sit down again. He then turned to address the Rajput. "*Maharaja* Jaswant Singh, please leave now. We will get in touch with you later."

Shamshuddin realized only too well that Shaista Khan could not openly punish Jaswant Singh. There were several Rajput officers with Rajput contingents in the camp, and if they all sided with Jaswant, it could turn into a civil war like situation for them.

Jaswant glared at Shaista Khan, whirled around and left in a huff.

Shivaji *Raje's* attack may have failed to eliminate Shaista Khan himself, but had achieved the objective of seeding mistrust and factionalism in the Mughal camp. Above all, it had scared the hell out of the Mughal General. If Seeva could suddenly appear inside Lal Mahal, seemingly out of nowhere, he or his family could never be safe. Did Seeva really have magical powers, as the credulous said? Every day brought new rumours about the Maratha King. They said he could leap great distances and jump up two storeys. *Allah* be merciful! Was Seeva really a sorcerer?

4
PAYBACK!

The Mughal officer's eyes widened in disbelief as he read the letter from the Maratha King Seevaji:

For the past three years, many renowned officers of the Mughal Empire have descended upon my homeland. The Emperor orders them to sieze my forts and annexe my lands, and they reply that this will be done. Why do they not understand that it is difficult to gallop the steed of imagination here, let alone conquer these lands? Unlike the forts of Bidar and Kalyani, which sit on the open plain, and which were easily captured by the Mughals, this country has lofty mountains, ragged terrain criss-crossed by streams difficult to cross. You cannot run trenches up to my hill-forts and capture them. The great Adilshahi General, Afzal Khan, came to Jawli and perished. Your own noble, Amir-ul-Umrao Shaista Khan, tried hard for three years, writing falsely to the Emperor that I had been completely defeated. But you have witnessed the calamity that befell him, compelling him to retreat in disgrace! That event is clearer than the sun itself. It is my eternal duty to guard my country, and I shall do so as long as I live. Let the wise beware the river of blood through which none have yet crossed to safety!

Every word stung with its truth, honesty and incisiveness. The letter, addressed to several Mughal officers, as well as the Emperor himself, neatly summed up the Mughal Deccan campaign led by Shaista Khan. Many of the Mughal officers campaigning in the Deccan, including Shaista Khan himself, never tired of writing lies to the Emperor about the 'victories' won against Seevaji, when, in reality, the campaign was a failure.

Terrorized by the Lal Mahal raid, Shaista Khan decided to shift his base from Pune. He handed over charge of the Pune camp to Jaswant Singh, and with the majority of the troops, proceeded towards Aurangabad, capital of the Mughal Deccan province. Having failed to conclusively defeat Shivaji *Raje* for three years, the final blow dealt to Shaista Khan himself, nearly put an end to the Mughal campaign.

Shivaji *Raje,* meanwhile, had turned his attention to the South. He marched to Kudal at the head of fifteen thousand troops, to consolidate his holdings in the south Konkan. The campaign concluded uneventfully as Bijapur seemed in no mood to counter his moves. The Adilshah had washed his hands off Kudal province, allowing the Marathas to keep it, thus making peace with them. The Adilshahi armies were, at the time, campaigning in the southern kingdom of Ikkeri, trying to annex it.

Badi Begum Sahiba, Ali Adilshah's mother and former Empress of Bijapur, who had ruled the kingdom with an iron hand after her husband's death, had embarked upon a pilgrimage to Mecca. In an overture of peace, Shivaji *Raje* ordered Raoji Somnath, his *Subadar* in the south Konkan, to escort her to Vengurle port. The Marathas were thus temporarily at peace with the Adilshahi.

THE MUGHAL CAMP ON THE ROAD FROM LAHORE TO KASHMIR, END APRIL 1663

Emperor Aurangzeb stared in disbelief at the man who had brought the news from the Deccan. His expression changed to pure rage as he heard of the raid on Lal Mahal.

"The *Amir-ul-Umrao* has finally paid for his careless and profligate behaviour," Aurangzeb said, seething at the General's failure. He knew only too well that not just Shaista Khan, but the Mughal throne itself, would become the laughing stock of the world. News like this travelled fast and furious.

"How did that *kafir* get past a lakh of Mughal troops to reach Shaista Khan's chamber? Were all our soldiers and Captains sleeping on duty?" Aurangzeb screamed at Hussain, the spy who had brought the detailed despatch from Pune.

"No one knows where he came from, Your Majesty, nor where he disappeared to after the raid. A gaping hole was found in the outer wall behind the palace. They must have entered through it."

"And there were no guards there? How careless could Shaista Khan be? How many did that wretched rat kill?"

"Over fifty dead in the palace, Your Majesty, including the General's son, his Captain-of-the-Guard, one of his wives, and eleven other women. Scores more were injured. The General himself lost three fingers of his right hand."

"Three fingers? He should have lost his head! He will pay for this humiliation!" Aurangzeb waved the man away angrily. Closing his eyes, he began turning his prayer beads. For some time he chanted the names of *Allah* to calm himself. He needed to think clearly. The Deccan campaign had ended in failure. Punishing Shaista Khan for his incompetence was one thing but he knew he would have to start afresh to deal with that *kafir* Seeva.

Aurangzeb summoned his scribe. "Compose a *firmaan* addressed to *Amir-ul-Umrao* Shaista Khan, ordering him to wind up operations in the Deccan. He is relieved of the *Subadari* of the Deccan province at once. Another *firmaan* should go to my son, Muazzam, ordering him to take charge as the new *Subadar* of the Deccan. These *firmaans* should be despatched at once."

Long after the scribe had left, Aurangzeb sat alone in his *shamiana*, deep in thought. The Maratha menace was growing day by day. He would have to organize another campaign in the Deccan now. Seeva had to be finished off, completely. He simply could not be allowed to prosper any more. Besides being a constant threat to the Empire's southern boundary, Seeva would undoubtedly upset his plans of southern expansion. He well knew that the Adilshah recognized Seeva's usefulness as a bulwark against the Mughals, and hence, was happy to let him be. For the Empire's safety and future, Seeva had to be removed.

Despite his hatred of the Maratha rebel, Aurangzeb, a warrior himself, couldn't help but admire his cunning, courage and audacity. Not in a thousand years could any of his officers have concieved such a plan, let alone execute it. Nor could he.

The attack on Shaista Khan's personal chambers caused considerable consternation in Aurangzeb's household. After all, he was family.

"That *kafir* is the devil!" Aurangzeb's sister Roshanara said of Seevaji Bhosale. "I've heard that our uncle's daughter, our cousin, is missing since the attack. The *kafirs* must have kidnapped her!"

"Seeva would never kidnap a woman during a raid, Roshanara." Aurangzeb wasn't prepared to believe the rumors. He felt he knew the *kafir* rebel quite well now. "He may be our enemy, but we must respect his good qualities. He is a God-fearing and pious man. He never molests women and strictly forbids his men from doing so. Don't you remember how he sent the Kalyan Governor's daughter-in-law back to her family?"

Roshanara jerked her head angrily. "How can you praise him?"

"He *is* praiseworthy, sister. Make no mistake, Seeva *is* different from all our other enemies. He never indulges in wine, women, music, dance or merry making, while our own esteemed nobles steep themselves in these vices. That is why we keep losing to him. Come to think of it, Seeva is much like myself; a pure soul. *Allah* be praised for sending such an able adversary."

RAJGAD PALACE, MID-1663

Shivaji *Raje* sat in his conference chamber with his *Peshwa* Moro *Punt* Pingale, *Muzumdar* Nilo *Punt* Sondev, *Dabir* Tryambak *Punt* Sonaji and *Surnis* Anaji *Punt* Datto. The chief administrators of the *Swarajya* had assembled to discuss matters of money and state with their sovereign. The situation was grim indeed.

"Your Highness, the government treasury is nearly empty," *Muzumdar* Nilo *Punt* said. "We do not have enough money to pay our troops."

Shivaji *Raje* did not react. He knew the problems. Battling enemy armies was one thing but generating enough money from within his kingdom, not merely to run his military machinery, but also to allievate the suffering of his people, was a harder challenge. He had succeeded in defeating Shaista Khan, but if, at the end of it all, his people did not have enough food, shelter and clothing, it amounted to nothing.

"Shaista Khan occupied our fief for three years and destroyed our lands, our people. This Mughal campaign has cost our *Swarajya* dear," *Raje* said bitterly.

"Our crops have been burned down by the Mughal armies. Large tracts of land have become uncultivable," Ananji *Punt* added.

"And there is no hope of revenue for the next year as well. Our people will need much longer to recover," Nilo *Punt* continued.

Raje sighed. After all the effort he and his comrades had put in, he could not bear to contemplate collapse of *Swarajya* for financial reasons. And if it did, it would be a victory attributed to the Mughals as part of their war strategy of adopting measures to bring about his kingdom's economic downfall.

"Jaswant Singh continues to stay put in Pune," Moro *Punt* remarked. "We must do something about him before he plans anything big."

"I am not worried about Jaswant Singh," *Raje* said. "He is not an able Commander. He may try to annex some of our forts, which he will not succeed in doing. Kondhana is nearest to his camp and he may besiege the fort. We could keep him occupied there so he doesn't cause trouble elsewhere."

The *Peshwa* nodded. Jaswant Singh could be tackled. They had far bigger problems at hand, within their own fiefdom. The men were quiet for some time.

"We must launch a counter campaign in Mughal territory, Sire," Moro *Punt* said finally.

"That we will have to do, Moro *Punt*," *Raje* agreed. "We must make the Mughal administration pay for what they have taken from our people and the *Swarajya*. But before that, we have to help our people. Moro *Punt*, open the government granaries and distribute the grain. See that our people do not starve. If they do, they will never support our rule, and without people we have no kingdom. The Mavals have been worst hit; help the Mavale population first. The coastal areas of the Konkan have been relatively spared and they have the sea as a refuge.

Nilo *Punt*, announce tax rebates for the next year. That should encourage the people to work harder in spite of the troubles they face. Anaji *Punt*, allot new plots to those farmers whose lands have become untenable. Cultivation must continue; we have no hope without it."

The men absorbed their King's orders, marvelling at his futuristic thinking. After centuries, the Marathi people been blessed with a ruler who thought of their welfare instead of his own.

"And I shall focus on filling our treasury," *Raje* said finally. "Moro *Punt*, summon Bahirji. Ask him to see me in private."

THE CITY OF SURAT, GUJARAT, SECOND HALF 1663

A lone beggar in ragged clothes, carrying nothing but a staff and a begging bowl, hobbled along the coastal road to the great Mughal trading post in the west – Surat. The road was crowded and the beggar attracted no attention. But though no one noticed him, he took note of everything. He saw the hundred odd trading ships anchored in the port, including those of the English, Dutch, Portuguese and French, the Arab dhows, and the Chinese junks. He saw foreign and Indian traders haggling with the porters to get their goods on and off their ships. He checked out the customs office where a bored Mughal officer ordered his men to check every box and consignment, and then stamped duties on them. He noticed the traders struggle through this first hurdle and then pass through the exchange office, where foreigners exchanged money and the more frequent visitors presented *hundis*.

The beggar then trudged along a tree lined road toward the city itself. There were sugarcane fields on either side of the road and, as he neared the city, he saw great gardens with shady trees, where the rich merchants came with their families to holiday.

The poor wretch was pushed around at the gates to the city, but managed to plead his way through, getting mercilessly kicked in the process. He bore it all and, emerging into the city itself, saw its grand bazaars with the shops and showrooms stocked to capacity with goods of every kind from across the oceans, with ornaments and precious gems. The market displayed goods as diverse as rich carpets, silk and embroidered cloth, spices, saffron, ivory and sandalwood.

The streets of Surat were busy from early morning till late at night. The beggar watched people of many nationalities and ethnicities in Surat's crowded markets. He saw the Mughal *amirs* being carried by in their ornate open palanquins, while their women followed in closed ones; Gujarati businessmen in cotton *dhotis* and loose coats; Parsis in knee-length coats and tall hats; Pathans in their oversized loose fitting coats, baggy trousers and cloth turbans; and Arabs in their white *dishdashas* and tied headcloths. He saw the white skinned British in their smart red uniforms, tight trousers and knee-high boots, seated with beautiful women, in open carriages which sparkled with gilded knobs and handles, drawn by horses. He saw the elaborate procession of the Mughal Governor, seated on a stately elephant, preceded and followed by platoons of smartly uniformed infantry and cavalry, heralded with trumpets and kettledrums, and flying banners of state.

No one noticed him squatting besides the traders, or idling in the market, as people gossiped about the rich merchants and their women, or the foreigners, or the Mughal Governor and his retinue. He imbibed every bit of information. Slowly but surely, he memorized every street in the city, every bazaar, and the richest shops in the bazaars. He found out who the richest merchants were, and where they lived. He even found out how much wealth they had! He inspected their mansions, surrounded by sprawling gardens with fountains.

The beggar mingled with the Mughal Governor's soldiers, doing odd jobs for them, and learnt how many troops were stationed there. He discovered that the Governor, Inayat Khan, was a corrupt and lazy drunkard, who would certainly offer no resistance if an army attacked Surat. He was told the Emperor had sanctioned a garrison of five thousand for the protection of Surat, which was a rich revenue source for the empire. But Inayat Khan, maintained only a thousand men and pocketed the rest of the sanctioned money.

Having spent two months in this strange, dynamic city, the beggar knew it like the back of his own hand. As he left Surat through its gates and joined the coastal road over which he had come, weeks ago, Bahirji Naik, Shivaji *Raje's* secret eye, turned to look back at the city and smiled in satisfaction. His King had sent him here on a mission and he had accomplished it.

Rajgad Palace, November 1663

"Your Highness, we could get untold wealth if we sack Surat," Bahirji summed up his report as he sat cross-legged on the floor in Shivaji *Raje*'s private chamber. "The Mughal garrison is hardly a thousand strong, and they have become used to a lazy, wasteful life. The city is practically unguarded. The Governor is a corrupt drunkard. The city has no wall or ramparts of note. There is a dry ditch in some parts, easily passable on foot. There are a few guarded gates, but those should pose no problem for us."

Raje laughed. "I am surprised Aurangzeb has left his richest city thus unprotected."

"He probably never expects anyone to raid Surat."

"What about the city itself?"

"It is situated on the south bank of the river Tapi, six *kos* inland from the sea. There is an old fort near the river, north of the town. It is a squarish structure with formidable walls and four bastions. I am told there is no platform on the inner side of the rampart and the guns are mounted on wooden scaffoldings. Should not be too difficult to assault and capture."

Raje listened intently.

"The English and Dutch factories are located to the north as well. So are the mansions of the two richest businessmen of Surat, Virji Vora and Haji Sayed Baig. It is said that Virji is the richest trader in the world, worth some eight million."

"Really?" *Raje's* eyes widened. "And he has all that wealth stocked in his house?"

"Yes, Highness. These rich merchants have large drums of gold, pearls and precious gems."

"What about the English and Dutch factories?"

"The factories have their own ramparts. They are manned by armed guards, businessmen officers, and Indian peons. Should we decide to storm these factories, we could easily do so in less than a *prahar*. I have heard the English have plenty of cash stashed in their factory. The customs office is another place where there is plenty of cash. It is near the port. The *serais* are on the south side of the town. The travelling businessmen and embassies from other lands are accommodated here."

Raje mused, a plan forming in his mind. "Any news of Prince Muazzam?" he asked.

"The Prince leads a life of luxury in Aurangabad, enjoying himself with wine, women and music. He seems to be the exact opposite of his father. We could easily divert his attention by feeding him false news."

Shivaji *Raje* considered for a while and then said, "We shall go to Surat. We will ride out in a month, with ten thousand cavalry. Bahirji, planning the raid is your job. Once there, you will direct our men within the city itself – where to raid, which mansions, bazaars, offices. It is your headache. See that our Captains are well instructed. As for our troops, no one should know our destination till we actually get there. Barring us and a handful of our Captains, no one is to know that our target is Surat."

"Understood, Highness."

"Surat is over a hundred and fifty *kos* from Rajgad. We will have to ride through Mughal territory all along the way. Once we have advanced, we will have no cover behind us, nor any safe haven to escape to. Do you think we can pull it off?" *Raje* asked.

Bahirji smiled, stroking his moustache with his fist. "My King," he said, "we pulled off the raid on Lal Mahal. After that, Surat should be child's play!"

AURANGABAD, NOVEMBER-DECEMBER 1663

You have utterly failed in the Deccan campaign and have fallen from grace. You are ordered by the Emperor Alamgir Aurangzeb to report to the subadari of Bengal at once. Your request for an audience with the Emperor has been denied and you are instructed to proceed to Bengal without further delay.

Shaista Khan was crestfallen as he read the *firmaan* from Aurangzeb. He had been dismissed from the Deccan *subadari* months ago, but he had procrastinated by sending several letters requesting the Emperor to allow him another chance in the Deccan. He had asked to meet Aurangzeb in person. But all his pleas had been summarily rejected. He now had no choice but to proceed to Bengal.

"Bengal is hell, well stocked with bread," Khan lamented. The Mughal province of Bengal was notorious for its unhealthy climate and hence, much hated by the nobles, who dreaded appointments there. This was now Shaista Khan's fate.

Jaswant Singh, who had taken over the command of Pune from the Khan, decided to try and do something himself. He laid siege to Fort Kondhana and over the next seven months tried his best to capture it. But Jaswant was a warrior of the plains. The Sahyadri mountains and forests posed unanswerable challenges for him. In an attempt to tire and starve the Maratha garrison in the fort, he waited. But they did not tire and they did not starve. Jaswant stayed put. Little did he know that while he thus sat inactive, the Maratha King would, for a second time, bypass his camp and ride into the Mughal Empire to bury a lance right into its heart!

Surat, 5 January 1663

The second *prahar* of the day ended. The markets in the heart of Surat were as busy as ever. Business was brisk and the streets were packed with people, animals, carts, palanquins and retinues. Mughal horse messengers had just arrived in the city from the South, with some sensational news. They announced that a large Maratha army had arrived at Gandevi, thirty miles southeast of Surat. They declared with sufficient alarm that it was Shivaji's army and the Maratha King planned to march on Surat in person.

The news spread like wildfire through the town and soon the streets and bazaars erupted in panic and commotion. People ran helter-skelter, some trying to get out of town, some across the river, and some into the fort for protection. Those most alarmed were the rich, who had the double task of saving their lives as well as their wealth, accumulated over years. They took some with them as they fled, but mostly tried, as best they could, to bury or conceal their gold, jewels and precious stones within the confines of their mansions.

Inayat Khan, the Mughal Governor, received the news as well, but instead of being concerned for his city, laughed at the stupidity of the Surat residents. How could it be Shivaji? Surat was over a hundred and fifty *kos* into Mughal territory. How could any Maratha army march that far without being noticed? He assumed it was some dacoit gang, pretending to be Shivaji and his men.

To make sure, Inayat Khan dispatched his riders south to find out more. They returned with the news it wasn't Shivaji at all, but a Mughal officer returning from a campaign in the Deccan. On hearing this, Inayat Khan laughed heartily, possibly from relief. He sent riders to rendezvous with the supposed Mughal officer, instructing him to avoid Surat as there was considerable panic in the city.

That night, the Mughal Governor of Surat slept comfortably, in the belief that he had averted a major ruckus in his city.

The plains of Udhna, six miles southeast of Surat, night of 5 January, 1664.

Shivaji *Raje* had finished his night meal and prepared to lie down in the makeshift tent that had been erected for him. His troops slept in the open, under the dark skies. A strict nightwatch was placed around *Raje*'s tent, and his closest comrades, Tanhaji Malusare and Yesaji Kank, slept outside his tent. They were in Mughal territory, out in the open. They could not take any chances with their King's safety.

The night was chilly and *Raje* pulled his blanket closer around himself as he considered the present operation. Things had gone well thus far. They had left Rajgad a month ago and ridden north across the Sahyadri range, mostly under cover of the forests. They rode silently at night to avoid raising an alarm. During the day they camped in the forests and lay low to avoid detection.

Along the way, his spies circulated rumors that theirs was a Mughal force with a Mughal officer at the helm. This served to dissipate any alarms raised in the territories they crossed, which were entirely Mughal ruled. The Marathas rode with minimal luggage and provisions. Their armies, on the march, had none of the pomp of the imperial Mughal or Adilshahi armies. The only belongings the soldiers carried were a couple of thick blankets and food for their own mounts. There were no heavy tents or bedding. The only ones to have tents on their campaigns were Shivaji *Raje* and some of his Commanders. The rest always slept in the open. This way, they remained light and could move at a much more rapid pace than the imperial armies.

Bahirji Naik's men were dispatched to Aurangabad to plant a rumor that Shivaji was preparing to march to the capital of the Mughal Deccan province. The *Subadar* of the Deccan, Prince Muazzam, believed this rumor to be true and stayed put in Aurangabad, waiting for the Marathas. 'Let the *kafir* come,' he thought. 'I will teach him a lesson!' This successfully prevented any mobilisation of Mughal troops towards Surat.

"Are you awake, My Lord?" Tanhaji poked his face in between the tent flaps.

"Yes, Tanhya, what is it?"

"Bahirji Naik is here. Our men on the northern outpost have arrested some Mughals who say they have a message from the Surat Governor, Inayat Khan."

Raje nodded. Bahirji followed Tanhaji inside and said, "Highness, Inayat Khan still seems to think that a Mughal army has arrived near Surat. He has sent messengers with an order not to venture near Surat. They say the news of our arrival has unnecessarily caused panic in the city."

Raje grinned, amused. "Looks like all our moves have worked. Let Inayat Khan sleep peacefully tonight. We will land at the gates of Surat tomorrow and surprise him."

As a result of the excellent work done by his spy network, Shivaji *Raje* and his ten thousand men had advanced unmolested to Udhna. Surat now lay within striking distance.

SURAT CITY, END OF SECOND PRAHAR OF THE DAY,
6 JANUARY 1664

The worst fears of Surat's residents had come true. Shivaji *Raje* had arrived at the city gates with a huge army! There were only a few Mughal sentries manning the gates and these were dispatched immediately. However, the Marathas had not entered the city. Instead, Shivaji *Raje* sent a messenger to Inayat Khan, who, having lost his bearings, had fled to the fort, where he locked himself in. *Raje*'s messenger duly arrived at Fort Surat and was produced before the Governor.

The three richest traders in Surat, Virji Vora, Haji Sayed Baig and Haji Kasam, should present themselves in my camp and finalize the terms and amount of levied contribution. This amount is to be paid immediately. If they do so, we will not enter the city, nor molest any resident. However, if not done, I shall order my men to enter and sack the city. No house, no trader will be spared. We cannot then be held responsible for the outcome of the raid.

Raje's chilling ultimatum to the Governor froze all those present. Instead of prudent words, the Governor said, "Finalize the ransom amount? Ha! Tell me, how much ransom should I demand from you?"

The Maratha messenger realized that Inayat Khan was not a man who would co-operate to save the city and its people from harm. He returned to his King with the Governor's hasty reply.

Meanwhile, the Marathas had set up camp in a garden outside the city gates. In his tent, *Raje* awaited word from the Governor. He did not want to enter and sack Surat, and was thus dismayed when his man brought back Inayat Khan's pompous reply. Summoning his chief officers, he ordered the sacking of the city.

"We had hoped the Mughals would settle the matter peacefully," he said. "But that does not seem likely to happen. We have no choice but to raid Surat now. Remember, we are here to get what is rightfully ours. For three years the Mughals have destroyed our lands, burned our crops and looted our people. We must be reimbursed. The Mughals must pay for what they have taken from us. But keep this in your mind, that even when we raid, we have our principles. We should not turn into renegades and ruffians like the Mughals themselves. No woman, child or elderly person should be harmed. If any of our men molests a woman, he shall be put to death! Do not kill anyone unnecessarily. Demand ransom only from the rich and leave the poor folk alone. Hand out written receipts to those who pay, so that no one demands payment from them again."

The Maratha Captains rounded up their respective units and relayed the King's orders. Thousands of Maratha troops then entered the city and began sacking it. Pandemonium ensued. Surat residents ran from pillar to post, some trying to escape the raiders, some trying to get into the fort for safety. Inayat Khan realized he was pitifully short of troops and incapable of defending his city, which was now at the mercy of the Marathas. Never one to forgo an opportunity to make some money for himself, he demanded payment from those who came to the fort seeking refuge, and let in only those who paid up.

The Marathas began levying contributions on the rich. Those who paid were left in peace. Those who refused were beaten up. Some were produced before the Maratha King. Locked houses were broken into and looted. Their owners, according to the Marathas, had lost the opportunity to pay a ransom and save their homes.

A Maratha party marched to the government customs office and sacked it thoroughly, procuring plenty of ready cash. Bahirji Naik led another party to Haji Sayed Baig's mansion. Baig had locked the mansion and fled to the fort with his family. The Marathas broke into the house and sacked it.

Fort Surat, about the same time

Inayat Khan paced his conference chamber, deep in thought, as the chief members of his staff stood by with arms folded. His Captain-of-the-Guard, though he had a non-committal expression, inwardly cursed the Governor. He knew only too well that with the meager troops at their disposal, they could do nothing to stop the Marathas. Had the Governor shown some presence of mind and negotiated with Seevaji, they could have got away with a peaceful settlement. Now there was no telling how much and for how long the sacking would continue. Had the Governor maintained the five thousand troops sanctioned by the Emperor, they could have given the raiders a good fight. How he wished he had more men!

An attendant arrived to say, "My Lord, the Captain on watch has sent a message that the English are marching through the streets."

"What the hell!" Inayat Khan exclaimed.

The men hurried to the ramparts and climbed onto a wooden scaffolding that supported one of the fort's guns, and peered across the city. The English, a mere hundred odd, were marching with beating drums and blaring trumpets. At the head was a smart officer holding the East India Company's checkered flag. Behind him, mounted on a horse was the English President, George Oxenden. As the party marched past the fort, Oxenden looked up to see the Mughals staring down at him from the ramparts.

Inayat Khan laughed contemptuously. "Does that idiot Oxenden think he can fight thousands of Maratha troops with his paltry force?"

Khan's young son smirked. "They will get massacred."

The Captain-of-the-Guard looked away, his frustration palpable. *At least applaud his act of brave defiance, you cowards!* He thought. But he could only stand in silence.

SHIVAJI RAJE'S SHAMIANA, OUTSKIRTS OF SURAT CITY,
LATE AFTERNOON 6 JANUARY 1664

"Highness, we have accosted an Englishman named Anthony Smith," Tanhaji announced, as he and Yesaji entered Shivaji *Raje*'s *shamiana*. "We have tried to make him pay ransom, but he insists he has no money. He is most certainly an Officer of the English factory here."

"Send him to his factory with some of our men, with a message to the English factory President: If you pay the ransom, we will not harm your factory. If you do not, we will be forced to attack you."

"Very well, Sire."

Yesaji too, had news of a foreign visitor. "Highness, a person who calls himself Reverand Ambrose, has come here and requests to see you in person." *Raje* nodded permission.

An elderly bearded man walked in, dressed in priestly garb. His white skin was tanned from exposure to the sun. He bowed slightly to the Maratha King and said, "Your Highness, I run a missionary centre in Surat, where I treat sick people and care for the poor and needy. We do not have any treasures. In fact, we survive on donations. Kindly spare us from any levies."

Raje studied him intently for a few moments. He was aware of the charity work done by the Christian missionaries. The man seemed genuine enough. "Go in peace, Reverand Ambrose," he said. "We will leave your center alone. My men will not harm your people."

"You are kind, O King!" Ambrose said, bowing again, and left.

A while later, Kudtoji Gujar, another of Shivaji *Raje*'s Captains arrived. The man was in his forties, tall and well built, with large expressive eyes and a thick moustache. He proudly wore a crescent *tilak* on his forehead, like his Lord. He had just returned from the city with plenty of loot and news.

"How are things progressing, Kudtoji?" *Raje* enquired.

"As planned, Sire. Ransom is being collected systematically and receipts are being handed out."

"Good! Do not use force on anyone who co-operates with us. Even those who do not, must not be seriously harmed. No one should be in peril of their lives. We are not barbarians."

Kudtoji nodded. "Highness, we came across the house of a Dutch merchant, who is long since dead. We were told his wife lives there now, with her children."

Raje raised his eyebrows and his expression hardened. What was Kudtoji suggesting?

Kudtoji realized that his Master had misunderstood him, and hurriedly added, "Sire, there is much commotion in the town right now. I am sure some bad elements in Surat will take advantage of that and do some looting of their own in our name. I am concerned about the safety of the Dutch lady and her children. Should we post a guard around her house?"

Raje's face softened into a smile and he nodded permission. "Post some of your men there and reassure the lady," he said.

FORT SURAT, 7 JANUARY 1664

A young Captain stood in front of the Governor with folded hands as he listened intently to his instructions.

"Discard your military uniform and dress as a diplomat. Pay that Maratha rat a visit and beg permission to meet him in person. Try to get near him, then attack him with a concealed dagger. If you manage to kill him, this entire raid will fall apart."

"Yes Sir," the Captain answered confidently. Inwardly, he knew it was a suicide mission. But the city was in peril and he had to obey the Governor's command.

SHIVAJI RAJE'S SHAMIANA, OUTSKIRTS OF SURAT,
EARLY SECOND PRAHAR, MORNING OF 7 JANUARY 1664

Yesaji Kank, Tanhaji Malusare and Kudtoji Gujar stood in front of their King with news of the early morning raids.

"Highness, we have sacked the house of Virji Vora, near the Dutch factory. We procured over eighty lakh in gold and cash, plus some twenty eight *ser* of pearls," Tanhaji beamed.

"Good," Shivaji *Raje* said, satisfied. "Anyone hurt?"

"No one, Sire. Vora, like Haji Baig, has fled to the fort. His house was unoccupied."

"How about the Dutch? Did they make any moves?"

"The Dutch have remained neutral so far," said Kudtoji.

"Highness, the English and Dutch have steadfastly refused to pay ransom. Should we storm both factories?" Tanhaji asked.

"No," *Raje* replied. "According to our spies, the man-strength in these factories is not more than a few hundred. We can reduce both factories to dust whenever we wish. As a matter of fact, we could do the same to the fort and arrest the Governor. But we are not here for battle or to annex territory. Even if we do, we will never be able to hold Surat for long. Why waste time and men? We are here for the loot and that we are getting in plenty from the rich traders of

Surat. But we can fire a few rounds at the factories and the fort, to discourage the inhabitants from sallying forth to create trouble. Do it under cover. I do not wish to lose any men."

"Yes, Sire!" Tanhaji said.

An attendant entered. "A diplomat has just arrived from Inayat Khan," he said, unable to keep the surprise from his voice.

The men exchanged looks. An envoy from the Governor? After all this time? What was the scoundrel upto now?

The man was ushered in. He was unarmed and dressed in the demure garb of a civil servant. Tanhaji stopped him at a distance from Shivaji *Raje* and instructed him to speak from there, while he stood beside him. Yesaji and Kudtoji stood to the man's left.

The man bowed courteously to Shivaji *Raje* and said, "Your Highness, I have come from the Surat Governor, Inayat Khan *sahib*, to discuss terms for a truce."

Raje raised his eyebrows. "Terms for a truce? Who is Inayat Khan to negotiate peace with me? His city is at my mercy. If he has any courage, ask him to step out of his fort and face me! He should beg for mercy, not negotiate for a truce."

"Shivaji *Raje*, you must realize that Surat is the Emperor's favourite city. When he learns you have vandalized Surat, he will never forgive..."

"I care not what the Emperor will do!" *Raje* said, interrupting this speech. "I know what I am doing. Now, if you have nothing sensible to say, do not waste my time."

"*Raje*, I do have something important to say. It is a personal message from the Governor, but for your ears alone. If I may come closer?" So saying, the man rapidly advanced toward Shivaji *Raje*.

Tanhaji and Yesaji smelled a rat immediately. In an instant, both drew their swords. The envoy had almost reached *Raje*'s *baithak*. In a flash, he drew out a dagger. Yesaji's eyes widened in horror and he threw himself at the man, slashing with his sword. The blade went clean through the man's forearm, chopping off his hand, still gripping the dagger. But the momentum of the man's charge carried him onto Shivaji *Raje*, drenching his *angarkha* in blood. *Raje* and the diplomat both crashed in a heap. As the stunned *Raje* gathered himself, Tanhaji, Yesaji and Kudtoji pulled the diplomat off him and hacked his body to pieces in frenzied rage, screaming as they did.

Hearing the commotion, the Maratha soldiers on guard outside the *shamiana* rushed in. They saw their King on the ground, drenched in blood, and the Captains attacking the Mughal envoy. Panicked, some of them rushed out screaming that Shivaji *Raje* had been attacked in the *shamiana* and been killed! The news spread like wildfire around the camp and beyond. Enraged, Maratha soldiers began hacking at some traders and others whom they had earlier taken prisoner, to extract ransom. Heads rolled and hands were chopped off. It was the frenzied reaction of a mob who had been told that the man they called King, and worshipped with all their heart, had been murdered.

Inside the *shamiana*, the assailant's hacked body lay in a pool of blood, while Tanhaji, Yesaji, Kudtoji and *Raje* stood speechless and stunned. The Mughal emissary had caught them unawares. Only Yesaji's swiftness had saved *Raje* from certain death. No one had expected such a suicidal attack from the Mughal camp.

"My King, are you hurt?" Tanhaji asked, visible alarmed.

"His blade never touched me, thanks to Yesaji's quick action."

Raje soon realized that pandemonium had broken out amongst his own men. He knew only too well the implications of such frenzy amongst armed troops. It was more than likely that his men would go on a murderous rampage through the city. He ran out shouting, "I am alright! I am alive! Do not kill anyone. Be calm!"

He did manage to pacify the men in the camp, but the news had been relayed right into the city. The Maratha platoons there lost their cool and went on a rampage till the news of *Raje* being safe finally reached them. In the meantime, however, many lives had been lost.

Raje returned to the *shamiana* and changed his garments. Though he maintained a calm face, he was fuming. How had Inayat Khan dared to commit such a brazen act? He fervently wished to attack the fort, but knew it would be a tremendous waste of time. Prudently, he chose to remain silent.

Surat, 7 & 8 January 1664

The murderous attempt on Shivaji *Raje*'s life inevitably had the effect of transforming a relatively controlled sacking of Surat into a more vengeful affair. The Marathas in the city now began torching houses in retribution. Messages from the King failed to stop them. The Maratha army was a motley band of troops from various sections of society, and the wilder elements in the army went berserk on hearing the news of the attack on their liberator. Through that day and the next, more houses were torched. Virji Vora's house was set afire and the flames rose to the skies, at one time even threatening the nearby Dutch factory.

The British continued with their obstinate stand, refusing to pay. A Maratha platoon tried some token firing at the factory, but were driven off. George Oxenden's stubbornness helped save not only his own factory and people, but also several other houses in the vicinity, as the Marathas now left this part of the town alone.

A few Maratha soldiers, angry at the Surat Governor's treachery, scaled the fort ramparts and began firing at the people inside. In response, the impulsive Inayat Khan ordered his men to fire the fort cannons at the raiders. The cannon shots missed the Marathas and landed outside the fort, destroying some adjacent houses.

Amidst this meleé, the sacking of Surat progressed to Shivaji *Raje*'s satisfaction. Thousands of sacks filled with loot were brought to his camp outside the city gates. These were neatly stacked and kept in readiness to move at a moment's notice.

Later, *Raje's* spy network brought news of a large Mughal army moving toward Surat. He immediately gave orders to wind up the operation.

Outskirts of Surat, 9 January 1664

The Marathas had brought several thousand spare horses with them, to transport the loot back to Rajgad. They began stacking over three thousand sacks of gold, silver, diamonds, pearls and ornaments onto these mounts. By the first *prahar* of the morning, Shivaji *Raje* and his army were ready to march out of Surat. Mounting his horse, he turned towards the city gates and said, "I have fulfilled my desire of many years to take back wealth from Surat. We have no enemity with the residents of this great city. The treasure we take with us is but a small compensation for the immense destruction of our land, crops and people by the Mughals."

"We have done to Surat what they did to our *Swarajya*," replied Tanhaji.

"The loss of business from Surat is bound to hurt the Mughal treasury and administration," *Raje* said with a slight smile. "I have pulled out a precious feather from Aurangzeb's crown!"

The Mughal Imperial Court, Delhi, a few weeks later

The court attendant bowed low, begging the Emperor's indulgence for interrupting the court proceedings. "An urgent despatch has just arrived from Commander Mahabat Khan in Surat. The man who brings it says it must be presented to Your Majesty without delay," he said hurriedly, fearful of the Emperor's displeasure.

Aurangzeb threw him an irritated look, but gave a slight nod. Moments later, the imperial messenger arrived with a pouch, which he said was from Mahabat Khan, currently lodged in Surat.

"What is Mahabat Khan doing in Surat?" the Emperor asked, frowning.

The pouch was handed to the *Wazir,* Jafar Khan, who opened the scroll. As he read, his eyes widened in horror:

The evil infidel Seeva has attacked Surat and looted it for four days, carrying away immense wealth. An eyewitness informed me that he saw the Marathas load thousands of bags of loot on their horses before they left the town. It is difficult to be exact, but the sons of dogs may have carried away over ten million in cash, gold, silver and gems.

Aurangzeb sat in stunned silence. The courtiers began murmuring and shifting restlessly, but the Emperor sat as if carved in stone. His eyes, red with anger, threatened to burn to ash the very chamber in which he sat.

Before leaving, the infidels torched thousands of houses. The fires were so devastating that they turned day into night with thick clouds of smoke. And when night fell, they turned night to day with the flames which rose to the skies. Surat continued to burn for many days and over two-thirds of the town is now in ashes. I fear the city may never return to its former prosperity."

"Enough!" the Emperor thundered, silencing the growing murmurs. The courtiers fell silent and intently regarded their feet, none daring to look up at the infuriated sovereign.

"What was Inayat Khan doing when that rat was looting the city?" Aurangzeb shouted at the imperial messenger, who stood trembling before him.

The man prayed the Emperor would not order his head to be struck off for bringing such dire news. "Sire, the Governor shut himself in the fort when Seeva entered the city with his troops," he stammered out. "The infidel had over ten thousand cavalry with him. The Governor had but a thousand men."

"I have personally sanctioned a garrison of five thousand for Surat. What were they doing? Sleeping with their women?"

"Majesty..." the man hesitated, knowing the Emperor would be further enraged by what he had to communicate. "Majesty, Inayat Khan maintains only a thousand men in Surat. They too, are not first class soldiers but cheap mercenaries."

"What the...?" Aurangzeb was furious but checked himself. It was evident the Surat Governor had been swallowing a large share of the imperial funds granted to him to maintain a garrison. "Are you part of the Surat garrison?" the Emperor asked the man.

"No, Sire," the man replied hurriedly. "I belong to Commander Mahabat Khan's army. We marched to Surat as soon as we received news of the loot. But because of the distance, we reached only a week after the Marathas had left. The Governor had not dared to step out of the fort till we reached the city. Only then did he come out to meet the Commander. The people of Surat derided him for his cowardice and threw dung at him. Angered, his son shot down a trader."

"Cowards!" The Emperor's cold voice was like a whiplash. "How do they even show their faces?" Aurangzeb fell silent. Closing his eyes, he began turning his prayer beads, composing himself.

When he opened his eyes again, he said quietly, "Jafar Khan, prepare imperial orders at once. Inayat Khan is dismissed from the Governorship of Surat with immediate effect. Have him brought to court...in chains. Ghiyasuddin Khan is appointed the new Governor of Surat. Arrange tax concessions for the people of Surat to offset some of their losses."

The *Vizier* bowed. "It will be done, Sire. Mahabat Khan further writes that the foreign traders, especially the English and Dutch, resisted the raiders with their paltry garrisons. They refused to pay ransom and even protected the houses in the vicinity of their factories. The Commander offered an award to Oxenden, the English factory President for his bravery, but he refused it, asking for a concession in customs duty instead."

"We shall think about offering such concessions later. Our Governors and Commanders have something to learn about bravery and self-respect from these foreigners." Abruptly, the Emperor signalled the end of the court session and retired to his chambers.

The news of the raid on Surat spread like wildfire not only in the Mughal capital, but across Hindustan, the Deccan, and beyond. The rulers and politicians of the land were stunned by the news. Foreigners, including the English, Dutch and Portuguese, were amazed at the audacity of the raid and furiously wrote to their own sovereigns across the seas, that a new power had risen in the land which even the great Mughal found hard to supress.

The incident caused bitter mortification in the Mughal court, which found the burden of humiliation exceedingly difficult to bear. Across the capital, people murmured that the Emperor was losing his grip on his Empire. Surat, the jewel in Aurangzeb's crown, the gateway to Mecca, had been utterly ruined. The immense flow of wealth from the city to the imperial treasury had ceased completely. As Mahabat Khan had said, it would be many years before Surat would return to its former state.

Months later, the news reached Shah Abbas, the Persian Emperor, who laughed at the Mughals. In an attempt to ridicule Aurangzeb, he wrote: *It seems you have lost the ability to govern your Empire. I will personally come to Hindustan with my army, to teach you how to do your job.*

This raised the alarm of a Persian invasion from the north-west. The disturbed Mughal Emperor paced his chambers in silence, thinking about whom to appoint as Head of the unconcluded Deccan mission. His uncle, the much decorated Shaista Khan, had failed against Seeva. His own son, Prince Muazzam too, had failed to reign in the Marathas, and as per reports, preferred to while away his time in hunting, games, wine and women. He had to be called back and a more responsible person appointed to the *Subadari* of the Deccan province.

It did not take Aurangzeb long to decide on the new General. The next morning, he sent an urgent *firmaan* to Jai Singh, the *Raja* of Jaipur, a long time faithful of the throne.

MARATHA MILITARY CAMP NEAR RAJGAD, EARLY FEBRUARY 1664

Bahirji Naik's face was grave as he entered the King's presence. He had just received terrible news, which he knew would plunge his Master into despair. The Maratha camp, flushed with its recent success in Surat, and happily carrying the burden of over three thousand bags of loot, would have to abandon its celebrations and mourn with their King.

The Maratha Chief of Intelligence stood before his King and bowed his head. So did the messenger who had ridden hard from the South.

"What is it Bahirji?" Shivaji *Raje* asked, concerned.

"Highness, my man has just arrived from Bengalur with sad news. His Highness, *Maharaj saheb* Shahaji *Raje*, is no more."

Raje gave a deep sigh and momentarily closed his eyes, uttering the Goddess' name. "How?" he asked.

"His Highness was out hunting in the forest near Hodigere, in Chitradurg district. While at a full gallop, chasing a wild boar, his mount got entangled in some undergrowth, throwing him off. *Maharaj saheb* landed heavily on his head. He fought for his life for two days, but ultimately succumbed."

Raje silently mourned for his father, a man he had hardly lived with, but whom he had greatly admired and respected. His mother would be shattered on hearing the news.

"Has word been sent to my mother?" he asked.

"Yes, Highness, the news has reached Rajgad."

Raje stood up, alarmed. "I must leave at once!"

"Highness, we can leave at first light..."

"No Bahirji! You do not know my mother as I do! I must be at her side as soon as possible."

Both men rushed out to prepare for the hurried departure.

RAJGAD, 5 FEBRUARY 1664

Shivaji *Raje* returned to a home plunged in grief. His staff tried to console him. His wives waited on Jijabai, devoid of rich apparel and adornments. It tore his heart to see his mother in the traditional white saree of a widow. But what alarmed him more was the vermillion smeared on her forehead and the plates bearing ritual offerings, placed in her chamber. *Raje*'s worst fears had come true. He realized painfully that his mother had resolved to immolate herself on a burning pyre, adhering to the age-old ritual of *sati*.

The grief of his father's death was momentarily forgotten as he struggled to come to terms with having to watch his mother on a burning pyre. Driving such thoughts from his mind, he threw himself at his mother's feet, drenching them with his tears. He begged her to change her mind, reminding her repeatedly that she had been the one to encourage him on this path to freedom. She had to remain with him to see his oath fulfilled.

The Queens joined him in attempting to change Jijabai's mind. Putala especially, wept inconsolably as she sat at her mother-in-law's feet, begging her not to leave them.

"Mother, do not abandon your children like this. It is not mandatory for every widow to become a *sati*." *Raje* tried desperately to change her mind.

Jijabai, however, was resolute in her decision. She sat upright, looking away into the distance. "I have been called..." she kept repeating. "Prepare to see me off."

"No, mother!" *Raje* begged. "I will plead with the Gods to pardon you. Father has left us suddenly. If you leave too, who will cherish my deeds?" Shivaji *Raje* clasped his mother's legs and wouldn't let her get up.

After much pleading, Jijabai's heart melted and she relented. She feared that her son would, in his grief, deviate from his destiny. That must never be. *Swarajya* came first. Her son had to be kept on the path to his true goal. She would live for that.

"Get up, Shivba," she finally said. "I will not leave you. Not yet."

Shivaji *Raje* let out a long sigh of relief. Taking his mother in his arms, he realised he had won the greatest challenge of his life.

Rajgad, third week April 1664

"The Rajput-Mughal force launched a massive attack on the fort early in the morning, but our garrison was alert. A thousand of our soldiers sallied out of the fort and fell upon Jaswant Singh's assault batallion. After much fierce fighting at close quarters, the Rajputs were beaten back. While this battle was being fought, some of our men crept right into the Mughal camp and lit up their ammunition dump. Their entire supply of gunpowder and rockets, and most of their artillery was blown sky high!"

Shivaji *Raje* grinned as he listened to the exploits of his troops garrisoned in Fort Kondhana, which had been besieged by Jaswant Singh for the last five months. Jaswant had been relatively quiet for some time now. He had again been caught napping when *Raje* passed close to his camp, this time on his way to Surat. He had received a rude shock when he heard of the Surat raid and immediately planned an assault on Kondhana, to show the Emperor that he was not sitting idle.

"The explosion ignited quarrels within the Mughal camp, as Jaswant blamed his brother-in-law, Rao Bhao Singh Hada, for the disaster," said Mahadev, the man who had brought the news from Kondhana, hiding a smile. "Right now there is plenty of dissension in the camp. I don't think they are capable of any concerted efforts to capture Kondhana."

Raje smiled. "Praised be our men who achieved so much! Jaswant Singh may be forced to abandon the Kondhana campaign."

Rajgad Palace, sometime in mid-1664

"Welcome to Rajgad, Pilajirao," Shivaji *Raje* said, welcoming his guest from Shringarpur. "I hope the journey was uneventful?"

"It was, Highness," Pilajirao said, bowing to *Raje* and Jijabai.

Raje seated the newcomer beside him. Also present in the conference chamber inside Rajgad Palace were Moro *Punt*, Tryambak *Punt*, Raghunath *Punt* and Niraji *Punt*. As he sat down amongst these dignitaries, Pilajirao wondered why the King had summoned him with a personal letter.

"Pilajirao, I hope Shringarpur is peaceful?" Jijabai asked him.

"With your blessings Queen Mother, it is," Pilajirao replied.

"Pilajirao, my father passed away recently..." Shivaji *Raje* said, broaching the subject of the meeting.

"Yes, your Highness, I am aware of it. My condolences are with you and the Queen Mother."

"Our *shastras* dictate that any festal rites in our household must be performed within a year of his death. My son Shambhu *Raje* is of marriageable age now, and we wish to conclude an alliance soon."

Pilajirao nodded. "A wise thought, Highness." He was still unsure why he had been involved in what was a family matter.

Shivaji *Raje* looked at Jijabai, who nodded. "Pilajirao, I wish to ask for your daughter Rajasbai's hand in marriage for my son, Shambhu. If it is agreeable to you, please say so. If not, I would appreciate it if you tell me so frankly."

Pilajirao was quite stunned. A marriage proposal from the King himself! This was high honour for his family. Not in a hundred years could he have said no. "Highness, you do my family great honour!" he managed to say.

Smiles appeared on every face. Shivaji *Raje* and Jijabai were overjoyed. *Raje* felt happy that the marriage would finally give his mother a reason to smile.

The marriage was soon concluded in Rajgad, with the customary royal fanfare. As the ceremoniously dressed young couple touched her feet to seek her blessings, Jijabai pulled them close and planted kisses on their foreheads. She cradled Rajasbai's beautiful face in her hands saying, "How beautiful you are Yesubai! Shambhu is a lucky boy."

As per custom, Rajasbai had been given a new name in her husband's household. Yesubai thus became the first wife of the Maratha Prince.

THE MUGHAL IMPERIAL COURT, DELHI, MID-1664

A tall, well-built man in his early fifties stood before the Emperor with his hands folded in front of his body and eyes downcast. Dressed in fine ceremonial clothes, he wore a turban adorned with pearls and rubies on his head. His clean shaven, round face sported a thick moustache which met his bushy sideburns. Pearls hung from his earlobes and around his neck. Precious gems sparkled on his fingers. To any onlooker it was evident the man was a noble of high rank, a royal. He was no stranger to the Mughal *durbar*, for he was Jai Singh, *Raja* of Amer, ruler of his home principality and a faithful Mughal vassal.

"Welcome, *Raja* Jai Singh!" the Emperor greeted his ablest noble.

Jai Singh finally raised his head when thus addressed. Despite his age, his eyes sparkled with the enthusiasm of youth. Ever since he was a boy of twelve, Jai Singh had toiled in Mughal military camps as a vassal noble and had proved his mettle many times over. He had fought wars across the length and breadth of Hindustan, and had tasted victory every time. A brilliant soldier, a capable General, and a clever diplomat, Jai Singh was master of the Urdu, Persian, Turki, Hindustani and Rajastani languages. In him, Aurangzeb saw an ideal leader of the composite army of Afghans, Turks, Rajputs and Hindustanis, that fought under the Mughal banner.

"The Master beckons and his servant comes, Your Majesty," Jai Singh replied with a courteous bow.

"Jai Singh, you are pre eminent amongst my nobles. The Empire is faced with a difficult problem in the Deccan. The Maratha rebel Seeva has challenged our imperial authority in these lands. He seems to have forgotten that he is a mere *zamindar* and has dared to raise his head against us. He has recently raided our richest town, Surat, and burned it to ashes. I want you to bring him to book; teach him a lesson he will not forget."

"*Jahaanpanaah,* it is an honour to be nominated for this campaign."

Aurangzeb's face broke into a rare smile. "I hereby appoint you the new *Subadar* of our Deccan province. You will leave immediately for Aurangabad, and take charge from Prince Muazzam, who has been recalled to court."

Jai Singh bowed in acceptance of the Emperor's orders.

"On this occasion, I award you with the high title of *Mirza.* From this day, you shall be known as *Mirza Raja* Jai Singh." Aurangzeb raised his hand to honour his noble.

Mirza... Mirza... the assembled nobles and officers chanted, raising their hands. *Umr darraaz rahe...*

Jai Singh nodded and bowed, accepting the title. Coming from the Emperor, it was a high honour indeed.

"*Mirza Raja* Jai Singh," continued Aurangzeb, "you will have the services of our best Captains and nobles, adequate finances, and a free hand with artillery and ammunition. Take what you wish, but bring me results. Reign in Seeva and annex his lands and forts. Avenge the insults he has subjected the Empire to."

Jai Singh bowed again. "Rest easy, Your Majesty. The day is not far when Seeva shall be presented before you. From this day I shall think of nothing but the task entrusted to me."

Aurangzeb nodded. If there was anything he demanded from his nobles, it was this, complete devotion to duty and undying fidelity. Having appointed his best and most experienced noble to the Deccan, he waited impatiently for the conclusion of the campaign against the infidel Seeva.

Aurangzeb sent word to Diler Khan, lodged in his own *jagir*, to appear before him in the capital. The tall and muscular, broad shouldered Pathani noble responded immediately to the summons. He was taken to the Emperor's private audience chamber. There was no third person present. Diler realized the Emperor wished to say something meant for his ears alone.

"Diler Khan," Aurangzeb said to his trusted man, "I have appointed Jai Singh to head the Deccan campaign. You are to join his camp with your Pathan contingent."

"Yes, Your Majesty." Diler raised his eyes to glance at his Master.

"Remember, though Jai Singh is the General, you are my most trusted man in his camp. Keep an eye on him. There is no doubting his military and diplomatic capabilities, nor his intelligence. But he is a *kafir* after all, just like that rat Seeva! It has been my experience that these *kafirs* often band together. If Seeva manages to corrupt Jai Singh's mind using their faith as a weapon, our entire campaign will fizzle out. You must guard against such treachery."

"As you command, *Jahaanpanaah*. Diler Khan will not fail you." Diler bowed and left the chamber.

Aurangzeb waited till another man quietly appeared from behind the draperies. It was his chief spy, Hussain.

"Hussain, keep an eye on both Jai Singh and Diler," the Emperor said to him.

Hussain was surprised. "Diler Khan too, Majesty?"

"Anyone can defect to the enemy, Hussain. A ruler has to be two steps ahead of his nobles and Captains! Plant your men around the chief nobles in our camp, but mainly around Jai Singh and Diler. If either plays mischief or defects, the campaign is over."

The Mughal administration went into overdrive to organize the new Deccan campaign under the Generalship of Jai Singh. Numerous Captains had been ordered to report to him with their retinues. Chief amongst them were Daud Khan Qureshi, Barq-andaz Khan, Ihtisham Khan Shaikhzada, Mulla Yahya Nayta (who had earlier that year defected from the Adilshahi), Qutb-ud-din Khan, Sujan Singh Bundela, Puranmal Bundela, Raja Nar Singh Gaur, and Jai Singh's own son, Kirat Singh. But towering over these, and of nearly equal stature to Jai Singh himself, was Aurangzeb's trusted noble, Diler Khan.

The initial strength of Jai Singh's cavalry, assembled in Delhi, was nearly fifteen thousand. This number swelled as he travelled to the Deccan, as more nobles joined him along the way. He had been given plenty of artillery, including heavy siege guns, and thousands of animals. An unbroken baggage chain had been established to maintain supplies to his vast army.

Delhi, 30th September 1664

The massive Mughal army snaked its way past the southern limits of the capital city and advanced as rapidly as its size would permit, toward the capital of the Mughal Deccan province, Aurangabad. Jai Singh was deep in thought as he lay back on the cushions in his palanquin, while the carriers laboured to keep up a brisk pace. Their immediate objective was to annex the Maratha dominions and eliminate the rebel leader Seeva, who had rapidly become a thorn in the Emperor's flesh. Privately, Jai Singh marvelled at both the genius and daring of the Maratha rebel. Not since the *Rana* of Mewar, Pratap Singh, had anyone defied imperial authority so boldly. He seemed to carry on with his audacious raids and guerilla strikes in utter contempt of repercussion from the Great Mughal.

Something within him mourned the fact that Seeva and his challenge would soon be annhilated in the face of this massive military campaign. He was loathe to kill such a fine warrior. He would give Seeva a chance to come over to the Mughals, he thought. Seeva deserved it. If he, Jai Singh, succeeded in procuring the Maratha rebel's loyalty to the Mughal throne, the Empire would gain not just an outstanding Commander, but scores of Maratha troops, to fight under the Mughal banner. If that happened, his second important objective, to attack and reduce the Deccan Sultanate of the Adilshah, would become easier.

Jai Singh was fully aware that subduing Seeva was not an easy proposition. The man had slain no less a monster than Afzal Khan, whom Aurangzeb himself had grappled with. Then he had followed it up by skillfully ruining Siddi Jauhar's life. Jai Singh had heard how Seeva and his spies had seeded mistrust between the Adilshah and Jauhar, resulting in the latter's death. The most recent events, including the raid on Shaista Khan and the sack of Surat, were still fresh in everyone's mind. Shaista Khan was a fool, thought Jai Singh, and had got what he deserved. Conceited and boastful, he lived steeped in luxury. Come to think of it, the Mughals had, till now, eliminated most rebellions with brawn. Seldom had they used ingenious tactics or clever politics. The might of the Mughal army, its sheer numbers and superior artillery, had overwhelmed most opposition. Faced with a smart thinking and calculating rebel like Seeva, Shaista Khan's shortcomings had been exposed.

For Jai Singh, this campaign would be different from most others. He had to win, of course, but he knew it wouldn't be possible with might alone. He would have to out-think Seeva, clip his wings, and demoralize him...to such an extent that the Maratha would never dream of raising his head against the Mughals again.

5
OLD FOE PUNISHED

ROYAL DURBAR, BIJAPUR CITADEL, OCTOBER 1664

The young Sultan of Bijapur, Ali, the Adilshah, sat upright on his throne, his right foot resting on a globe. On either side stood tall muscular *hashams* with unsheathed swords. Two slaves fanned him tirelessly from behind the throne.

A dark skinned noble stood in front of him, in a posture of abject servitude, eyes to the ground, hands clasped in front. He had been summoned to this *durbar* with a *firmaan*. The other nobles stood silently in rows on either side of the hall.

The Adilshah bent forward to place his right elbow on his raised right knee, smiling slightly from the corners of his mouth. "Khawas Khan, I have decided to entrust a very important campaign to you. Seevaji has occupied large tracts of land in the Konkan. You will march to south Konkan and free it from the Marathas."

Khawas Khan bowed and finally raised his gaze to look at his sovereign. "Your wish is my command, Excellency! I will begin preparations at once."

"The *Desai* of Kudal, Lakham Savant, will assist you. So will Baji Ghorpade of Mudhol. *Firmaans* have been despatched to Savant and Ghorpade, ordering them to join your camp with their retinues."

Ali looked at Khawas Khan hopefully. He was amongst the pre-eminent nobles of his court. Khawas Khan's father, Khan Muhammad, had once been the Bijapuri *Vizier*. Back then, the short sightedness and impulsiveness of Ali's mother, *Badi Begum*, then the Regent, and the vindictive nature of Afzal Khan, had resulted in Khan Muhammad's murder. But years later, Ali had gained control over the administration and sidelined his mother, winning the trust and faith of the nobles once slighted by his mother. Khawas Khan had rapidly risen to a high stature at his court. He had successfully repelled the advance of Seevaji's *Sirnaubat,* Netoji Palkar, in the aftermath of Afzal Khan's defeat.

Khawas Khan made haste to organize his campaign and leave Bijapur. His objective was to cross the Sahyadris and emerge onto the Konkan coastal strip before Shivaji could get a whiff of the campaign.

RAJGAD, A FEW DAYS LATER

Bahirji Naik squatted on the floor as he informed his King of the latest movements in Bijapur.

"Khawas Khan is already on his way from Bijapur," he said. "He should cross the *ghats* before we can get to him."

Shivaji *Raje* listened intently. Adilshah had been active in the Konkan for the last five months. His earlier campaign under Aziz Khan had resulted in the loss of Kudal. But the Adilshahi forces had failed to shake the Maratha hold over South Konkan. The campaign had fizzled out, due to Aziz Khan's untimely demise, and the rains. The Adilshah had now appointed Khawas Khan, a proven General, to wrest South Konkan from him.

"What is his strength?" *Raje* asked.

"Not over five thousand, Highness. Half of those are foot soldiers. He has a fair amount of artillery and ammunition, though. There is news that Lakham Savant will join him in the Konkan, with ten thousand infantry."

Raje stroked his beard, deep in thought. The Mughal frontier had been quiet since Shaista Khan had returned to Aurangabad, and now, with Jaswant Singh too, turning back, they could breathe easy till Aurangzeb organized another campaign. He felt the time was right to turn his attention to Adilshahi. If he could successfully repulse this latest move from Bijapur and keep his hold over the Konkan, he might be able to convince the Adilshah to refrain from further campaigns against him. He would have to silence Bijapur decisively in order to give his full attention to the Mughals, who would no doubt turn on him with a vengeance.

"Savant needs to be taught a lesson," *Raje* said harshly.

"Highness..." Bahirji leaned forward to give his King some crucial information. "Baji Ghorpade too, has been ordered to join Khawas Khan, with fifteen hundred infantry."

Shivaji *Raje's* eyes turned cold at the mention of the name. Baji Ghorpade had, for decades, fostered enemity with his father. Over a decade and a half ago, Ghorpade had connived with Mustafa Khan and Afzal Khan to dupe and arrest his father. Ghorpade had chained Shahaji himself. His father had remained in captivity for nearly a year. Much later, after Shahaji's release from prison, he had written to his son: *If you are my son, you will never forget these insults and will avenge me!* Shivaji *Raje* had neither forgiven Ghorpade those insults, nor had he forgotten. Mustafa Khan and Afzal Khan were dead. It was time to put an end to the third conniver.

"Where is Baji Ghorpade now?" *Raje* asked Bahirji.

"Still in Mudhol."

"Summon our *Sirnaubat* and Captains, Bahirji. We will march to Mudhol right away."

The principality of Mudhol lay a hundred and twenty-five *kos* south-east of Rajgad. Shivaji *Raje* rode into Baji Ghorpade's stronghold like a typhoon, with over five thousand cavalry in tow and summarily routed Ghorpade's paltry force stationed there. *Raje* himself, with Tanhaji Malusare, Yesaji Kank, Sarjerao Jedhe, Hiroji *Farzand* and other Captains, stormed Ghorpade's palace. Despite knowing that his end was near, Baji Ghorpade resolved to stand his ground and fight Shahaji's son.

Baji Ghorpade and Shivaji *Raje* faced each other with gleaming swords. *Raje* gritted his teeth as his eyes bored into the ageing face of his father's arch enemy. Ghorpade's anger knew no bounds as he charged at Shivaji *Raje,* vengeance in his heart. He had always hated the Bhosales, and this upstart rebel son of Shahaji made his blood boil with rage. *Raje* calmly took Baji's blows on his shield, looking straight at him.

Raje's Captains spread out on all sides, isolating the battling duo from Baji's men and guarding against a surprise assault on their Lord. They were not perturbed by Baji himself; Shivaji *Raje* was more than capable of dealing with the ageing man.

Ghorpade did all he could to break Shivaji *Raje*'s defence, but *Raje* blocked every move. Tanhaji looked back over his shoulder with a hint of impatience. He knew, had *Raje* really wished, he could have finished Ghorpade off within moments. Tanhaji knew *Raje* was prolonging Ghorpade's torture, tiring him out. He wished his Lord would wind up matters quickly.

As he parried with Ghorpade, Shivaji *Raje* replayed the scene of his father's humiliation in his mind. After all these years, he would settle the score. Baji was tiring fast. He decided to launch a final decisive attack on his tormentor. Gnashing his teeth, he rushed at his opponent. Shivaji *Raje* took the blow on his shield and the very next moment plunged his sword into Baji's belly. Baji staggered, gave an agonized cry, and dropped his sword and shield. *Raje* too, dropped his shield and, clutching Baji's *angarkha*, pulled him towards himself. His bloodied sword emerged through Baji's back. *Raje*'s cold eyes locked on Baji's as he watched life ebb away. Baji Ghorpade finally fell dead at his feet.

Raje stared at him and then said simply, "Today I have fulfilled another of my mother's wishes." Turning to Tanhaji, he said, "Find and kill every member of Ghorpade's family. Sack this place and burn it to ashes. Sack the town."

Shivaji *Raje* thus annihilated the Ghorpades of Mudhol and clipped one of Khawas Khan's wings.

Now for the other...

The victorious Maratha army now marched to Kudal, seventy *kos* due west of Mudhol. En route, Bahirji's spies arrived with definite news of Khawas Khan's movements. The Khan had crossed Amboli Hill Pass and reached the Konkan, but had, for some inexplicable reason, camped close to the hills. Shivaji *Raje* had expected him to march on quickly and join Savant's forces. But the Khan had stayed back.

"He is probably waiting for Baji Ghorpade," Bahirji's man said with a half-smile. "Ghorpade was supposed to bring plenty of money with him."

"The Khan has five thousand men with him. Savant waits further west, with ten thousand," *Raje* summarised. "We should not allow the two forces to meet."

The Maratha Captains, assembled in *Raje*'s tent, nodded.

"*Sirnaubat,*" Raje turned to Netoji Palkar. "You will lead a detachment of three thousand cavalry and attack Khawas Khan's camp. Mind that he has plenty of artillery and rockets with him. You too, equip yourselves with musketeers and rocketeers."

"It will be done, Highness," Netoji assured him.

"Use surprise to the fullest. Remember, Khawas Khan is a tough General. You have experienced his skill before. The battle is likely to get extremely messy. Do not hesitate to withdraw if your forces are being overwhelmed."

Netoji shifted uneasily. He never felt comfortable when advised to withdraw as part of his King's guerilla tactics. Khawas Khan had thwarted him before, and he was itching to pay him back!

"I will lead the remaining ten thousand men and take on Lakham Savant," *Raje* continued outlining his plans. "I am confident we can take him out in a single assault. Once Savant's force has been dispersed, Khawas Khan will have lost both of his reinforcement units. He will not be able to withstand us then."

Netoji and the others now realized what their Lord had in mind. Netoji's assault on Khawas Khan would be to keep him engaged and prevent him from going to Savant's aid, while *Raje* eliminated the former *Desai* of Kudal.

Raje rose purposefully. "Prepare the men. We march at dawn."

Late the following evening, the Maratha force, led by their *Sirnaubat,* approached close to Khawas Khan's camp. The Khan's scouts had been inept, thus allowing the Marathas to surprise them. Netoji launched a ferocious attack on the Khan's camp. His horsemen rained rockets and shot on the enemy. The camp was in pandemonium as the Khan's men struggled in the thick smoke and smell of gunpowder. Being regular levies of Bijapur, the trained soldiers regrouped quickly and handed a fitting reply to the Maratha *Sirnaubat*. The battle waged for over a *prahar,* with losses to both sides. The Bijapuris finally managed to drive Netoji's forces back toward the hills, but Khawas Khan had suffered heavily, losing his chief officers, Siddi Sarvar, Shaikh Miran and Shah Hazrat, in the meleé.

Meanwhile, the same night, Shivaji *Raje* fell upon Lakham Savant, stationed in Kudal. Another pitched battle was fought there. Savant had little artillery with him and had been waiting for Khawas Khan to join him. Their combined forces would have increased their strength many fold. But the Khan had decided to wait for Baji Ghorpade. Their forces had thus remained divided and Shivaji *Raje* had taken full advantage. Within a short while, Savant realized he was being overwhelmed, and fled south toward Portuguese ruled territory.

Shivaji *Raje* wasted no time in Kudal. He left a detachment to secure the district and turned back on Khawas Khan with his full force. The Khan received the news of the fall of Mudhol and the rout of Savant's forces on the same day. He now faced a large Maratha force under Shivaji, approaching him from the west, while the Maratha *Sirnaubat* lurked in the hills to the east. His own force was depleted after the earlier battle. The Khan realised he had been pitifully outsmarted by the Marathas. Reluctantly, he ordered his men to pack up and quietly retreat towards Bijapur.

Bijapur had lost another campaign against the resilient Marathas, who had retained their hold over the Konkan. Krishna Savant, a kin of Lakham Savant, joined the *Swarajya* as a vassal. Shivaji Raje conferred the *Deshmukhi* of Kudal upon him. Lakham knew he was being hunted by Shivaji's men and hid in Portuguese territory. The Portuguese, however, were reluctant to antagonize the Maratha King and this made Lakham's life difficult.

Following their tremendous success over the Bijapuri forces, Shivaji *Raje* and his Marathas marched into the uplands and burst into the south-west Adilshahi territory. They plundered the rich trading towns of Hubli, Khanapur and Bommasundara, besides several smaller towns. They collected plenty of booty, which, together with the wealth acquired at Mudhol, amounted to nearly three million rupees. But, besides collecting precious money, these raids had another objective. The trade in these parts of the Adilshahi Sultanate would be paralyzed, thus disrupting the supply of taxes to the Bijapur coffers. That would affect Ali Adilshah's decisions on future campaigns against the Marathas. The Sultan, meanwhile, could do little but bang his fists in frustration. He did not have the resources to launch another campaign against Shivaji.

The Maratha Navy had by now developed into a strong arm of Shivaji *Raje*'s forces. He felt the time was ripe to use the Navy to exert more control over the western shores, so he issued orders to his Navy Chief, Darya Sarang, to attack and loot the trading ships sailing from faraway lands like Persia and Muscat, to the Adilshahi ports. Darya Sarang sprang into action and mobilized ninety frigates, which sailed the high seas and spread terror not only amongst the overseas traders, but across the coastal lands. This pillage affected trade across the Adilshahi ports and further compromised Bijapur's tax collections.

Shivaji *Raje* now turned his attention to the Portuguese *firangis*. He marched to Bardesh, in the Portuguese dominions south of Kudal, and spread terror, forcing the Portuguese Viceroy at Goa to sue for peace. A treaty was finally concluded between the Portuguese and the Marathas.

MALVAN, END-1664

Shivaji *Raje* gazed at the sea as it stretched out to the bright line of the horizon. High tide was setting in, so was the sun. The waves slowly crept toward him as the slanting rays cast a golden light over the water. The sea seemed abuzz with a dormant energy, ready to explode into life as the tide reached its high point.

Across the water he spotted a large, dark shape. Curious, he turned to Maynak Bhandari, his Naval Captain. "What is that dark shape in the water, Maynak?"

"An island, Highness, about half a *kos* offshore. It is called Kurate Island by the locals." Maynak informed him.

"Interesting..." *Raje* was lost in thought. "Does the island have a fresh water supply?"

"Yes, it does."

Raje's eyes lit up. "Can you arrange for us to visit the island tomorrow?"

"Of course, My Lord."

The following morning, *Raje* stood on a small hillock on Kurate Island, that gave him a bird's eye view of the place and the sea around it. He had roamed the island for the greater part of the last *prahar*, and loved it. Turning to Maynak, he asked, "How would you like to build a fort on this island, Maynak, a fort to rival Janjira of the Siddis?"

Maynak smiled. "A brilliant idea, Highness! A strong sea fort here, close to the coast, would immensely strengthen our hold on the western sea."

"Ingenious, My Lord!" Tanhaji, who had been listening, added. "We could put the money from Surat to good use here."

Raje nodded. Tanhaji had voiced his own thought. "Maynak, arrange for priests right away. We will perform the *bhumipoojan* for our new fort tomorrow. Let us get this project started."

Mahabaleshwar, 6 January 1665

Shivaji *Raje* sat in a *shamiana* erected near the Mahabaleshwar temple. Despite being mid-day, it was chilly on the plateau. With him sat his mother, Jijabai, shrouded in a woollen shawl, and Shivaji *Raje*'s now retired administrator, Sono *Punt*. *Raje*'s Queens, Soyara, Putala and Sakvar, busied themselves with their maids, getting things ready for the ceremony.

"*Raje*," Sono *Punt* said, "what was the need to involve me in this ceremony? It is Her Highness, the Queen Mother's prerogative."

Shivaji *Raje* smiled affectionately at his ex-*Dabir*. He was fond of the old man. In the past decade and a half, Sono *Punt* had played a stellar role in his administration, besides being an advisor beyond compare. Age had forced him to retire, but *Raje* had placed Sono *Punt*'s equally able son, Tryambak *Punt* in his post. Tryambak *Punt* was now a part of *Raje*'s Council and core group.

"Sono *Punt*, your work has contributed in no small measure to the existence of our *Swarajya*. You have been a father to me. The honour belongs to you too."

Tryambak *Punt* entered the *shamiana* with the head priest. "Your Highness, we are ready. It is almost time," he said, smiling.

Shivaji *Raje* rose and helped Jijabai to her feet. He led her out of the *shamiana*, followed by the Queens, Tryambak *Punt* and Sono *Punt*. A large crowd had gathered outside the Mahabaleshwar temple. The locals had come to see their King and the ceremony, but mostly to collect alms and donations, as they had been told their King would give away plenty that day. Shivaji *Raje*'s ministers, administrators and military Captains were there for the ceremony. *Sirnaubat* Netoji Palkar stood smartly dressed in all his finery for the occasion.

The assembly bowed as the royals emerged from the *shamiana*. Within moments, the skies darkened, the wind died down and the air turned progressively colder. Everyone looked to the skies, to watch the sun as it slowly vanished from sight. A solar eclipse had been predicted by the royal astrologers, and, as per tradition, Shivaji *Raje* had ordered a special *tula* ceremony in which his mother would be weighed against gold, silver and grain, which would then be donated to the poor. A large weighing scale had been placed in front of the temple. *Raje* led Jijabai to the scale and helped her sit in one of its pans. His smiling *Peshwa*, Moro *Punt* moved forward and placed a bag of gold coins in the other pan. One by one, *Raje*'s ministers, his *Sirnaubat,* and then his Captains, moved forward and placed more gold coins in the pan, till its weight balanced that of the Queen Mother. The *tula* was repeated with silver, and then grain. Jijabai was then helped off the scale and *Raje* bent to touch her feet.

"*Aukshavanta wha...*" Jijabai's voice trembled with emotion as she placed her hand on her son's head. A *tula* ceremony was considered a mark of great wealth, generosity and righteousness in Hindu tradition. Jijabai felt infinitely proud of Shivba's achievements. For a brief moment she remembered the day her sixteen-year-old son had walked into her chamber and announced that he would take the oath of *Swarajya*. That day, her Shivba had barely a hundred boys with him, no army or wealth to speak of. Now, as she looked at the heaps of gold and silver being weighed against her and then donated, at the hundreds of office bearers and military Captains, and thousands of armed soldiers around her, Jijabai realized that her son had come a long way in fulfilling her and her late husband's dream of a free state.

Shivaji *Raje* ushered Sono *Punt* onto the scales. The weighing ceremony was repeated. It was a supreme recognition of Sono *Punt*'s contribution to the cause of their *Swarajya*.

MUGHAL MILITARY CAMP, NORTH BANK OF THE NARMADA RIVER

Jai Singh sat cross-legged on the floor in front of a *homagni* and made offerings of *ghee* into the ritual fire as the priest chanted *mantras* in Sanskrit. The Mughal General was clad in a silk *dhoti* with a sacred thread slung across his naked left shoulder and torso. A *tilak* painted with sandalwood paste adorned his forehead and pearl earrings adorned his ears. Having made the offerings, he folded his hands in reverence as the priest continued to chant.

Jai Singh had ordered an elaborate *havan* and *poojan* in preparation for his campaign against the Marathas. He wished to seek the blessings of the Almighty for a victory.

Half a *prahar* later, the ritual was over, and Jai Singh had retired to his *shamiana,* while the priests continued to distribute *prasad* to the assembled Hindu gentry.

A storm raged in Jai Singh's mind. Normally, he was calm before a campaign, but this time he felt unusually disturbed. He wondered why. Was it because his adversary was the wily Maratha, Seeva, who had thus far defeated, killed or disgraced every Adilshahi or Mughal General sent against him? Was he worried about faltering against Seeva? Or was it because of Diler Khan's presence in his camp? The powerful Pathan made him feel uncomfortable. It was common knowledge that he was amongst the Emperor's most trusted men. Without doubt, Aurangzeb had sent Diler on this campaign to keep an eye on him.

Jai Singh knew he would have to tackle the hot-headed Pathan with caution. Diler, probably here on direct orders of the Emperor, would be an unwilling subordinate. To force Diler to obey his commands, Jai Singh would need the Emperor's written order, granting him absolute and final authority on all decisions military and administrative, including those of payments to the troops, punishment for defectors, and grants of land in the Deccan. Jai Singh summoned his scribe and dictated a letter to the Emperor.

"Dispatch this immediately. It must reach the capital as soon as possible," Jai Singh commanded the scribe, who bowed and left.

Rajgad, late January, 1665

The Maratha King's Council was in session at the Rajgad palace. Bahirji Naik had arrived with news of the latest movements of the Mughal armies.

"Jai Singh has crossed the Narmada and is well on his way to Aurangabad," Bahirji said. "His army is huge, and is expected to swell further with the addition of the levies at Aurangabad."

Shivaji *Raje* pondered in silence. Another Mughal campaign! The northern front had been quiet these past two years, ever since the attack on Shaista Khan. But it was insufficient time for the land and his people to have recovered from the earlier Mughal depreditions.

"How big?" Moro *Punt*, the *Peshwa* asked.

"Over a lakh; amongst them are seventy thousand troopers. He has plenty of artillery; some really big guns."

Moro *Punt* seemed disturbed by the news. Jai Singh's reputation and capability was well known to all. "Highness, this is likely to be tough for us," he said quietly.

"Let them come!" Netoji snarled. "We sent back Shaista Khan, did we not? We will send Jai Singh back as well, to Rajputana!"

"Jai Singh is no Shaista Khan, *Sirnaubat*," *Raje* cautioned. "He is a proven military General, a clever politician, and an astute diplomat. Moro *Punt* is right… this will be tough."

"Our men in the field expect him to reach Aurangabad in two weeks," Bahirji added.

"His march seems quite fast for a Mughal army," *Raje* quipped.

"He has not wasted a day, Highness," Bahirji said, nodding. "Jai Singh is on the job. There is no Mughal lethargy about his camp."

"Well, he will arrive at the boundary of our *Swarajya* some day," *Raje* said, looking at his men. "Meanwhile, we need not sit back and relax. After Khawas Khan's defeat, the Adilshah has been quiet. Let us give him a jolt by launching a new campaign in his coastal towns."

"A good idea," Netoji said approvingly. "Give us the order to march, Sire. Let us fill our coffers before the Mughals get here."

Raje nodded. "Exactly my thought, *Sirnaubat*. But this time we shall not march."

The men looked at him questioningly.

"We shall sail!" *Raje* said with a grin. "Our Navy looks quite robust now. It is time to put it to test by launching our first naval campaign."

"A naval campaign! Darya Sarang and Maynak Bhandari will be overjoyed when they hear this," Netoji said.

Raje turned to his Chief of Intelligence. "Bahirji, send word to Darya Sarang, ordering him to keep at least three large ships and plenty of small frigates, ready at the Malvan jetty. We will sail from Malvan in a fortnight, with six thousand men."

"Yes, Sire. But where will we head to?"

"Basrur. We will sail from Malvan and raid that rich trading town. From there, we will sail north to Gokarna, and then to Ankola."

"Consider it done, My Lord!" said Bahirji.

WESTERN SEA, OFF THE MALVAN COAST, 8 FEBRUARY 1665

The Maratha Navy sailed south from Malvan in great strength. Darya Sarang had readied three large ships and eighty-five frigates near the jetty, fully loaded with provisions and ammunition. Six thousand Maratha troops boarded the vessels. Shivaji *Raje* sailed in the lead ship with Darya Sarang and Maynak Bhandari, his chief naval officers.

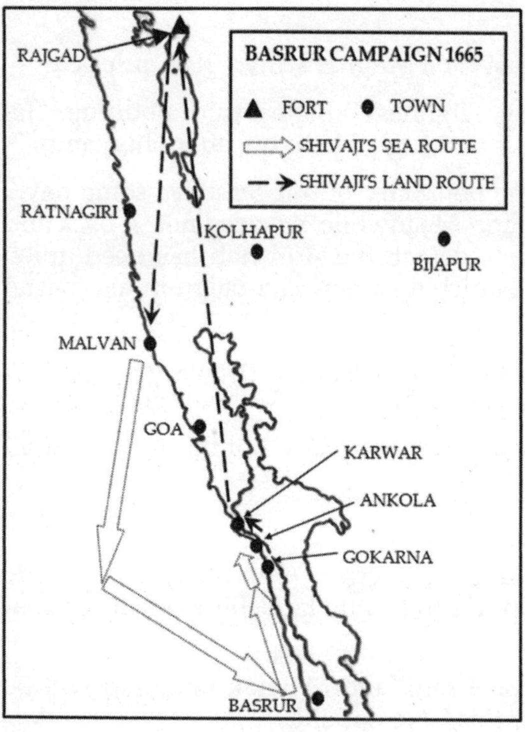

The sun disappeared beyond the horizon and the vast expanse of sea was enveloped in near darkness; some light being afforded by the moon. *Raje* stood on the front deck, his hands resting on the ship's bow. The cool night breeze made him shiver as the ship silently cut through the calm waters. He felt immensely proud of his Navy. No indigenious ruler had ever concieved the idea of building ships and harbouring a special force on the seas. His naval force already excercised control over the western sea and the coastal lands, checking the movement of the British, Dutch, Portuguese and Abyssinian traders. *Raje* had been particularly concerned about the unchecked growth of the Siddis of Janjira. These Abyssinian warlords behaved like independant Kings, and committed untold atrocities on the people. They were famous for their slave trade, for which they regularly abducted men, women and children from the coastal towns and villages. *Raje* had been unable to check their activities. But now, with his naval force taking shape, he hoped to put an end to the Abyssinian menace on the western coast.

Shivaji *Raje* tried to focus his thoughts on the raids ahead of him. His spies had reliably informed him that Basrur was poorly garrisoned by the Adilshah and so, should not offer much resistance to the raid. *Raje* was acutely aware that his practice of campaigning in the Adilshahi and Mughal territories to collect levied contributions was a temporary measure at best. In the future, he would have to develop trade and businesses in his own *Swarajya*, to increase its indigenious income. But for that to happen, his kingdom had to have peace for extended periods, which was presently impossible with both the Adilshah and the Mughal organizing repeated campaigns against him. Each campaign meant depredition, loss of crops and business, and people. To protect his boundaries he needed more troops, who had to be paid, more ammunition, and above all, good artillery. He had to repair and garrison strong forts and place big guns on their ramparts. His monetary requirements were endless, and with his own tax collections being insufficient, there was no option but to campaign in enemy territory.

"Looks like it will be a long night, Darya Sarang," *Raje* said.

"The sea is quite calm tonight, My Lord. Our journey should be uneventful."

Raje nodded and smiled. Placing a hand on Darya Sarang's shoulder, he said, "You have done a great job, Navy Chief! I am proud of you and your men."

The dimunitive looking man smiled broadly at this praise from his King. "I but do my duty, Highness. We should reach Basrur early in the morning."

Shivaji *Raje* retired to his cabin. Darya Sarang stayed back on deck to give some final instructions to his men.

Basrur Port, early morning of 9 February 1665

The Maratha warships docked at Basrur Port midway through the first *prahar* and thousands of Maratha infantrymen leapt onto shores. Led by their King, they marched into the town and began sacking it systematically. As in Surat, Bahirji Naik and his men had crucial information about the town's prominent traders ready. This, coupled with the fact that the meagre Bijapuri garrison of the town fled at first hint of Shivaji *Raje*'s arrival, ensured the raid was peaceful and thorough.

By evening, a large stash of cash, gold, silver and valuables had been collected on the ships. *Raje* inspected the booty and smiled, satisfied. He would now have money to fund his upcoming campaign against the Mughals. His reasoning was straight forward. The Adilshah and the Mughal compelled him to maintain a large military force to protect his kingdom. They would have to pay for that through such levied contributions from their trading towns.

The next morning, the Maratha fleet sailed north and headed for the coastal town of Gokarna. *Raje* made a brief halt there, with the sole intention of visiting the famous shrine of Lord Mahadev. He performed an elaborate *pooja* and *abhishek* to the Lord. After spending a couple of quiet days near the shrine, he gave the order to sail.

The Maratha fleet now sailed further north to Ankola, where *Raje* disembarked and, having sent the fleet away, rode north towards Karwar, with four thousand soldiers. His naval expedition had come to an end, but the campaign continued further north, on land. By the next day, the Marathas had reached Karwar, though the news of their impending arrival had reached the town, especially the English factors, earlier. Having heard of the Surat raid, these factors were wary of the Marathas and decided to load all their goods onto a ship, ready to sail at the first hint of danger.

The Governor of Karwar was a prominent Adilshahi noble, Bahlul Khan. He was, however, away from Karwar at the time, with most of his garrison. His subordinate officer, Sher Khan, had just arrived in Karwar with a small retinue. Learning of Shivaji *Raje*'s arrival, he realised that he had insufficient men to take on the Marathas, and sued for peace.

A ransom amount was fixed between the prominent traders and *Raje*'s emmisaries. This was paid in full. Even the English factors pitched in with a contribution. *Raje* then ordered his men to strike camp and head northeast to Rajgad. He had hoped to sack the English factory, but his plans had been thwarted by the mediation of Sher Khan.

As he looked back at the town from his mount, *Raje* quipped, "Sher Khan has spoilt my fun. The English factors should be grateful to him."

MUGHAL MILITARY CAMP, PUNE, MARCH 1665

Jai Singh sat in conference in his command tent, with his chief Captains, chalking out the campaign against Shivaji *Raje*. Before them was spread a large map of the Deccan. Holding a long wooden pointer, Jai Singh stared at the map, pondering.

"We will have to establish military stations to secure our position and limit the Maratha moves," he said to his men. Placing his pointer north of their Pune camp, he said to one of his Captains, "Qutb-ud-din Khan, you will march north to Junnar, with seven thousand men. Set up posts at the foothills of Fort Lohgad, and at Nardurg. Create mobile units to patrol that entire region and prevent the Marathas from creating any trouble. We must guard our north to keep our supply lines open. If Seevaji's troops ouflank us, they could cut off our supplies."

Qutb-ud-din Khan nodded, confident he could do the job for his General.

Jai Singh now addressed another young Captain. "Ihtisham Khan, you will stay back in Pune with four thousand men. Set up a post between Pune and Lohgad. Be on guard!"

"Yes, *Mirzaji*!"

"I will move south toward Purandar, with the rest of our army." Jai Singh said, placing the pointer on the map. Casting a glance at the beefy Pathan who sat quietly across the table, he added. "Diler Khan will go with me."

"All that is fine, *Mirza*," Diler Khan remarked, stroking his beard as he addressed the General without the customary honorific, "but what is your actual plan to deal with Seeva?"

Jai Singh stared back at his interlocutor, intending everyone present to know who was in charge. "We will set up our main camp near Purandar," he said. "That will serve to keep Bijapur in check, lest they decide to join hands with Seevaji. From that position, Seevaji's capital fort, Rajgad, is due west, and Seevaji's movements will be hampered by our presence. We will create mobile units and send them throughout Seevaji's dominions to raze villages to the ground and take his people captive."

Diler smirked. "What will that achieve? Seeva remains safe in his fort. By killing his people and destroying villages, we cannot win. Shaista Khan tried the same thing and failed miserably."

"He did, but his planning was not up to the mark. I am convinced our strategy will work."

"Seeva's strength is in his hill forts, *Mirza*. We must capture his forts," Diler said forcefully.

"Seevaji's strength is in his people, Diler Khan! Make no mistake about that. We must break his people first. Shaista Khan needed over two months to take Fort Chakan, which is on the plains. Capturing Seevaji's hill forts could take years. We can get faster results by destroying Seevaji's lands and people. Once we do that, his revenue will stop. He will have to come out of his fort. Besides, the misery of his people will force him to surrender."

Diler was not convinced of Jai Singh's strategy. He waved his hand dismissively at the Rajput General. Jai Singh realized this was the first hint of dissension within the camp. In exasperation, he asked, "What do you suggest, Diler Khan?"

"We should attack Fort Purandar and capture it! Once we have taken Purandar, we will turn west towards Rajgad."

"Capturing Purandar is easier said than done, Diler Khan. It will be an unnecessary waste of time and men."

"Let me take Purandar, *Mirza*. I will show you how to take Seeva's forts." Diler said, openly challenging Jai Singh's authority.

Jai Singh gritted his teeth and swallowed the rebuke. He did not want an open confrontation at the very commencement of the campaign. After a thoughtful pause, he replied, "So be it, Diler Khan. You may proceed to Purandar with your Pathani contingent.

I will follow shortly. We will put my plan into action along with yours. We will use both strategies at once."

The meeting broke up much later, after the plans had been finalised.

6
DEFEAT AND HUMILIATION

Rajgad, March 1665

News of the Mughal campaign began pouring in from all quarters. Shivaji *Raje*'s spies brought him fresh information daily, making him increasingly despondent. Mobile units of Mughal horsemen were ravaging the Mavals, forcing the people to flee. Villages were being razed and crops burned. The countryside, which had just begun to settle down after the earlier Mughal depredations, was being destroyed again.

"Diler Khan is moving toward Purandar at great speed, Your Highness," Bahirji Naik told him. "Jai Singh has, however, delayed his departure from Pune."

"Jai Singh is guarding against any possible movement of our troops into Mughal territory, while Diler Khan wedges himself between us and Bijapur." Shivaji *Raje* said, quickly analysing Jai Singh's strategy.

"He has sent Syed Abdul Aziz Khan to Shirwal, with three thousand cavalry. Chandrarao More's son, Baji, is with him," Bahirji continued.

"Jai Singh's planning is immaculate. I salute him! He has isolated Rajgad from the rest of our fief to cramp our movements." *Raje* sank deep into thought.

"Jai Singh has ganged up with all our enemies, Sire. He has invited Fazal Khan to the Mughal camp to avenge his father's death. The Mores are already with him. He has also begun corrupting the local *Deshmukhs* and *Desais*."

Raje laughed ironically. "Jai Singh seems more eager to avenge Afzal Khan's death than does Khan's son."

"What should be our course of action, Highness?" Moro *Punt*, who had been quiet thus far, asked.

Raje looked at him, unable to find an answer. "This will be a hard campaign for us, *Punt*. Netoji is already in the field. He will no doubt try to counter the Mughal moves, but I doubt if that will have any effect. The Mughals simply have too much reserve. If they attack Purandar, which I think they will, Murarbaji *Deshpande* and his garrison in the fort will have their hands full."

"Purandar is a strong fort, Highness," Moro *Punt* opined. "We can be reasonably assured that Murarbaji will defend it successfully."

"I do not doubt Murarbaji's capability. But Diler Khan is an equally brave and obstinate soldier from all I have heard. Besides, we may not be able to send any help to the fort."

"Any moves from the Adilshah, Highness?"

"Ali Adilshah has sent a secret communication expressing his willingness to help us, albiet discreetly. Obviously, he cannot openly side with us."

"He is merely trying to use us as a bulwark against the Mughals," Moro *Punt* said, trying to decipher the Adilshah's moves.

"Yes, he is. The Adilshah harbours no goodwill towards us. In fact, he hates us. But, at the moment, he feels helping us may protect Bijapur from a direct invasion by the Mughals. I am sure he has simultaneously sent another envoy to Jai Singh!"

"The Mughals will invade Bijapur some day," Moro *Punt* said.

"Yes, they will. But at the moment they have focussed their offensive against us." *Raje* made up his mind to do the best under the circumstances. "Bahirji," he said to his chief spy, "send word to all forts in the Sahyadris to be war ready. Send word to Murarbaji, that he is to defend Purandar to the end, or till he receives further instructions from me. Moro *Punt*, see that our forts get all the provisions they need."

Bahirji and Moro *Punt* nodded. This Mughal campaign would test not only Shivaji *Raje's* capability but the resilience of the Marathi populace.

Environs of Fort Purandar, Southeast of Pune, end-March 1665

The Mughal army had moved south from Pune to the hills near Saswad, and camped there. From here, the path went through a mountain pass. Jai Singh was wary of exposing his main army in the mountain passes. His knowledge of Shaista Khan's campaign and Kartalab Khan's defeat in Umbarkhind, had made him cautious. He sent a vanguard of Pathans under Diler Khan to cross the pass and camp on the other side. Once he received news that Diler Khan had crossed safely, he decided to move the main body of his army. Again, as a precaution, he left a rearguard under Daud Khan's command, at the mouth of the pass.

While Jai Singh prepared to move his army, Diler Khan scouted for a good location to set up camp. In doing so, he strayed near the fort. The Maratha outposts were alert and they opened fire on the Mughals with rockets and muskets. Diler Khan was surprised at this sudden move by the Maratha defenders, but quickly organized a counter attack. The Mughals succeeded in driving the Marathas towards the fort, but stayed put at a safe distance.

On hearing of the attack on Diler Khan's contingent, Jai Singh hurriedly dispatched a reinforcement of three thousand Rajputs under the command of his son, Kirat Singh, with several other Captains. Meanwhile, Diler Khan ordered entrenchments and began systematically beseiging the fort, without waiting for Jai Singh to arrive.

Fort Purandar, at the same time

A tall, muscular man strode confidently toward the northern rampart of Purandar with several Captains in tow. He was dressed simply in a white *angarkha* and *dhoti*, with a red *dushela* tied around his waist. His left hand rested firmly on the hilt of his sword. On his head, he wore a red turban, held in place by a cloth tied below his chin. He sported a thin curved moustache on a clean shaven face. Murarbaji *Deshpande*, Commander of Fort Purandar, grimly surveyed the approaching Mughal troops from his vantage point.

"The Pathans appeared suddenly on the slopes. I gave the order to open fire," Murarbaji's young Captain, who had been involved in the earlier skirmish with Diler Khan's contingent, related.

"You did well," Murarbaji said. "Let the Mughals get a taste of the Maratha sword! If they think they can take Purandar easily, they have a surprise in store."

The Captain pointed to the Mughal entrenchments to the east. "Looks like they are wedging themselves between Purandar and Vajragad."

"They will try to take Vajragad first," Murarbaji said, narrowing his eyes. "Send reinforcements and ammunition to the lower fort right away."

"Yes Sir!" The Captain disappeared to carry out his orders.

The sudden arrival of the Mughals had created quite a buzz at Purandar. Every Captain and soldier was immediately on alert. Purandar was one of the strongest forts in the Sahyadris and among the most difficult mountains to scale. Purandar's upper fort or *bala-i-qilla* rose high above sea level. A long, narrow hillock called Kandakada, extended eastwards from the upper fort. On the northern face of the mountain, some distance from the peak, was a ledge, fortified by ramparts and bastions. This was the lower fort or *machi*. To the east of the upper fort was a narrow ravine called Bhairav Khind, beyond which the hills rose once again, peaking in another fort. This was the Vajragad, Purandar's twin fort. Vajragad commanded Purandar's *machi*. If Vajragad fell to the enemy, Purandar's lower fort would become untenable.

Murarbaji fixed his cold gaze on the enemy trenches. Nearly a decade ago, he had joined Shivaji *Raje*'s *Swarajya*, and had never regretted his decision. Years ago, he had been made Commander of the fort, a responsibility he had accepted and fulfilled wholeheartedly. He had watched Shivaji *Raje*'s rise to fame and power with awe, and had developed a fierce devotion towards his King and Liege.

He knew the Mughals had opened a new campaign against them under the Generalship of the Rajput, Jai Singh. Shivaji *Raje* had sent him a directive to defend the fort for as long as possible. He had also sent provisions. Murarbaji had a garrison of nearly two thousand men, and grain and ammunition supplies sufficient to defend the fort for months. He now resolved to defend his fort to the death.

Diler Khan had completed his deployment and besieged the fort. The main Mughal camp was spread a short distance from the north face of the mountain, near Narayanpur village. Diler Khan himself was camped here with his Pathani regiment and several Captains. Chief amongst them were Turktaj Khan, Atish Khan, Sayyed Maqbool Alam, and Diler's nephews, Gairat and Muzaffar. To the south of the fort were camped Rasool Baig Rozbhani, Muhammad Salih, Ram Singh, Sher Singh Rathod, Rai Singh Rathod and others. Daud Khan, who had been moved forward from the rearguard, was entrenched in front of the southern or Kedar gate of the fort. Mitrasen and Chaturbhuj Chauhan were camped to the north of Vajragad, while Indraman Bundela had camped to the south.

Kirat Singh and some of the other officers now began erecting wooden platforms or *damdamas,* in front of the north gate of the lower fort, in order to mount their guns and fire at the *machi*.

Shortly thereafter, Jai Singh moved in with his Rajput regiments and pitched their tents near Diler Khan's camp, to the north of Purandar. With him, were his Captains Nar Singh Kunwar, Karan Rathod, Jagat Singh and others. The artillery was moved to this camp. Jai Singh immediately inspected the trenches and camp positions around the fort, and studied the topography. The same evening he convened a war council in his command tent.

"We have to make Vajragad our first target," Jai Singh voiced his opinion to the assembly of Captains. "Purandar itself is too difficult to storm. Vajragad, on the other hand, may fall to us more easily. Once we have that fort, we can bombard Purandar's lower fort from Vajragad."

The men nodded. The General's plan was sensible. Diler Khan was quiet, thinking hard. He had received a jolt the previous day when the Maratha outposts had opened fire. He realized he had been caught unawares, and that had, in part, prompted him to complete the siege preparations before Jai Singh's arrival.

"Diler Khan," Jai Singh's words broke into Diler's brooding. "I think we should move our big guns to the top of the hill opposite Vajragad and begin firing on that fort."

Diler mused for a while before nodding. "I agree, *Mirza*. I will get my men on it immediately."

Jai Singh let out a silent sigh of relief. Having Diler agree to his ideas was like traversing a field of nettles. "We have received intelligence that Netoji Palkar has moved toward Fort Paranda. A detachment of our forces will go after him. Sharza Khan, Jagat Singh and Hasan Khan will be the Captains in-charge."

The three Captains left to begin their preparations.

"Kirat Singh," Jai Singh said, addressing his son, "how are the *damdamas* progressing?"

"We should have the guns mounted on the platforms in two days at the most."

"Good. We can then begin to bombard Vajragad and the lower fort of Purandar at the same time."

After three days of immense toil, Diler Khan's men managed to drag the massive gun named *Abdullah Khan* to the top of a hill opposite Vajragad. The effort had been so exhausting that many of Diler's men gave up, saying it was an impossible task. But Diler was nothing if not obdurate, and finally the job was accomplished. The cannon was docked and ammunition moved up. The gunners began bombarding Vajragad's northern rampart.

But there was no respite for Diler's men. He had immediately ordered moving the second gun, named *Fath Lashkar*, up the same hill. His Captains cursed him, but got on with the job.

Meanwhile, Kirat Singh had completed erecting the *damdama* in front of Purandar's *machi*. Some medium-sized guns were moved up to the platform and began firing in earnest. Murarbaji's garrison on the lower fort tried to destroy the *damdama* by firing rockets, but could achieve little. The firing by the Mughals made life difficult for them.

Three days later, Diler Khan's men had succeeded in moving *Fath Lashkar* to the top of the hill and, in two more days, a third gun named *Haveli,* was dragged up. Incessant bombardent of Vajragad continued for nearly a fortnight. Finally, the Mughals succeeded in demolishing one of the bastions of the fort. Diler Khan ordered his Pathans to scale the mountain and take control of the demolished bastion. This, they did with great losses. The slope was steep and narrow, only two men could move up, abreast. Yet Diler persisted, and finally the Mughals set foot in the fort and planted the Mughal banner.

The next day, the Pathans pushed into the inner fort. As more enemy soldiers poured into the fort, the few hundred Marathas in Vajragad lost heart and surrendered.

Rajgad, mid April 1665

"Vajragad has fallen to the Mughals, Your Highness," Bahirji said dejectedly. "Our garrison fought valiantly, but their losses proved too great to continue the resistance."

Shivaji *Raje* momentarily closed his eyes, feeling despondent. He knew that once the Mughals had captured Vajragad, Purandar itself would become vulnerable.

"How many men did we lose?" he asked Bahirji.

"Over half the garrison, Sire."

Moro *Punt* wished he could offer some advice to help the situation, but their minds seem to have become collectively numbed by the Mughal onslaught.

"Do we continue to resist on Purandar, Highness?" *Punt* finally asked quietly.

"Yes we do, for now." *Raje* placed his right elbow on his knee and rested his chin on his hand, deep in thought.

"Our requests for help from Bijapur have been turned down," Moro *Punt* said.

"Yes, but that was due to the influence of the Pathani faction under Bahlol Khan. It is no secret the Pathans support the Mughals. The Deccani faction is sympathetic towards us, but short of full military support from Bijapur, nothing is likely to help us in our current situation. And the Adilshah does not seem willing to give us such support against the Mughals. What that fool fails to realize is that the Mughals will surely turn on Bijapur once they are done with us."

"The Portuguese have helped us, albiet under cover," *Punt* said.

Raje nodded. "But their help is limited to ammunition and artillery. Right now, we need men!"

"What instructions should I send to our men, Highness?" Bahirji, who had been quiet, asked.

Raje looked at him and sighed. "Send word to Murarbaji to continue the defence of Purandar, and to Netoji to continue his raids and try to cut the Mughal supply lines. Perhaps it would be to our advantage if the Mughals stayed at Purandar for a while."

"The monsoon?" Moro *Punt* had read *Raje*'s mind.

"Yes *Punt*, the monsoon. Right now, most of their army is stationed around Purandar. Once the rains start, the siege may slacken."

"Our Purandar garrison will struggle with supplies," Bahirji said.

"Then we shall have to help them."

Murarbaji *Deshpande* walked back to his fort headquarters after inspecting the guard on the ramparts of Purandar fort. Two young Captains followed him.

"The fall of Vajragad could hurt us," one of the Captains said.

Murarbaji stopped in his tracks and turned around, locking blazing eyes on the young man's face. The man stammered in defence. "I mean...the *machi* is in danger of falling, Sir!"

"Purandar will not fall as long as I live!" Murarbaji barked. "Have no doubt about that!"

The Captain swallowed and lowered his eyes. The Commander's bravery and anger were equally legendary.

Inside the fort, Murarbaji stood before a large map of Purandar and its environs, deep in thought. "They are bombarding us from the north and south. Soon, they will begin pounding us from Vajragad as well." Murarbaji pointed at the map as he spoke.

The Captains remained quiet. Their relative inexperience was obvious. They had little advice to offer their Commander.

"I doubt if their cannons on Vajragad will be able to reach Purandar's ramparts," Murarbaji mused, stroking his chin. "We must deal with the guns on the north and south sides. Organize a raiding party of forty of our best men. I will lead them myself. We will leave the fort in the dead of night and attempt to disable their cannons by hammering nails into the touch holes." After a brief pause, he added, "We will lead another sortie on the south side tomorrow."

Mughal military camp north of Purandar, a few days later

Jai Singh paced the limited confines of his command tent, his hands clasped behind his back. A senior Captain stood to one side. He was Daud Khan Qureshi, who had been camped to the south of Purandar for the last few weeks. The events in the southern military camp in the past few days had forced Jai Singh to summon Daud Khan to the main camp. The Mughal General was worried. Since they had taken Vajragad over two weeks ago, things had slackened. A large number of their troops had become disheartened just when they needed to intensify the battle to take Purandar. Diler Khan was hell bent on storming the fort, but an increasing number of his Captains seemed to disagree with him.

Meanwhile, the obstinate Commander of Purandar continued his stoic resistance. The Marathas had carried out several sorties on the entrenched Mughal troops at night. A few days ago, they had managed to disable some of the guns that had been so laboriously hauled up the mountains. But the real cause for the present tension in the camp was something that had happened the previous night.

The towering figure of Diler Khan, the Pathani Commander, now barged into Jai Singh's tent, obviously angry at the way things had turned out on the southern side of the siege. Completely disregarding Jai Singh's presence, he walked straight up to Daud Khan and fixed him with a scorching gaze. "Is this how you go about your military duties, Daud Khan?" Diler kept his voice low, but the tone was menacing enough to freeze a man's blood. "What have your men been doing on the southern side?"

Daud Khan returned the Commander's stare coldly. "We have been doing our job, Diler Khan."

"Is that so? How then did those Maratha rascals succeed in spiking your guns a few days ago? What do your men do on night watch? Sleep?"

"Mind your words, Diler Khan!" Daud Khan warned, becoming increasingly agitated. "My men have been working very hard for many weeks now."

"Last night, the Marathas smuggled three hundred sacks of grain and provisions into the fort from the south side. How the hell did they manage to do that?"

Daud Khan fell silent and looked away. However much he resented being questioned by Diler Khan, he simply had no answer to that. In a series of events, the garrison in Fort Purandar, had conducted night raids, spiked some guns and, quite incredibly, the previous night, managed to sneak provisions into the fort.

"How did they manage that, I ask you?" Diler repeated. "I cannot imagine how they could have done it without your knowledge!"

"Diler Khan!" Daud Khan's voice rose. He could not stand silent while Diler Khan cast doubts on his integrity. "I have not committed any treachery, so mind what you say!"

"*I* should mind what *I* say?" Diler mocked. "While the rest of the Mughal army toils day and night to capture Purandar, you and your men commit costly errors that bring our efforts to nought."

"This entire campaign has gone in the wrong direction Diler Khan! We should never have besieged Purandar. Do you think it is easy to storm that fort? We have wasted time, money and men. Look around your own camp and see how many men agree with your battle plans. What a waste of imperial money, supplies, ammunition and lives!"

"I suppose you know better how to conduct this campaign against the Marathas?" Diler continued his tirade.

"Diler Khan, calm down..." Jai Singh, who had thus far been quiet, intervened between the two.

"Do not ask me to calm down, *Mirza*. Pull this man up for his glaring mistakes which have jeopardized us all!"

"We must deal with this situation with calm heads. Sit down Diler." Jai Singh gently pulled him away from Daud Khan. The last thing he needed was dissention in his own camp. If fights broke out between his Captains and Commanders, the entire campaign would suffer.

Reluctantly, both Diler and Daud sat down, facing each other. Jai Singh sat on a couch between the two. "Look, we cannot fight amongst ourselves. This campaign has been hard on everyone. I agree Purandar is a difficult fort to capture, but we are too far into this battle to give up now."

"Diler Khan will never capture Purandar!" Daud Khan said bluntly. "*Mirzaji*, your strategy of devastating Seeva's lands and people was the right way to go about it."

Diler glared at Daud, but said nothing. Despite capturing Vajragad, his efforts to storm Purandar had failed thus far. He was at a loss for new ideas; only his obstinacy prevented him from giving up.

"You doubt my ability to take Purandar?" Diler asked, supressing his rage. He lifted his turban and held it out in front of him. "I vow I shall not place this turban on my head till I have captured Purandar!" Rising abruptly, he stormed out of the tent.

Jai Singh gritted his teeth at this open disregard of his authority as the Imperial General. Being the King of a Rajput state, Jai Singh was unused to such blatant disrespect. Suppressing his anger, he turned to Daud Khan.

"Daud Khan, I appoint you to a new charge. Ride out into Seeva's territory and devastate his lands. Burn down villages and crops. Kill his people. Bring away as many animals as you can. You can take seven thousand cavalry with you. I will appoint Sharza Khan, Raja Rai Singh, Amar Singh Chandrawat, Mohammed Salih and some others, as your subordinate officers."

Daud Khan's face showed his approval. "Your orders will be carried out, *Mirzaji*," he assured the General.

Jai Singh nodded. "Good. Hand over charge of the southern camp to Shubhkarn Bundela and Purdil Khan. Send riders to summon Qutb-ud-din Khan from Junnar, and Lodi Khan from the Konkan. They can devastate the Mavals."

Daud Khan nodded and took his leave. For a long time after he had left, Jai Singh sat alone in his tent and contemplated the campaign. He was increasingly worried by Diler's aggression and insubordination. His men were getting demoralized, there was dissention in his camp, yet he was nowhere close to laying hands on Seeva. He also knew the real danger lay with the Adilshah. If Bijapur decided to join hands with Seeva, and both armies marched on him, the Mughals would be sitting ducks here. Seeva would no doubt have realized this as well and tried to affect a coalition with Bijapur. Jai Singh knew he had to somehow bring the campaign to a swift and decisive conclusion.

RAJGAD, EARLY MAY 1665

The mood was tense as Shivaji *Raje* sat in conference with his ministers and his mother, Jijabai. Bahirji had arrived with the latest news from the Mughal front.

"Daud Khan has devastated our lands in the environs of Purandar, Your Highness," he apprised them. "He has seven thousand cavalry with him. He then moved west toward Rohida and Raigad. A few days ago, they torched fifty villages in a day."

Jijabai looked up sharply at Bahirji.

"They looted four townships and took innumerable prisoners. Countless girls and young women have gone missing."

Shivaji *Raje* looked away, clenching his fists in frustration.

"Qutb-ud-din Khan did the same in Paud Khore. He later joined forces with Daud, and the two moved to Lohgad. Our garrison sallied out of the fort and attacked them, but their numbers were pitifully insufficient to shake the Mughals. They had to flee back. The Khans camped near Lohgad and continued depredations, burning crops, killing and imprisoning people, and taking away animals. They have carried the devastation to the environs of Visapur, Tung and Tikona forts..."

"Enough, Bahirji!" Jijabai said, raising her voice. "I cannot hear any more..." Her eyes were moist and her voice trembled with anguish and fury. "How did we become so helpless?" she asked her son.

"The Mughals are simply too powerful, mother. Besides, Jai Singh is an astute General. He has cleverly used his numbers to cramp us and devastate the *Swarajya* at the same time."

"What have we done thus far?" Jijabai asked him tersely.

"Mother, we are doing all we can with the troops at our disposal. We succeeded in driving Daud Khan away from the environs of Rajgad. I had hoped to hold on till the onset of the monsoon, but that seems difficult now."

"What options do we have?"

"To sue for peace," *Raje* said, looking at her. The pain in his eyes was like a knife in her heart. She knew her son was torn between battling the Mughals and saving his people.

"Highness, from what I have heard, I do not think Jai Singh would be interested in any peace proposal," Bahirji said.

Raje sighed. "Moro *Punt,*" he turned to his *Peshwa*. "Open the Rajgad granaries to our people in the Mavals. Help them in any way we can."

Moro *Punt* nodded. Jijabai rose and walked out of the chamber, heading for the *devghar.* It was time for her evening prayers. She would ask the Goddess why she continued to test her son and her people.

A long line of peasants presented themselves at Rajgad fort to collect the grains they had been promised by the King himself. The hardened Mavales waited patiently for their turn as the Rajgad officials went about the task of distribution.

Shivaji *Raje* emerged from the palace and the people bowed to him. He was simply dressed in a dhoti and kurta, with a shawl draped over his shoulders. The regal dress, the pearl and ruby adorned turban, were missing. He wasn't there to impose his authority but to ask forgiveness from his people. He stood with folded hands as his men handed over grain to the peasants. They bowed to him and some touched his feet. An old man, bent over a walking staff, collected his share of the grain in a cloth and looked at *Raje* through teary eyes. *Raje* could sense the unvoiced complaint in the man's expression. Before he could say anything, the man began sobbing and fell at his feet.

Raje quickly bent and raised the old man by his shoulders. "Do not cry *baba,* better days shall return."

"The Mughals have taken everything from me, Your Highness. They killed my only son and kidnapped my daughter-in-law right before my eyes," the man sobbed. "My wife died of grief soon after. Our villages and crops lie in ashes. We have nothing left in this world now."

Raje's eyes filled with tears as he listened to the horrors of Mughal depredition. "Forgive me *baba,* for letting things come to this. I have failed my people."

"Do not ask for our forgiveness, my King," the man said, looking up. "You must fight them! Fight the *yavans* and destroy them, for you are destined to do it. You are the only one who stands between us and them. Do not worry about us. Your people shall not break. We will stand behind you till the end."

Shivaji *Raje* stood with folded hands, tears in his eyes as attendants lead the old man away.

"Fight them, my King! Do not give up!" The old man's final words kept ringing in *Raje*'s ears long after he was gone.

Fort Purandar, about the same time

Having secured Vajragad, the Mughals realized their gunfire from that fort would not reach Purandar's rampart. They now began moving into Bhairav Khind, the ravine between the two forts. After much exertion, they positioned their cannons on the hill in Bhairav Khind, thus reducing the distance to Purandar. Kirat Singh and Diler Khan personally supervised the erection of *damdamas* targeting the *Safed Buruj*, the lower of the two main bastions. In a few days, cannons were mounted on these and firing began in earnest. The *Safed Buruj* and the ramparts on either side, now within reach of the gunfire, suffered serious damage.

The Maratha garrison in the lower fort fought back with vengeance. They mounted their own guns on the ramparts and did their best to target the *damdamas*. There were casualties on both sides.

Frustrated by his inability to take the lower fort, Diler Khan ordered his men to dig an underground trench from their camp to the ramparts, with the aim of blowing them up. But his efforts were in vain, for several days later, as the trench advanced close to the rampart, the Marathas got wind of the plan. The defenders dug their own trench from behind the rampart and advanced to meet the Mughal trench. They then poured water into the trench, thus soaking the gunpowder planted by the Mughals. When Diler's men tried to torch the mine, it simply wouldn't blow.

Murarbaji and his garrison had defended Purandar bravely and frustrated Diler Khan. But in his heart, the Maratha Commander knew he could not hold the lower fort for much longer.

The fatal night arrived. To defend the *Kala Buruj,* situated at a higher level, the garrison mined the area between it and *Safed Buruj,* which was lower. In the heat of battle, the mines were set off by accident and a large amount of gunpowder was ignited. Eighty Marathas from the garrison were blown to smithereens. A gaping hole resulted in the rampart, making the *Safed Buruj* untenable. Diler Khan was delighted by the Maratha mishap and immediately ordered his Pathans to scale the slope and occupy the bastion. This they did with minimal loss and planted the Mughal banner on the *Safed Buruj*.

The Mughals stayed put in the lower bastion through the night. The next morning, they mounted their guns and began firing at the *Kala Buruj*. Fighting continued through the day, but in the end, the Maratha garrison was forced to vacate the *Kala Buruj* as well. The survivors fell back to the upper fort or *Bala-i-Qilla*. Murarbaji had lost the lower fort or *machi* to the Mughals, but Purandar's upper fort still stood firmly out of enemy reach.

Purandar, mid-May 1665

Murarbaji peered down from the north-eastern rampart of Purandar's *Bala-i-Qilla* to inspect the movement of Mughal troops in the lower fort. A large batallion of Pathans had assembled and were getting ready for an assault. Guns were being positioned and ammunition stocked piled.

"They are planning a *sultan-dhawa* on the upper fort," Murarbaji snarled.

"Should we stock ammunition on this side?" his Captain asked.

Murarbaji nodded. "Let us give them a rude shock! We will sally forth and attack them before they launch their *sultan-dhawa*."

"Sir, that would be suicidal," the young Captain said, his face turning pale.

Murarbaji glared at him and barked, "Get seven hundred of our best men ready for the assault! Right now!"

"Move those guns further up!" Diler Khan shouted at the men positioning the cannons to begin firing at the upper fort. Since early that morning, he had begun preparations for a final assault. Three thousand of his Pathani troops had been assembled, with many more in reserve, in case the need arose for reinforcements. Battalions of archers and musketeers were busy getting their weapons ready.

Diler rounded up his assault Captains. Turktaj Khan, Atish Khan and his nephews, Gairat and Muzaffar, stood at attention, as he instructed them. "Our guns will begin firing soon. As soon as we have softened the garrison on the rampart, all units will scale the slopes and assault the upper fort in unison. The Marathas should not be able to withstand our attack."

The Captains nodded their understanding. Just then, a din rose from the direction of the main gates of Purandar's *Bala-i-Qilla*. The men looked in the direction of the noise and were shocked to see the main gates open and hundreds of Marathas sallying out, screaming *Har Har Mahadev*!

The alarm was raised and there was commotion in the Pathani ranks, who were not ready yet. They had been preparing for an assault but had not expected the Maratha garrison to emerge from the fort and attack them before they had even made a move.

Murarbaji emerged from the open gates and ran down the slope, swords in both hands, screaming for blood. His seven hundred men followed him, each knowing he would probably not return alive. It was a suicide mission. But not once did they falter. Their Commander had ordered them to attack, and that was exactly what they would do.

The Marathas charged down the slope and fell upon the Pathans. Their initial assault was so fierce that in a short while they had managed to cut down over three hundred Pathans. Murarbaji cut through the Pathani ranks like a force of nature. With tremendous speed, he whirled around in circles, operating both swords with such skill that they formed a virtual ring of cutting metal around him. His hungry blades sliced through Pathani limbs and bodies with such deadly effect that Diler Khan's entire battalion was shaken. Diler Khan himself watched in wide-eyed disbelief as the Maratha Commander felled his men like a demon of death. He had never seen such fighting skill, such valour!

Diler could see the entire scene of battle from his vantage point on the bastion. He stood speechless for some time, mesmerized by Murarbaji's swordsmanship. But finally he came to his senses and began shouting orders. The Pathans regrouped and retaliated. A pitched battle began on the slopes of Purandar.

Murarbaji had spotted Diler Khan on the bastion. Gritting his teeth, he decided to charge the Mughal Commander himself. The Pathans had surrounded Murarbaji, but were still unable to seriously wound him. With a vengeance, he fell upon them in an attempt to get to Diler. Two Pathans charged him at the same time, one from the front and one from the rear. In a swift move, Murarbaji blocked the sword of the Pathan in front with his left sword, and at the same time, buried his right sword into the man's body. As the Pathan grew limp, Murarbaji removed his sword and slashed the neck of the Pathan behind him. Both men dropped almost at the same time.

Murarbaji now leaped onto a rock. More Pathans charged at him. Screaming for their blood, he slashed at the first one to reach him, with both blades. The Pathan proved quite resilient and returned his charge. When, after several strikes he couldn't get past the Pathan's defence, Murarbaji suddenly bent down and struck him on his legs. The hefty man collapsed, screaming. Murarbaji jumped from the large rock on which he had stationed himself, and finding an opening between the Pathani ranks, charged toward Diler's position. On the way, his sword claimed two more.

Diler watched with increasing unease as the Maratha Commander approached his position. He was dangerously close. On an impulse, he shouted to the Maratha, "Halt, o brave soldier! Stop fighting!"

Diler's Captains shouted to their men to fall back. Murarbaji glared at Diler, hatred in his eyes. Both his blades dripped Pathani blood. He himself bore many wounds. Yet no part of him was willing to stop the massacre.

"You are the bravest soldier I have ever seen, and the most skilled swordsman! Join us, brave one! You will be well rewarded. Join the imperial forces and surrender your fort to us!"

Murarbaji's blood boiled with rage as he heard the Pathani Commander offer him a bribe to defect. He pointed a sword at Diler and yelled, "I am a soldier of the Maratha King Shivaji *Raje*, and I will remain faithful till my death! Do you really think Shivaji *Raje*'s men can be bought so easily?" With a blood curdling yell, Murarbaji fell upon the Pathan nearest him. Before he could retaliate, Murarbaji's sword had cleaved his skull in two. More Pathans rushed forward to stop the Maratha, but he kept cutting them down.

Diler, unsettled by the Maratha Commander's dangerous advance towards him, picked up his bow and cocked an arrow. Pulling the bowstring back, he took aim and let the arrow fly. The shaft struck Murarbaji in the neck and emerged through his spine. His swords dropped from his hands. In moments, the brave Maratha crashed to the ground, lifeless. After nearly a decade of faithful service to his Master, Murarbaji had made the final sacrifice.

His garrison fought on, but had to finally withdraw due to increasing retaliation by the Pathans. By the time the surviving

Marathas withdrew into the fort, more than five hundred Pathans had been cut down. The Maratha garrison had lost three hundred men. The carnage had lasted less than a *prahar*.

Diler Khan stood bemused on the bastion, watching the Marathas struggle back up the slope to the fort gates. He did not have the heart to order his savagely mauled battalion to pursue them. He had finally had a taste of Maratha warfare.

RAJGAD, THE NEXT DAY

Shivaji *Raje* listened quietly as Bahirji Naik narrated the events of the previous day.

"Murarbaji fought like a man possessed. Alone, he must have cut down at least thirty Pathans. In the end, Diler Khan killed him with an arrowshot."

"How many of our men?" *Raje* asked.

"Over three hundred, Your Highness."

Raje rose from his seat and began pacing the chamber. "What is the condition of the upper fort?"

"Not much damage to the upper fort rampart. Diler Khan was preparing to storm it but Murarbaji's suicidal mission thwarted his plan. The officers at the fort have sent a message, Highness."

Raje turned to him questioningly.

"They say: *The fall of Murarbaji Deshpande does not change anything. We shall continue to fight to the last man.*"

Shivaji *Raje* felt tears well in his eyes, and turned away, his back to his men. "Murarbaji...." he murmured disconsolately, "I have lost my bravest man. Three hundred soldiers lost in a single morning...eighty more lost the other day in the blast...thousands of commoners killed and imprisoned... Lord Mahadev! Is there no end to this destruction?" *Raje* could no longer hold back his tears.

Moro *Punt* gently helped him back to his seat. The assembly sat in silence, with heads hung. No one had any thoughts to offer.

Shivaji *Raje* composed himself and said, "For nearly five years a large part of *Swarajya* remains occupied by the Mughals. To this day, they continue their depreditions. Our men continue to die and our people suffer untold atrocities. I am wholly responsible for this disaster. It has to stop. I cannot bear the suffering of my people and the massacre of my soldiers any longer. I will sue for peace with Jai Singh."

"Jai Singh has thus far refused to accept any peace proposal," Moro *Punt* reminded his King. "We have offered to pay tribute and even cede some forts."

Shivaji *Raje* firmly pushed aside his grief. Jai Singh was proving to be a tough customer. He had steadfastly turned down their peace overtures. That could only mean that he was convinced he could completely wipe out the Maratha resistance. Could they somehow plant a doubt in his mind; let him know they were planning something with the Adilshah's connivance? It might make him more open to negotiations.

"Bahirji," *Raje* turned to his Intelligence Chief. "Can you plant information in Jai Singh's inner circle?"

"Certainly, Highness."

"Good. Then let Jai Singh know that we intend to make a final attempt at peace with the Mughals, failing which, we will cede a large part of our holdings in the Konkan to the Adilshah, and enter into an open alliance with him."

Bahirji smiled. "It shall be done, Highness."

After more than two decades of struggle, the Maratha rebellion under Shivaji *Raje* had hit a major obstacle. An obstacle called *Mirza Raja* Jai Singh, the ablest military Commander serving the Mughals. In less than three months, the astute Jai Singh had managed to counter the brains and military tactics of Shivaji. Having successfully neutralized major campaigns under Fateh Khan, Afzal Khan, Siddi Jauhar, Shaista Khan and Khawas Khan, Shivaji *Raje* had tasted his first major defeat.

JAI SINGH'S COMMAND TENT, MUGHAL MILITARY CAMP,
20 MAY 1665

Jai Singh sat on a comfortable *baithak*, twirling a jasmine flower between two fingers, as he regarded Shivaji Bhosale's envoy. Dressed in the traditional garb of a *Brahman* diplomat, the man stood in abject humility, with bowed head.

"*Mirza Raja* Jai Singh, Shivaji *Raje* is willing to cede more forts and offers a healthy tribute to the Emperor in exchange for peace," Raghunath *Punt* said.

"I do not have the liberty to negotiate with your Seevaji *Raja*," Jai Singh said tersely. "Only the Emperor can negotiate terms."

"In that case *Rajaji*, this campaign could reach a stalemate. You have yet to capture Purandar. It could take you years to capture all our hill forts."

"Do not have undue faith in your hills, *Punt*! The Sahyadris will be trodden flat by the hooves of the imperial cavalry."

"*Rajaji*, my King is inclined toward a peace treaty. I humbly suggest you consider it."

"If Seevaji *Raja* is willing to come to my camp unarmed, like a common criminal, and ask for pardon, maybe the Emperor, who is akin to the Almighty, may grant him a pardon."

Raghunath *Punt* was dismayed but his face showed no emotion. "I shall convey your message to my King, *Rajaji*."

"....the Emperor, who is akin to the Almighty?" an astonished Shivaji *Raje* repeated what he had just heard from Raghunath *Punt*.

"His exact words, Your Highness."

"Every bone of his body, every thought on his mind, is steeped in servitude!" Jijabai said in disgust. "Why do people like Jai Singh serve the Mughals? Why do they not even think of freeing themselves from foreign rule?"

"Mother, if all the Rajput Kings of Rajputana decided to rebel, the Mughals would not stand a chance. They would be blown away like dried leaves in autumn."

"But who can make them see this?"

Raje shook his head. "No one. Sadly, the Rajputs will never unite, and hence the Mughals will always remain powerful." After a brief pause, he added, "Just like we Marathas can never unite. Imagine if the Marathas and Rajputs united against these imperial rulers..."

"That may never happen, Your Highness. Presently, we must think our way out of this mess," Moro *Punt* said, pulling the brooding King back to present realities.

"Highness. Jai Singh has demanded that you visit his camp, unarmed. We have to give him an answer," Raghunath *Punt* added his voice to the *Peshwa*'s.

"Raghunath *Punt*, go back to Jai Singh and ask him if he will give us an assurance, under oath, of safety to my person while in his camp. If negotiations fail, I must be allowed to return unharmed."

The *Punts* looked at each other with grim faces.

Jijabai looked up. "Shivba, is it safe to visit the Mughal camp in the present circumstances?"

"No, mother, it is not. But I am willing to take my chances if Jai Singh gives his word. He is an honourable warrior."

Jijabai looked away in frustration. "Once again you seek to willfully place yourself in the enemy's jaws. And I will be left behind to suffer the anxiety silently. How many times will I have to bear this?"

Raje placed a comforting hand over his mother's. "Jai Singh is a Rajput King. If he gives his word under oath, he will keep it. I am willing to risk a visit to the Mughal camp on his word."

"Diler Khan is an entirely different matter, however!" Tryambak *Punt*, the *Dabir*, who had been silent thus far, said.

The men frowned. Tryambak *Punt* was right. While Jai Singh could be trusted with an assurance of safety, the hot-headed Pathani Commander could not. In any case, it was well known that the two men did not see eye to eye.

"Must you go personally?" Jijabai asked, her voice laced with concern.

"Mother, Jai Singh is disinclined to negotiate. Maybe, if I go, we can strike some sort of a bargain. Besides, I plan to appeal to Jai Singh's reason and try to make him defect."

"Defect?" Raghunath *Punt* said, astonished. "Highness, Jai Singh will never defect. It is not in his nature to do so."

"Did he not change sides when Dara Shukoh and Aurangzeb were fighting for the throne?"

"That was different, Your Highness. Jai Singh would have sensed an impending victory for Aurangzeb and rationalised his defection as remaining faithful to the throne. He will never side with a rebel Maratha King."

Raje nodded thoughtfully. "It will be interesting to meet *Mirza Raja* Jai Singh in person. *Punt*, prepare to visit the Mughal camp."

Jai Singh looked thoughtfully at Seevaji Bhosale's envoy. The man had returned after consulting with his King. Seevaji had agreed to come personally, provided Jai Singh assured his personal safety. Jai Singh silently weighed his options. He realized all too well that capturing Seevaji's hill forts was an arduous task, which could take years. Getting his hands on Seevaji himself was even more difficult. If he let this opportunity slip, it could take him an eternity to conclude this campaign. Besides, just the previous day he had received intelligence that Seevaji was in talks with the Adilshah. If those two forged an alliance, his worst fears would come true.

On the other hand, he knew Aurangzeb would not be pleased if he negotiated a peace treaty with Seeva. It was of paramount importance that he communicate with Aurangzeb, but that could take weeks. In the meanwhile, if Seeva succeeded in wooing the Adilshah, the matter would become very sticky indeed.

"*Rajaji*?" Raghunath *Punt* prodded gently.

Jai Singh looked at him. He knew what he had to do. The time for procrastination had passed. Jai Singh rose from his seat and walked to where he had set up a small shrine in his tent. Burnished idols of Hindu Gods, that he worshipped every morning and evening, sat on a small table, with offerings of flowers and sweets. Jai Singh picked up a *bael* leaf and approached Raghunath *Punt*.

"Raghunath *Pandit*," he said, holding the leaf in his palm, "I swear by this *bael* leaf that Seevaji *Raja* will be safe in my camp. He can come without fear." So saying, he placed the leaf in Raghunath *Punt*'s palm.

Raghunath *Punt* was relieved to receive this assurance from the Rajput King. He touched the leaf to his forehead, in reverence. "*Rajaji*, Shivaji *Raje* has also requested an assurance that he will be allowed to return to Rajgad should the talks fail."

"I promise he will be allowed to return to his fort unharmed." Jai Singh placed both hands over Raghunath *Punt*'s, and said solemnly, "This is my promise as a Rajput."

Raghunath *Punt* bowed. He knew a Rajput's promise could not be broken. "I will carry this *bael* leaf to my Master and convey your message. Shivaji *Raje*'s safety is in your hands, *Rajaji*."

JAI SINGH'S TENT, MUGHAL CAMP,
EARLY MORNING, 11 JUNE 1665

"Do you really think Seevaji *Raja* will risk a visit to our camp, *Rajaji*?" A diminutive looking man in a simple full-sleeved *sadara* and *dhoti*, sporting an oversized turban on his head, asked. The man was Jai Singh's *Munshi*, Udairaj, who stood on one side as his master relaxed on a *baithak*, fingering some dry fruits placed before him in a plate.

"He has little choice Udairaj," Jai Singh said thoughtfully. They had received a message from Rajgad, that the Maratha King would visit Jai Singh's camp that day. "He has almost lost Purandar, his fief is devastated, and the movements of his army have been neutralized. I suspect he is desperate to sue for peace."

A sly smile appeared on Udairaj's clean shaven face. "*Rajaji* has successfully brought him to his knees."

Jai Singh did not smile. He knew the job was far from done. He was too shrewd a General to assume victory at this stage. "Seevaji is like a wounded tiger now. We must deal with him cautiously. Any wrong move by us could drive him into Adilshah's arms."

"True, but the Pathani faction in Bijapur is on our payroll. They will do their best to prevent the Adilshah from joining hands with the Marathas."

"Do not underestimate Seevaji," Jai Singh said, looking straight at his *Munshi*. "He is no ordinary man. For two decades he has successfully held the Adilshahi at bay and carved out his own kingdom."

Udairaj nodded. His master was clearly enamoured of the Maratha rebel King. Just then the tent awning was lifted by the guards outside and light flooded into the tent.

Raghunath *Punt* entered and bowed to Jai Singh. "*Rajaji*, Shivaji *Raje* has arrived to meet you. He has halted at a distance and requests permission to enter the camp."

"Has he come alone, as promised?" Jai Singh asked.

"*Raje* has come with six administrators, besides the carriers of his palanquin."

"No bodyguards?"

"None, *Rajaji*." Raghunath *Punt* smiled in assurance.

Jai Singh nodded and turned to his *Munshi*. "Udairaj, go forth and meet Seevaji *Raja*. Advise him that he need come further only if he is willing to surrender all the forts in his possession to His Majesty, *Alampanah* Aurangzeb *Padishah*. If not, he should turn back and return to his mountainous abode."

Udairaj supressed a smile and bowed. "Certainly, *Maharaja*."

Raghunath *Punt* and Udairaj left the tent. Jai Singh clapped to summon his attendant. "Summon Jani Beg immediately."

The man bowed and turned to leave. As an afterthought, Jai Singh stopped him and said, "Summon my Rajput bodyguards as well. I want at least four armed men in my tent."

Some time later, Jai Singh's attendant entered the tent to say Seevaji *Raja* had arrived.

Jai Singh turned to his *Mir Bakshi*. "Jani Beg, ensure that Seevaji is thoroughly searched for weapons and then usher him in. His administrators can wait outside for now. Allow only Seevaji and Raghunath *Pandit* to enter."

Mir Bakshi prepared to exit but Jai Singh called after him, "Jani Beg! Don't forget to check his palms and sleeves."

Jani Beg smiled and left to carry out his General's orders.

Shivaji *Raje* alighted from his palaquin in front of Jai Singh's command tent and looked around. The tent was heavily guarded by armed Rajput *hashams*. Soldiers stood around the camp, watching the entourage curiously. *Raje* looked over his shoulder toward Purandar, which loomed over the camp. Sounds of battle and cannon fire were clearly audible even at this distance from the main fort. He knew the Mughals were gaining ground every day and that his men were being slaughtered. Only two days ago, his men in Purandar's upper fort had foiled a determined assault by Diler Khan's Pathans. Eighty Marathas had been slain, but the Pathans had been driven back. Purandar remained unconquered. But for how long?

"Welcome to the Mughal camp, Seevaji *Raja*!"

Raje turned his face to find a Mughal officer offering him a nominal bow. The bearded man wore a half-smile but he seemed strangely restrained in his welcome.

"I am Jani Beg, *Mir Bakshi* of the Mughal army," he said.

Raje nodded. "Do I have permission to enter?"

"Not until you have been disarmed, *Rajaji*," Jani Beg replied with a broad smile this time, showing his teeth.

Shivaji *Raje* laughed wryly and proceeded to remove his *Bhavani* from his *dushela*. He held it out to the *Mir Bakshi* saying, "That is the only weapon I am carrying."

Jani Beg took the sword and handed it over to a *hasham*. "Raise your arms, *Rajaji*," he ordered peremptorily.

Raje was still smiling as he raised his arms and allowed his person to be searched. Jani Beg thoroughly frisked him for hidden weapons. *Raje* burst out laughing when his palms and sleeves were also checked.

Having satisfied himself, Jani Beg ushered the rebel King towards the tent. "You may enter, *Rajaji*."

Raje entered Jai Singh's tent, followed by Raghunath *Punt*. The other administrators were stopped outside. *Raje* found himself in a plushly decorated tent with comfortable *baithaks*. At the far end sat a Rajput of imposing physique. His thick, greying moustache accentuated his warrior appearance. His piercing eyes were locked on Shivaji *Raje*, regarding him with equal measures of curiosity and suspicion. On either side of the Mughal General stood two Rajput *hashams*, holding unsheathed swords. Two more Rajputs guarded the entrance.

Raghunath *Punt* moved forward and bowed to Jai Singh. "The Maratha King, Shivaji *Raje* Bhosale," he said. Turning to his King, he said, "Your Highness, this is *Mirza Raja* Jai Singh, King of Amer and General of this imperial Mughal army."

"Shivaji comes in peace and friendship; why this excessive security, *Rajaji*?" Shivaji *Raje* asked the man before him.

"The story of your meeting with Afzal Khan is still fresh in our minds, Seevaji *Raja*," Jai Singh said in all seriousness.

Shivaji *Raje* laughed. "*Rajaji*, I make my plans according to the person I must meet. I carried concealed weapons to meet Afzal Khan, yet I come unarmed to meet *Mirza Raja* Jai Singh."

Jai Singh smiled for the first time and rose from his seat. Spreading his arms, he said, "Come, Seevaji *Raja*, let us embrace in friendship."

As Shivaji *Raje* moved forward, the Rajput bodyguards gripped the hilts of their swords, ready to strike at any hint of trouble. The Maratha King and Mughal General embraced warmly. Jai Singh then gestured for Shivaji *Raje* to be seated on a *baithak* next to his. Raghunath *Punt* positioned himself near his King, while Udairaj and Jani Beg stood beside the General. In the distance, a cannon boomed.

Shivaji *Raje* turned to Jai Singh, his brows raised. Before he could utter a word, the Mughal General said, "*Abdulla Khan*." Seeing the look of confusion on *Raje*'s face, he explained with a grim smile, "The cannon that just fired is known as *Abdulla Khan*. It will not stop firing till Purandar's ramparts have been destroyed. Diler Khan has taken a vow to that effect."

"*Rajaji*," Shivaji *Raje* pleaded, "pray stop the battle. I surrender Purandar to you this moment. Do not kill any more of my men."

Jai Singh regarded the Maratha intently. His situation must be desperate, Jai Singh thought, or he would not have surrendered the fort thus quickly. "Seevaji *Raja*, the battle will stop when the treaty is concluded. If our talks fail, I will let you return and the battle will continue," Jai Singh replied.

"*Rajaji*, whether our talks succeed or fail, I am willing to surrender the fort to save my men."

Jai Singh thought a while and nodded. Turning to Jani Beg he said, "*Mir Bakshi*, send word to Diler Khan to stop the bombardement. Tell him Seevaji *Raja* has surrendered the fort."

Purandar foothills, some time later

"Stop the bombardment?" Diler Khan glared at the foot soldier who had brought Jai Singh's message. "Is *Mirza* out of his mind? We are close to capturing the fort. I will not stand down."

The soldier swallowed. Diler Khan's temper was known to all. "Seevaji *Raja* has surrendered the fort," he stammered. "He will order his men to evacuate immediately."

"Surrendered?" Diler shouted. "I don't need Seeva to surrender the fort for I will take it from him by force!" He pumped his fist in anger. "Go back and tell *Mirza* that my Pathans will continue to battle the Marathas."

Diler fumed as he watched the soldier take his hurried leave. He was convinced this was a deliberate attempt by Jai Singh to upstage him. The Rajput simply wanted to prove to the Emperor that his negotiations had succeeded in getting Fort Purandar for the Mughals, where Diler had failed in battle. He cast a frustrated glance at his turban, sitting on a small table in his tent. Inwardly, he had to admit the Maratha garrison in the fort had proven too tough for him to subdue. All his military might had failed to capture the fort. Diler gritted his teeth and resolved to lead a final assault. He would not let Jai Singh's diplomacy rob him of a well deserved victory.

Jai Singh and Shivaji *Raje* sat alone in the General's tent. Having sufficiently warmed up to his guest, Jai Singh was finally convinced that Seevaji was not up to any dangerous tricks. He had dismissed his bodyguards. Diplomats from both sides were haggling about the terms of the treaty, in another tent. Save for Jai Singh's attendants, who remained behind the curtains at all times, there was no one else in the tent.

Shivaji *Raje* sat quietly, deep in thought. With every passing moment it was becoming clearer that he would eventually lose a large part of what he and his comrades had built in the last two decades with their sweat and blood. Jai Singh would stop only after he had crippled the *Swarajya*.

"You look morose, Seevaji *Raja*," Jai Singh remarked. "Cheer up! You are about to profess your alliegance to the Emperor. Once he grants you pardon and takes you into his fold, the sky is the limit for you. The vast resources of the Empire will be at your disposal. You can achieve whatever you aspire to, and more."

Raje smiled ruefully. How could he explain to Jai Singh that he could never achieve what he aspired for under the Mughal banner? "*Rajaji*," he said, "the eternal misfortune of our great land has been that its sons dream only of personal aspirations and goals. No one thinks of the future and the greater picture."

"What greater picture do you speak of, Seevaji *Raja*?"

"The day when there will be no foreign rule in our land."

"That is an impossible dream, my friend," Jai Singh said with conviction. "Do not make the mistake of going against the Mughals. They are too powerful. If you do, you will only be left with death and destruction."

"They are powerful because we choose to make them so. Millions of our people are ruled by a handful of Mughals, Persians and Turks. Just imagine what could happen if these millions decide to say *no* to foreign rule!"

Jai Singh laughed indulgently. "You live in a dream world, Seevaji *Raja*. That will never happen. I admire your courage though. I have seen many a rebel in my day, but none as obstinate as you."

"Unite the Rajputs under your banner, *Rajaji*." Shivaji *Raje*'s blunt statement wiped the smile off Jai Singh's face. He became instantly serious as *Raje* continued, "I promise you support of the entire Maratha might. Together, we can blow the Mughals away."

"Beware what you say, Seevaji *Raja*!" Jai Singh's face had hardened. "You are talking to the General of the imperial Mughal army, not another vagabond rebel."

"I am fully aware of that *Rajaji*, and also of your stature in Rajputana. I am certain that all the Rajput Kings would answer your call. Think about it, the imperial throne could be yours if we overthrow the Mughals."

Jai Singh was momentarily stunned by what *Raje* had said. He quickly recovered and said, "Why me? Do you not harbour the dream to sit on the throne of Hindustan?"

"*Rajaji*, I rebelled because I object to foreigners ruling us. If you are my King, I will gladly serve you and safeguard the throne."

Jai Singh laughed. "Seevaji *Raja,* that was a good attempt, but be warned that Jai Singh is a faithful servant of His Majesty. Do not even think of suggesting treachery. It is not in my blood."

Raje sighed. "*Rajaji,* for a brief moment take your mind a hundred years into the past. It was your grandfather, was it not, who fought against the *Rana* of Mewar? Had the armies of Amer and Mewar united, with their respective allies, would Emperor Akbar have succeeded in subduing Rajputana?"

Jai Singh was not amused at being reminded of the past. While it was true the *Rana* of Mewar was much revered in Rajputana for stoically refusing to accept Mughal suzerainty, Jai Singh was proud of his own family's history and tradition. For generations they had been allies of the Mughals, and had even wed their daughters to Mughal royalty. He certainly had no intention of breaking this tradition. Seevaji *Raja* spoke nonsense.

"How I wish the great *Rana* Pratap had lived now," Shivaji *Raje* said dejectedly. "Maybe he could have made you see reason."

"That is enough, Seevaji *Raja*!" Jai Singh said curtly. "Enough of this treasonous talk! Do not forget that you are here to submit to the Mughals. Pray, for the future of your people, that our respective diplomats reach common ground and ink out a treaty. If not, you will face annhilation." He rose from his seat and clasping his hands behind his back, said firmly, "I think you should retire to your tent to rest."

Shivaji *Raje* rose, bowed his head, and turned to leave.

Negotiations between the Mughals and Marathas had been in progress for the entire day. Raghunath *Punt* led the talks for the Marathas and Udairaj *Munshi* for the Mughals. But the two parties had not reached an agreement. Udairaj was adamant that Shivaji *Raje* surrender all his forts and territory to the Mughals and become a vassal. He informed Raghunath *Punt* that the Emperor had placed this condition to concluding the campaign. Raghunath *Punt* repeatedly declined these demands, insisting that if no acceptable terms were reached, Shivaji *Raje* would leave the camp and the Mughal campaign would be faced with a stalemate.

That evening, Udairaj called on Shivaji *Raje* to have a word with him. Though *Raje* had received regular feedbacks from his team, he was eager to hear what Udairaj had to say to him in private.

"*Rajaji,*" Udairaj said earnestly, "*Mirza Raja* Jai Singh realizes that your position is severely compromised. You must submit, else you may not even be left with your personal freedom."

"It is not my personal freedom that concerns me, *Munshiji,*" *Raje* replied scornfully. "All my life I have strived for my people's freedom. If they are to be enslaved again, I do not wish to live."

"*Rajaji,* I plead with you, submit to the Emperor. Surrender your entire fief."

"My entire *Swarajya*?" *Raje*'s voice rose sharply. "Never! Never in a hundred years. My men and I will die fighting if need be, but we will never surrender our *Swarajya*! *Munshiji,* I am here to negotiate a treaty, not to surrender. I have not surrendered! Do not think that my means are that limited. Before leaving Rajgad, I made provision for my administration to run in my absence, for our struggle to continue without me. My men are prepared to face the eventuality that I do not return alive from your camp. So is my mother. Need I say more?"

Udairaj frowned and fell silent. The Maratha could not be persuaded, even for his own good. He would have to consult his Master before making his next move.

"I do not think Seevaji *Raja* will surrender all he has, *Rajaji.*" Udairaj said to Jai Singh. "We will have to reduce our demands."

Jai Singh thought hard. Udairaj had just informed what had transpired and Seevaji's utter refusal to surrender. Jai Singh knew he had succeeded far beyond what anyone else had managed to achieve against the Maratha in two decades. He now had the man at his mercy. But pushing him too far would be ill advised. If he snapped, who could tell what he would do? Here was a golden opportunity to conclude this campaign, and he was loathe to let it slip from his hands.

He would have to downsize his demands but in such a way that the Mughal gains would look dazzling despite the compromise, leaving Seeva with just enough for him to feel inclined to agree. The only thing was to convince the Emperor that under the circumstances, this was the best option, because he had left the capital with strict orders to eliminate Seeva.

Jai Singh finally made up his mind. "Udairaj, ask for a large part of the old Nizamshahi territory and forts, which Bijapur ceded to the Prince Aurangzeb eight years ago. That treaty was never fully honoured by the Adilshah. Seeva took advantage of this and usurped most of those lands. Ask him to return that territory."

Udairaj understood what his Master had in mind. If Seevaji agreed to this, the Mughals would regain what had been their's, and the Maratha King's fief would be reduced significantly.

Jai Singh's tent, Mughal camp, 12 June 1665

Following another day and night of negotiation, the two parties at last reached an agreement on the terms of the peace treaty. These terms would now be read out for all concerned to hear and consent to. *Mirza Raja* Jai Singh sat at the head of the assembly, commanding the proceedings. Shivaji *Raje* and Raghunath *Punt* sat to his left, while Udairaj, the *Munshi,* sat to his right. Also present were Jani Beg, the *Mir Bakshi,* and Ugrasen Kachwah, another of Jai Singh's office bearers.

"After extensive deliberation, both parties have agreed upon the following terms," Udairaj said, initiating the official proceedings. He opened the scroll that had the terms written on it and looked at Jai Singh. The General nodded.

"This treaty, being concluded between the General of the Mughal imperial forces, *Mirza Raja* Jai Singh, on behalf of His Majesty, the Emperor Aurangzeb *Padishah,* and the Commander of the Maratha forces, Seevaji *Raja,* will effect a lasting peace between the two peoples. It is agreed that from the old Nizamshahi territory ceded by the Adilshah to His Majesty, eight years ago, Seevaji *Raja* will surrender twenty-three forts, with their appurtenent territories, yielding an annual revenue of four hundred thousand *hons*. Seevaji *Raja* will retain twelve forts and their appurtenent territories, yielding an annual revenue of a hundred thousand *hons*."

Shivaji *Raje* and Raghunath *Punt* glanced at each other uneasily. The terms were tough and would certainly take away a major chunk of the *Swarajya,* and with it, much needed revenue. But they had little choice and had to remain silent.

Udairaj continued, "Seevaji *Raja*'s son, Sambhaji Bhosale, will accept service at the Mughal court as a *mansabdar* of the rank of five thousand *dhat,* five thousand *sawar* and five thousand *du aspa sih aspa*. Seevaji Raja himself will be exempted from holding a *mansab* but will be bound to perform any military duty assigned to him by the Emperor in the Deccan."

Jai Singh nodded and said, "That sounds appropriate to me. It only remains for us to get His Majesty's approval." He looked at Shivaji *Raje*. "Seevaji *Raja,* do we have your approval?"

Raje nodded reluctantly. This remarkable Rajput had in three months undone what he and his comrades had achieved through their sweat and blood over two decades. Jai Singh had, with this swift, well planned and brutal campaign, reduced his beloved *Swarajya* to almost nothing. It was true that he would still hold a small part of his territory with a few forts, but he could see clearly that his administration would struggle with expenses. In any case, what he was left with had been devastated by the Mughals.

Udairaj's voice broke into *Raje's* thoughts: "I will now name the forts to be handed over to the Mughal Empire – Purandar, Vajragad, Kondhana, Khandakala, Lohgad, Visapur, Tung, Tikona, Rohida, Nardurg, Mahuli, Bhandardurg, Palaskhol, Kohoj, Vikatgad, Prabalgad, Manikgad, Karnala, Sagargad, Mrugagad, Ghangad, Songad and Mangad."

Raje sat in silence. He had nothing to say. A large part of his kingdom was being taken by the Mughals. It was as if a part of his own body was being hacked away. Kondhana, the jewel of the Sahyadris, would no longer be his. Purandar would fly the Mughal banner. Murarbaji's valiant sacrifice was in vain.

"Seevaji *Raja* will now place his seal on the treaty." Udairaj's words brought Shivaji *Raje* back to the present.

The formalities were completed in a short while. Jai Singh smiled. This marked the end of another successful campaign for him. It was another feather in his cap. "Seevaji *Raja,*" he said, "I have one more condition you must agree to."

What more could this shrewd man want from him, wondered *Raje*. Jai Singh had already taken his heart's blood.

"We have learned from past experience that treaties of this kind are often not fully honoured. Hence I have decided to keep a surety with me till all forts and territory are handed over."

"Surety?" Shivaji *Raje* raised his eyebrows. "What surety do you want, *Rajaji*? I am at your mercy. What more do you want?"

Jai Singh's smile vanished and his face hardened. His eyes bore menacingly into Shivaji *Raje*'s, as he said slowly, "Seevaji *Raja*, your son Sambhaji will remain with me, in my camp, till the formal handing over of the forts is complete."

Raje was stunned! Shambhu in the Mughal camp! Lord Mahadev! "*Rajaji*, my son is but a child. How can I leave him alone in your military camp? I simply cannot accept this. If you so wish, *I* shall remain in your camp as surety."

"You cannot stay here, *Raja*, for your presence is required in Rajgad, so the treaty can be executed quickly. Sambhaji will remain here as surety. Arrange to send him to my camp as soon as possible." Jai Singh rose from his seat, indicating the conference was over.

"*Rajaji*..." Shivaji *Raje* tried to protest, but Jai Singh silenced him by raising his hand.

"The treaty is concluded, Seevaji *Raja*. I shall send it to His Majesty immediately. All that remains is his seal of approval."

Shivaji *Raje* and Raghunath *Punt* left Jai Singh's tent with heavy hearts. *Raje* could feel his world collapsing around him. It remained to be seen if he would prove strong enough to rise again from this disaster.

Diler Khan's camp, Purandar foothills, 13 June 1665

"*Huzoor*, Seevaji *Raja* has come to see you," Diler Khan's attendant uttered cautiously, lest he trigger his Master's temper.

Diler Khan was busy sharpening his dagger. He stopped what he was doing and shot an angry look at his *quorchi*. The man hurriedly lowered his eyes, half expecting his Master's dagger at his throat any moment. In the past few weeks, his Master had become increasingly irritable, lashing out at the slightest aggravation. The *quorchi* well knew how his Master hated Seevaji, the Maratha. For nearly three months now, Diler Khan had tried every means at his disposal to capture Fort Purander, but had failed. And now General Jai Singh had signed some treaty with the Maratha King, without his Master's knowledge. That was certainly cause for a display of unchecked rage.

Diler remained unnaturally quiet as he checked the sharpness of the blade on his thumb. "Is he alone?" he asked.

"No, *huzoor*. He comes seated on an elephant, accompanied by *Raja* Rai Singh and his Rajputs."

Diler Khan nodded and the man hurried out to usher in these unexpected guests.

Raja Rai Singh, the Rajput Chieftain, entered Diler Khan's tent, followed by Shivaji *Raje*. Diler Khan remained seated, regarding the Maratha calmly, still holding his unsheathed dagger in his right hand. Two of his bodyguards stood to either side, while his *quorchi* stood behind him, partly hidden behind a curtain. Who could tell what would ensue? Diler's men knew he was prone to rash acts of anger and, of late, his mood had been irritable at best. The man he had battled for the past three months, whose men had thwarted all his attempts at capturing Purandar, now stood unarmed in front of him, at his mercy. Would Diler Khan vent his pent up anger and kill the Maratha King?

"*Huzoor* Diler Khan," *Raja* Rai Singh said, breaking the silence, "this is Seevaji *Raja*, the Maratha King. He has signed a treaty with *Mirza Raja* Jai Singh, agreeing to surrender twenty-three forts and attached territory to us. Fort Purandar has been surrendered. *Mirzaji* has asked you to end hostilities."

Shivaji *Raje* gave Diler Khan a disarming smile. "I am fortunate to meet a great soldier like you, Diler Khan. No ordinary man could have got the better of my Captain, Murarbaji *Deshpande*."

Diler gave him a half smile, and put aside his dagger. Rising from his seat, the burly Pathan advanced toward *Raje* and spread his arms to give him the customary embrace. Momentarily, Shivaji *Raje* was reminded of his meeting with Afzal Khan. The hands of Diler's bodyguards hovered over the hilts of their swords, as did *Raja* Rai Singh's.

This day, however, turned out differently from the fateful day at the foot of Pratapgad, over five years ago. Diler Khan gestured for Shivaji *Raje* to be seated beside him and the formal talks began. Shivaji *Raje* coaxed the Khan to order a cease fire in his presence, promising to hand over Fort Purandar personally. The Khan, in return, graciously gifted *Raje* a bejewelled sword and dagger, precious cloth, and two fine horses, one of which was adorned with gold trappings.

Peace was thus finally concluded with the Mughals. Shivaji *Raje*'s *Swarajya*, or rather, what was left of it, would see peace after years of war. The Mughal front would finally be quiet.

Rajgad, 15 June 1665

Jijabai stared silently at the floor as Raghunath *Punt* finished recounting the events of the past few days in the Mughal camp and the clauses of the treaty the King had just signed with the Mughals.

"A dark day indeed for our *Swarajya*," she finally said. "But we must look at the positives. We still have a part of our kingdom, and Shivba *Raje* has not been compelled to formally accept the Emperor's service."

Shivaji *Raje* stood by a large window which faced west, gazing forlornly at the sky which had turned orange as the sun dipped toward the horizon. It seemed as if the sun was setting on his *Swarajya*, and would soon plunge them into darkness. Raghunath *Punt* felt his heart fill with sadness as he watched his King. *Raje* had been strangely quiet these past few days, ever since they had left the Mughal camp. The previous day, he had personally handed over charge of Kondhana to Jai Singh's son, Kirat Singh. Though he had spoken little, Raghunath *Punt* knew it had burned a hole in the King's heart. They all knew how much *Raje* had loved and once coveted Kondhana, and now he had been compelled to surrender it. It must have rent his heart.

Soyarabai, Sakvarbai and Putalabai, *Raje*'s Queens, were present also at this private meeting being held in *Raje*'s chamber.

Soyara felt her husband's pain and wished she could do something to lessen his grief. She walked up to him and said quietly, "Your Highness must not get discouraged by this defeat. By the grace of the Goddess, we shall see success against the Mughals again."

Raje did not look at her. It was not that he had never experienced defeat, but this reverse against Jai Singh had been particularly hard to swallow, coming as it had after the loss of so many good men. *Raje* was unable to look at his wife, fearing to see disappointment in her face. "I fear the Goddess has turned her face away from me, though I do not know why," he said.

"She would never do that, Highness," Soyara replied gently. "In the hardest times, when it seems she had abandoned us, she actually carries us in her loving arms."

Raje had to fight back his tears. He began to pace the chamber, hands behind his back.

"Shivba, why have Jai Singh's people accompanied you to Rajgad?" Jijabai asked.

"Jai Singh wants some surety that we will abide by the terms of the treaty," *Raje* told his mother.

"Surety?" Jijabai raised her brows. "Is not the word of a Maratha enough for the Mughal? What kind of surety?"

Raje looked at Raghunath *Punt,* who sighed and looked down at his feet. Seeing both King and diplomat silent, Jijabai grew impatient. "Shivba! What surety does he want?" she asked sternly.

"He wants us to send Shambhu to the Mughal camp till we hand over all the forts."

A collective gasp came from Jijabai and the Queens, as they covered their mouths in horror.

"There is no way I will send Shambhu to the Mughal camp!" Soyara said angrily, confronting her husband. "How did you ever agree to this condition?"

Putala and Sakvar simply covered their faces with their hands, unable to speak.

Jijabai rose from her seat and looked at her son, tears forming in her eyes. "Shivba, how could you? Do you have no heart left in your body?"

"Mother, I was helpless," *Raje* said, wondering how he could explain to his women why he had agreed to send his only son to the enemy camp. "For the sake of our people, we must abide by the terms. There is little else we can do at the moment."

"*Raje,* Shambhu is only eight years old! He is but a child! How can we send him to the enemy camp? Wasn't it enough that we had to bear the torture of you going there?"

Shivaji *Raje* walked over to his mother and held her affectionately in his arms. "Mother, Jai Singh has assured me of Shambhu's safety.

Did he not keep his promise to me? He is a Rajput. He will keep our child safe."

As she looked into his eyes, Jijabai could clearly see her son's despair. She realized that at this moment she had to support, not fight him. She laid her head on his chest in submission and wept. *Raje* held her close, fighting back his own tears.

Turning to his Queens, he said, "Get Shambhu ready for the trip. He leaves for Jai Singh's camp in two days."

The Queens hesitated and Putala looked to Soyara for strength. Glaring defiantly at her husband through her tears, Soyara said in a calm voice that belied the storm raging inside her, "Highness, if anything happens to Shambhu..."

"He will be safe," Shivaji *Raje* said firmly. "Now get him ready. That is your King's order."

RAJGAD, 17 JUNE 1665

Eight-year-old Sambhaji Bhosale strode confidently into his father's chamber and offered obeisance. He was smartly dressed in fine clothes, as befitted a Prince. A bejewelled sword was stuck into his *dushela*. He stood upright and regarded his father. He had been told by his sobbing step-mothers that he would be sent to the Mughal camp for a few days. The news had hardly bothered him. While he could see that people all around him were worried sick for his safety, he felt secretly excited since, for the first time, he would get to see a Mughal military camp!

Two men stood at attention to one side, watching this meeting between father and son. One was the *Sirnaubat*, Netoji Palkar; the other the faithful Captain, Baji *Sarjerao*.

Shivaji *Raje* looked at his son, wondering if this was the last time he would ever see him. He struggled to keep his emotions in check, as he said, "Shambhu *Raje*, you are leaving on an important diplomatic mission. Remember, in the Mughal camp, you are the Maratha Prince. Be mindful of the etiquette that has been taught you. *Mirza Raja* Jai Singh is the General of the Mughal army. You must give him due respect. Be fearless, but not careless. *Sirnaubat* Netoji Palkar and Baji *Sarjerao* will accompany you. Be sure that one of them is always near you."

"I will remember what you have said, Father," little Shambhu assured him.

"Are you afraid?"

"Certainly not!" Shambhu said indignantly. "I am a Maratha!"

"You will spend the next few weeks among our enemies. Does that not scare you?"

"Not in the least."

"Why not?"

"Because I am the son of the bravest man on earth!"

Shivaji *Raje's* eyes moistened as he looked at his confident eight-year-old. He rose and came forward. Kneeling in front of his son, he took him in his arms. Shambhu hugged him tightly, betraying for a moment his anxiety at leaving the safety of their home. But none of it showed on his face when father and son looked at each other again. It was *Raje* whose eyes filled with unshed tears.

"Do not worry about me, Father," Shambhu told him. "I will not let you down. I will uphold our family's royal traditions while I am in the Mughal camp."

Raje laughed. "Who taught you to talk like that?"

"Elder mother did."

"What else did she tell you?"

"That I must be brave like my father."

Raje smiled. Soyara had handled their son well. "Did you see your grandmother?"

"Yes, and she blessed me too!"

Raje rose to his feet and regarded his son seriously. "Prince Shambhaji Bhosale, it is time to leave now. May the Goddess be with you."

Sambhaji bowed to his King and departed on the first mission of his life.

After he had left the room, *Raje* turned to his men. "Netoji, Baji, I entrust you with my son, your Prince. Remember, he is your future King. Keep him safe."

"Do not worry, Highness," Netoji assured him. "As long as Netoji and Baji are with the Prince, he will be safe."

Raje nodded. "Come back safely, all of you."

The men bowed and left. Alone in his chamber, Shivaji *Raje* closed his eyes and pictured the Divine Mother, Goddess Bhavani. *I have sent him to you, mother. Keep him alive.*

The regally dressed Maratha Prince walked confidently through the awning and entered the *shamiana* of the Mughal General. He was preceded by his father's *Sirnaubat*, who now stood respectfully to one side. Sambhaji cast his curious gaze upon the figure seated on a *baithak.*

The Rajput's face broke into a smile "Welcome to the Mughal camp, Sambhaji *Raje*."

Sambhaji bowed slightly, then he walked up to Jai Singh and bent down to touch his feet. "Bless me so I can be a great warrior like you, *Dadaji*."

"*Dadaji*?" Jai Singh was intrigued by the boy.

"My father said that when he was in your camp, you treated him like a son. That makes you my *Dadaji*, doesn't it?" said Sambhaji.

Jai Singh laughed heartily at the boy's ready wit and clasped him in an embrace. Placing his hand on Sambhaji's head, he said, "May Lord Mahadev bless you with a long life, *Kunwar* Sambhaji."

Jai Singh seated Sambhaji next to himself. As the boy stared back, Jai Singh couldn't help but notice the same fearlessness in his eyes that he had seen in his father's. "Sambhaji *Raje*, you will be a Mughal *mansabdar* soon. This visit to the Mughal camp is a golden opportunity for you to learn how the Mughals conduct a military campaign. Make the most of your visit!"

"I will, *Dadaji*!" Sambhaji said, his eyes alight. "I may never get to see another Mughal camp!"

Jai Singh's smile waned. *The boy never intends to be in another Mughal camp,* he thought. Jai Singh wondered for a moment if he really was only eight years old.

The Mughals spent the months after the Purandar treaty taking charge of the forts surrendered by Shivaji *Raje*. During this time, Prince Sambhaji remained in Jai Singh's camp. Jai Singh was quite impressed with Shivaji's son. Notwithstanding his tender age, Sambhaji's erect posture, regal mannerisms, and wit far beyond his years, had created a favourable impression on the Mughal General. *The son is as remarkable as is his father*, he thought. Jai Singh had arranged for Sambhaji to be put up in his own tent, partly because of his fondness for the lad, and partly because he felt the boy would be safer near him. He had assured Seevaji that his son would be safe, and he intended to keep his word.

Jai Singh also kept up a regular flow of letters to the Emperor, informing him of the developments in the Deccan. It was important to keep Aurangzeb apprised of events. The keys to the forts were despatched to the Mughal capital as well. Having successfully concluded his campaign against the Marathas, Jai Singh began preparing in earnest for the second stage of his Deccan campaign, against the Adilshah.

Delhi, the Mughal capital, early September 1665

Aurangzeb impatiently turned the prayer beads in his right hand as he listened to his *Wazir*, Jafar Khan, read Jai Singh's elaborate despatch from the Deccan. He grew increasingly restless as he realised that Jai Singh had not been able to achieve the goals he had set out with. He had told Jai Singh to finish Seeva and his resistance, yet the Rajput had agreed to a truce with the Maratha instead. But as he heard the clauses of the treaty, Aurangzeb realised the terms were quite favourable to the Empire. Jai Singh had managed to clip Seeva's wings. But, the shrewd politician that he was, Aurangzeb knew Seeva would survive this and create more trouble for him later. Why hadn't Jai Singh killed Seeva while he had the chance?

Jafar Khan finished reading the despatch and handed the scroll to an attendant. The antechamber where they sat, was quiet. Jafar Khan threw a cursory glance at Mohammed Amin, the *Mir Bakshi*, who stood in front of him. Amin let out a sigh as he returned the *Wazir*'s glance. Both knew the Emperor well enough to realise he would not be happy with Jai Singh's settlement in the Deccan.

"*Mirza Raja*..." Aurangzeb said the title with such spite that had Jai Singh heard it, he would have feared for himself. "I ordered that *kafir* to kill Seeva! And all that he can manage is a treaty? *A treaty*! Why am I stuck with such short-sighted fools? For all his military expertise and political wisdom, Jai Singh has failed to gauge the danger of letting Seeva live. Jai Singh sees Seeva as a person and thinks that subjugating him will do the job. What Jai Singh does not realise is that Seeva is instigating millions of people into rebellion."

"Should we refuse the terms of the treaty, Your Majesty?" Jafar Khan asked.

"No! We cannot do that. Our expenditure in the Deccan is mounting. We must focus on Bijapur now. If Seeva is quiet, it will serve our purpose for now. We can deal with him later."

The chamber was quiet again as the *Wazir* and *Mir Bakshi* awaited the Emperor's orders.

"Send a *firmaan* of acceptance to Seeva. We must close the Maratha matter. Send strict instructions to Jai Singh that he must oversee the handover of the forts personally. I do not want a repeat of the fiasco that occured with the Adilshahi treaty." After a brief pause he added, "Write to Jai Singh that he should persuade Seeva to appear in my *durbar*."

Jafar Khan threw another glance at Amin and said gently, "Majesty, there is no clause in the treaty about Seeva having to appear in court. The *kafir* may not agree."

"Then tell Jai Singh to *make* him agree, by whatever means!" Aurangzeb shot back. "I want to see Seeva kneel before me."

Aurangzeb sat alone in his personal chamber as Hussain emerged from the shadows and gave him the latest intelligence from the Deccan camp. "The *Mirza* seems to have grown quite fond of Seevaji," he said. "My men have heard that he often praises the Maratha *kafir*."

"I was afraid that would happen," Aurangzeb said quietly. "No wonder Jai Singh agreed to a treaty. What has Diler Khan been doing?"

"Obsessed with capturing Purandar, he completely disregarded what was happening in the *Mirza*'s camp."

"Diler Khan wasn't able to take Purandar?" Aurangzeb was surprised at the apparent failure of his most trusted man.

"No, Your Majesty. The Maratha garrison in Purandar seems to have neutralised all his efforts. They suffered heavy losses but refused to surrender. Seevaji surrendered the fort personally, in Jai Singh's camp."

"Tell your men to be alert, Hussain. Dangers will mount. As per the clauses of the treaty, Jai Singh will order Seeva to join the Mughal camp in the war with Bijapur. The risk of the two *kafirs* joining hands will be great."

Outskirts of the Mughal camp, 30 September, 1665

The rains had finally receded and the skies had lightened. The sun came out in all its fury to scorch the rain drenched countryside. A small party, on foot, traversed the lightly wooded path that led to the imperial camp set up a *kos* away from Jai Singh's military camp. In the lead was Kirat Singh, son of Jai Singh, with a few of his Rajput *hashams*. They were followed by the Maratha King, Shivaji *Raje,* and his diplomat, Raghunath *Punt*. Accompanying them was Jani Beg, the *Mir Bakshi* of the Mughal army.

In due time, the party reached the imperial camp set up for the small ceremony. Shivaji *Raje*'s eyes caught sight of the *firmaanbadi,* the unusually tall open canopy erected on poles. They were asked to halt as horns and trumpets blared from the far side. Rank upon rank of armed Mughal *hashams* stood on either side of a pathway leading to the *firmaanbadi*. In a short while, a regally caparisoned camel ambled through the path flanked by the soldiers. The rider led his mount straight under the canopy of the *firmaanbadi*.

Shivaji *Raje* was now led by a couple of Mughal guards to the imperial rider, seated on the camel, holding a silk pouch. Jani Beg advanced and said, "This is Seevaji *Raja*. You may hand over the Emperor's *firmaan* to him."

The imperial rider gently kicked his mount and the animal folded its legs and sat down. The officer alighted and moved forward to confront the receiver of the Emperor's favour. Shivaji *Raje* stood in his place, rigid and unmoving. He remembered what Jai Singh had instructed him to do: *You must kneel before the messenger, lower your head and raise your hands to receive the firmaan*. *Raje* had felt disgusted merely hearing it. His mind went back twenty-five years, to the time when he had watched his father kneel before the Adilshah. How he had hated that! Now, he would have to do the same in front of a mere messenger who held the Emperor's *firmaan*! *I shall not kneel...I shall not serve...* he had said then. Now, he would have to do the very things he had vowed never to do. He would have to swallow his pride and follow Mughal etiquette in receiving the Emperor's *firmaan*.

"*Raja* Seevaji," Jani Beg prodded. "You must kneel now."

Shivaji *Raje* looked at him and nodded. Slowly, he knelt, bowed his head and raised his palms towards the messenger. The man simply placed the silk pouch in his hands. *Raje* rose and, still holding the *firmaan* over his head, left the *firmaanbadi*, retracing his steps to the Mughal military camp.

Raghunath *Punt* felt a lump in his throat as he saw his Master's pain. But Shivaji *Raje* did not flinch as he went through the motions. A *prahar* later, the party had returned to Jai Singh's camp, where, in the General's command tent, the *firmaan* was read with customary fanfare. The Emperor had affixed his seal of approval to the treaty of Purandar. The Maratha's past sins had been pardoned and his son accepted into the Mughal fold as a *mansabdar*. The Emperor had also sent the much coveted robes of honour for him.

In the eyes of Jai Singh, the King of Amer and General of the Mughal army, not only was his own victory complete, but so was Shivaji *Raje*'s advancement and honour at the Mughal court.

In the eyes of Shivaji *Raje,* the proud Maratha King, his defeat was complete, as was his humiliation.

Once the *firmaan* had been read, Shivaji *Raje* left for Rajgad.

Back in his palace, he headed straight for his chambers and locked himself in, refusing to see anyone, even his mother. He wished to be alone that night.

Raje felt no sense of relief now that the treaty had been concluded with the Mughal. Instead, he felt stifled; his heart yearned to break free from the heavy burden that seemed to have been placed on it. His dreams and aspirations, his desperate desire to free his homeland from the clutches of the Sultans, had received a huge setback. His mind went back to a rainy day, twenty years ago, when Tanhaji and Yesaji had led the assault to take Fort Torna…their first conquest. How thrilled and proud they had been; the day they had defiantly declared they would no longer bow to any Sultan! Since that eventful day, they had won many victories, achieved much. They had come far...

But now, after two decades, they had lost a large part of their blossoming kingdom. Peace had been achieved, but at horrendous cost. This Mughal campaign had spelt only destruction, humiliation and disaster for the Marathas.

It remained to be seen whether Shivaji *Raje* and his followers would pick themselves up again; whether the *Swarajya* would rise again from the ashes of Shivaji *Raje*'s dreams.

7
A VETERAN HUMBLED

THE MUGHAL MILITARY CAMP AT PURANDAR, NOVEMBER 1665

Shivaji *Raje* sat in conference with Jai Singh in the General's command tent. Jai Singh had summoned the Maratha King to apprise him of recent developments in the Deccan campaign.

"The Emperor has sent a *firmaan* ordering me to annex the Adilshahi territories," Jai Singh said to Shivaji *Raje*. "Soon, we march against Bijapur. As per our treaty, you will have to join our military camp and take active part in this campaign."

Raje nodded silently. He had expected this and had prepared himself for the new campaign.

"You will provide us with ten thousand troops," Jai Singh continued. "You will personally lead your contingent, with your *Sirnaubat*, Netoji, as second-in-command."

Raje nodded again. "I am bound to obey your commands, *Rajaji*. When do we leave?"

"In two weeks. Complete your preparations by then."

Shivaji *Raje* fingered the jewelled ring on his right hand and said, "*Rajaji*, I wish to make a formal offer to the Emperor."

Jai Singh regarded him curiously. "What offer, Seevaji *Raja*?"

"I hold part of the Adilshahi territory in the Konkan, which yields about four hundred thousand *hon* in revenue anually. I can also conquer, at my own expense, additional Adilshahi territory in the uplands of Balaghat, which could yield five hundred thousand *hon* in annual revenue. I wish to proposition the Emperor to allow me to keep this territory after the present Adilshahi campaign."

Jai Singh continued to regard him as he gently rubbed his chin. Having given the matter due thought, he said, "*Raja*, you are now a vassal of the Emperor. How then can you expect him to grant you these lands?"

Shivaji *Raje* replied quickly, "I will hold these territories as a vassal, of course. Officially, they will be part of the Empire. I am also willing to pay the Emperor a handsome sum for these lands."

"Is that so?" Jai Singh was intrigued. "How much will you pay?"

"Four million *hon,* in instalments of three hundred thousand *hon* a year."

Jai Singh's indulgent smile vanished. In the past few weeks he had come to know this extraordinary Maratha well. He was amazed not just by Seeva's military skills, but also by his political ingenuity. He marvelled at Seeva's confidence about raising such a sum, simply to retain control over the Konkan. As he gave the proposal more thought, he could see the advantages. If the Emperor agreed, it would serve three purposes. First, it would alienate Seeva from the Adilshah. Second, it would spare the Mughal army the arduous task of campaigning in the difficult Konkan terrain, and thirdly, it would yield four million *hon*.

"It is a good proposal, Seevaji *Raja*." Jai Singh's smile returned. "I will communicate it to the Emperor. Perhaps he will agree."

The two were quiet for some time before Jai Singh said somewhat hesitantly, "*Raja,* the Emperor has issued an order, for you."

Shivaji *Raje* raised his eyebrows. What he saw on Jai Singh's face made him uneasy. What had the Emperor ordered?

"The Emperor wishes you and Sambhaji *Raje* to attend his *durbar* in the Mughal capital."

Raje's face only momentarily betrayed the dismay he felt on hearing this. Though he had never agreed to visit the Emperor's *durbar* in person, he knew he was in no position to negotiate with the Mughal at the moment. If it was the Emperor's order, he would have to consider it seriously.

"But *Rajaji,*" Shivaji *Raje* protested, "our treaty makes no mention of my personal visit to the Emperor's *durbar*."

"I am aware of that, Seevaji *Raja*. But if the Emperor so wishes, you cannot, or rather *should not,* demur." Seeing *Raje* pensive, Jai Singh continued, "Think of the positives of a visit to the capital, Seevaji

Raja. You have recently forged an alliance with the Mughals. An audience with the Emperor will strengthen it. If the Emperor is pleased with you, he may grant you new lands and *jagirs*; maybe even the *Subadari* of the Deccan."

"*Rajaji*, a visit to the Mughal capital is too risky for me. Who can guarantee my safe return?" Shivaji *Raje* voiced his concerns.

"Seevaji *Raja*, you may have faith in me. I will entrust your security to my son Ram Singh, who serves the Emperor. You will return safely."

Shivaji *Raje* was quiet for some time. He could not agree to this in a hurry. It was simply too big a decision to take.

"What goes on in your mind *Raja*?"

"I need time to think about this *Rajaji*."

"Certainly. In any case, your visit can only be scheduled after the campaign against Bijapur."

Shivaji *Raje* left Jai Singh's camp the same day, his brow creased with a new worry.

20 November 1665

The Mughal army set out from Purandar to annex the Adilshahi territories. Jai Singh had placed Diler Khan in command of the vanguard, comprising seven and a half thousand Pathani cavalry, and another thousand Rajput cavalry provided by the *Rana* of Mewar (which he was obliged to do as per a previous treaty with the Mughals). The left and right wings, comprising six thousand cavalry each, were placed under the command of Daud Khan and *Raja* Rai Singh Sisodiya respectively. The main body of the Mughal army was made up of twelve thousand cavalry, under Jai Singh's personal command. The left wing of the main body comprised ten thousand Marathas, under Shivaji *Raje*. The right wing was placed under the command of Kirat Singh, son of Jai Singh, while Qutb-ud-din Khan was entrusted with the command of the rear guard.

The Mughals had established their supply lines and planned their advance well. Their numbers were massive and they had impressive artillery at their disposal. A Mughal victory seemed a foregone conclusion.

Jai Singh had prepared well, but for the most important aspect of planning a military campaign of such colossal proportions – intelligence. Jai Singh's spies had informed him that Bijapur city was running low on provisions; the Adilshah's court was immersed in factionalism; their army disunited; that most of the Adilshah's officers would defect once the Mughals reached the gates of Bijapur. Nothing could have been further from the truth. Contrary to the information supplied by Jai Singh's intelligence network, the young Sultan Ali had rallied his officers and troops well, and had chalked out a clever plan to oppose the Mughals.

Jai Singh was in for a surprise and would, in the months to come, suffer the worst reverse of his illustrious career.

Citadel of Bijapur, first half of December 1665

A top secret war council was in progress in the private audience chamber of the Bijapur Sultan, Ali Adilshah. The Sultan sat on a high seat, in front of a table on which was spread a map of the Adilshahi Empire. Five men stood at attention around the table and pored over the map. In the middle, stood the Bijapuri *Vizier*, Abdul Mohammed, the most faithful of the Bijapuri nobles, and Ali's principal support. To Abdul's right stood a tall and lanky Pathan; he was Abdul Karim Bahlol Khan, leader of the Pathani faction in Bijapur. Next to Bahlol stood Siddi Masud, a powerfully built, dark-skinned noble. He was Abyssinian by birth and leader of the Abyssinian faction, who controlled the north-eastern part of the Adilshahi Empire. Masud was the son-in-law of Siddi Jauhar, who had, years ago, led an unsuccessful campaign against Shivaji *Raje*. Another dark-skinned noble stood to the *Vizier's* left. This was Khawas Khan. Though of Abyssinian descent, he was now the leader of the Deccani faction of nobles in Bijapur. The fifth noble was Sharza Khan, who stood next to Khawas; he belonged to the Deccani faction.

Factionalism had forever been the bane of Bijapur as its nobles competed for control, and influence with the Sultan, doing their best to influence decisions in their favour. Such one-upmanship never helped the Sultanate however, making it vulnerable to invasion. Defections, chiefly to the Mughals, were common.

For the present, however, the various factions had temporarily buried their differences and decided to join hands to deal with the

Mughal threat, which was literally at their door. Ali had succeeded in rallying his nobles, convincing them to unite under the Bijapuri banner. He wished to teach the invading Mughals a lesson they wouldn't forget in a hurry.

Adbul Mohammed placed a pointer at a spot on the map and said, "The Mughals have camped on the banks of the Nira river, Your Excellency. Phaltan district is now untenable; so are several forts in the northern part of our kingdom."

Ali nodded. He had already received this information from his personal spy network. Jai Singh seemed to be heading south, straight for his capital.

"Should we send our forces to intercept the Mughals?" the *Vizier* inquired.

"Not yet," Ali said. "We will allow the Mughals to advance unhindered till they are near Bijapur. Send word to our forts along their line of advance not to resist the Mughals."

"But Your Excellency, that way we will allow them to penetrate deep into our lands."

"Yes, and further from their chief bases in Aurangabad and Burhanpur. Once they are deep into Adilshahi territory, we will send mobile units to outflank them and cut off their supply lines at the rear." Ali looked to his men to make sure they had absorbed his plan. It was crucial they did so as they would implement it in the field.

"Form units of swift cavalry under Sharza Khan and Khawas Khan," Ali continued. "These will take to the field once the Mughals are within striking distance, and engage their vanguard. Be mindful never to engage fully. Withdraw each time the Mughals gain the upper hand. Leave the fight, allow them to turn back towards their main camp, and then attack and harass them again. We can thus wear them down."

The nobles nodded. Ali looked at his *Vizier*. "Abdul Mohammed, you will direct the field operations against the Mughals. Bahlol Khan will stay in the city to defend it." He raised his hand, gesturing to the pointer. Abdul placed the pointer in his Master's hand. Ali marked out a broad zone around the capital limits and said, "Convert this land around the city into a desert! Empty every reservoir, fill every well with earth, and chop down every tree. Make sure that when the Mughals arrive to take our capital, they do not find a drop of water in these parched lands, nor any shade from the sun. At the same time, cut off their supplies of grain and fodder. Let them die of hunger and thirst!"

Ali narrowed his eyes. He hated the Mughal scum, who had in the past repeatedly invaded the Kingdom of his great ancestors, but always failed. He would make sure they failed yet again. "Move our people out of this zone to safer areas. See that they suffer as little as possible."

"The thirty thousand Karnataki infantry that you requested from our vassals in the south, will be in Bijapur in a couple of days, Sire," the *Vizier* informed him. "That should bolster our strength immensely."

Ali nodded. "Stock the city with food and ammunition. If the Mughals persist and lay siege to our city, we should be prepared for a battle lasting many months."

"Do we have any news from the Qutubshah, Sire?" Bahlol spoke for the first time.

"The Qutubshah is still ruminating over our proposal to make a united stand against the Mughals. He is an idiot! Does he not realize that this Mughal campaign against Bijapur is but a precursor to a Mughal invasion of the entire South? If Bijapur falls, what hope does the Qutubshah have of defending his kingdom? When will he see sense?"

"I think he will, Your Excellency," Bahlol replied. "I believe he will eventually help us."

"That infidel Seeva was a thorn in our flesh, but nevertheless an effective bulwark against the Mughals. Now that Jai Singh has subdued him, our northern borders are exposed," the *Vizier* remarked. "Else we could have thought of a three-way alliance against the Mughals."

"Seeva will be a persistent problem for us, mark my words! He will never be a real ally. We must always be wary of him. He now stands against us with the Mughals." The Sultan's view differed from his *Vizier*, but he was quick to add, "But you are right; we were better off with Seeva between us and the Mughals."

The men looked at each other grimly. The Mughal threat was very real and each recognised the imminent danger to their existence. They would have to implement their battle plans meticulously. One foot wrong and they would face annihilation.

The Mughal army advanced unopposed for nearly a month. During this period, they annexed a significant part of the northern Adilshahi territories. Jai Singh despatched Netoji Palkar with his Maratha troops to capture the Adilshahi forts along the way. Netoji succeeded in annexing Phaltan, the *jagir* of Shivaji *Raje*'s brother-in-law, Bajaji Naik Nimbalkar. Bajaji surrendered to Jai Singh and accepted his offer of Mughal service. The forts of Tathawada and Khatav were taken without much effort, so was Fort Mangalwedha, which stood twenty-five *kos* north of Bijapur.

Finally, after a month of uninterrupted marching, Jai Singh received the first news of approaching Bijapuri troops. The Bijapuris made no attempt to engage during the day, however. Jai Singh waited for them to make a move, which they did, at night. In classic Deccani style warfare, the Bijapuris, under the command of Khawas Khan and Sharza Khan, fired rockets at the Mughals through the night, harassing them. By morning, Jai Singh had resolved to repulse this enemy force and despatched Pathani and Maratha troops under the command of Diler Khan and Shivaji *Raje* himself. Both Captains distinguished themselves in the ensuing battle and succeeded in scattering the twelve thousand strong Bijapuri force. The Bijapuris seemed to withdraw, but no sooner had the combined Mughal division turned back towards their camp, than the Bijapuris returned to harass them. At this point, Netoji Palkar's division formed the rear guard and so bore the brunt of the Bijapuri attack from the rear. He was so hard pressed that he had to send for urgent reinforcement from the Mughal camp. These soon arrived in the form of Jai Singh's son, Kirat Singh, who bailed Netoji out.

After a two-day rest, the Mughals continued their march and soon had their next encounter with the Adilshahi troops. This time, Jai Singh marched out in person, to take the enemy head on. Again, the Bijapuris baffled the Mughals by breaking up into several swift mobile groups which attacked the Mughal front at various points; engaging and fleeing repeatedly. The Mughals pursued them for nearly four *kos*, but failed to crush them decisively.

The Bijapuri night attacks on the Mughals continued, harassing them endlessly. The Mughals failed to force a decisive battle. Despite this, Jai Singh advanced and reached within five *kos* of Bijapur city. But as they camped there, debating their next move, Jai Singh became increasingly aware that he had lost the initiative and was now in a rather compromised position.

When he had first received Aurangzeb's order to invade Adilshahi, Jai Singh knew he would have to expedite preparations and march as fast as possible, to arrive at the gates of Bijapur before the Adilshah had a chance to bolster his defences and rally his troops and nobles. An element of surprise would work best. His spies had informed him that most of the Bijapuri nobles were keen on defecting to the Mughal side, so he had acted on this.

But Jai Singh had been forced to waste a precious month at Purandar camp, waiting for release of funds from the imperial treasury. When the money did finally arrive, he had hurriedly organized the campaign and marched out. In his haste, he had failed to procure large guns from the Mughal forts in the Deccan. Now, entrenched five *kos* from his objective, he realized that his parially depleted force was insufficient to lay siege to the Adilshah's capital. He had no siege guns with him, but was faced with monster guns like the *Malik-i-Maidan* on Bijapur's ramparts. Twenty thousand Bijapuris hovered around his camp, striking repeatedly, mostly at night, while the Mughlas sat in the open like sitting ducks for their rockets. The Bijapuris had also cut off their supply lines and they could not find a single source of water. As the Adilshah had predicted, Jai Singh's men were dying of hunger and thirst.

As Jai Singh thus sat bemused in his tent, he was about to receive a jolt from his own camp.

Diler Khan's massive form barged into Jai Singh's tent, brushing aside Jai Singh's Rajput guard. Jai Singh stared at the Pathan's angry face as he stood fuming in front of him. "What seems to be the matter, Diler Khan?" he asked as calmly as possible.

"*Mirza*, I am going to kill that infidel Seeva!"

"Seevaji? Why?"

"He is responsible for our debacle in this campaign."

"Diler Khan, calm down. How can Seevaji alone be responsible for our situation?"

"Seeva has secretly connived with the Adilshah. He makes only a show of battle each time we engage. Why else would our massive army face such indignity against the Bijapuris?"

"Diler Khan, you are mistaken. We cannot hold Seeva responsible for our lack of success."

The tent awning rustled again as Daud Khan and Kirat Singh entered together.

"*Mirzaji,*" Daud Khan said, "we are severly compromised and must retreat."

"Retreat?" Diler thundered. "I will have Seeva's head before I retreat!" He left the tent in a huff.

Kirat Singh spoke up. "Father, I think we must seriously think of retreating. Our position is fast becoming untenable."

"I am aware of our position, Kirat. But we have invested far too much in this campaign to back out now."

"We have received intelligence that the Qutubshah has sent a large force to assist Bijapur. That army may arrive here any day."

"I am afraid we may lose too many lives if we persist." Daud Khan said. "Taking Bijapur city is impossible now. The men's morale has been broken by hunger and thirst."

Jai Singh was pitifully aware of these facts. He sat down with a sigh. Never before had he experienced such humiliation in battle. After a successful campaign against the Marathas, this campaign against Bijapur was supposed to be his crowing glory. How had things gone so wrong?

Diler's threat of killing Shivaji *Raje* was a new headache for Jai Singh. If the hot-headed Pathan really did carry out his threat, the Marathas would most certainly rise in rebellion. There would be a civil war right here in his own camp. The Purandar treaty would become history and the already compromised imperial army would be faced with an angry Maratha state.

In an attempt to diffuse the tension and warn the Maratha King, Jai Singh asked Kirat Singh to personally summon Shivaji *Raje* to his tent.

When *Raje* appeared, Jai Singh apprised him of Diler Khan's accusations. He felt personally reponsible for the Maratha's safety. Besides, he had grown quite fond of him.

Raje sat for a while in thought and then said, "*Rajaji*, My presence in your camp is not without danger. I feel I should leave."

"Seevaji *Raja*, if you leave now, it will only serve to aggravate Diler Khan's suspicions. If he succeeds in reaching the Emperor's ear, you will lose any ground you have gained with His Majesty."

"In that case, appoint me to a fresh campaign, to Fort Panhala."

"Panhala?"

"Yes, *Rajaji*. Panhala was under my control and I have stayed there for several months. I know the fort's strengths and weaknesses well. I am sure I can capture Panhala for His Majesty in a short time. That will give us success on a new front."

Jai Singh considered this and then threw a cursory glance at his son. Kirat Singh nodded slightly, indicating his agreement.

"Very well, Seevaji *Raja*. Proceed to Panhala with your contingent. But do you have sufficient men here? Netoji Palkar is in the field with half your troops."

Raje nodded. "I will send word to Netoji at once, ordering him to join me at Panhala."

Raje left Jai Singh's tent and the Mughal General heaved a sigh of relief. He wasn't really convinced that Shivaji *Raje* could storm Panhala, but the very fact that the Maratha was moving away from the unpredictable Diler Khan, relaxed him.

Environs of Fort Panhala, third prahar of the night, 15/16 January 1666

Shivaji *Raje* waited impatiently for his *Sirnaubat* as he crouched in the forest around the base of Fort Panhala. Netoji had been campaigning around Bijapur city, on Jai Singh's orders. *Raje* had sent word, ordering him to come here. According to his instructions, Netoji should have reached the previous evening. *Raje* waited, hidden in the forest for over three *prahars*. Still there was no sign of Netoji. *Raje* realized that waiting any longer was futile. Though he had insufficient men with him and desperately needed Netoji to bolster his own force, he knew that every passing moment increased their risk in battle. Their presence was sure to be discovered by the fort garrison sooner or later. By daybreak they would have lost the initiative. He had to attack under cover of darkness.

Raje summoned his Captain, *Sarjerao* Jedhe, and said to him, "*Sarjerao*, we cannot wait for the *Sirnaubat* any longer. Rally the men and move forward. We will assault the ramparts at once."

Jedhe nodded and went off to assemble the Captains. A short while later, the Maratha force emerged and advanced towards the fort. *Raje* had expected to reach the ramparts and begin scaling them in the dark. He had no reason to believe the garrison had been alerted since this attack had been planned only a few days ago. None other than Jai Singh and Kirat Singh knew of it.

Unfortunately for the Marathas, the Panhala garrison was alert and they were spotted before they had even reached the ramparts. Volleys of arrows and shot rained down upon them as the fort defenders sought to repulse them in earnest. Unperturbed, Shivaji *Raje* urged his men on, valiantly carrying on with the assault. Only a short distance now lay between them and the ramparts.

Suddenly, the fort gates opened and thousands of Bijapuri defenders poured out of the fort. The attack, which came from the Maratha right flank, was so terrible that several hundred Marathas were cut down before they could regroup and collect their wits. Once they did, they fought back spiritedly. *Raje* flung himself headlong into the thick of battle. His *Bhavani* moved around him like a flash of lightning, cutting down enemy soldiers with a vengeance. His Captains joined him and a pitched battle began at the base of the fort.

As day broke in the east, bathing the environs of the fort in first light, Shivaji *Raje* found himself standing amongst too many of his own dead. While the Bijapuri defenders were still in great strength, his own men were tiring and dropping fast, and Netoji's reinforcements were nowhere in sight. *Raje* realized it would be madness to continue and reluctantly gave the order to retreat.

The Marathas retreated towards Fort Vishalgad, pursued for a great distance by the Panhala garrison. This was the second time Shivaji *Raje* had been pursued down the same path. And this time too, he managed to reach the safety of Fort Vishalgad.

Fort Vishalgad, evening of 16 January 1666

Sirnaubat Netoji Palkar arrived at the fort several *prahars* late. He knew his Master would be displeased. News of the debacle at Panhala had reached him and he felt personally responsible even though he knew there was little he could have done.

Shivaji *Raje* sat brooding in his chamber. Having seen his men massacred earlier, he simply did not wish to speak to anyone. *Raje* mourned his dead comrades alone, ruing their consummate defeat at Panhala. The past few months had been hard on him. He had seen failure like never before, and had begun to doubt his own capabilities. What an utterly crazy mission he had embarked upon. How could he and his men even think of overthrowing the powerful Sultans? Were they any match for their massive armies, their superior artillery, or the endless money at their disposal? In the past three and a half centuries, had anyone even thought of attempting such an impossible task?

Shivaji *Raje* held himself at fault for the wanton loss of lives in the last few months. A part of him cried out, telling him to stop; to end this hopeless journey. *Raje* sat on a *divan*, facing a window that looked to the west. The skies darkened with every passing moment as the sun disappeared behind the hills. *Raje* rested his chin on his hands and closed his eyes, allowing tears to bathe his face. Times of introspection like this were the most difficult to bear, and he preferred to be alone, away from his comrades.

An attendant entered silently. "Your Highness, the *Sirnaubat* has arrived and wishes to see you."

Shivaji *Raje*'s anger sparked at the mention of the *Sirnaubat*. He said nothing, only nodding silently.

Netoji Palkar entered. Bowing, he stood in silence, his head lowered. Shivaji *Raje* rose and walked up to him. Fixing his blazing gaze on his Commander-in-Chief, he asked, "*Sirnaubat*, why could you not reach the designated place in time?"

Netoji looked up and locked eyes with his Master. Beads of sweat had formed on his forehead. "Highness…" he stammered, "I was far distant...far to the east..."

"You had five days, yet you could not reach in time?"

"Sire, I did my best, but the men were exhausted after so many months of campaigning."

"Poor timing has always been your problem has it not?"

Netoji looked away, saying nothing. *Raje* was far too angry and anguished for any reasonable argument.

"Do you know how many men we lost today? One thousand, Netoji; one thousand good men, slaughtered before my eyes! Had you been there, they would still be alive, rejoicing in a victory!"

Sirnaubat Netoji Palkar had no response to offer. He had certainly misjudged the time, but he had been helpless. He simply could not have pushed his men any harder. Yet, not reaching a battle scene on time was a cardinal sin, never forgiven by his Lord. And *Raje* was right, had he reached on time, they would not have lost so many men.

"*Swarajya* cannot survive with a *Sirnaubat* who is so irresponsible..."

Netoji looked at his Master, fearing the worst.

"Netoji Palkar, you are hereby relieved of your post of *Sirnaubat* of the Maratha army. You are also removed from service. Leave now and find yourself another employer!"

Netoji was stunned by Shivaji *Raje*'s verdict. He would have willingly accepted any punishment, but being banished seemed too harsh to swallow.

"Your Highness, do not remove me from your service! Demote me, but do not send me away..." Netoji pleaded with the man he worshipped next to God.

"I have said what I have to say, Netoji. Leave now."

"Your Highness, I have given my blood for *Swarajya* these past ten years. I admit I have made errors. Punish me, but do not send me away."

Shivaji *Raje* turned his back to Netoji and clapped his hands for his attendant. "Show Netoji Palkar out," he said tersely.

Netoji's face flushed with humiliation and anger. He could not believe that his Master had sacked him. The attendant quietly opened the door and stood aside. Netoji cast one last glance at the man he had given everything to and risked everything for. Then he whirled around and stormed off without offering obeisance.

A forlorn Mughal General looked around at the barren landscapes from the *howdah* as his war elephant slowly trudged its way north. His dispirited and disheartened army followed. Jai Singh rued his lost chances in the campaign against Bijapur. He felt he had had a good chance of forcing a victory and annexing the entire Adilshahi to the Empire. He had over seventy thousand troopers, artillery, ammunition and the vast resources of the Empire at his disposal. The long list of his Captains boasted names like Diler Khan, Daud Khan, Shivaji *Raje* Bhosale and Netoji Palkar, among others. The man he had pitched himself against was a young inexperienced Sultan, who had recently lost two major campaigns against Seevaji. Ali's own camp was forever immersed in factionalism and infighting. Yet, incredibly, Ali had risen over his past failures, to frustrate and defeat him! Ali had defeated Jai Singh, a war veteran, a master of the battlefield and diplomacy, the man who had subdued Shivaji.

Now, Jai Singh faced an even bigger task than swallowing his pride and defeat. He would have to explain to the Emperor the reasons for his failure and justify the immense resources wasted in the entire exercise. The campaign against the Adilshah had indeed caused a massive drain on the imperial treasury. It had cost the Mughal Emperor over three million rupees, and Jai Singh had neither territory nor forts to show for it. His recent acquisitions in Bijapuri territory were untenable once their army retreated. Jai Singh had no choice but to order his men to evacuate those holdings. To add to it all, Jai Singh had spent over twenty million rupees of his own funds, which he had no hopes of recovering from the Emperor.

After two weeks of marching north, Jai Singh and his army reached the banks of the Bhima river, close to the southern boundary of the Empire.

8
A TIGER ROARS IN AGRA

RAJGAD, FEBRUARY 1666

Shivaji *Raje* had returned to Rajgad. After the particularly hectic campaign in Adilshahi, he was enjoying some quiet time with his family. The hurt of his defeat at Jai Singh's hands had not eased yet. To that was added the grief of watching a thousand of his men slaughtered before his own eyes at Panhala. *Raje*'s mind had been numbed by these reverses and he needed some time away from campaigns to heal the wounds, not just to his body, but also to his soul.

He also needed some time to consider the impending visit to the Mughal capital, in solitude, and with his advisors. He had per force given it much thought. Jai Singh seemed to have an honest interest in advancing his cause with the Emperor. *Raje* himself had no intention of serving the Mughal Empire. He wanted to be an independent ruler in his own realm. But, for the present, he needed some peace and stability in his fiefdom. He had to stop warring for some time and let his men have a few quiet years. His kingdom and his people needed time to recover from the ravages of war.

The Purandar treaty had achieved an effective cease fire with the Mughals. What harm would it do if a visit to the Emperor's court could achieve something more? What if he could extract permission for the *Sirdeshmukhi* rights in the Mughal Deccan, which he had been trying to get for years? Or better still, what if he could impress the Emperor enough to make him grant the *Subadari* of the Deccan province? To a great extent, that could offset the costs of maintaining his army. Besides, he could get access to the resources of the Empire, particularly its artillery. He could use these to annex more territory from the Adilshah. Then, a few years later, at an opportune moment, he could cast off the cloak of this make-believe subservience and lock horns with Aurangzeb again.

But a visit to the Mughal capital was fraught with serious danger. Aurangzeb was an unpredictable person, given to breaking his promises. What if the assurance of safety turned out to be false? In any case, it was Jai Singh who had promised him safety, not Aurangzeb. What if the Mughal decided to put aside Jai Singh's promises and imprison him... or worse, kill him?

Yet, to achieve any political success, he would have to visit the Emperor's *durbar*. He would have to bow to Aurangzeb.

The Maratha Council pondered the impending visit of their King to the Emperor's court. Shivaji *Raje* and Queen Mother Jijabai, sat at the head of an assembly that included the most powerful men of the Kingdom. To *Raje*'s right, as always, sat his *Peshwa,* Moro *Punt* Pingale. Next to Moro *Punt* sat Tryambak *Punt,* the *Dabir;* Nilo *Punt,* the *Muzumdar,* and Anaji *Punt,* the *Surnis*. To the left, sat Raghunath *Punt* and *Raje*'s trusted Captains, Tanhaji Malusare, Yesaji Kank, Kudtoji Gujar, Hiroji Farzand and *Sarjerao* Jedhe. The seat to Jijabai's immediate left was vacant.

The mood was sombre. The past year had seen the fledging Maratha kingdom face tremendous difficulties. They had faced their worst ever defeat since their struggle had begun two decades earlier. They had witnessed untold destruction of their lands, spoiling of crops, and killing of their people by the Mughals. The treaty had arrested the depreditions; they had borne the tensions of their Prince being in custody at the Mughal camp, and their King campaigning for the Mughals against Bijapur. The final insult had been the crushing defeat at Panhala...a thousand men lost... and an empty seat at their Council.

"Aurangzeb cannot be trusted, Your Highness," Moro *Punt* said, voicing the worries of the Council. "It would not be prudent for you to risk your life going to Agra."

Though the Mughal Capital was at Delhi, a court order had recently arrived, summoning Shivaji *Raje* to the imperial presence at Agra instead. Aurangzeb's father, the ex-Emperor Shah Jahan, had left for his heavenly abode a few weeks earlier and Aurangzeb had shifted his base to Agra Fort. Celebrations of Aurangzeb's fiftieth birthday would now be held there and *Raje* was required to attend *durbar* on that auspicious day.

"I agree," said Tryambak *Punt*, the *Dabir*. "It would be wiser to send a diplomatic mission with suitable presents instead."

"My King, you continue to take grave risks. You must remain safe here at Rajgad," Tanhaji said, worry creasing his forehead.

The men began discussing the subject animatedly, each trying to convince the King against going to Agra.

Shivaji *Raje* was quiet. He calmly turned to look at his mother. Jijabai had been unusually withdrawn ever since he had informed her about the Emperor's summons to him and Shambhu. Deep inside, she knew her son had already taken the decision to go on this perilious journey, and that she would have to endure the torture of waiting for him to return. She looked at him sadly but remained sitting erect in her seat. With an almost imperceptible nod to her son, she raised her hand to silence the Council. "Listen to what your King has to say," she said.

Shivaji *Raje* turned to his men. "My faithful Ministers and Captains," he began, "dangerous as this journey is, I must go. Not just because I am now bound to obey the Emperor's summons, but also to secure through diplomacy that which would not be possible without me. Our fiefdom has been reduced by two-thirds, so has our revenue. My chief objective is to try and convince the Emperor to allow me to open a fresh campaign against the Deccani Sultanates. If I succeed, it will serve several objectives. First, we will achieve a lasting peace with the Mughals; second, the imperial grants will help our forces subsist, and third, we will have the best chance of annexing the Adilshahi. As matters stand, without the vast resources that only the Mughals can provide, we stand no chance against Bijapur. And if we do indeed succeed, we can strengthen ourselves and later shake off this make-believe subservience to the Mughal."

"Pardon my impudence, Your Highness, but there are so many 'ifs'," Moro *Punt* countered firmly. It was his job as *Peshwa* to advise his King wisely on political matters. "Besides, we must remember that Jai Singh, with all the Mughal might behind him, failed miserably against Bijapur."

"He did, but that was because of his poor knowledge of the Deccan," *Raje* said. "His intelligence network failed completely. I am sure we can do a much better job against the Adilshah...we have in the past."

"But Your Highness, both the King and the Crown Prince placing themselves in such danger, at the same time, is unwise," the *Peshwa* said.

The men nodded. The Council became a raucous cacophony as each Councillor tried to add his voice to the objections. Finally, Shivaji *Raje* raised his hand and the men fell silent.

"My men, I must do this. Believe me, I too, take no pleasure in such risks. But right now, I have little choice. Jai Singh has sent me this latest *firmaan* from the Emperor. *Raje* handed a scroll to his *Peshwa*, who read out the salient points:

...Begin your journey without delay with a composed and confident mind and arrive here to salute the threshold of my durbar. *After you have offered obeisance to my Royal Self, you will be glorified and allowed to return home with splendid favours. Behold the* khilat *that I send you...*

Raje looked at the grave faces before him. "A refusal to obey this *firmaan* will spoil our relations again. Jai Singh and his Mughal army are still right here, in our fiefdom. Who can say what orders Aurangzeb may issue if I disobey? Right now, our people need peace...so do our soldiers. They are tired after years of warfare."

There was a quiet pause as the men pondered. Raje continued, "I agree it is not wise to take Prince Shambhu with me, but I must. He is officially a Mughal *mansabdar* now. His presence in the *durbar* is mandatory."

The men sighed. The King had made up his mind and the decision to go, had been taken. There was nothing they could do.

"The administrative arrangements in my absence must be immaculate. As always, the Queen Mother will be Chief Regent. Her immediate subordinates will be Moro *Punt* Pingale, the *Peshwa*, Nilo *Punt* Sondev, the *Muzumdar*, and Anaji *Punt* Datto, the *Surnis*. The *Sirnaubat* will be the fourth person with authority, in charge of our armed forces." *Raje* looked at the empty seat to the left. "Except that we have no *Sirnaubat* at the moment."

The men shifted uneasily in their seats. The sacking of Netoji Palkar had not gone down well with them. Quite a few harboured the belief that their King had erred in removing Netoji from the force, yet none dared question his authority openly.

Raje nodded firmly and said, "It is time we give our forces a new Commander-in-Chief." He looked across the chamber at his Captains, seated at the far end. His eyes fixed on a man who sat erect, returning his Master's gaze confidently. "Kudtoji Gujar," *Raje* said finally, "I hereby appoint you *Sirnaubat* of the Maratha forces. Come forth and receive your formal appointment."

Kudtoji's chest swelled with pride as he rose and came forward to offer obeisance to his King. *Raje* summoned an aide, who brought forth a ceremonial sword and the robes of honour. *Raje* rose from his seat and handed the sword to Kudtoji, formally confirming his appointment. "I confer the title of *Prataprao* upon you. From this day, you shall be known to all as *Prataprao* Gujar."

The men's faces broke into smiles as they nodded at each other, concurring with this important appointment. After days filled with worry, following *Raje*'s return, this was a rare moment to smile. Kudtoji Gujar was a fierce soldier, an expert in guerilla warfare, and a capable leader of men. In him, the *Swarajya* had an able Commander for its armed forces.

"*Prataprao*, take your rightful place in Council," *Raje* said, pointing to the empty seat.

Prataprao Gujar bowed again and took his place to the Queen Mother's left. The Council was complete once again.

"Moro *Punt*, it is the Council's responsibility to run *Swarajya*. I may be gone a few months and my absence must not be felt." Moro *Punt* nodded his agreement.

"*Prataprao*, tighten the security and defend our boundaries well. While I am away, you must marshal the forces alone."

"His Highness need not worry," *Prataprao* replied. "I will secure our boundaries."

"Make sure all our forts are adequately stocked with grain and ammunition; our garrisons placed on alert. Discipline must be strict in all our forts. The gates must be closed from sunset to sunrise without exception. Despatch written orders to all fort Commanders."

"Yes, Your Highness."

"*Raje*," Jijabai said gently, "who goes with you to Agra?"

Raje paused for a moment and then replied, "The Emperor has sanctioned one lakh rupees for our expenses. I think I can easily take three hundred chosen men with me. Raghunath *Punt* Korde, Tryambak *Punt* and Niraji Raoji, amongst our diplomats, will go with me. The Captains will be Yesaji, *Sarjerao* Jedhe, Hiroji *Farzand* and Ragho Mitra. Jiva Mahala will go as well." *Raje* had chosen his oldest and most trusted Captains for the journey.

"May the Goddess bring you all back safely," Jijabai said, rising to leave.

The men rose and bowed. The all important Council meeting had concluded.

Outskirts of Aurangabad, mid-March 1666

A large number of people had gathered at a clearing on the outskirts of Aurangabad, capital of the Mughal Deccan province. Word had spread in the town the previous day that Shivaji *Raja*, the Maratha King, would soon arrive and camp at Aurangabad, on his way to Agra. Hundreds of curious people had taken time off from their daily routines to see the famous Maratha who had challenged the might of the Sultans, killed the giant Afzal Khan, and raided Shaista Khan's residence at night; the man they called a sorcerer.

By mid-day, half the town seemed to have gathered. Shortly thereafter, a cloud of dust was seen in the distance and the crowd began buzzing with activity as people jostled to get a view of the approaching caravan.

Shivaji *Raje*'s entourage trudged its way towards the city gates. In the lead was a large elephant, proudly carrying the saffron standard of the Maratha *Swarajya*. Following it was a platoon of Maratha cavalry, smartly dressed in white, with red turbans and *dushelas,* mounted on the choicest of horses with silver and gold trappings. The cavalry was followed by the infantry, marching in organized ranks. Following the infantry was a *sukhpal,* a special empty palanquin with a dome, completely covered by silver plates. Right behind the *sukhpal* was another grand palanquin, covered in engraved silver plates. Covering the pegs were gold plates. In it sat the King himself, looking resplendent in a ceremonial, embroidered *angarkha*. On his head, he wore a turban decorated with pearls and rubies. On his fingers were rings glittering with precious stones, and around his neck were strings of pearls. His calm face sported a full beard and moustache, and sideburns. He was fairer than his men, and to the onlookers it was apparent that he was a ruler of men. Even in the fleeting glimpses they caught of him, his spirit and manliness were apparent.

Following the King were more palanquins, carrying his son, Sambhaji, his ministers, and chief officers. Finally came the rear guard, and the *banjaras,* the stragglers who followed with their pack-oxen. There were several bullock carts and camels as well, to carry provisions.

The caravan halted outside the city limits as the gathered crowd cheered the Maratha King. A small Mughal contingent, awaiting the arrival of Shivaji *Raja,* moved forward. A young officer gently nudged his mount and approached the *Raja*'s palanquin. "On behalf of the Governor of Aurangabad, *huzoor* Safshikan Khan *sahib*, I welcome you, Seevaji *Raja,*" he said courteously.

Shivaji *Raje* nodded. "The Governor is not here?"

"*Rajaji,* he awaits you in the audience chamber at his residence. I have come to take you to him."

Raje realised at once that this was a slight by the Governor. He was dismayed by this deliberate breach of protocol, but kept his composure. "Who are you, young man?" he asked the officer.

"I am the Governor's nephew," the young man replied.

"In that case officer, I will go straight to my designated residence in *Mirza Raja* Jai Singh's house. My men are tired after a long journey and have earned their rest. Do inform the Governor on my behalf." With a sardonic smile and a curt nod, *Raje* gave his men the signal to move on.

The caravan slowly coiled its way into the town and headed for Jai Singh's residence.

Safshikan Khan, the Governor of Aurangabad, listened quietly as his nephew narrated the incident with Seevaji *Raja*. The Maratha is wily, he thought, and quick thinking. Safshikan Khan had, a few days earlier, received a *firmaan* from the Emperor, ordering him to make arrangements for Seevaji *Raja*'s stay, and to treat him as he would an imperial Prince. The *Raja* was to be put up in a suitable place with full honours. Food and provisions were to be arranged for his entourage. Yet Khan, in a moment of egoistic gloating, had declared to his men that Seeva was but a mere landowner. What was the need for so much respect? He declared that he would not receive the Maratha himself, but send his nephew to usher the Maratha to his presence. But Seeva had turned the tables on him by going straight to Jai Singh's house. Now, Safshikan Khan would have to go to him because if he did not, it would amount to disregarding the Emperor's *firmaan*. And that was never done.

The Governor swallowed his pride and set out to meet the Maratha King everyone talked about. Shivaji *Raje* received the news of his arrival but, instead of going out to receive him, remained in the audience chamber. When the Governor finally walked in, *Raje* went forth as far as the carpet under his feet extended and waited. Safshikan Khan stared at the Maratha standing and regarding him fearlessly, and realized his own folly. The man he had insulted was no ordinary man.

There followed some formal discussion between the men, after which the Governor rose to leave. He courteously extended an invitation to the *Raja* to visit his residence the following day. Shivaji *Raje* graciously accepted the invitation and did indeed visit the Governor the next day.

MULUKCHAND'S SERAI, OUTSKIRTS OF AGRA, 11 MAY 1666

After a hard march, the Maratha contingent finally reached the outskirts of Agra. They were directed to a modest place meant for travelers, a *serai* owned by a certain Mulukchand. It certainly was not the kind of arrangement Shivaji *Raje* had expected from the Mughal Emperor. As a state guest, he had expected more respect and full Mughal honours. But he said nothing and consented to retire for the night in the small chamber provided. His mind was now fixed on the next day when he would, finally, meet the Great Mughal. Aurangzeb's fiftieth birthday celebration was to be held the next day and he had been told to be present at the *durbar* for the occasion.

There was a light knock on *Raje*'s door. Two men entered and bowed. They were Tej Singh, a representative of Jai Singh, and Gazi Beg, a representative of the Emperor. Both had accompanied *Raje* and his entourage from Rajgad, to help organize the arrangements for the trip.

"I hope *Rajaji* is comfortable?" Gazi Beg enquired with a sly smile.

"I am a soldier, Gazi Beg," *Raje* replied. "I can be comfortable even under the stars. But I had expected a more gracious welcome to his guests by one who is the Emperor of Hindustan."

"Certainly, *Rajaji*. I apologize for the deficiency. I have as yet no knowledge why a formal camp was not set up. Unfortunately, we have no time to waste. Pray rest here tonight. We must leave early tomorrow to reach the *durbar* in good time."

Raje nodded. He too, had to mentally prepare for tomorrow. He had no time to waste in complaining about protocol.

"Is there anything I can get you, *Rajaji*?" Tej Singh asked. As Jai Singh's official on duty, he was aware his Master had personally vouched for the Maratha King's safety at court. The King had also been promised appropriate respect and honour, and the Emperor was certainly not living up to that part of the bargain.

As Shivaji *Raje* shook his head, Shambhu entered the chamber, bringing smiles to everyone's faces.

"The Prince is in high spirits," Gazi Beg remarked.

"I am merely alert, Gaziji. One must be, when one has so many enemies." The nine-year-old, possessed of a maturity far beyond his years, had charmed everyone in camp.

Gazi smiled at the lad. "But there are no enemies here, Prince Sambhaji. The Emperor is now a friend of the Marathas."

"That remains to be seen," Shambhu concluded firmly. He remembered every word his father had said to him before the trip.

Shivaji *Raje* smiled indulgently at his son and then turned to the Emperor's man. "Gazi Beg, why has no official from the Mughal court come to receive me?"

"*Rajaji*, once again I apologize for this breach of protocol. Unless I get an official intimation, I cannot answer your question."

Raje frowned. The cold reception was worrying him.

There was a knock on the door. Raghunath *Punt* entered and said, "Highness, a man has arrived from Ram Singh's office. He says he was sent by his Master to meet you and has brought gifts. Would you wish to step out into the courtyard?"

Raje nodded and Raghunath *Punt* led them to the outer courtyard, where a middle-aged man, dressed in the usual garb of a clerk, awaited them, his head bowed humbly. He offered obeisance to *Raje* and proceeded to kneel in front of him. He then opened a cloth pouch and emptied its contents into his palm. He extended his hand to show *Raje* the offering of nine gold coins. Then he ceremoniously poured the coins over the Maratha King's feet.

Politely, the man said, "*Rajaji,* my name is Giridhar Lal, *Munshi* to *Kunwar* Ram Singh. My master has sent a thousand apologies for his inability to come in person to receive you. But he is held up on official guard duty at Salimgarh, and cannot move from there until dismissed by His Majesty himself."

Raje looked questioningly at Gazi Beg, who promptly intervened with an explanation. "Highness, Salimgarh is the official residence of the Emperor, inside Agra Fort. The officer on guard duty cannot leave unless allowed to do so by the Emperor himself."

In an instant *Raje* understood what was happening. News of their arrival had been conveyed to Agra Fort, and hence to Aurangzeb, who had then intentionally left Ram Singh on duty so he would be unable to receive *Raje*.

"Allow me to offer you these gifts from my Master, Your Highness." Girdhar Lal bowed again and turned to his men, who stepped forth with a plate. Girdhar offered it to *Raje*. "A formal *sar-o-pa,* Your Highness." Then a fine horse with silver trappings was produced and paraded before *Raje*. "A royal gift for a royal guest," Girdhar Lal said with an empty smile.

Raje accepted the gifts, his face hard and unsmiling. He instructed his men to offer Girdhar Lal two hundred rupees and a robe in return. The *Munshi* left with a promise that his Master would come as soon as he was free.

"*Rajaji,* if there is nothing more you require, we will leave you to rest," Tej Singh said. The men bowed and left.

Alone, father and son regarded each other. *Raje* affectionately caressed his son's cheek saying, "Scared?"

"Never!" Shambhu shot out his answer instantaneously.

"We will be in Agra Fort tomorrow, in Aurangzeb's *durbar*..."

"The Emperor does not scare me. I am scared of only one person in the whole world."

"And who is that?" *Raje* asked, intrigued.

Shambhu lowered his head to look at the floor. "My father."

Raje laughed and pulled him into an embrace, planting a kiss on his forehead. "Listen carefully, Shambhu. Keep your eyes and ears open tomorrow. This is your chance to see the Mughal capital, Aurangzeb's fort. Remember, he is our future enemy. Learn as much as you can while we are here."

Shambhu nodded. "I will, Father."

Early morning, 12 May 1666

The Maratha contingent was ready early the next day. They had been informed that the first *durbar*, held in the *Diwan-e-Aam*, would begin early in the second *prahar*. Shivaji *Raje* and Sambhaji *Raje* had to be present at this *durbar*, and that meant they had to leave early. *Raje* waited for the formal escort from the Emperor to arrive, to conduct him to Agra Fort. *Raje* was the Maratha King and now vassal of the Empire, but not an official *mansabdar*, hence not in the Emperor's service, except as the terms of the Purandar treaty dictated. He had come to Agra as a state guest, and as such, expected a royal welcome.

Girdhar Lal had said that Ram Singh would be there to escort him as well. As per protocol, *Raje* expected a high ranking officer as escort. Ram Singh, though the son of *Mirza Raja* Jai Singh, was a low ranking *mansabdar*, heading a contingent of two thousand horse. His presence would be at his father's behest, not the Emperor's.

As *Raje* sat lost in these and other disquietening thoughts, Raghunath *Punt* announced, "Highness, the *Munshi* has arrived with a small retinue of forty mounts."

Raje looked at him in disbelief. "No officials?"

"None, Your Highness."

"Ram Singh?"

Raghunath *Punt* shook his head. *Raje* let out a sigh and nodded for the *Munshi* to be shown in.

Girdhar Lal arrived, bowed courteously, and once again offered nine gold coins at *Raje*'s feet. "Our sincere apologies, Your Highness," he said. "*Kunwar* Ram Singh has not yet been relieved from Salimgarh. He has sent me to conduct Your Highess to Agra. He shall make haste to join your retinue as soon as he is off duty. But we cannot wait for him as we must reach His Majesty's *durbar* in time."

"Why has no other official from the court come?" *Raje* asked the *Munshi* pointedly.

"Your Highness, I am but an employee of *Kunwar* Ram Singh and know nothing of the Mughal offices."

Raje's face remained grim. He had been deliberately insulted. But now was not the time to fret and complain. The *durbar* would begin soon and he had to be there in time. He gave Raghunath *Punt* the nod to get his entourage moving.

SALIMGARH, AGRA, ABOUT THE SAME TIME

Kunwar Ram Singh, Prince of Amer, a principality of Rajputana, stood at attention outside the royal chamber of the Mughal Emperor Aurangzeb. He had been worried since the previous evening. Having received news of the arrival of Seevaji *Raja,* he had prepared to set out to receive him. But he had been summoned by the Emperor instead, and been ordered to stand guard at Salimgarh with his Rajputs. The order had confused Ram Singh. News of Seevaji *Raja*'s arrival had no doubt reached the Emperor, who knew that Ram Singh was to ride out to receive the Maratha. Why then had he been ordered to stand guard? Had the Emperor chosen to send some other officer to receive the *Raja*?

Much later, Ram Singh was informed that no one had been sent to greet Seevaji. Rather reluctantly, Ram Singh sent his own *Munshi* with presents to pacify the *Raja*. He knew only too well that a person of Seevaji *Raja*'s stature was usually received with fanfare and honours. His father, Jai Singh, had written to him many a times about this remarkable Maratha, who had dared stand alone against the might of the Empire. No ordinary man would have dared do so. He deserved respect as both a King and a great warrior, yet here he was in the Mughal capital, being deliberately insulted by the Emperor.

Ba-adab ba-mulahizah hoshiyaar... the *quorchi*'s shout brought Ram Singh back to the present and he stiffened to attention. Despite being at the Mughal court for over a year now, Ram Singh could never quite get used to being around the Emperor. He was terrified of the gaunt and stern monarch, and the absolute authority he commanded. Ordinarily, Ram Singh would have been in Amer, his fiefdom, but when his father had been appointed General of the Deccan campaign, he had been ordered to report to court. No doubt, Aurangzeb wanted to keep Ram Singh in the Mughal capital as surety against possible treachery by Jai Singh. After all, Jai Singh had been sent against another *kafir* chieftain. Auranzeb's ever suspicious mind did not permit him to trust Jai Singh completely.

The massive doors of the Emperor's bedchamber opened and he strode out confidently, regally attired for the auspicious *durbar*. He was followed by his personal attendants. The select assembly awaiting him boasted high ranking *mansabdars* and Princes, who bowed low in obeisance. In that power packed congregation, Ram Singh felt miserably out of place and stood behind everyone else, with his eyes to the ground.

Prince Muazzam moved forward and greeted his father. "Greetings to His Majesty on the auspicious occasion of his fiftieth birthday. May he live long for the welfare of his people!"

Ameen... Ameen... the others joined in.

"Age is but a number, *Shehzaade* Muazzam. One must count one's achievements, not years." Aurangzeb gave his son a typically cryptic response.

The grand *Wazir* Jafar Khan then moved forward. "Greetings, Your Majesty. May we be blessed by your ever gracious presence for another fifty years!"

Ameen... Ameen...

Aurangzeb nodded and began walking towards the *Diwan-e-Aam*, then stopped. "Jafar Khan, has Seeva arrived?" he asked his *Wazir*.

"*Jahanpanah*, the last news received was that the *kafir* is at the *serai* outside Agra. Ram Singh should know more."

Reluctantly, Ram Singh moved forward and bowed. Holding his hand in front of his mouth, as royal etiquette demanded, he said, "Your Majesty, I was on guard at Salimgarh and could not go to receive Seevaji *Raja* in person. I sent my *Munshi*. He should be conducting the *Raja* to Agra as we speak."

Aurangzeb smiled inwardly. Things had worked out perfectly. A mere *Munshi* had gone to receive the cursed *kafir*. "Ram Singh," he said, "you are dismissed from duty. Go forth to receive Seeva and conduct him to my presence. Take Mukhlis Khan with you."

"At once, Your Majesty!" Ram Singh bowed, retraced his steps and left. As he walked back to his station to summon Mukhlis Khan, he heaved a sigh of relief.

Outskirts of Agra

Shivaji *Raje*'s entourage snaked its way into Agra city. Leading the way was Girdhar Lal, and his men, followed by an elephant carrying *Raje's* saffron standard, then the Maratha cavalry and infantry. Shivaji *Raje* and Prince Shambhu followed, mounted on the finest horses with gold and silver trappings. The Maratha ministers followed, similarly mounted. The procession advanced slowly as Girdhar Lal lead them into Agra by a relatively less travelled road, via the Dahar-Ara garden.

At about the same time, *Kunwar* Ram Singh and Mukhlis Khan were on their way out of Agra via the main boulevard, hoping to encounter Shivaji *Raje* on his way, thus enabling them to conduct him into Agra. Accompanying them was a fairly large entourage, comprising caparisoned elephants, cavalry, mounted musicians and trumpeters. Ram Singh felt personally responsible for the lacunae in *Raje*'s welcome and had wanted to undo the damage to the extent he was able. From what he knew, the Maratha King was a fiercely self-respecting man, proud of his own achievements. He would expect to be welcomed appropriately as a state guest. But they had now crossed Firoza Garden, yet Shivaji *Raje*'s party was nowhere in sight. Ram Singh raised a hand, signalling his men to halt.

Mukhlis Khan caught up with him. "What is the matter, *Kunwar*?"

"Something's not right," Ram Singh said, rubbing his chin. "We should have caught up with Seevaji *Raja* by now."

The two officers looked at each other. In moments they both realized their folly. Girdhar Lal would have led the *Raja* by the alternate route. "The *Munshi* must have taken the road past Dahar-Ara garden."

"If we divert now, we will waste too much time," Mukhlis said.

Ram Singh nodded. Making up his mind, he signalled to a Rajput *hasham* behind him. "Dungar Mal, make haste and ride to the Dahar-Ara garden. Catch up with Girdhar Lal and the *Raja* and apprise them of the confusion. We have taken two different routes and hence missed each other. Instruct the *Munshi* to continue along the road and halt at Nurganj Garden. We shall retrace our steps and catch up with them there."

"*Rajaji, Kunwar* Ram Singh will be here soon." Girdhar Lal, having been informed of the route mix-up, was doing his best to pacify Shivaji *Raje,* who was visibly irritated. They had been on their way for over a *prahar* and still there was no sign of the welcoming party. Having arrived at Nurganj Garden, Girdhar Lal had cried a halt and they had been waiting for some time now.

Ram Singh's welcoming party arrived some time later. As the two officers halted some distance away from Shivaji *Raje,* Girdhar Lal pointed to a fair, well built Rajput seated on a chestnut horse adorned with precious trappings, and said, "*Rajaji,* that is *Kunwar* Ram Singh, Prince of Amer."

Raje nodded, but remained where he was, mounted on his horse. Girdhar Lal then rode up to Ram Singh and pointed in Shivaji *Raje*'s direction, saying, "*Kunwarji,* that is *Raja* Seevaji."

Ram Singh too, stayed put. For a few brief moments no one moved. Girdhar Lal, getting increasingly uneasy, said to his Master, "*Kunwarji,* Seevaji *Raja* wishes you to approach him."

Ram Singh nudged his horse with his foot and the animal trotted forward. Mukhlis Khan followed.

Ram Singh brought his mount to a halt near *Raje*'s and said, "*Rajaji,* welcome to Agra. You are here on His Majesty's invitation as a state guest, but you are also my personal guest. Your safety and comfort are my reponsibility."

Shivaji *Raje,* whose face had worn a grim expression since morning, smiled at his host. "*Kunwar* Ram Singh, you are like a brother to me. While I was in your father's camp, he treated me like a son, and my son as his grandchild. Your father is a remarkable man."

Ram Singh smiled. "Come *Rajaji,* let us embrace in friendship." The men moved their horses close and exchanged a formal embrace while still mounted.

Mukhlis Khan then moved forward. "*Rajaji,* we should proceed towards Agra now. We must be at the *durbar* on time."

"That we must," *Raje* agreed. Pointing to the line of elephants he added, "*Bhaiji,* leave the elephants behind. They will slow our progress unnecessarily."

Within moments, Ram Singh's men turned around and began marching toward Agra, followed by their guests and the rest of the entourage.

Agra Fort, at the same time

The courtyard outside the *Diwan-e-Aam* had been covered with a massive decorative canopy, held up by numerous poles wrapped in gold and silver cloth. Hundreds of men stood at attention, dressed splendidly for the occasion. There were Princes and *Umraos,* nobles of every rank, and state guests from vassal fiefdoms. Ladies of the *zenana* viewed the proceedings from behind the *jali* windows above the Emperor's throne.

In the centre of the courtyard, a large balance had been erected, with gold plates on either side. In one sat the master of all he surveyed – Emperor Aurangzeb *Alamgir*. In the other, were stacks of gold and silver coin. As the court attendant added another bag of coins to the plate, the balance tipped, elevating the Emperor into the air. Immediately the assembly broke into applause and cries of *Mubarik* and *Subhan Allah* filled the air.

The Emperor alighted from the scales and left the courtyard. The assembled men made their way into the pillared audience hall, adorned with exquisite curtains, tapestries, chandeliers and strings of pearls. They quickly took up their designated positions, according to rank. The Princes and the *Wazir* stood in front, closest to the throne. Then came the *Umraos,* the nobles of highest rank. The others stood in rows behind. With eyes to the floor, they waited the arrival of their Lord and Master.

Ram Singh's camp, Agra

Shivaji *Raje's* entourage had been led to a secluded place. The *Kunwar* alighted and led *Raje* into a modest building. Inside, an audience hall had been prepared to welcome an important guest. Decorative jars of wine and water stood beside comfortable *baithaks*. Plates of fruit and sweets had been laid out.

"Welcome *Rajaji*," Ram Singh said with a slight bow as he led *Raje* to a *baithak*. "Come, Prince." He ushered in Shambhu as well. As soon as his guests were settled, he ordered his servants to ceremoniously wash their feet in rose water.

Raje's diplomats and officers were ushered in too and everyone was offered refreshments while a group of musicians, seated in a corner of the hall, began playing soothing music.

Shivaji *Raje* smiled politely as he accepted a delicacy from the plate offered to him. Turning to Ram Singh, he inquired, "*Bhaiji*, where have you brought me?"

"*Rajaji*, I deeply regret the deficiency in your welcome, and humbly beg your pardon. Please understand that I was helpless. This is my personal residence in Agra. I brought you and the Prince here to welcome you in the customary manner."

Raje laughed. "*Bhaiji*, be assured that I have no ill feeling towards you. But we should not delay here. We must reach the court in good time."

Ram Singh had long realized they would be late for the *durbar*. He had been instructed to conduct Seevaji *Raja* to court on time, which meant before the arrival of the Emperor. But that could not happen now. They would certainly be late and in all probability miss the *durbar* at the *Diwan-e-Aam*.

Some time later, the men rose and prepared to leave for Agra Fort.

...Abul Muzaffar Muhi-ud-din Mohammed, Aurangzeb Alamgir, Padishah-e-Gazi... the *quorchi* shouted, announcing the arrival of the Emperor. The assembly of the most powerful men in the Empire bowed and offered obeisance as Aurangzeb, regally dressed, took his place on the elevated throne. The ceremonial turban on his head sparkled with rubies and diamonds. A heavy gold ring, engraved with an image of a tiger and encrusted with rubies, adorned

his right hand. It was the ring of Timur, his legendary ancestor. Aurangzeb's face looked much younger than his fifty years; his jaw firm and resolute, his piercing eyes gazing down upon those who bowed to him. At his side was his eagle-hilted, engraved sword, another family hierloom

After his father, the ex-Emperor Shah Jahan's death four months earlier, Aurangzeb had settled at Agra Fort and had ordered his offices and treasuries to be shifted there. Agra had thus become the new capital of the Mughal Empire. But now, as he sat on his throne on the day of the *durbar*, Aurangzeb experienced disquiet. Jai Singh had subdued the troublesome Maratha, Seeva, and the southern boundary of his Empire promised to be quiet. Jai Singh had sent Seeva to Agra and the infidel would be produced before him at this very *durbar*. Seeva would certainly not dare create trouble here in the heart of the realm. Yet, the stories he had heard said Seeva could leap across a distance of several *guz!* Aurangzeb gripped the hilt of his sword.

The *Wazir,* Jafar Khan, conducted the proceedings of the special *durbar*. The Princes and prominent nobles presented the Emperor with expensive gifts and received gifts in return. New appointments were made, promotions and high titles granted in commemoration of this auspicious day. All those present prayed to the Almighty for the long life of the Emperor.

Towards the end of the second *prahar*, the *durbar* session concluded. As Aurangzeb left the hall, he summoned the *durbar* attendant and asked, "Why has Seeva not reached the court?"

"I have no news yet, Your Majesty," the man replied.

Aurangzeb silently cursed Ram Singh. The man was a fool.

At about the same time as Aurangzeb left the *Diwan-e-Aam,* a platoon of horses trotted up the sloping wooden drawbridge across the wide moat around Agra Fort, and arrived at its massive western gate. Ram Singh, his attendants, and Mukhlis Khan, dismounted and approached the sentries, informing them the Maratha King, Seevaji *Raja,* had arrived for royal audience, on direct orders of the Emperor. The gates were opened. The guests left their horses behind and entered on foot.

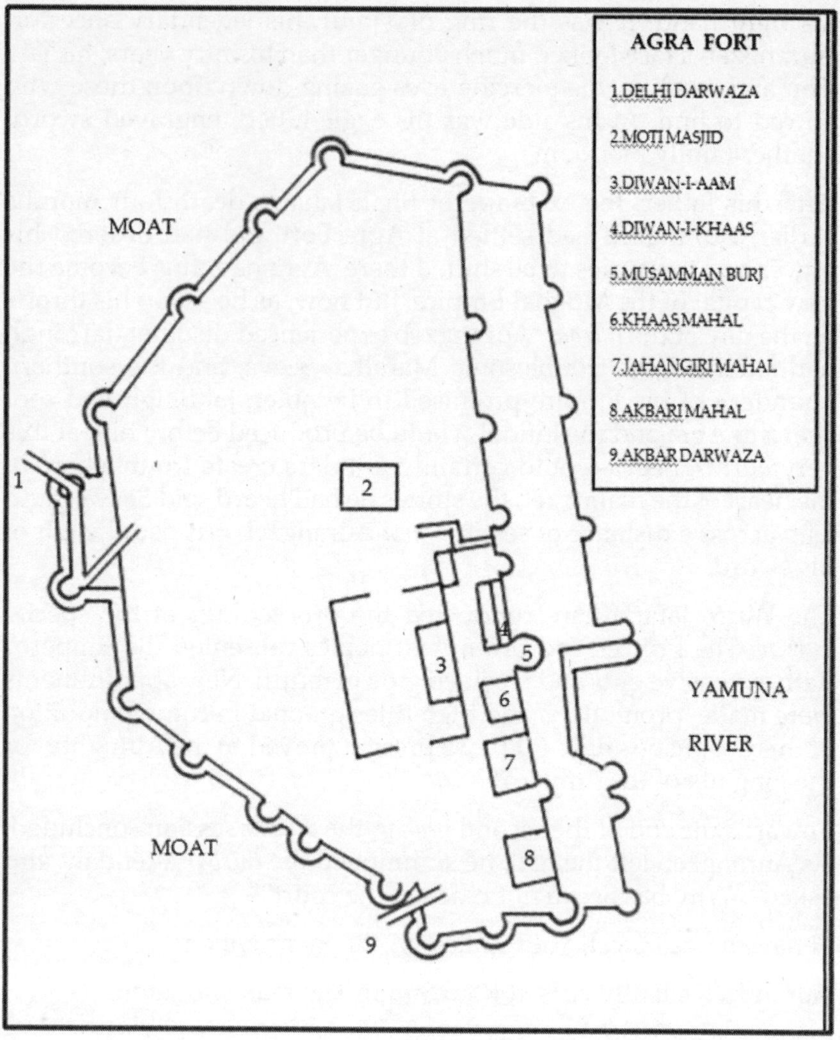

For the first time ever, Shivaji *Raje* stepped into Aurangzeb's world. With Shambhu beside him, he followed Ram Singh and his men through two battlemented gateways and then up a paved walkway leading to a wide courtyard, lined by neatly trimmed lawns and flower beds. *Raje* halted a moment and looked around to marvel at the impregnable gates he had just traversed. Whoever had constructed them was a genius, he thought. The inclined ramp would make it difficult even for elephants to break through the outer gate. Even if they did, the approach to the inner gate was at an angle that made charging the inner gate difficult. *Raje* looked around; as far as his eye could see, stretched massive ramparts of red sandstone.

"*Rajaji,*" Ram Singh prompted him gently, "we must hurry to reach the *durbar*."

Shivaji Raje and Shambhu quickened their pace.

By now, the special session in the *Diwan-e-Khaas* had commenced. As the name suggested, this session was reserved for ranking officers and special dignitaries. The Princes and the *Wazir* were, of course, present. The Emperor sat on a special throne studded with diamonds, rubies, topazes and other precious stones. Over the sparkling golden throne was an impressive canopy, supported by carved gold pillars. A fenestrated gold railing ran along the base of the throne. Festooned across the arches on either side and behind the throne, hung exquisite silk curtains. The throne itself was placed on a recessed balcony of white marble, decorated with inlays of precious stones, at a higher level than the floor of the hall, thus placing the Emperor above everyone else. The Emperor sat cross-legged on a plush *baithak* of embroidered silk, leaning against bolsters.

The *Diwan-e-Khaas* was a smaller hall compared to the *Diwan-e-Aam,* but much more splendidly decorated. The walls, pillars and arches had exquisite carvings, painted in gold and silver and inlaid with gems. Expensive curtains, tapestries and hangings adorned the walls, while the pillars were hung with gold brocade. Flowered satin canopies were raised over the entire hall, fastened with silken cords from which were suspended tassels of silk and gold. The floor was covered in thick, soft carpet. The splendour was enough to dazzle the most premier of the Emperor's nobles and the most royal of his guests and dignitaries.

The Princes stood on the throne balcony, on either side of the Emperor. The *Wazir,* Jafar Khan, stood below the balcony, closest to it. The imperial standard bearers too, stood below the balcony, carrying the royal ensigns of a fish, a dragon, a lion, a pair of scales, and a yak's tail. On either side of the balcony, and behind the throne, stood the Emperor's personal bodyguard, armed with unsheathed swords. The courtiers stood in rows, heads bowed, their eyes to the ground. Those who stood in the front ranks were the *amirs* and *umraos*, officers of the high rank.

As the court proceedings began, the *quorchi* appeared to one side of the throne and whispered, "Your Majesty, I have received news that Seevji *Raja* has arrived in the fort."

Aurangzeb nodded slightly and raised his hand, indicating that he be summoned. The Emperor touched his sword, the *Alamgir*.

Shivaji *Raje* and Shambhu followed Ram Singh across a great pillared hall, now empty. Ram Singh turned to whisper, "*Rajaji*, this is the *Diwan-e-Aam*, where the first *durbar* was held. We missed it. The second *durbar* is being held at the *Diwan-e-Khaas*, where we shall go now."

As they moved east, *Raje* caught sight of another, smaller pillared hall. It had a flat roof with four *chhatris* in the corners. Five arched pillars marked the front face of the hall, which appeared to be packed with men.

Ram Singh stopped and turned to *Raje*. He appeared nervous, as if he had forgotten to do something important. "*Rajaji*, I have failed to inform you of the proper court etiquette, and there is not much time for instruction now. The Emperor has been informed of your arrival and we are expected."

Raje smiled reassuringly. "Do not worry, *Bhaiji*. I will not embarass you."

"*Rajaji*, Prince Sambhaji, please listen! When in the Emperor's presence, look at the floor. Do not raise your eyes to him. *Nazar bar qadam*...do you understand? When you speak to him, hold your hand in front of your mouth like this..." He demonstrated the proper way to address the Emperor. "And yes..." he slapped his forehead in panic, "when presented to him, offer the *sijda*."

"What is that?" *Raje* asked.

"You must kneel and kiss the ground in front of His Majesty."

"I will do no such thing, *Bhaiji*!" *Raje* retorted angrily.

Ram Singh's eyes widened in horror. "*Rajaji*, you must! It is compulsory court etiquette."

Raje shook his head firmly. "I will offer a formal obeisance while standing, but that's it. I will not kneel, nor will my son."

"*Rajaji,* listen to me..." Ram Singh pleaded, but stopped as they caught sight of the *quorchi* walking their way.

"*Kunwar* Ram Singh, His Majesty awaits Seevaji *Raja*. Pray make haste."

"Yes, yes…" Ram Singh was quite flustered by now, as he realised his own dual responsibility. Not only had his father entrusted him with Shivaji *Raje*'s security, but he also had the added responsibility of ensuring the Maratha King obeyed all Mughal customs and etiquette, and behaved in court.

The party moved again, this time with the *quorchi* in the lead. Uniformed armed guards stood at every point of entry into the hall. Shivaji *Raje* and Sambhaji *Raje* were asked to wait outside the hall, at the central entry arch.

The *quorchi* rushed up to the throne, bowing as he did, and informed the Emperor, "Seevaji *Raja*!" To that, Aurangzeb nodded. The *quorchi* signalled to Ram Singh to bring the guests forward.

Aurangzeb sat calmly on the throne, turning beads in his right hand. The silence in the *durbar* was palpable. The only sound was the muffled flutter of the *punkahs,* as the attendants tirelessly fanned the sovereign. The *durbar* proceedings had been called to a halt as everyone waited for the arrival of the most notorious rebel in the history of the Empire.

Aurangzeb had wanted Seeva to be presented at the *Diwan-e-Aam,* but somehow, Ram Singh had bungled things. He had arrived late and Seeva was being brought into the *khaas durbar*. The list of Seeva's crimes was long... the looting of Junnar and Ahmednagar, the defeats of Kartalab Khan and Namdar Khan, the night raid on Shaista Khan, and above all, the demeaning sack of Surat! *His* Surat! Aurangzeb boiled with inner rage when he thought about it. He had wanted the *kafir* dead and had hoped Jai Singh would do the job for him. But the Rajput seemed to have developed a strange fondness for the Maratha. He had let Seeva return alive from his camp, much to Aurangzeb's displeasure. So Aurangzeb had decided to summon Seeva to Agra, to finish what Jai Singh had not.

The courtiers too, waited with a mix of curiosity and excitement, for the man who had so blatantly challenged the Emperor's authority.

They had heard many tales of the *kafir*... that he was a sorcerer, a magician. Now they would see the man himself.

Aurangzeb caught sight of a small party entering the hall under the central arch. In the lead was Ram Singh, who bowed to the ground and kissed the floor. Aurangzeb smiled slightly. It was only right the *kafirs* kissed the ground the Emperor walked upon. That was their rightful place. But he wasn't really interested in Ram Singh. The Rajput and his father were his servants. He wanted Seeva to do the same. He waited.

Shivaji *Raje* walked forward, Shambhu beside him. But neither was his head bowed, nor were his eyes on the ground. Back straight and head held high, he looked the Emperor in the eye.

Ram Singh, head still bowed, glanced at his guest and was horrified to see Shivaji *Raje* upright, looking at the Emperor! "*Rajaji*, bow your head! Look down!" he hissed urgently.

Raje, however, was not looking at him. In that moment, his mind went back twenty-five years, when, as a twelve-year-old, he had refused to bow to the Adilshah. The scene was being repeated.

Kneel now! commanded Aurangzeb in his mind. But Seeva did not kneel, and neither did his son. Aurangzeb's smile vanished as he saw the *kafir* walk up to him, his head held high, his eyes gazing directly into his own. *Bow your head, kafir*! Aurangzeb commanded again in his mind.

Seeva offered obeisance three times, still standing. Shambhu emulated his father. As *Raje* straightened, his eyes locked with those of the Emperor. The greatest adversaries in the land faced each other. Aurangzeb's blazing eyes locked on Seeva's. There was murderous rage in theEmperor's gaze; a cold, calm defiance in the Maratha's. Had it been anyone else, even an Imperial Prince or the Grand *Wazir* himself, they would have trembled in fear, for they well knew the Emperor's merciless judgements. The Emperor wanted the rebel to submit, kneel, prostrate, kiss the ground before him. Yet the rebel stood his ground and stared back at the Emperor! Leisurely, he summoned Ram Singh's attendants, who carried in gifts. *Raje* graciously offered these to the Emperor.

Aurangzeb was boiling with rage, but maintained a stoic demeanour. Raising his right hand slightly, he acknowledged the gifts, which were then carried away. Young Sambhaji then offered his gifts to the

Emperor, who accepted them with an almost imperceptible gesture.

"Akil!" Aurangzeb summoned a courtier.

Akil Khan scrambled up to the throne balcony and knelt beside the throne with bowed head. Aurangzeb whispered something to him. Akil nodded, descended from the balcony and walked up to Shivaji *Raje*.

"Come *Rajaji*," he said courteously. "You must now stand with the nobles while the *durbar* proceeds with business."

Akil and Ram Singh retraced their steps with heads bowed. Shivaji *Raje* and Sambhaji did the same, their heads held high.

Akil Khan led the guests to a designated spot in the fourth row of courtiers. As Shivaji *Raje* took his place with Shambhu by his side, his mind was in turmoil. He had expected a more gracious welcome in Aurangzeb's court. Jai Singh had sent him here to cement his newly established alliance with the Mughals. Jai Singh had also promised him Aurangzeb's favour and glory at court. He had been made to believe he could hope to command the Mughal Deccan province. But in reality, he had been slighted since his arrival outside Agra. There had been no royal welcome; he had been made to stay in a *serai;* a clerk had been sent to receive him. At court, Aurangzeb had not spoken a word to him and now he had been made to stand in the fourth row of courtiers.

Raje's legendary temper rose. He looked around for Ram Singh. He found the Rajput standing three rows behind him. *Raje* knew Ram Singh held the rank of a two thousand *mansabdar*. That meant that he himself had been made to stand amongst those who held five thousand horse rank. When had he become Aurangzeb's *mansabdar,* he wondered? *Raje* considered himself a state guest, who had come to the *durbar* on the invitation of the Emperor himself. To his own people, Shivaji *Raje* was a King, which meant he should be given the status and welcome due a royal guest. Yet, Aurangzeb had deliberately and repeatedly insulted him.

"Akil!" Aurangzeb's deep voice echoed in the pillared hall. "The *khilats*!"

Akil Khan instructed the court attendants to bring forth the royal robes of honour. Each attendant would approach the throne with the *khilat* placed on a gold plate. He would raise the plate to the Emperor who would then raise his hand slightly in a symbolic gesture. Akil Khan would then guide the attendant to the recepient, who was expected to touch the plate in acceptance and bow to the Emperor.

The *khilats* went to the Princes, the *Wazir*, and some high ranking *mansabdars*. Increasingly restless and agitated, Shivaji *Raje* waited in his place. The last attendant with a *khilat* plate walked in his direction, but the *khilat* went to the *mansabdar* who stood directly in front of him. The noble accepted the *khilat*, bowed to the Emperor, and then, turning slightly, flashed *Raje* a mocking smile.

This final insult was impossible to bear for the proud Shivaji *Raje*. The *khilat* too, had been denied him. He could no longer take the slights dealt him by the Mughal. His anger boiled over and in an agitated voice, he called out to his host, "Ram Singh!"

The call broke the soft silence of the court and stunned everyone. Ram Singh, who had been on tenterhooks ever since his royal guest had refused to prostrate himself before the Emperor, nearly jumped when he heard his name called.

"Ram Singh!" *Raje* called louder this time.

Ram Singh, sweating and trembling in fear, shuffled up to *Raje* and whispered, "*Rajaji*, please speak in whispers. No one is allowed to speak loudly in court. You are insulting His Majesty!" Ram Singh was acutely aware that Seevaji *Raja* had completely disregarded court etiquettes till now. He had not just refused to offer *sijda*, but had not even bowed his head to the Emperor. In a place where even a Prince or the *Vizier* never raised their heads, this Maratha had looked straight at the Emperor! And now he had broken established decorum by raising his voice when none was allowed to speak unless permitted to by the Emperor.

"Ram Singh, who stands ahead of me?" *Raje* asked tersely.

"*Rajaji*, please speak in whispers. His Majesty will be offended. In front of you stands *Maharaja* Jaswant Singh, King of Jodhpur."

"Jaswant Singh?" *Raje's* voice rose on hearing the name. "The man who fled the battle at Fort Kondhana? He tasted defeat at the hands of my foot soldiers, yet I am asked to stand behind him?"

"*Rajaji*, pray calm down! Speak softly. The Emperor will be angered by such behaviour!" Ram Singh realised the situation had gone out of control. The Emperor was sure to have heard this loud tirade from the Maratha and would most certainly lose his own temper soon. And once he did, there was no telling what he would do. Seevaji *Raja* would be punished, and so would he. Ram Singh had been caught in a storm against his own wishes. At that moment, he fervently wished his father had not sent Seevaji *Raja* to Agra at all.

"Do not ask me to calm down, *Bhaiji!* Ever since I arrived in Agra, I have been subjected to insults. I was put up in a *serai,* and who was sent to welcome me? A *munshi*! And here, in court today, your Emperor does not even speak to me, or even offer me the basic respect due a state guest. Since when did I become a Mughal *mansabdar*? Why am I made to stand in this back row?" *Raje* was shaking with rage now, his face flushed and eyes bloodshot. Little Shambhu, sensing his father's anguish at being insulted, stood by his side, holding his hand tightly.

"*Rajaji,* pray calm down..."

"*Bhaiji,* both your father and your Emperor are aware of my capability, yet I have been insulted thus! I came here as a guest, as the King of my people. I have not accepted Mughal service. I signed a treaty with your father. A treaty! I expect to be treated as an equal!"

"Ram Singh!" Aurangzeb's voice boomed.

Ram Singh once again jumped out of his skin. He hurried up to the throne, bowing repeatedly.

"What is the matter, Ram Singh? What has angered Seeva?"

"Your Majesty, Seevaji *Raja* is displeased as he was not awarded a *khilat,*" Ram Singh stammered. "May I beg forgiveness on his behalf? The *Raja* is not accustomed to formal court etiquette."

Aurangzeb smiled disdainfully, then called out to Akil Khan. "Akil, award *khilat* to Seeva." Akil bowed and left to make arrangements for another robe of honour. "Ram Singh," Aurangzeb continued, "bring Seeva to my presence."

Ram Singh retraced his steps and joined Shivaji *Raje* in the ranks. "*Rajaji,* the Emperor has ordered you to approach him. Pray follow me."

"I refuse to stand in front of him again," *Raje* said bluntly.

"Seevaji *Raja,* no one *refuses* the Emperor!" Ram Singh was horrified.

"I just did, *Bhaiji.* I prefer death to such insult. The Emperor may kill me if he so wishes, but I will not stand in front of him again."

There was a buzz as the courtiers murmured in astonishment at this senseless talk. How could anyone disregard the rules of the *durbar*? No one ever looked into the Emperor's eyes. How could anyone be so disrespectful, so uncouth? How could anyone be so...*brave*?

Abruptly, *Raje* decided to leave the *durbar*. He walked through the ranks till he emerged from amongst the nobles who still stood in abject servility, throwing amazed looks at him.

"*Rajaji,*" Ram Singh pleaded once again, trying to restrain him, but *Raje* shrugged him off. He looked toward the throne one last time. Aurangzeb's furious eyes were still locked on his.

Raje then did the unthinkable. As the entire assembly looked on in shock, he turned his back to the throne and strode away, followed by his son.

Shivaji *Raje* had left the *Diwan-i-Khaas,* but he stopped just outside, near a railing, shaking with rage.

Shambhu held out a hand, asking, "Father are you alright?" He too, realised they had been insulted at court and agreed with his father's decision to leave.

Ram Singh rushed up to them, looking pale. "*Rajaji*! What have you done? You turned your back to His Majesty!" Ram Singh could not believe what he had just seen.

Raje said nothing. In a fit of rage he had done the unthinkable. Only time would tell how the Emperor would react.

In the *durbar,* the attendant had arrived with the *khilat,* and stood awaiting the Emperor's orders.

"Akil, present Seeva with the *khilat,*" he said. "Bring him back in front of me."

Akil bowed and left with the attendant in tow. When they arrived outside, they found the Maratha King sitting on a railing, his son by his side and Ram Singh pleading with him.

"Seevaji *Raja,*" Akil said. "His Majesty has sent this *khilat* for you. Accept the honour and return to the *durbar*. His Majesty has ordered you back."

"I have said this before and I say it again now, I will not stand in front of the Emperor again. I will not go back!" *Raje* declared with finality. "As for this *khilat*, I never aspired to it. I award such gifts to my officers every day. I refuse to accept His Majesty's robe of honour."

Akil was taken aback, but refrained from saying anything. He merely nodded and retraced his steps to the *durbar*. Back in front of the Emperor, he said, "Your Majesty, Seevaji *Raja* will not return. He is like a wild beast, out of control."

Aurangzeb cursed the Maratha under his breath, but said calmly, "Tell Ram Singh to take him away and pacify him. He shall be produced in court again when I order so."

Ram Singh heaved a sigh of relief when he was told of the order. He had no heart left to stand in front of the Emperor again and explain why Seevaji *Raja* refused to return to court! "Come *Rajaji,*" he said to Shivaji *Raje*, "the Emperor has excused you from the *durbar*. Let us go back to my camp. You can rest there."

Back at Ram Singh's residence, Shivaji *Raje* quietly contemplated the day's events. The visit to Aurangzeb's court had not gone well. He had come here to win the Mughal's approval and gain further grants, troops and supplies in the Deccan, with a view to overthrowing Adilshahi. He was confident that given support, he could achieve what Jai Singh had failed to do. Jai Singh's magnanimous assurances had also given him the impression that Aurangzeb was in principle agreeable to such support being given to him. But the recent events had made it quite clear to *Raje*'s shrewd mind that Aurangzeb had invited him to court merely to insult him in front of his courtiers; to show him that his place was at the Emperor's feet! The fact that *Raje* had disregarded court protocol and insulted the Emperor, would weigh against him. *Raje* was aware that Aurangzeb was an unpredictable person, and that he was at his mercy in Agra.

Ram Singh sat across from *Raje*, wondering how he was supposed to talk some sense into this brash yet exceedingly brave Maratha.

He looked at Shivaji *Raje* in wondrous amazement. This small framed man had done what everyone else considered unthinkable. He had travelled nearly four hundred and fifty *kos* from his own home, to the Mughal court, and stood at the Emperor's mercy. Yet he would not bow his head or suffer insults. In Aurangzeb's *durbar*, this man had looked the Emperor in the eye and even turned his back on him, both unpardonable acts! The Emperor would doubtless be fuming and who could tell what he would do in retribution?

Raje's diplomats and attendants, who had not been allowed in court, rejoined him when he emerged. They were then apprised of events. Raghunath *Punt* and Tryambak *Punt* were instantly concerned. Being diplomats, they were used to obeying court customs, bowing and prostrating before sovereigns, and agreeing to every extravagant wish of these monarchs. Pleasing them meant half their work done. But they could not expect their fiercely proud King to do the same...and he hadn't. They recognised they were not just in trouble, but in grave danger now.

"*Rajaji,* you should not have lost your temper in court," Ram Singh broke the uneasy silence. "The Emperor will be extremely displeased. You should have at least gone back in front of him and accepted the *khilat*."

Raje gave him a sardonic laugh. "*Bhaiji,* why speak to me about my behaviour in court? Your Emperor does not understand the basic etiquette of welcoming a state guest!"

"*Rajaji,* you have unwittingly placed your own, and your son's life, in danger. Heed my advice, come back to court with me and apologise to His Majesty," Ram Singh pleaded.

Raje shook his head. "I will not go back, *Bhaiji*. Death beckons me, it seems. The Emperor may kill me, but I will not bow to him."

Ram Singh turned away in frustration.

"But I will send my son to court. You may take him with you, *Bhaiji*. He will bow to His Majesty as a Mughal *mansabdar*."

Raghunath *Punt* stood by quietly. His King had, in a fit of rage, committed treason in Aurangzeb's court. *What have you done my King?* he wondered.

After Shivaji *Raje*'s departure from the *durbar*, Jaffar Khan, the *Wazir,* had quietened the buzzing assembly and made an attempt to proceed with court business. But Aurangzeb was too disturbed by what had occurred. He could not get his mind off Seeva. Unable to concentrate, he raised his hand saying, "*Takhliya,*" thus signalling an end to the *durbar*. He rose from his throne as everyone bowed low, and left the throne balcony by a door at the rear, followed by the *quorchi*.

Behind the *jali* windows, the leading ladies of the Emperor's harem fumed. Jahanara *begum,* the Emperor's sister, was worried by this open show of insubordination by the Maratha rat. If more vassal chieftains of the Empire behaved like Seeva, it could augur trouble. She thought her brother should order Seeva's beheading. Ever since the *kafir* had raided Surat, her personal income, which came from the city's octroi collection, had ceased completely. She wanted to see Seeva punished.

Aurangzeb strode out of the *Diwan-e-Khaas* and entered a much smaller chamber called the *Ghusalkhana,* which was really an antechamber leading to the harem quarters. His chief courtiers followed him. This chamber was reserved for private discussions. Only a chosen few were allowed entry.

Aurangzeb sat down on a comfortable *baithak*. He was fuming within but maintained a calm face to show his courtiers that Seeva's antics in court were too insignificant to be taken notice of. But the assembled men were less restrained as they tried to instigate their ruler against the Maratha rebel. Aurangzeb's *Wazir* Jafar Khan, Prince Muazzam, the *Mir Bakshi* Mohammed Amin, and *Maharaja* Jaswant Singh were amongst those assembled.

Jafar Khan spoke first. "That *kafir* Seeva has grossly misbehaved in court and must be punished."

"Seeva has displayed such rudeness and contumacy in court," Muazzam said, "that the news will spread across the Empire and encourage others to misbehave in front of His Majesty."

Jaswant Singh was equally furious. After the fiasco of Shaista Khan's campaign, he had wanted to show some mettle by capturing Fort Kondhana. But the Maratha defenders had put paid to all his efforts. He had been compelled to abandon the siege, which had stretched on for many months and cost them heavily. In court, Shivaji *Raje* had insulted him by reminding him of that defeat.

"He is a mere *bhumia,* yet he dared to behave in such an uncouth manner in court," Jaswant Singh said, feeling aggrieved. "If His Majesty wishes to forgive him, he may do so, but I think Seevaji must be punished!"

The *Mir Bakshi,* Mohammed Amin, stood quietly. A thinking diplomat, he realised that punishing Seeva would be a tricky proposition for the Emperor. For one, he had come here with the assurance of no less a noble than *Mirza Raja* Jai Singh. The Emperor would think twice before upsetting Jai Singh. Secondly, Jai Singh had openly declared that Ram Singh was responsible for Seeva's security, which meant the Rajput Prince would surely stand in the way if the Emperor tried to punish Seeva. Strong headed obstinates, these Rajputs were. To keep a promise they would even do away with their own lives.

The assembly in the *Ghusalkhana* could discuss nothing but Shivaji *Raje*. Finally Aurangzeb, still quiet, rose and left the chamber.

In the harem, it was no different. The ladies could not stop talking about the rebel's atrocious behaviour in court. Jahanara *begum* encouraged her brother to punish Seeva severely, saying, "Seeva plundered Surat, carried away our uncle's daughter, and has now insulted you in your own *durbar*. Yet you let him live! How far is this policy advisable?"

Aurangzeb looked at her. "I am aware of the facts, my sister. But I do not agree with you that Seeva abducted Shaista Khan's daughter. I have said so earlier. He is not that kind of man. Seeva is different from other rebels."

Jahanara jerked her head in irritation. "Deal with Seeva *now,* Aurangzeb," she said. "You may not get another chance!"

Aurangzeb refrained from saying anything. He too realised, like his *Mir Bakshi,* that punishing Seeva would not be easy. He would die of course, but it would have to be thought through. He needed to be alone. Lifting his hand, he dismissed the women.

Later, as he sat in his bedchamber, the one man he relied upon to do his dirty work, stood before him. "Hussain," Aurangzeb said to his chief spy, "post your men around Seeva's camp. Keep an eye on him. Do not let him out of your sight till I decide how to kill him."

"Understood, Your Majesty!" Hussain replied.

"And keep an eye on Ram Singh as well!" the Emperor added as an afterthought.

9
THE EAGLE HAS FLOWN

DIWAN-E-AAM, AGRA FORT, EVENING OF 13 MAY 1666

The evening *durbar* was in progress when the *quorchi* approached the throne and said, "Your Majesty, *Kunwar* Ram Singh has arrived with Seevaji's son, for an audience."

Aurangzeb nodded permission. Ram Singh approached the throne, offered a formal *sijda* and presented Sambhaji *Raje* to the Emperor. Sambhaji offered obeisance, but did not kneel, as he had been instructed to do by his father. As he straightened, he looked at the Emperor.

Aurangzeb smiled slightly at the young boy standing with his head held high. Like father, like son, he thought. The son has the same fire in his eyes. "Ram Singh, has Seeva come with you today?" he asked.

"No, Your Majesty. Seevaji *Raja* has taken ill. He had fever this morning. I will bring him to court when he is better."

Aurangzeb knew this was a lie but he let the *Kunwar* be. Raising his hand, he summoned Akil Khan. "Akil, present Seeva's son with a *sar-o-pa* and gifts. He seems to be a brave lad." Aurangzeb smiled at Sambhaji. "Sambha Bhosale, you are a Mughal *mansabdar*. Conduct yourself well and you may receive further favours from us."

The *quorchi* appeared with gifts, which included a bejewelled dagger and a pearl necklace. Aurangzeb raised his hand and waved towards the lad. The gifts were offered to Sambhaji, who touched the plates and bowed in acceptance, keeping his eyes fixed on Aurangzeb.

The Emperor was amazed. Never before had he seen a nine-year-old so composed, so fearless!

Ram Singh's residence, the same evening

Ram Singh's informant stood in front of him in his chamber. Both men were grim faced. The man had just brought information that the Emperor had ordered Seevaji and Sambhaji to be removed to Rad-andaz Khan's mansion in Agra. Ram Singh was worried. This meant, without doubt, that the Emperor had finally decided to execute Seevaji. Rad-andaz Khan was the Commandant of Agra Fort. His reckless bravery was matched only by his cruelty. Besides, he was a diehard faithful of the Emperor. His Majesty could not have chosen a better man to eliminate Seevaji. Deep in the bowels of his massive mansion, Rad-andaz Khan would no doubt torture the Maratha, his son, and his officers, before ending their lives. Ram Singh shuddered at the thought. Seevaji *Raja*'s safety was his responsibility and he could, under no circumstances, allow anyone to lay hands upon the Maratha while he lived. He rose and said to his man, "I will visit the *Mir Bakshi*. He is the only sensible man around His Majesty."

Later that evening, Ram Singh sat in Mohammed Amin's house. "I have heard that His Majesty has ordered Seevaji and his son to be taken to Rad-andaz Khan's mansion. Is this true, *Mir Bakshi sahib*?" he asked, knowing it to be true.

Mohammed Amin looked at his guest uncomfortably and nodded. Both knew what the order meant.

"Then please request His Majesty to execute me before he touches the *Raja*," Ram Singh declared.

Mohammed Amin was taken aback. Of all the things he had expected the Rajput to do, this was the most surprising. He knew the hidden meaning behind the supposed request. What Ram Singh actually meant was that he would not allow anyone to touch Seevaji as long as he himself lived.

"*Kunwarji*, have you considered what you have said?" the *Mir Bakshi* asked.

"Yes, I have. My father sent Seevaji *Raja* to Agra with an assurance of safety, under my security. It is a Rajput's promise, and it shall be kept at all cost. Now, tell me *Mir Bakshi sahib*, will you take my plea to the Emperor?"

Mohammed Amin sensed the Rajput Prince's determination and nodded quietly. Somehow, he would have to convince the Emperor to change his mind.

The *Mir Bakshi* requested a private meeting with the Emperor to discuss a matter of importance. His request was granted the next day, and at the appointed hour, he presented himself to his sovereign.

"Your Majesty, Ram Singh will not stand down if we try to grab Seeva's person. Further, if the other Rajput chieftains in Agra join him with their contingents, it could turn into an ugly situation. We will overpower them, but it would cause much bloodshed." Mohammed Amin analysed the situation for the Emperor.

Aurangzeb was quiet for a while. He realized Mohammed Amin was right. He would have to rescind his order. Suddenly, a thought struck him and he said, "Ask Ram Singh if he is ready to stand surety for Seeva. If Seeva attempts any mischief or tries to leave without permission, Ram Singh will be held responsible. He must sign a bond to that effect."

The *Mir Bakshi* left to convey the Emperor's order to Ram Singh.

Ram Singh's residence, evening of 14 May 1666

Ram Singh sat in conference with Shivaji *Raje* and his diplomats, Raghunath *Punt* and Tryambak *Punt*. Also present were Ram Singh's men, Ballu Sah and Maha Singh Shekawat. Tej Singh, Jai Singh's man, who had accompanied *Raje* to Agra, was present too.

Raje, who had been apprised of the events of the previous day, realized that Ram Singh had intervened to somehow convince Aurangzeb to take back an order to kill them. He looked affectionately at the Rajput Prince, whom he had addressed as 'brother' from the day they had met. Whatever his capabilities and rank in the Mughal administration, there was no mistaking Ram Singh's honest intentions and genuine concern for *Raje*'s safety.

"*Bhaiji*," *Raje* said, "I regret having put you in a difficult position with the Emperor but I am dismayed and disillusioned by your father. He gave me false promises. The Emperor never meant to give me any further grants beyond what has been stated in the Purandar treaty. *Mirzaji* should never have sent me here!"

Privately, Ram Singh agreed with Shivaji *Raje*, but not for his life would he have voiced those thoughts. Instead, he said, "*Rajaji*, you could have avoided this calamity if you had remained calm at court, or at least apologized to the Emperor later."

"That is out of the question, *Bhaiji*. I will never go into his presence again. I do not care about my own life."

Raghunath *Punt* was quiet, but thought to himself: *You must care about your life, my King, for the sake of our* Swarajya, *our people, for the Queen Mother... you will have to care. Shed your indignance,* Raje, *and behave like the politician you truly are.*

Shivaji *Raje* turned to Tej Singh. "I am surprised that people like you did not advise *Mirzaji* while we were in the Deccan. There are so many intelligent people around your Master, yet none advised against going on the disastrous campaign against the Adilshah! He was ill-prepared and Diler Khan was never in agreement with him. His defeat was pre-ordained."

Tej Singh looked uncomfortably at Ram Singh and said, "*Raja* Jai Singh never heeds another's advice. There is only one person he does listen to, and that is his *Munshi,* Udairaj. That crafty secretary of his knows this only too well and so influences the *Raja*'s decisions as he thinks best."

"You should have reasoned with him; dissuaded him from sending me here."

The men were quiet again. Ram Singh broached the subject of the bond the Emperor required him to sign. Shivaji *Raje* realised Ram Singh's predicament. On the one hand he could not go against Aurangzeb, while on the other, he was bound by his father's oath to protect him.

Raje rose, saying to Ram Singh, "*Bhaiji,* take me to the temple."

Ram Singh was confused by this request, but nodded and led the men to the small temple inside his residence. Shivaji *Raje* knelt before the *Shivling* and touched his head to the ground. He willingly did in front of Lord Mahadev what he had refused to do before the Emperor.

Rising, *Raje* folded his hands in prayer. Finally, he picked up a *bael* leaf from those offered at the shrine and turned to face his host. "*Bhaiji,* give me your hand," he said gently.

Ram Singh held up his upturned palms. *Raje* placed the *bael* leaf in them and placed his own palms over Ram Singh's. "*Bhaiji*, your father assured Raghunath *Punt* in this manner when asked to give surety of my life. I give you the same solemn promise. Before Lord Mahadev, I assure you I shall do nothing to put you in danger while your surety is in force. By all means sign a bond for His Majesty."

Ram Singh was moved. He gazed at the Maratha King, seeing only honesty in his eyes. Despite being in peril of his own life, this remarkable man was ready to give an assurance that he would not try to escape, simply to allow Ram Singh himself to save face with the Emperor!

Shivaji *Raje* left Ram Singh's residence shortly thereafter. As Ram Singh watched him disappear beyond the gates, Maha Singh Shekawat said, "He always speaks the truth, this Maratha *Raja*. Nobody need say anything after he has voiced his thoughts, because his words are so precise and correct. He is a true Rajput!"

DIWAN-E-KHAAS, AGRA FORT, 15 MAY 1666

The second *durbar* of the morning was in session when Ram Singh arrived with the signed bond as ordered by the Emperor. He handed it to Mohammed Amin, who placed it before the Emperor. Aurangzeb briefly glanced at the bond and handed it to his attendant. Looking at Ram Singh, he said, "*Kunwar* Ram Singh, I have appointed you to a campaign in Kabul. You will take Seeva and his son along with you. You have a week to depart, so commence your preparations and summon your Rajputs."

Ram Singh bowed. "As Your Majesty commands. I will begin preparations immediately."

"Remember that you have signed this bond and accepted responsibility for Seeva's actions. Do not let him out of your sight," the Emperor warned, his voice stern. "You are now excused from court." Aurangzeb waved him away.

As Ram Singh exited the *Diwan-e-Khaas,* he heard someone call his name. Ram Singh turned to face Rad-andaz Khan, the brutal Commander of Agra Fort. "I have been told to command the vanguard of your army to Kabul," he said, smiling maliciously.

It dawned on Ram Singh that this new move by the Emperor was merely a pretext to get Seevaji *Raja* out of Agra. Rad-andaz

Khan was still in the picture and would certainly kill the *Raja* and his son somewhere on the way to Kabul. Amongst thousands of Mughal troops, and without his own men, Seevaji *Raja* would be defenceless.

SHIVAJI RAJE'S CAMP, AGRA, 16 MAY 1666

Ram Singh had ordered his men to set up an elaborate camp for his guests in a vast open space in front of his own residence. A small stone building was procured for Shivaji *Raje* himself and was suitably furnished, as befitted the status of his guest. Tents for *Raje*'s entourage were put up around the building, thus giving *Raje* himself a degree of safety among his own men. Ram Singh's men had been ordered to see to *Raje*'s comfort at all times and to make arrangements for ample provisions.

Shivaji *Raje* sat in his bedchamber with Raghunath *Punt*, Tryambak *Punt*, Niraji *Punt*, Bahirji Naik, *Sarjerao* Jedhe, Yesaji Kank, Hiroji *Farzand* and Ragho Mitra. His trusted team gathered around him to brainstorm a way out of the fresh move by Aurangzeb. Jiva Mahala, Shivaji *Raje*'s bodyguard, stood at attention behind him.

"We cannot allow this campaign to materialize," Raghunath *Punt* said. "If His Highness is taken to Kabul, it will be the end."

"I agree," said Tryambak *Punt*. "Aurangzeb was thwarted by Ram Singh the other day. He simply wants to move us away from Agra to cut Ram Singh off from the other Rajput vassals."

"We must make our own moves to stay here," Shivaji *Raje* said.

"What does Your Highness suggest?" Raghunath asked.

Raje thought a while and said, "Let us begin diplomatic visits to Aurangzeb's top courtiers." He turned to his diplomats. "Make a list of the most influential nobles at court and bribe them well. Convince them to speak to the Emperor about our plight and secure a pardon from him."

"Bribe the Emperor's nobles right under his nose?" Tryambak *Punt*'s eyes widened in surprise.

Raje smiled. "Yes. Money has great convincing power, *Punt*! Besides, I have heard that every single noble who stands in Aurangzeb's *durbar* is corrupt. The same courtiers who speak *against* us today, shall speak *for* us if we show them some gold. Conclude your visits in a couple of days. Leave the *Vizier* out of your list, however."

"Why leave out the *Vizier*, Highness? He is likely to have the greatest influence on Aurangzeb."

"Yes, indeed. That is why I will visit him in person."

The men shifted uneasily. *Raje* moving out into the streets of Agra was an added security challenge. In the current situation, it seemed ill advised.

"Bahirji," Raje turned to his chief spy. "Spread word among the masses that Aurangzeb holds Shivaji *Raje* unjustly in Agra. Let the people know how I was given false promises and how the Emperor now plans to kill me. Also, spread your men around Agra and its outskirts. Begin preparations for our exit from this damned city!"

Bahirji nodded. Once again his intelligence skills would be put to the test in preparing the ground for *Raje's* escape from Agra.

"Hiroji, Yesaji, Ragho and *Sarjerao*... we are in constant peril from Aurangzeb. There is no telling when he will order his men to sieze me and Shambhu. Place your men around this building, on constant guard."

The meeting ended and the men left to perform the allotted tasks.

Jafar Khan's mansion, night of 18 May 1666

"*Rajaji*, I cannot tell you how surprised I am to see you here," Jafar Khan, the Mughal *Wazir* said to the Maratha King who sat in front of him in his spacious and richly furnished audience chamber.

"Khan *saheb*," Shivaji *Raje* replied, "you must plead with the Emperor on my behalf for a pardon. Beg him to forgive my crimes. I will forever be his faithful vassal if he allows me to return to my homeland."

Jafar Khan stroked his beard, looking intently at *Raje*. This was just the second time he had set eyes upon the famous Seevaji. The first time he had been, like most others, stunned by the *kafir*'s behaviour in court. But now, six days later, the man before him seemed genuinely repentant.

"The Emperor is extremely displeased, *Rajaji*. It will be difficult to pacify him."

"You hold sufficient influence over him, Khan *saheb*. None but you can do this for me. Besides, it would not do His Majesty's prestige any good to have his own state guest killed. Remember, the Emperor has invited me here. If I am murdered while on the Kabul mission, the news will spread to all your vassals and no one will ever trust the Emperor's invitation or word again."

The kafir is clever, thought Jafar Khan. *He plays his cards well.*

Raje looked at Hiroji, who was standing by quietly, and nodded. Hiroji summoned the attendants, who entered with plates loaded with gifts for the *Vizier*. Hiroji proceeded to remove the silken covers and display the gifts. There were bejewelled daggers and cups, a pile of gold coins, and the choicest of sweets from Agra's markets. The *Wazir*'s eyes widened in amazement, and then in greed. *The kafir is rich*, he thought.

"A few humble gifts from me, Khan *sahib*. Pray speak for me."

As Jafar Khan accepted the expensive gifts, his personal attendant entered and whispered into his ear, "The *begum* asks you to see her immediately." Puzzled and intrigued, Khan excused himself and went to his wife's bedchamber.

"Are you out of your mind?" the Khan's *begum* spat out as soon as he entered the chamber.

Jafar Khan was taken aback. "What is the matter, *Begum*? Why are you so agitated?"

"That *kafir* appeared out of thin air in *bhaijaan's* bedchamber and attacked him! And now he sits next to you fully armed. Why did you even let him into the house?"

Jafar Khan was thus reminded that he had unwittingly let the dangerous Seevaji, the man who had so spectacularly assaulted his wife's brother, Shaista Khan, into his own house, armed! He began to pace restlessly.

"I have heard that man is a magician! Now get him out of our *haveli*!" His irate *begum* looked at Jafar Khan angrily.

The *Wazir* left to rejoin his guest. Back in the audience hall, he said, "*Rajaji*, rest assured I will speak to His Majesty about your request for a pardon. I am sorry, but I must leave now as I have been called away on some important business."

Raje was surprised by this abrupt end to their meeting but immediately rose to his feet. "Very well, Khan *saheb*. I shall take your leave. But do accept these few presents." Thus gently reminding the Vizier of the offerings, *Raje* left the mansion.

The political moves initiated by Shivaji *Raje* began having effect in a few days. The nobles his diplomats had managed to bribe, changed their tone in the Emperor's presence and pleaded in veiled words for a pardon for the Maratha. The age-old rivalry between the Kachhwah Rajputs and the Rathores was rekindled. The Rathore camp, which was essentially anti-Jai Singh, supported harsh punishment for the Maratha King. Jaswant Singh was the front runner of this camp, seeking to revenge his own lack of success in the Deccan. Where he had failed, Jai Singh had succeeded and this was a sore wound he wished to heal by seeing Seeva punished. The Kachhwahs, on the other hand, rallied behind Ram Singh and his father. Shivaji *Raje* had come to Agra on the latter's assurance and they would do their best to see Jai Singh's promise was honoured. Besides, standing up against the Rathores was reason enough.

The Emperor was also fed a steady flow of reactions from the general public. There was a growing rumour among the common people that Shivaji *Raje* had been duped by the imperial government with false promises and was now being unlawfully held on the Emperor's order. The Emperor could not be trusted, they said. He would kill the Maratha King at the first opportunity.

Aurangzeb's many Hindu feudatories began echoing these sentiments. Shivaji *Raje* had, in fact, met with some of them and fed them similar thoughts. Aurangzeb felt the heat of these political battles around him as he realized the number of those demanding punishment for Seeva was diminishing every day. Hussain faithfully brought him news of Shivaji *Raje's* visits and gifts to his nobles and, shrewd man that he was, Aurangzeb quickly guessed that Seeva was bribing his men. But he was nevertheless stunned when, one evening, his *Wazir* presented Seeva's petition for pardon. That infidel had somehow managed to corrupt his *Wazir*!

Aurangzeb decided to diffuse the situation by postponing the mission to Kabul and temporarily agreeing to spare Seeva's life. In the interim, he sought to find out from Jai Singh exactly what promises had been made to Seeva. A *firmaan* was dispatched to Deccan immediately.

Aurangzeb's second order to execute Shivaji *Raje* was thus thwarted, this time by *Raje*'s sharp political mind.

GHUSALKHANA, AGRA FORT, 24 MAY 1666

Mohammed Amin, the *Mir Bakshi,* was reading the petition sent by Shivaji *Raje* to the Emperor. "Seeva proposes to pay His Majesty a sum of two crores of rupees if he is allowed to return to his fief and retain the forts and territory he ceded in the recent treaty of Purandar. He also pledges to fight under the Mughal banner against the Adilshah." Amin rolled up the scroll which bore Seeva's seal.

A small assembly of prominent nobles stood before the Emperor in the antechamber. Aurangzeb wrinkled his brow in irritation at this atrocious demand from Seeva. "Has he gone off his head?" he thundered. "How can he go back?"

Amin shifted uneasily and threw a helpless glance at Jafar Khan. Over the past few days, the two had tried to influence the Emperor's mind to pardon Seeva and diffuse a potentially sticky stand-off with the Hindu vassalage in Agra, especially the Kachhwah Rajputs. However fervently they all wanted the infidel executed, they could not do it openly in Agra. It would have to be done away from the public eye. Amin was convinced the Emperor would see the potential hazards of killing Seeva.

"I have heard that Seeva and his *Brahmans* have paid visits to quite a few of my nobles," Aurangzeb said, watching his courtiers closely. The men stared at the floor, avoiding his gaze, lest he catch the guilty look in their eyes. Most had, in fact, received 'gifts' from Shivaji *Raje*.

"Jafar Khan..." Aurangzeb called to his *Wazir*.

"Your Majesty..." Jafar Khan stammered. "He did pay me a visit but I drove him out immediately!"

Aurangzeb gave him a cold stare and continued, "Restrict Seeva's movements. Confine him to his camp. He should not even be permitted to visit Ram Singh."

"As your Majesty wishes," Jafar Khan said, nodding his head.

"Send Fulad Khan to my chambers immediately." The Emperor rose from his seat and his courtiers bowed low.

Later, Fulad Khan, the *Kotwal* of Agra, stood before the Emperor in his chambers. "Fulad Khan, place a thousand of your best men around Seeva's camp," Aurangzeb instructed. "He should not be allowed out of his camp. Issue passes to his men and allow only those with passes through your posts. Ram Singh and his men may be allowed in, but no one else. I repeat, no one else should go in without my permission."

"Understood, Your Majesty," Fulad Khan replied and bowed. "I will set up the watch immediately."

"Watch him closely, Fulad Khan. On an appropriate day, I will order you to sieze him and his son and move them elsewhere. Be prepared."

SHIVAJI RAJE'S CAMP, MORNING OF 25 MAY 1666

Early the next morning, as Shivaji *Raje* was finalizing the diplomatic activities for the day with his officers, they heard a commotion from the camp periphery. *Raje* rushed out with his diplomats and little Shambhu in tow, to find his panicked men running around the camp, shouting and scrambling for weapons. *Raje* was alarmed to see hundreds of Mughal soldiers converging upon the camp.

Bahirji rushed towards them, worry writ large on his face. "Your Highness, we have been betrayed by Aurangzeb! Our worst fears have come true. Hundreds of Mughal soldiers have surrounded our camp."

Shivaji *Raje* looked at him, his face grim. The ingenious political web he had been trying to weave around Aurangzeb had come to nought if Aurangzeb had ordered his army to arrest them.

"Get inside your residence, *Raje,*" Bahirji said. "We shall prepare to defend you with our lives."

Raje took Shambhu by the hand and rushed inside. Over his shoulder, he could see Bahirji and his Captains shouting orders to rally the men around his residence. Once in, the doors were bolted. Shivaji *Raje* stood staring at Raghunath, Tryambak and Niraji, his diplomats. Their minds numbed, none could say anything. Fists were clenched and hearts beat faster by the moment. *Raje* sat down on his bed to collect his wits. How was he going to get out of this?

Shambhu walked up to him and placed a hand on his shoulder. "Father, what do we do now?"

Raje looked at his son. Anytime now, Mughal soldiers would barge into their chamber and grab them. How far could his few men resist the Mughal thousands? There was no fear on Shambhu's face. He too, was ready to go out and fight. *Raje* pulled his son to him and clasped him to his bosom, lamenting, "How did we get into this mess, Shambhu? I erred gravely in coming here. Aurangzeb never meant to honour me or grant me any favours. He always meant to kill me. How could I have been so blind? What have I done?"

Shambhu put his arms around his grieving father and held him for a moment. Even as *Raje* cursed himself for bringing his son on this perilous trip, Shambhu pulled away and said, "Father, let them come! We will fight them till the end." Shambhu pulled his sword from its scabbard.

The metallic scraping of his son's blade seemed to send a spark through *Raje*'s mind, for he rose, a fierce determination evident in his face and form. Shambhu was right. Let the Mughals come. They would never capture him alive! *Raje* picked up his *Bhavani* and unsheathed it. His diplomats too, armed themselves, each one resolved to fight to the end.

As the men waited, the commotion outside died down. Nothing seemed to happen after that. The Mughal soldiers did not attack *Raje*'s residence, and no one came in. Some time later, they heard a knock on the door and a voice saying, "Your Highness, please open the door." It was *Sarjerao* Jedhe.

Raghunath opened the door to find *Sarjerao*, Yesaji and Bahirji standing outside. With them was a Mughal officer.

"This officer would like a word with His Highness," *Sarjerao* said. *Raje* nodded permission and Raghunath let them in.

A burly, bearded man in formal Mughal attire and a plumed turban signifying he was an officer of high rank, waddled into the chamber to face Shivaji *Raje*. Jiva Mahala and Yesaji took up positions on either side of their King, ready for any false move by the Mughal.

"Highness, this is Fulad Khan, the *Kotwal* of Agra," *Sarjerao* said, introducing the officer.

Fulad Khan curtly nodded his head and said, "*Rajaji,* His Majesty had ordered me to place a guard around your camp and restrict your movements. From this moment, you will not be allowed to leave your camp."

"Why not just say His Majesty has ordered you to place me under arrest, Fulad Khan?" *Raje* retorted sternly.

"Believe me, *Rajaji,* this is for your own safety. My men mean no harm to you or your son. Besides, only you are to be detained. Your son and your men are free to come and go as they please, as long as they have passes. But know this, no one else will be allowed into the camp to meet you."

"Not even Ram Singh?"

"*Kunwarji* and his chosen men will be allowed in, but no others."

Raje looked away angrily. "Your Emperor has betrayed me. I was called to Agra with false promises and now he has placed me under arrest! Who will believe the Emperor's word after this?"

Fulad Khan's expression remained inscrutable as he said, "If you require anything *Rajaji,* your men should get in touch with me directly. I am in charge of your camp now. Your men will be issued passes today."

Fulad Khan departed, leaving behind worried minds.

Later, Shivaji *Raje* sat in conference with his men. They spoke in hushed tones lest they be heard by the Mughal soldiers patrolling outside. Aurangzeb would no doubt have planted his spies around *Raje*'s residence.

"The situation is quite grave, Your Highness," Tryambak *Punt* said. "We have no choice but to secure a written pardon from Aurangzeb. I do not see any other way."

Bahirji nodded gravely. "Escape will be difficult. There are a thousand pairs of eyes watching our every move."

"And yet, we shall escape!" *Raje* said with determination.

The men looked at each other, used to their King's audacious plans.

But an escape from Agra seemed an impossible task. What was *Raje* planning to do?

"We do not care about our lives, Highness," Yesaji said. "It is enough if you and the Prince get away. We will stay back and handle the aftermath."

"No! We will all get away from here. Every one of us!" *Raje* said with conviction. "We will leave right in front of them and they will never know! Aurangzeb shall know what Shivaji is capable of."

How were over three hundred men supposed to leave camp when they were being detained and guarded by the Emperor's order?

"Now listen carefully..." *Raje* said in a low voice.

The men leaned forward to hear his plan.

Ram Singh had been greatly alarmed when he learnt of Fulad Khan's deployment around Shivaji *Raje*'s camp. Having lived in the capital for some time now, he realized that this was but a preliminary move by the Emperor, in preparation for the Maratha King's arrest. Restricting his movements was a prelude to siezing him at a later date. There was also the possibility of the *Raja* being murdered at night, at the behest of the Emperor. Ram Singh was in a fix. While he could not openly oppose the Emperor, he was under orders from his father to protect the *Raja* and his son.

After giving it due thought, Ram Singh concluded that Shivaji *Raje*'s life was in great peril and resolved to put his own neck on the line for him once again. He placed a cordon of his own men around *Raje*'s residence, inside the ring of Mughal soldiers. His Rajputs were under strict orders to protect Shivaji *Raje* and his young son, at all cost. "Watch *Rajaji*'s bed at night," Ram Singh instructed his Captains. "The Emperor's spies may ambush him in the dark."

Ram Singh's move thwarted Aurangzeb's plans once again. He realized the Kachhwah Rajputs were prepared for a confrontation. Wanting to avoid such a stand-off, he postponed his plans to arrest Shivaji *Raje* yet again, choosing instead to simply keep him under watch.

Having received this reprieve, *Raje* put his own plan into action. When Ram Singh visited him one evening, he said to him, "*Bhaiji*, request the Emperor to cancel your bond. You must do it now."

Ram Singh was intrigued by this request. He knew the *Raja* was under oath to behave himself while his own bond to Aurangzeb was in force. Now that the *Raja* was requesting him to have the bond cancelled, was he planning something? "What are you planning, *Rajaji*?" Ram Singh asked his guest directly.

Raje gave him a disarming smile. "I am in no position to plan anything, *Bhaiji*. It does look like I will be here a while. The Emperor does not seem to be in any mood to grant me leave any time soon. Fulad Khan is in charge of my camp. Why then should your bond still be in force? Get it cancelled."

Ram Singh gave it some thought, then said, "I will petition the Emperor tomorrow."

"*Bhaiji*, I have one more request. In the past few days, I have run out of money. Would you be kind enough to advance me a loan? I will send a *hundi* to Rajgad, so the money is repaid to *Mirzaji* immediately."

"Certainly, *Rajaji*. I will arrange for the money immediately." As he rose to leave, he added, "For your own sake *Rajaji*, please do not do anything rash."

Shivaji *Raje* gave him a reassuring nod. Once his guest had left, *Raje* summoned his men. Addressed his diplomats, Tryambak *Punt* and Raghunath *Punt*, he said, "Send a request to the Emperor to grant official leave to all our men. Everyone must be sent back with official passes."

"Everyone?" Tryambak *Punt* asked, surprised.

Raje nodded. "You will stay back; so will Raghunath *Punt* and Niraji *Punt*. Hiroji, Madari Mehtar, Yesaji, Sarjerao and Jiva will remain as well. Detain only a handful to run errands. But procure passes for everyone. In fact, try to manage a few extra passes with false names."

"Bahirji, select a desolate spot near the exit route from Agra. On the designated day, you will wait there with horses and clothes for disguise. Shambhu and I will join you there. Plant our men along the road to Mathura."

"Mathura, Highness?" Bahirji was confused. "That will take us further away from Rajgad." Mathura was north-west from Agra. If they had to escape, thought Bahirji, they should ideally take the straightest and shortest route south to Rajgad. But then his King never thought straight.

"Yes, Mathura. When our flight is discovered, Aurangzeb will send his men after us. They will no doubt assume we have taken the straight road south from Agra. But we will travel north first, and then take a circuitous route back to Rajgad."

The men understood the plan. It made sense…if they managed to get out of camp undiscovered, that is.

"Besides," *Raje* continued, "some of our *Peshwa*'s relatives live in Mathura. They will no doubt help us." *Raje,* with incredible foresight, had planned for this eventuality even before he had left for Agra. Moro *Punt*'s brothers-in-law lived in Mathura and *Raje* had asked Moro *Punt* to send word to him to be ready in case *Raje* needed his help.

"Find out where we can get large cane baskets," *Raje* told them. "And find out where we can buy the best sweets in town."

"Baskets…sweets… Highness?" Bahirji inquired, bewildered.

"Yes. First, the baskets will go out of our camp filled with sweets. But one day, they will carry a King and a Prince."

Aurangzeb received Ram Singh's petition to cancel his bond the next day and having considered the matter, granted his request. Where would the rat go with a thousand men guarding him? Ram Singh was thus officially relieved of responsibility for Shivaji *Raj*e, though he was still under moral obligation to fulfil his father's promise to the *Raja.*

Before dismissing him, Aurangzeb said to Ram Singh, "Convince Seeva to hand over his entire fief, including his forts and become a Mughal *mansabdar*."

"I shall do my best, Your Majesty," Ram Singh promised, knowing the earth would end in *pralay* before the Maratha did so.

That evening, Aurangzeb received a curious request from the Maratha King. Jafar Khan read the petition in the *Ghusalkhana.* "Seevaji requests His Majesty to grant leave to his men, so they can return home. He wishes to send back most of them, save for a few," Jafar Khan said.

Aurangzeb was surprised by this petition. The *kafir* certainly seems to have lost his mind, he thought. If he sent his men away, who would watch his back? But this served his own plan nicely. With Seeva's men out of the way, it would be that much easier to plan his execution. At a later date, he would remove Ram Singh and his Rajputs from the picture as well. So the Emperor agreed, saying, "Let them go back. The fewer men in his camp the better. Grant them passes to leave!"

Shivaji *Raje*'s incredible plan to escape from the clutches of the Mughal Emperor had been put in action. The Emperor had himself, unwittingly, granted permission for the first move.

A couple of days later, Aurangzeb received news that Seevaji had taken ill and was confined to bed. His spies informed him that Seevaji's men had fetched a *hakim* from Agra to examine him and were running errands to fetch medicines and provisions.

That evening, Aurangzeb received another petition from the Maratha.

I no longer have any interest in politics or matters of state, Seeva had written. *I wish to resign from this world and spend the rest of my days as a religious medicant in Benares. I request His Majesty to grant me leave to depart from Agra.*

"Very well," Aurangzeb quipped to his *Wazir*, "if he wishes to turn *faqir*, let him live in Allahabad Fort! Bahadur Khan our *Subadar* will treat him well there."

Allahabad Fort was famous as a place for housing and torturing criminals. By choosing such a place, Aurangzeb had made his intentions clear. Jafar Khan exchanged a quick look with Mohammed Amin. Was the Emperor finalizing his plan for the Maratha? They hadn't yet received a reply to the Emperor's *firmaan* from Jai Singh and it would not be prudent to act before that. But he refrained from voicing his opinion. Who could hope to change the Emperor's mind about anything?

A few days later, the Mughal administration granted passes to Shivaji *Raje*'s men to leave Agra. Relieved of this responsibility, *Raje* now set the second stage of his plan into action.

Ram Singh continued the practice of taking Sambhaji to the Emperor's court. One such day, in the *durbar*, the Emperor inquired about *Raje*'s health, to which Ram Singh replied, "Seevaji *Raja*'s health worsens by the day. I am worried about him."

Another twist of fate to suit his plans, thought Aurangzeb. Let the *kafir* die on his own; a slow death in captivity. No one would accuse him of treachery then. Later that night, he summoned Rad-andaz Khan to his private chambers and said to him, "Seeva is unwell and we need to move him to a better house so he can spend his last days in peace."

Rad-andaz understood what his sovereign was hinting at. "Your Majesty, the construction of my new house should be completed shortly. It is in a quiet area of Agra...suitable to shift the *kafir* and his son to," he replied.

Aurangzeb smiled. "Good. Have the work finished quickly. You will have a royal guest soon."

Days passed and Shivaji *Raje's* health showed no signs of improvement. How could it, when the man feigning illness was, in fact, well and waiting to flee? *Raje* played the part of a sick man so well that not just Fulad Khan and his men, but even Hussain's spies, planted in his camp, were convinced the Maratha King was nearing his end. *Raje* would spend the entire day in bed, covered by a sheet, his back to the only window in his chamber. Fulad Khan's men, who habitually peeped into his chamber, finally got used to the sight of him asleep with his back to them. They also got used to the sight of the gold bracelet he wore on his wrist. Fulad Khan would visit *Raje* occasionally, but discontinued his visits when he was informed that *Raje*'s condition had worsened.

When the *hakim*'s medicines showed no effect, *Raje* requested permission to donate alms and sweetmeats to the poor. This request was conveyed to the Emperor, who failed to see through it. *Give all the alms and sweets you want kafir, you will not get out of this alive,* Aurangzeb thought as he nodded assent.

The process of sending sweetmeats began in earnest. Every day, by noon, several large cane baskets, filled with sweets and other delicacies from the finest shops in Agra, would be brought to Shivaji *Raje*'s camp. The baskets, each carried on a pole between two men, would be checked by Fulad Khan's men on their way in. They would then be taken to *Raje*'s bedchamber, where he would, still lying down, touch them in a symbolic gesture. The baskets would then be taken away and Fulad Khan's men would recheck them on the way out of camp. Outside, the sweets would be taken to different parts of Agra for distribution amongst the poor.

However, the poor were not the only ones to benefit from *Raje*'s generosity. Some of the baskets reached the homes of Aurangzeb's prominent nobles, once again reminding them to be sympathetic to his cause and plead for leniency from the Emperor. The nobles enjoyed the sweets, not realizing they would give them a bout of indigestion later.

Aurangzeb's private chambers, night of 16 August 1666

Jafar Khan, Mohammed Amin, Rad-andaz Khan and Fulad Khan stood in front of the Emperor as he spoke.

"Seeva is to be shifted to Rad-andaz Khan's new mansion the day after tomorrow. It will be a more suitable place for him and his son. Fulad Khan, prepare to hand over charge of your prisoner to Rad-andaz Khan.

"As Your Majesty wishes," Fulad said, bowing.

"Your Majesty, *Kunwar* Ram Singh may create trouble during the transfer," Rad-andaz suggested.

"Then see that he does not find out about it. I will arrange to send him away on an errand." The Emperor waved them away.

The final order in the matter of the *kafir* prisoners had been issued. They would be shifted to the secluded place and then killed.

That night, a man arrived at Ram Singh's residence with a secret message from the *Mir Bakshi*. "Seevaji Raja is being shifted to Radandaz Khan's mansion the day after tomorrow," the messenger told him.

Ram Singh was convinced this was a final move by Aurangzeb to confine the Maratha *Raja* and then kill him. But try as he might, he could not think of a way to change the course of events this time. Short of a full scale armed confrontation with Fulad Khan's men, there was no way out. He fervently wished he could get in touch with his father for advice, but that was impossible. The least he could do was to alert the Maratha King of the impending move by the Mughals. So Ram Singh summoned Tej Singh and asked him to go inform Shivaji *Raje*.

A tense Shivaji *Raje* summoned his men that night. Raghunath, Tryambak, Niraji Raoji, Hiroji, Yesaji, Sarjerao, Jiva and Madari Mehtar, sat on the floor, close to his bed. Shambhu sat beside his father. The men spoke in whispers.

"We must make our move tomorrow. It is do or die now," *Raje* said to them. Having received the latest news from Ram Singh, they had little choice.

"Raghunath *Punt*, Niraji *Punt* and Tryambak *Punt* will leave camp in the morning on the pretext of meeting some Mughal nobles. The baskets will arrive by noon. Shambhu and I will escape in the baskets. Yesaji, Sarjerao and Jiva will accompany us out. Hiroji will take my place here on the bed, and Madari will stay back to serve him. Only a few more need remain. Hiroji, Madari, remember, you two will be the last to leave camp. You will have to work out some ruse to get out."

Hiroji nodded. "Do not worry about us, Highness. We will gladly lay down our lives if you can escape from here."

"No!" *Raje* hissed at him. "No one gets left behind. Once you have given us a head start, get out of the camp! I have sworn that I will get all my men out of Aurangzeb's clutches, and I intend to see that happen. Promise me that you will get out of here alive."

"I promise, my King," Hiroji assured him.

"Good. Send one person to Bahirji tonight with these instructions. He is to wait for us at the designated spot at noon tomorrow. He should light a haystack to create a smoke signal to guide us. He should also send a man ahead tonight to inform our advance units to be ready."

Raje turned to his diplomats. "It will be difficult for the three of you to get out of town. Many people here know you by now, especially the Mughal officers. Getting past the Agra outposts may prove tough."

"That is the least of our worries, Highness. We will keep the administration occupied till you get out of Agra safely," Tryambak *Punt* said.

"One of us will have to mislead Fulad Khan as well," Raghunath *Punt* reminded his collegues.

The details having been worked out, the men retired for the night.

Raje was alone in his chamber with his son. "We flee Agra tomorrow, Shambhu. Remember you must be very still and quiet in the basket."

Shambhu nodded. He understood how grave the situation was, but he wasn't scared, knowing his father would be with him. "The Goddess will see us through this, Father," he said.

Raje smiled. "Go, get some sleep, my son. Tomorrow is going to be a long long day."

Shivaji Raje's camp, Agra, 17 August 1666

The last of Shivaji *Raje's* men in the camp were tense beyond words. The diplomats had left early to make their usual round of Mughal offices with petitions. The objective of their visits that day was to mislead the Mughals into believing it was just another day at *Raje*'s camp. No one could get so much as a hint that something was afoot.

Hiroji, Yesaji, Sarjerao and Jiva went about the camp doing the daily chores, keeping up the façade of a normal day. They had been busy, working out the finer details of the plan.

By noon, it was time for the baskets to arrive. Tryambak *Punt* had stationed himself in Fulad's office, distracting the *Kotwal*, lest he venture out to check the baskets himself. Hiroji and Madari had stayed put in *Raje*'s chamber. Sarjerao, Yesaji and the others hovered around the checkpost to distract the Mughal sentries.

The baskets arrived as usual and were let in by the guards, this time with only a cursory check. Yesaji looked at Sarjerao and gave him the most imperceptible of nods. Perfect. The ground had been laid for this over the last week. The guards, used to the sweetmeats arriving and leaving every day, had become complacent. In any case the prisoners would be transferred the next day and their job would be done.

The baskets were taken into *Raje*'s bedchamber, one by one. The first basket was let out without being opened. The second basket was carried in. A Mughal guard walked by the window and peeped in. He saw the *Raja* lying on the bed, covered by a sheet. As he watched, he saw the *Raja* extend his hand and touch the basket, the gold bracelet on his wrist glittering in the sunlight streaming in from the window. The basket was soon carried away.

But *Sarjerao* realized the man could cause trouble and moved forward casually. "Hot day, isn't it?" he remarked.

The guard nodded. "How is your *Raja* doing today?" he asked.

Sarjerao shook his head sadly. "His health has deteriorated further. We are very worried about him."

The guard made a sympathetic sound and moved away. *Sarjerao* walked beside him, chatting and leading the man away. The third basket had by then, been taken into *Raje*'s chamber.

"*Kotwal saheb,* you look relaxed today," Tryambak *Punt* said to Fulad Khan as he sat in the latter's tent, which also served as his office. He had been in there for a while now, attempting to prevent the *Kotwal* from going to the checkposts.

"Just another day, Tryambak *Punt,*" Fulad said, trying hard not to show relief at handing over Shivaji *Raje*'s charge to Radandaz Khan the next day. "So tell me, who have you been visiting today?"

"Oh, I went to see the *Mir Bakshi,* but he was too busy to give me time. He seems sympathetic to our cause so I wanted to request him to plead for a pardon from the Emperor."

Fulad let out a guffaw. Pardon from the Emperor? He almost told the affable Tryambak *Punt* that his King would soon be shifted to a hell house from where there was no return.

"Why do you laugh, *Kotwal saheb*? Do you not feel for my ailing King?"

"Sure, sure…" Fulad answered, amused.

A guard entered the tent and bowed. "*Huzoor,* the baskets have arrived as usual."

Tryambak *Punt* stiffened. Fulad laughed again. "Your sweets do not seem to have served any purpose beyond fattening some already fat nobles, my friend!" He raised his corpulent self and picked up his sword.

Tryambak *Punt*'s heartbeat quickened. "*Kotwal saheb*, why do you bother yourself with such a trivial matter? The baskets will enter and leave the camp as usual. Some will go to the poor and some to the rich."

Fulad paused, nodding agreement. "But it does no harm to have a look, does it?" he said.

The third basket was placed beside *Raje*'s bed. Hiroji peered out of the window to make sure no guard was nearby. "Now!" he whispered.

Shivaji *Raje* quickly rose from his bed. Hiroji took off his own footwear, and *Raje* quickly slipped them on. In one swift move, Hiroji lay down on the bed and Madari covered him with a sheet. *Raje* removed his gold bracelet and fastened it onto Hiroji's wrist. The basket was opened. It was full of small parcels of sweets. The men quickly emptied the basket. *Raje* gave Hiroji a last look and stepped into the basket. The packets of sweets were put back so they covered *Raje*. The basket was closed and carried away.

The fourth basket was carried in and opened. The same process was followed. Shambhu jumped in and was smilarly covered by the sweets. The basket was carried away. The entire drama had been enacted in mere moments, giving the Mughal guards outside no reason to suspect anything was amiss.

The fifth and sixth baskets were carried in and out as usual, with Hiroji now playing *Raje*'s part in touching them.

The baskets had been placed in a line in the courtyard outside, with the most precious two in the middle. The carriers, who were *Raje*'s own men in disguise, positioned themselves, ready to move.

Fulad Khan arrived at the outer checkpost just in time to see the first basket being carried out. He had been vigilant the first few days and had supervised the checking of all baskets. But he soon tired of the daily routine and left it to the guards. The guards too had tired of the same fruitless exercise and had begun letting the baskets through without checking. Yet, on this crucial day, Fulad developed an interest in the baskets and cried out, "Halt!"

The guards stiffened as they saw their Chief approach and immediatey stopped the carriers. Fulad Khan walked up to the first basket and ordered, "Put it down!"

The carriers put the basket down. Inside the cordon of Mughal soldiers at the checkpost, Yesaji and *Sarjerao* tensed. Would Fulad Khan discover the fugitives?

"Open the basket!" Fulad ordered the carriers. The men proceeded to open the lid. Fulad checked the contents and waved them off. He moved to the next basket.

Yesaji had his hand on his sword as he glanced at *Sarjerao*. If Fulad discovered *Raje* in the third basket, they would charge. Jiva calmly walked towards the guards with the same intention.

Fulad ordered the second basket to be opened. He checked its contents and moved to the third one.

Mahadev! Yesaji, Sarjerao and Jiva prayed silently.

Fulad paused at the third basket and looked at it intently. Finally, deciding against opening it, he waved the carriers away, telling the others to hurry up and be gone too as they did not have all day to check what sweets the shops were making that day.

Yesaji, Jiva and Sarjerao heaved silent sighs of relief.

The men made haste to carry the baskets away from the camp. Once out of sight, the party split up. Two baskets were carried by a separate route to a desolate area of town. The others were taken by the usual route to their designated destinations – some temples, and the mansions of some prominent nobles.

In a short while the two precious baskets had moved away from prying eyes. The lead carrier desperately looked around for the sign he had been told to look out for. He kept going in the direction he had been told, with only his instincts to guide him. Then he saw it. In the distance, smoke billowed up into the sky. The man smiled. His chief, Bahirji Naik, had done his job. It was now his responsibility to get his King to the spot safely.

Bahirji paced impatiently as he waited for his King and Prince. He had kept everything ready, as instructed. Even the smoke signal was up. By his own calculation, the baskets should have arrived by now. What was holding them up? Bahirji looked up at the sky and closed his eyes. "Lord, get the King out safely. I will take him home from here," he prayed.

As he opened his eyes, he spotted the baskets. In the lead was his best man, whom he had trusted with this risky task. Bahirji smiled. The baskets arrived and the men put them down. Bahirji and the men quickly opened the lids and out stepped Shivaji *Raje* and Prince Shambhu. Bahirji exulted, raising his folded hands to the sky in gratitude. He bowed to his King and then gathered Shambhu in an embrace.

Raje, smiling in delight, patted Bahirji on the back. "Well done, Bahirji! So far so good! Let's not waste any time here. You never know when our escape will be discovered."

The men changed their clothing, donning the disguises Bahirji had provided. Shivaji *Raje* even shaved off his beard and moustache. Then they mounted the horses and rode to the south gate of Agra city. Though it was suitably guarded, they had no trouble getting past as they had official passes to leave Agra. Even *Raje* himself had a pass, procured under a false name. Once past the gates, they rode south for a few miles. Then, at a secluded spot, they left the road going south and turned first east, and then north. Finally, crossing the Yamuna river, they rode northwest towards Mathura.

Shivaji *Raje* and Prince Shambhu had escaped the Emperor's clutches. The eagle had flown. Aurangzeb would never set eyes on Seeva again.

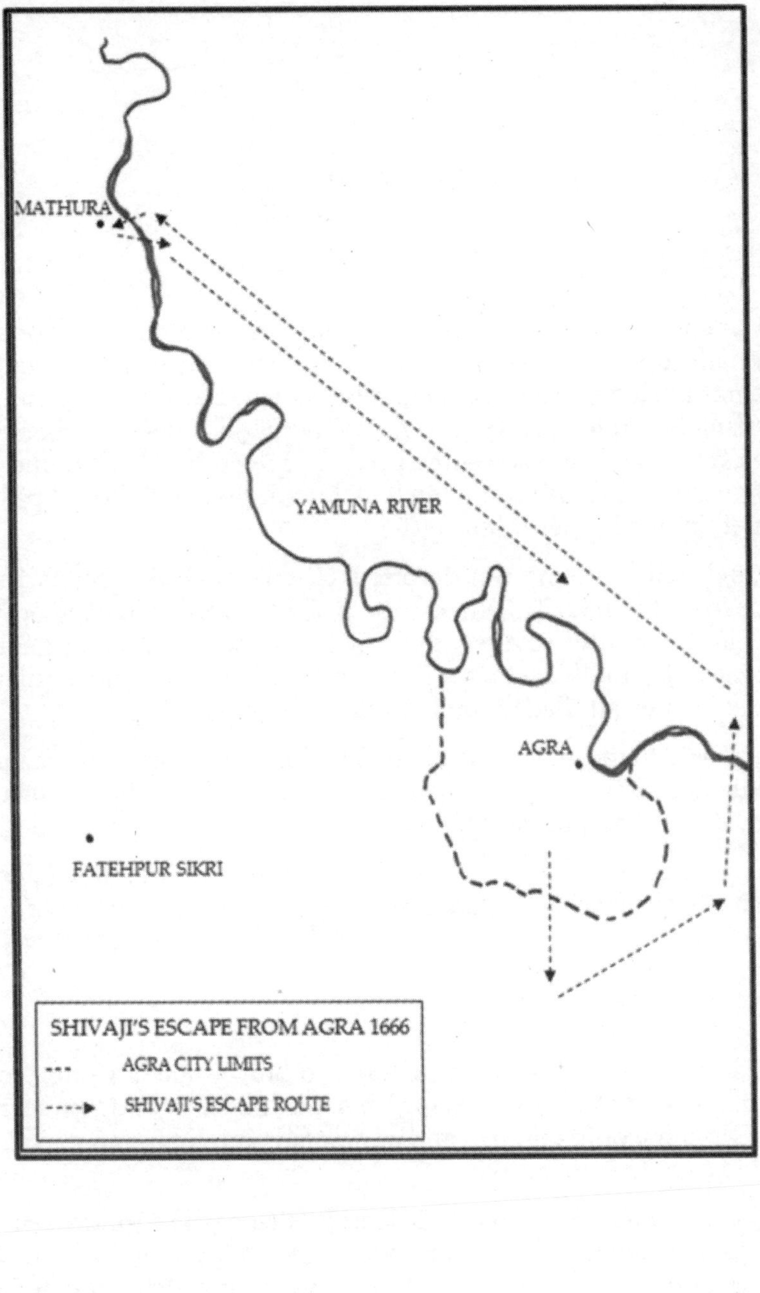
MATHURA
YAMUNA RIVER
AGRA
FATEHPUR SIKRI
SHIVAJI'S ESCAPE FROM AGRA 1666
AGRA CITY LIMITS
SHIVAJI'S ESCAPE ROUTE

10
LIFELONG REGRET

Back at the camp, the men went about their activities as if nothing had happened. Hiroji, lying on the bed, did not rise. Madari Mehtar busied himself massaging his feet and fussing over him, as he usually did for the King. *Sarjerao,* Yesaji, Jiva and the others left the camp one by one, on some pretext or the other. Each found his way out of Agra without a hitch. After all, they had official passes issued by the Emperor himself!

By nightfall, the camp was deserted. Hiroji signalled to Madari and rose from the bed. Together, they placed several cushions on the bed and carefully covered them with the sheet. Leaving behind Shivaji *Raje*'s footwear by the bedside, they left the chamber quietly. Outside, they strolled casually to the checkpost.

Hiroji said to the guard, "We are off to the *hakim*'s place to get some medicines. Shivaji *Raje* has just fallen asleep. Please do not disturb him. We will be back shortly."

The guards nodded, disinclined to disturb the Maratha *Raja* or themselves. Hiroji and Madari left the camp and disappeared into the night.

Late that night

The Mughal guard at the checkpost to Shivaji *Raje*'s camp woke with a start. He had been dozing for some time now and was scared his Captain would barge in and admonish him. He began pacing to and fro just to keep awake.

The camp was immersed in a deathly silence. The guard sensed rather than saw that something was amiss. Why was there no one in the camp? Whenever he had been on night watch here, he had seen at least a few Marathas around. They would even come up and chat with him. But today, there seemed to be no one. He roused his mate, who was dozing in a corner of the checkpost.

"What is it?" he asked, rubbing his eyes.

"There seems to be no one in the camp."

"No one? How can that be?"

Together, they walked in and checked the camp. There wasn't a soul in sight. The men panicked and fetched the Captain of the night guard. The Captain, on hearing what the men had to say, checked the tents for himself and then went straight to Shivaji *Raje*'s residence and peered through the window. It was dark. There seemed to be no one inside. In the light of their *mashaals*, the men saw someone asleep on the bed, covered by a sheet.

The Captain was certain something was wrong. But he knew if he raised the alarm, he would get into trouble himself. "Listen, you two," he said to his guards, "carry on with your night watch as if nothing has happened. You never called me here and we never inspected the camp. In the morning, we will simply hand over charge to the Captain of the morning shift and leave. Let them sort out things in the morning."

"Do you think the *Raja* is in there, asleep?" the first guard asked.

"Has the *Raja* escaped?" The second guard voiced the more terrifying possibility.

"I do not know, and I do not care. Now, back to your post and remember, nothing happened here tonight."

The Captain went back to his tent. He was sure the Maratha *Raja* had somehow escaped. He had heard stories of his sorcery in Agra and had laughed at them. But at the moment, he felt inclined to believe every word. The cursed *kafir* had simply disappeared! One thing he was sure of, he wasn't about to let this be discovered on his watch. Fulad Khan himself would discover the truth tomorrow.

SHIVAJI RAJE'S CAMP, THE MORNING OF 18 AUGUST 1666

The morning guard took over and set up their posts. The Captain then went about his routine task of checking the camp. He was shocked to find no one inside. He raised the alarm and sent a man rushing to fetch Fulad Khan. The *Kotwal* nearly threw a fit when he was told there was no one in Shivaji *Raje*'s camp.

When he arrived at the camp, hundreds of Mughal soldiers had already gathered there.

"There is no one in the camp," the Captain informed him.

"What do you mean?" Fulad Khan barked at him. "How can they just disappear?"

"I don't know how, but they have!"

"Did you look in the *Raja*'s chamber?"

The Captain shook his head. He had waited for the *Kotwal* to check on the *Raja* himself. Fulad Khan rushed inside Shivaji *Raje*'s bedchamber, to find someone asleep, covered by a sheet. *Raje*'s footwear was on the floor beside the bed. Fulad hoped against hope that at least the *Raja* was indeed there though he knew in his heart that it was not likely. With a trembling hand he pulled the sheet away to find only cushions underneath. He froze in fear as it finally dawned upon him that the Maratha *Raja* had escaped!

Panicked and fearful at having to face the enraged Emperor, Fulad gave orders to tear the camp apart while he himself rushed to fetch Ram Singh.

A bewildered Ram Singh followed Fulad back to the camp and inspected Shivaji *Raje*'s chamber for himself. He was stunned by the *Raja*'s sudden disappearance. Only the previous morning he had checked on him personally. His health seemed to have deteriorated considerably. Ram Singh had privately doubted that he would survive long, given the circumstances. And now...he was gone!

"Well?" Fulad demanded of the Rajput Prince. "Where is Seevaji *Raja*?"

Ram Singh threw him angry look. "How should I know? He was under your watch wasn't he?"

"Your men formed the inner circle of posts around the *Raja*!"

"I withdrew my security bond days ago, approved by the Emperor himself. Since then Seevaji *Raja* has been your sole responsibility. Do not try to blame me for this, Fulad Khan!"

Fulad Khan was terrified of the Emperor's displeasure and furious at Ram Singh at the same time. He strongly suspected Ram Singh of having connived with the Marathas. "Very well," he said, glaring at Ram Singh, "let us go and inform the Emperor. Let His Majesty decide for himself."

Ram Singh returned his stare. He knew beyond the shadow of a doubt that Seevaji *Raja*'s disappearance would not go down well with the Emperor. Both he and his father could be in serious trouble over this fiasco. He decided to send an express message to his father immediately.

By the time Fulad Khan and Ram Singh reached Agra Fort, the Emperor had left the *Diwan-e-Khaas*. As he relaxed in the *Ghusalkhana,* listening to Jafar Khan present some petitions, his mind wandered to the problem of Seeva. The wily Maratha and his son would be shifted to Rad-andaz Khan's house today. Finally, having waited so long, he would have the chance to wipe out this menace and end Maratha resistance forever. No one rebelled against him and lived! Aurangzeb contendedly turned the beads in his right hand.

The *quorchi* interrupted the *Wazir* to whisper something to him. Putting away the scroll he was holding, Jafar Khan addressed the Emperor, "Your Majesty, Bakhtawar Khan requests permission to interrupt court proceedings. He says he has some important news about Seevaji *Raja*."

Aurangzeb was mildly surprised. What news could Bakhtawar possibly have that was important enough to disturb his session with the *Wazir*? He raised his hand, signifying permission. Had the *kafir* died? Better that way, he thought, smiling to himself.

Bakhtawar Khan appeared and offered *sijda*. As he rose, he said, "Your Majesty, *Kunwar* Ram Singh and Fulad Khan have arrived with important news. The *Kunwar* says that Seevaji *Raja* has disappeared from his camp!"

Bakhtawar's words struck the *durbar* like a bolt of lightning. The nobles present shifted uneasily even as they looked at Bakhtawar in shock. Aurangzeb's eyes widened first in disbelief and then in anger as he ordered Fulad Khan to be presented before him. Ram Singh was, however, not summoned.

Aurangzeb's face and demeanor were calm when Fulad appeared and said, "Your Majesty, Seevaji *Raja* has disappeared from the camp. He was certainly in his bedchamber till last night, but now he is nowhere to be seen."

"Fulad Khan, a thousand of your men were on watch around his camp, yet Seeva has disappeared?"

Fulad Khan glanced briefly up at the Emperor and saw his blazing eyes locked upon himself. "*Jahanpanah*," he pleaded, "I know not if the ground swallowed him or whether he flew off into the skies. I simply cannot understand."

"Have you searched the camp?" Aurangzeb enquired.

"I did so myself, Your Majesty, yet found no answer to this bewildering question." Fulad knew he was in a deep mess and quickly needed to find a scapegoat. After a brief pause, he added, "The *Kunwar*'s men were posted inside my posts. They were nearer to the *Raja*. They should know what happened. I suspect the *Kunwar*'s hand in this matter." To save himself, Fulad openly accused Ram Singh of conniving with the Marathas.

Aurangzeb's hard eyes glittered dangerously. For days now he had felt that Ram Singh and his father, Jai Singh, had been thwarting his attempts to get rid of Seeva. If Ram Singh had indeed helped the *kafir* escape, it would amount to treason. Yet he had to deal with the matter with prudence. An open conflict with the Rajputs was ill advised.

"Majesty, should I summon the *Kunwar* to your presence?" Jafar Khan's words interrupted Aurangzeb's thoughts.

"No!" Aurangzeb refused Ram Singh an audience. "Tell him to go search for Seeva and produce him before me! And if he cannot, then tell him to go wherever that *kafir* has gone!" The Emperor's words were curt and authoritative. "Fulad Khan, close all exits from Agra. Put your men on high alert. Search every corner of Agra and find that infidel! He may still be here or close by. Arrest all Ram Singh's men who were on watch last night, and make them talk. Leave!"

As Fulad hurried off with his orders, Aurangzeb said to Jafar Khan, "Send *firmaans* to all *Subadars, Fauzdars* and *Kotwals* of the Empire. Order them to keep a strict watch for Seeva and his men. They are to stop and question every person passing through their territories, especially those dressed as *fakirs* and *sanyasis*."

"Yes, Your Majesty," Jafar Khan replied.

"*Takhliya*."

The assembly was dismissed.

Aurangzeb was seething with anger as he returned to his inner chambers. His personal attendant offered him refreshment, but he refused. Dismissing the man, he began pacing. He had planned Seeva's arrest with such care; to put an end to the miserable rat's life. Yet the Maratha had somehow escaped! There was a guard of a thousand men around him, yet he had fled. Aurangzeb wondered how it was possible. He cursed Fulad Khan for his incompetence. Had Fulad been alert and watchful, as he was ecpected to be, Seeva could never have pulled this off... not even with Ram Singh's help.

Aurangzeb recollected all the rumours about Seeva. That he was a magician who could disappear and appear at any place he desired. Could that really be true? Certainly not! All that talk was nonsense! His rational mind prevented him from believing such rumours. And yet, had he not, a few years earlier, managed to get past nearly a lakh of Mughal soldiers to suddenly appear inside Shaista Khan's bedchamber? Could he do the same now? What if Seeva was still in Agra, waiting for an opportunity to sneak into his own chamber? For a brief moment, Aurangzeb was unusually disturbed and fetched his *Alamgir*. Unsheathing the legendary sword of his ancestors, he gazed at its gleaming blade and then looked around the empty chamber. Calling out to his attendant, he said, "Summon the Captain of the Guard at once! And send word to Hussain as well."

Moments later, the Captain hurried into his chamber and bowed. "Double the guard around *Salimgarh* immediately," Aurangzeb ordered curtly. "I want all Captains on high alert. Post guards inside this chamber as well."

"*Inside* His Majesty's bedchamber?" The Captain was surprised, as the Emperor had never given such an order before."

"Yes. I want to see armed guards around me at all times." The Captain left and moments later, Hussain appeared.

"Hussain," Aurangzeb said to his Chief of Intelligence, "plant your best men around my chamber. You will have heard that Seeva has fled. Spread your men around Agra and along the roads to the Deccan. Find that infidel!"

A man of few words, Hussain, bowed in silence and departed.

Aurangzeb thus cocooned himself inside a ring of armed guards. Shivaji *Raje's* flight from Agra had tremendously disturbed the usually unflappable Emperor.

Nearly three *prahars* after they had escaped from the camp, Shivaji *Raje* and his men reached an old temple on the outskirts of Mathura. It was pitch dark and the temple was deserted, as were the surroundings. This was the scheduled meeting point with *Raje*'s diplomat, Niraji Raoji, who had left Agra earlier, to rendezvous with them here. They found him waiting, accompanied by a stranger.

Niraji *Punt* pointed to the stranger. "Highness, this is Kashi *Punt*, brother-in-law to our *Peshwa*."

The *Brahman* bowed. *Raje* patted him on the back and said, "Kashi *Punt*, I trust Niraji *Punt* has explained the situation to you? The Mughals will look for Shivaji and his son. To throw them off, I have decided to leave Shambhu with you in Mathura."

"I understand, Highness," Kashi said. "I will take utmost care of the Prince."

"It is a grave risk for you and your family, Kashi *Punt*. I hope you realize that." The man nodded. "Shambhu may have to stay here for a few months. I will send word when it is safe for you to bring him back to Rajgad. Bring your family as well, and settle in our *Swarajya*. I will reward you well for this service."

Shambhu, a boy who did not scare easily, was nevertheless unsettled when he was told he would have to stay back alone in Mathura. His eyes filled with tears as his father explained their predicament.

"We cannot travel together, Shambhu," *Raje* was at pains to explain. "Aurangzeb's men will find us easily if we do so for they are looking for a man and a boy. We must separate. You must stay here. I will send for you when it is safe."

Shambhu bravely swallowed his tears and looked at *Raje*. "Do not worry about me, Father. I will do as you say."

"Shambhu, I am sorry it has to be this way..."

"Do not be, Father. Return safely. Our *Swarajya* needs you right now, not me. Tell grandmother not to cry."

Raje laughed and pulled his son into an embrace. For a few brief moments, father and son held each other, neither willing to let go. As they separated, *Raje* looked at his son, wondering if he would ever see him again.

Kashi *Punt* left with the Maratha Prince, while the King looked on helplessly. *Promise me, you will take care of Shambhu; that you will protect him and keep him out of harm's way.* He remembered Saee's words to him on her deathbed. He had promised her then; but today he had been forced to break his promise. He looked up to the skies and murmured, "Forgive me, Saee."

Relieved of responsibility for his son, Shivaji *Raje* now set about planning the return journey. His remarkable brain, combined with Bahirji Naik's unbelievable skills in reconnoitering, deception and disguise, worked out a plan to throw any pursuing Mughals off their tracks. They first travelled far to the southeast of Agra, to Gaya, three hundred *kos* away. They were thus travelling further away not just from Agra, but also from the direct road to the Deccan. Beyond Gaya, they turned southwest and travelled through Gondwana and Golconda, well beyond their own fiefdom, before finally turning northwest toward Rajgad. The Mughal officers had not considered such a circuitous route. Common sense told them that anyone fleeing towards his own lands, would take the shortest route back. But they could never hope to match Shivaji *Raje*'s genius and thus never accosted the Marathas.

The Maratha party travelled by night and rested in secluded spots by day. They changed disguises often, even dressing as Mughal soldiers at times.

The main force of Shivaji *Raje*'s men, who had left Agra before him, travelled along the regular route to Deccan, spreading many rumours about him. Some even told Mughal officers along the way that the Emperor had released Shivaji *Raje* and allowed him to return home. At a place called Narwar, some hundred and seventy *kos* south of Agra, a Maratha Captain presented himself as Shivaji and even produced an official pass with the seal of the *Kotwal* of Agra! Ibadullah Khan, the *Fauzdar* of Narwar, had no choice but to let him go. He later sent a message to the capital that Seevaji *Raja* had crossed Narwar on his way to the Deccan.

The profusion of rumors and false reports making their way back to the Capital from numerous places placed Aurangzeb in a quandary. Neither he, nor any of his men, could decide upon a plan to arrest the escaped Maratha. But not for a moment did anyone dream that the wily man they were chasing had fled east. Nevertheless, several of Shivaji *Raje*'s men were arrested at various posts and sent back in chains to Agra to be questioned.

Three days after *Raje's* remarkable escape, his diplomats Raghunath *Punt* and Tryambak *Punt,* were arrested by Fulad Khan's men. The two had somehow failed to cross the city gates and had no choice but to remain hidden as the massive search operations were launched. But they could not conceal their presence for long. Fulad Khan began torturing them for information on Shivaji *Raje.* He lashed their bodies and burned their skin; denied them food and water for days. Yet the two fierce devotees of their King said nothing. They knew Shivaji *Raje* would take weeks to reach Rajgad and they had to endure the torture.

Fulad, knowing his best chance of getting useful information was from these two, put his heart into the matter. Standing menacingly before the half dead men strung to the ceiling of the dungeon by their wrists, he said, "Speak up, Raghunath! Why do you wish to bear such pain? I will release you the moment you tell me where Seevaji is."

Raghunath could barely open his eyes. He peered through slits at his tormentor. "You will never understand why I willingly bear this pain, *Kotwal*!"

Fulad signalled to his man. In moments, plates of food were brought in and held before Raghunath and Tryambak, so the men could smell the enticing aromas. They hadn't eaten for days. "Look!" Fulad said, tempting them. "Some information and this food is yours!"

Raghunath gave a tired smile. "Go feed your dog, *Kotwal*."

Fulad growled in anger and slapped Raghunath hard across the face. "Get the salt water!" he shouted.

The food was taken away and the guards fetched hot salt water. Holding Raghunath's head back by the tuft of hair on his crown, they poured the salt water into his nostrils. Raghunath choked and screamed in pain, but the screams died out within the dark dungeon and were never heard by anyone outside.

Ram Singh's men on watch around Shivaji *Raje*'s residence were arrested as well. Fulad Khan proceeded to whip them and forced them on pain of death to give written declarations that Ram Singh had helped Seevaji escape. The men were then sent to Fidai Khan, one of the nobles engaged in the search operations. When Fidai Khan questioned the men alone, they admitted that Ram Singh had no role to play in Seevaji's escape and that Fulad Khan had only made them say so under duress. The men were dismissed.

Notwithstanding these events, Aurangzeb's supicion fell upon Ram Singh. The Rajput Prince was first debarred from court and later stripped of his *mansab*. The Emperor ordered Ram Singh, with his platoons, to go in search of Seeva. The Prince marched to the banks of Narmada River, but failed to accost the Maratha King. Aurangzeb, fearing that Ram Singh would travel south to join his father and thus present him with a new problem, summoned him back to Agra.

Frustrated, the Emperor shot off a *firmaan* to Jai Singh, blaming his son for the treachery: *Have you seen what your son has done? He has allowed Seeva to escape. Through endless exertions, you sent Seeva to my presence and I entrusted his custody to Ram Singh, thinking he is trustworthy and of sound mind. But the Kunwar has disregarded the path of service and seeking of royal favours, and has allowed Seeva to escape. I wished to punish him by blinding and parading him through the streets of Agra. But I did not do so considering your faithful service over the years. Thank your God for that.*

Jai Singh was extremely pained when he received the *firmaan* and did his best to assure the Emperor that his son was innocent. *He is from your family Sire,* Jai Singh wrote back to the sovereign. *He is one of your own. How can he dare to deceive you? And where in heaven's name will Seeva go? I will personally arrest him soon!*

Aurangzeb's anger was not appeased by these assurances from Jai Singh. He kept up the pressure on his own men to investigate and search for Seeva, but drew a blank. As the days passed, he realized with increasing certainty that he would never get his hands on Seeva again. Shivaji *Raje*'s escape from Agra caused lifelong regret for the Great Mughal.

Rajgad, evening of 12 September 1666

The Queen Mother sat in her chamber, by the window, looking at the sun disappear beyond the hills. For over six months she had endured separation from her son and grandson, waiting endlessly for them to return. Bahirji's men had kept up a steady flow of news initially, but for the past few weeks, no one had made it to Rajgad. Jijabai was worried. She remembered how often she had in the past, spent such anxious days and sleepless nights. The battle with Afzal Khan, the raid on Surat, the attack on Lal Mahal...all potentially life threatening missions for her son. Yet, he had come through unscathed each time. The Goddess willing, he would this time too. But this time, Shivba had an added burden on his shoulders... Shambhu! Jijabai's eyes moistened as she thought of her grandson. Already, the little one had gone through much at a tender age. First, the stay at Jai Singh's camp, and then Agra. How much more would *Aai Bhavani* subject him to?

Jijabai's personal attendant entered and said, "Highness, there is word from the main gate that some *sanyasis* have arrived at the fort, asking to see the Queen Mother."

Jijabai waved a hand. "Ask someone to give them alms and food, and then send them on their way. I am in no condition to see anyone now."

The woman departed, leaving Jijabai alone to brood, But the woman reappeared a little later to say, "Your Highness, the *sanyasis* are unwilling to accept alms from the staff. They insist the Queen Mother attend to them."

How strange! thought Jijabai. She had no interest in meeting the ascetics, yet could not refuse. The blessings of such *sanyasis* sometimes worked in one's favour. Jijabai sighed and rose. The attendant followed as she slowly made her way to the courtyard.

A small group of ascetics, dressed in saffron robes and holding wooden staffs and beads, stood in the courtyard. Their faces and foreheads smeared with ash, they chanted Sanskrit hymns. Jijabai moved toward the first *sannyasi* and bowed to touch his feet.

The *sanyasi* immediately bent to raise her up, lifting his hand to bless her. "May your prayers be answered, Queen Mother."

Jijabai smiled at him as she straightened herself. "I pray for my son's return, *baba*. I pray I will see him soon."

"*Tathastu*!" the sanyasi replied.

Jijabai moved forward to touch the next man's feet, but the man quickly held her hands and pulled her up. Jijabai was taken aback by this odd behaviour. Looking at him, she thought his eyes and face were strangely familiar...

"A mother should never touch her son's feet," the *sannyasi* said to her, his eyes filling with tears.

In that moment Jijabai recognized her son. "Shivba!" Jijabai cried, falling into his arms. Shivaji *Raje* clasped his mother to his chest and held her tight as the tears, long suppressed, wet his cheeks.

In moments, as the Rajgad staff realized their King had returned, there was great rejoicing. In the fast diminishing light of the setting sun, *Raje*'s arrival had illuminated the palace as no lamps could do. Shivaji *Raje*'s Queens rushed out to welcome him with tears of relief and happiness. *Pooja thalis* were procured hastily and Soyara, Putala, Sakvar and the other Queens, applied vermillion tilaks to *Raje*'s forehead, offered the ceremonial *diva*.

Moro *Punt* was summoned from his residence and soon arrived, his face beaming. He heaved a sigh of relief as he set eyes upon his King. *Raje* had indeed returned. He looked tired, but he was well and unhurt! "Fire the cannons!" Moro *Punt* ordered the guards. "Let the world know the Maratha King has returned!"

"Distribute sweets to everyone in the fort," Soyara instructed.

"Moro *Punt*," Shivaji *Raje* said solemnly. "There is no need to fire the cannons. Do not offer sweets to the people. There is no cause to rejoice."

"No cause? Highness, what better reason could there be for our people to rejoice?"

"Moro *Punt*, we are in mourning," *Raje* said, hanging his head.

Jijabai's smile vanished at *Raje*'s words and a sickening feeling overcame her. "Mourning? Shivba, where is Shambhu?"

Raje did not answer, looking away. Niraji Raoji, the first ascetic Jijabai had offered her respects to, now moved forward. "Your Highness, Prince Shambhu *Raje* got sick on the way back. He could not tolerate the rigours of the journey."

"Where *is* he?" Jijabai could no longer tolerate the suspense. "Shivba, tell me!"

"Mother..." *Raje* hesitated, knowing the news would shake the very earth beneath the women's feet. "Shambhu *Raje* is no more."

The words stunned everyone. Jijabai broke down and rushed up to her son. Holding him by the shoulders, she demanded an explanation. "How? Why did you allow him to die?" Jijabai spoke through her tears and pain. "You, his father! Why did you not care for him? Why did you take him along in the first place?" Overcome by her grief, Jijabai collapsed in her son's arms. Her attendants quickly carried her away to her chamber.

As they did so, *Raje* stole a glance at his Queens, who were similarly devastated. The sooner he told them the truth, the better, he thought. They should not have to endure this for too long. But the drama was necessary to set the rumour of Shambhu's death into motion. After all, the rumour had a long way to travel to Aurangzeb's ears.

Sometime later, *Raje* entered Jijabai's chamber. He had summoned the Queens as well. As he entered, he found the women immersed in grief and cursed himself for putting them through this. He dismissed all the attendants and closed the doors and windows. Soyara gave him a questioning look and he returned a reassuring smile. Instantly Soyara understood that her husband had something up his sleeve.

"Mother," Shivaji *Raje* said tenderly, sitting down beside Jijabai, "listen to what I have to say."

"Go away, Shivba," Jijabai said to him roughly. "Nothing you can say will relieve me of my grief."

"Mother, Shambhu is alive and well, in Mathura!" *Raje* looked at the women and saw their expressions change from sorrow to surprise, and then happiness. "What I said earlier was untrue."

"A lie! Shivba, who lies about his son's death?" Jijabai asked.

"A father who must protect his son," *Raje* replied gently. "Mother, I intend for this rumour to reach Aurangzeb's ears, so he will call off the search parties, thus making it safe for Shambhu to return."

"Highness, your ways are beyond us!" said Soyara, smiling.

Raje laughed. "Getting away from Agra was no mean task. I had to leave Shambhu behind at Mathura, knowing the Mughals would be looking for Shivaji and his son. We simply could not travel together. Besides, our return journey was extremely hectic and demanding. It was tough even on the men."

He looked at his mother, who turned away in anger. "Mother, forgive me. I had to do this. The truth about Shambhu must not go beyond this chamber. No one must know. I will perform his last rites at Rajgad soon, so the news will be believed by all."

Jijabai looked at her son incredulously. "You will perform the last rites for your son, who lives?"

"Yes, mother! And may the Goddess forgive me."

Jijabai looked at her son, her anger dissipating as she understood his incredible plan to get his son back safely. "Your father would have been proud of you today, Shivba," she said. "Only you can think like this!"

11
INTERLUDE

Shivaji *Raje*'s return to Rajgad ended months of anxiety for his family, and his people. But the rejoicing was rudely curtailed as the news of the Prince's death cast a pall of gloom over the *Swarajya*. The news spread quickly, as bad news will, and reached Agra in a matter of weeks.

The difficult and arduous journey home had taken a toll on *Raje*'s health. He fell ill and remained in bed for a long time. His health improved, but then he relapsed, sending alarm bells ringing throughout *Swarajya*.

Aurangzeb received news of Shivaji *Raje*'s return to Rajgad from his envoy at the Qutubshah's court. He would have ordinarily expected Jai Singh, his Deccan *Subadar* to send him the news, but Jai Singh had learned of the *Raje*'s return rather late. This further angered Aurangzeb, who wrote to him in a *firmaan*:

I am dismayed at your failure to inform me that Seeva has returned to his land. This news came to me in u despatch from Bhaganagar...

When Aurangzeb then received the news of Prince Sambhaji's demise, he called off the search parties. One of the fugitives was in his fortress, the other dead.

The heat having thus died down, Shivaji *Raje* sent word to Mathura, asking Kashi *Punt* to bring Sambhaji home. Three months after their flight from Agra, the Maratha Prince returned to a rousing welcome. There was much rejoicing in the Rajgad palace, and across *Swarajya*. Shivaji *Raje*'s ingenuity had seen them through a grave situation, escaping certain death.

Shivaji *Raje*'s escape from Agra had frustrated Aurangzeb no end. He had hoped to end the Maratha menace once and for all, but the incompetence of his officers and Rajput obstinacy had put paid to his plans. He had read the infidel Seeva well. He had long been convinced that Seeva was a man of unusual abilities. Such men were a boon if they worked for the Empire, but could prove to be a thorn in the flesh if not. Seeva had to be either subjugated or finished. And Aurangzeb had achieved neither! Now, with Seeva back in his own realm, the Maratha problem still loomed large on the Empire's southern frontier.

In a rearguard action, Aurangzeb ordered Jai Singh, who was still in the Deccan, to arrest Netoji Palkar, lest the ex-Maratha Commander rejoin Shivaji *Raje* and create further problems for the Empire. Accordingly, Jai Singh arranged for Netoji' arrest. Netoji, who was working for the Mughals, did not suspect this move and fell easily into Jai Singh's trap. Jai Singh then sent Netoji to Agra in Diler Khan's custody, for the Emperor to decide his fate.

Jai Singh had, however, failed against the Adilshah. The Mughal Bijapur war waged on, albiet half-heartedly on the Mughal side. Jai Singh's army had been depleted and he had received no reinforcements from the Emperor. Besides, his personal finances had suffered greatly. The Adilshah wasted time in negotiations, refusing to conclude a treaty, while his officers continued to harass Jai Singh's troops. All this made the Rajput General anxious and restless. But, despite his problems, he stayed put in the Deccan and continued to assure the Emperor that he would somehow kill Seeva.

I will not fail to exert myself against Bijapur, the desperate General wrote to the Mughal *Wazir,* Jafar Khan. *As for that wretch Seevaji, I am trying to induce him to come and meet me again, and when he does, my men will have him killed on the way here or as he returns. If His Majesty so agrees, I shall send a proposal of marriage for my son with Seevaji's daughter. Though Seevaji's pedigree is so low that men like me cannot even eat food touched by him, I shall suffer this indignity to achieve my objective. Being of low caste, Seevaji will jump at such an alliance. But great care must be taken to keep the plan secret...*

This devious plan never materialized, however, as Shivaji *Raje* paid no heed to Jai Singh's invitation to meet him. Not appeased by Jai Singh's entreaties, Aurangzeb decided to remove him from the *Subadari* of the Deccan. Jai Singh's ambitious campaign thus ended in failure and humiliation. He had hoped for high success and honours at court, but had instead been sacked from his post.

Despite his anger and frustration, Aurangzeb had no respite to launch a fresh campaign against the Marathas. Events along the northwest frontier of the Empire demanded his full attention and he had little time for Shivaji *Raje* or the the Adilshah.

The Persian Emperor Shah Abbas had ceremoniously insulted Tarbiyat Khan, the Mughal Ambassador at his court. In open *durbar*, and in Tarbiyat Khan's presence, Shah Abbas had suggested marching to Hindustan to teach Aurangzeb a lesson in warfare. This set alarm bells ringing in Agra and the usually unperturbed Aurangzeb was greatly disturbed. He immediately recalled his chief officers to court and despatched Prince Muazzam and Jaswant Singh with twenty thousand troopers to the Persian frontier. Aurangzeb himself left Agra with an even larger army, intending to join the Prince later.

However, in the interim, there arrived the news of the Persian Emperor's death. Shah Abbas' son, Safi Mirza, had been crowned the next Shah. This removed the threat of a Persian invasion, at least temporarily. Aurangzeb, who had reached Delhi, changed his plans and ordered Prince Muazzam to stay put in Lahore and not advance any further.

This, however, did not end Aurangzeb's troubles. The Afghan tribes in the Empire's northwestern reaches, had rebelled against the imperial Mughal officers. These tribes had never been fully subdued, and despite Mughal overlordship, continued to exact toll on the roads to Lahore and Kabul. A number of expeditions against these tribes had failed in the past and the Mughal administration had finally decided to let the situation be, in order to keep the roads open.

Now, however, the Yusufzai tribe which inhabited the mountainous tract flanking the road from Lahore to the Khyber Pass, and had practically declared war. They had crossed the Sindhu River and overrun the plains east of the river, exacting forced contributions from the populace. They followed this by pillaging territory on the banks of the Kabul River.

Following close on the heels of the Persian threat, this Afghan revolt jolted Aurangzeb and alarmed him enough to order Amir Khan, Governor of the province, to counter the Afghan rebels with five thousand men from his local force. He followed this order by despatching another force of nine thousand troopers under the command of Mohammed Amin, the *Mir Bakshi*. But before these forces could take action, the brave Mughal *Fauzdar* of Kabul, Kamil Khan, marched against the rebels with whatever forces he could muster. In a spirited attack, he suceeded in defeating the rebels, who fled across the Sindhu to the west. By then, Amir Khan's detachment had arrived on the scene under the command of Shamshir Khan. The bolstered Mughal force then crossed the Sindhu, marched into Yusufzai country and defeated the rebels in a series of battles. Mohammed Amin arrived later, and, crossing the Kabul River, devastated more rebel country.

Aurangzeb's officers thus managed to quell this rebellion. However, the Emperor's peace of mind had been wrecked and his resources significantly sapped.

Meanwhile Prince Muazzam had returned from Lahore. Aurangzeb despatched him to the Deccan as the new *Subadar*. The beleagured Jai Singh, who had never tired of requesting his sovereign for another chance in the Deccan, was finally compelled to hand over charge of the Deccan to the Prince. Grieving and defeated, the proud Rajput turned north, to return to Amer, his home principality. But fate had other designs. He injured his leg mounting his elephant, and the wound quickly festered, leading to a protracted illness. Soon after reaching Burhanpur, this master of a thousand battles, died.

Kirat Singh suspected Jai Singh's *Munshi*, Udairaj, of having poisoned his father. Fearing for his life, Udairaj fled to the *Subadar* of Khandesh, and promptly embraced Islam. Kirat Singh had to give up his plan to personally slaughter the traitor as it was impossible for him to harm a neophyte.

Diler Khan presented the imprisoned Netoji Palkar before Aurangzeb and the Emperor ordered him to embrace Islam. The former Maratha *Sirnaubat* refused, upon which he was thrown into the dungeons. Several days in prison, however, broke Netoji's resolve and he submitted to the Emperor. He embraced Islam and even convinced his wives to do the same. Aurangzeb renamed him Mohammed Quli Khan, and awarded him a suitable post in the Mughal armed forces. Not trusting him entirely, Aurangzeb placed him under strict watch by senior Mughal officers.

Meanwhile, in the Deccan, there was a three-way deadlock between the Marathas, the Bijapuris, and the Mughals. The depleted Mughal force was barely able to hold on to their recent gains and refused to take on new challenges. Prince Muazzam, having taken charge from Jai Singh, was quite happy to let Shivaji *Raje* be and did not launch any active campaign. The Adilshah was, on the one hand, desperately trying to hold onto the South Konkan, and on the other, regain territory lost to the Mughals.

Shivaji *Raje* tried to patch a truce with Aurangzeb, while at the same time attempting to dislodge the Bijapuris from the South Konkan. He ordered his officers to raid Bijapuri territory in the uplands to create a diversion. Not to be outdone, the Adilshah despatched Bahlol Khan and Vyankoji Bhosale, Shivaji *Raje*'s half brother, into battle. The duo besieged Fort Rangna. When he heard of this development, *Raje*, who had by now recovered his vitality, attacked them in person, breaking the siege.

At last, Shivaji *Raje's* Marathas forced the Bijapuris out of the South Konkan, regaining that district. The Adilshah followed this reverse by signing a fresh treaty with Shivaji *Raje*. The Maratha-Bijapur conflict thus lulled into an uneasy peace.

Swarajya's southern boundary now touched the Portuguese dominion. A clash with these Europeans became imminent.

The Portuguese in Goa were never comfortable having Shivaji as their neighbour. They tried various political ploys, professing to help the Mughals against the Marathas, but as relations between Shivaji *Raje* and the Mughals improved, they backed off and instead, made friendly overtures to the Marathas.

With Shivaji *Raje* firmly occupying the South Konkan, the *Desais*, who were the local landlord chieftains, were pushed out of their realm. One of these was Lakham Savant of Wadi, who had earlier backtracked on a treaty with *Raje*. Savant and the other *Desais* took refuge in nearby Portuguese territory and from there, led a series of depredations into Maratha territory. Fed up with these conflicts, *Raje* led a strong contingent into Bardesh, with the sole aim of flushing out the recalcitrant *Desais*. The territory being Portuguese, it brought him into direct conflict with them. He however, desisted and made peace with the Europeans. One of the clauses of the subsequent treaty was that the *Desais* would be driven out of

Bardesh and Goa. The Portuguese Viceroy agreed and did just that. Lakham Savant and the others, now devoid of protection, were forced to submit to Shivaji *Raje,* who pardoned them. They did not dare to raise their head against him again.

Later, Shivaji *Raje* launched an offensive against the Siddis of Janjira, with the aim of wresting this strategically important fort from them. Unable to assault the fort directly, he resorted to besieging it with his naval vessels. The Siddis, brought to their knees, approached the Portuguese for help. The Portuguese did help them, thus precipitating a war with the Maratha navy and enraging *Raje* yet again. But once again, *Raje*'s political moves bore fruit as the Portuguese Viceroy made a second peace treaty, agreeing not to help the Siddis, and allowing small Maratha vessels to sail in waters controlled by the Portuguese.

The desperate Siddis approached the English at Mumbai, for help. The latter, wary of instigating Shivaji *Raje,* dilly-dallied with their response.

Shivaji *Raje* was unwilling to confront the Mughals any time soon. He would certainly do so in the future, but his tiny Kingdom, his people, and he himself, needed a breather. He maintained friendly relations with Prince Muazzam and the Mughal Deccan administration. He even sent a letter to the Emperor, asking to be forgiven for his past crimes and requesting release of his imprisoned diplomats. Aurangzeb too, thought it prudent for the present to keep Seeva quiet by appeasing him. So he ordered the release of Raghunath *Punt* and Tryambak *Punt,* who had been languishing in prison for nearly eight months. The duo returned to Rajgad, broken in body but not in spirit. *Raje* received them affectionately and showered praise and rewards upon them.

Through Shafi Khan, the *Diwan* of Mughal Deccan province, and later through Prince Muazzam himself, Shivaji *Raje* kept up a steady flow of letters to the Emperor, professing his loyalty to the Empire. He requested first the grant of *Sirdeshmukhi* rights in the territory he had recently ceded to the Mughals. These rights were granted, enabling *Raje* to collect at least some revenue from the lost territory. *Raje* then requested Sambhaji's former rank and status as a five thousand *mansabdar* to be reinstated. Aurangzeb initially refused, but later agreed, after being pressed by Prince Muazzam himself. Sambhaji's rank was thus reinstated and he was granted the district of Varhad, east of Aurangabad, in lieu of salary, to maintain troops.

Shivaji *Raje*'s diplomatic moves thus managed to reverse at least some of the losses of the disastrous war against Jai Singh. The Purandar treaty, which had been disregarded, was once again revived, bringing a much needed respite to Shivaji *Raje*'s *Swarajya.*

Raje received a *nishan* from Prince Muazzam, informing him of the Emperor's will. He wrote: *Raja Shivaji. His Majesty has graciously agreed to grant you the high title of 'Raja', which was the greatest of your desires. In recognition of this favour from the ever benevolent Emperor, you must strive harder in imperial service to show your loyalty...*

With the conclusion of this treaty between Shivaji *Raje* and the Mughal Emperor, the Adilshah was isolated. He now decided to make his own peace with Aurangzeb, by ceding the fortress of Solapur in tribute. This being successful, peace finally returned to the Deccan.

But the ambitions of men being like the restless sea, the peace was temporary. Shivaji *Raje* would never forego his dream of freedom, while the imperial rulers could never forget that a local landlord, son of a mere *jagirdar,* had raised his head to challenge their authority. And Aurangzeb would never disregard his burning ambition to subjugate the Adilshah, the Qutubshah, and Shivaji, and bring the entire Deccan under Mughal rule.

Yet the tenuous peace continued for some time. The Maratha country and its people breathed easy and nursed their wounds. Two years later, a series of events would end the peace and rekindle the ambition of the man who had set about challenging the imperialists. Shivaji *Raje* would put all treaties aside and embark upon a mission to reconquer lost territory and more.

12
RECONQUEST

RAJGAD, EARLY 1670

A tense atmosphere prevailed as the Maratha Council sat in session in the Rajgad palace. Shivaji *Raje* sat at the head of the Council, with his *Sirnaubat Prataprao* Gujar to his left, and his *Peshwa,* Moro *Punt* Pingale, to his right. Also present were Tryambak *Punt* the *Dabir,* Niraji Raoji the *Nyayadhish,* Raghunath Punt the *Panditrao,* Nilo Sondeo the *Muzumdar,* Anaji Datto the *Surnis* and Bahirji Naik, Head of Maratha intelligence.

"Your Highness, the Emperor's move is in direct violation of the peace treaty between us," *Sirnaubat Prataprao* Gujar said. "Our contingents in Aurangabad and Varhad were inactive and respectful of Prince Muazzam's orders."

As per the clauses of the Purandar treaty, Shivaji *Raje* had ordered two contingents under *Prataprao* and Niraji Raoji, to be stationed at the behest of the Mughal Prince. Muazzam had ordered the contingent under *Prataprao* to be moved to Sambhaji's designated *jagir* in Varhad. A few days earlier, Muazzam had received news from his own agent at the imperial court that the Emperor had issued a *firmaan* to arrest both *Prataprao* and Niraji Raoji. This news, having arrived secretly before the *firmaan* itself, had alerted the Prince, who, owing to the good relations between him and the Marathas, had advised Niraji Raoji to flee Aurangabad. Word had also been despatched to *Prataprao*. The two Maratha officers had managed to get back to Rajgad.

"Quite true, Highness," Niraji Raoji said. "There was absolutely no reason for the Emperor to issue such an order."

"I agree," Shivaji *Raje* said. "Prince Muazzam has taken a grave risk by informing us. He could be accused of treason if this reaches Aurangzeb's ears."

"Highness, there is news of temple desecration from all parts of the Empire," Bahirji Naik said. "Aurangzeb seems to have issued orders to all provinces to demolish Hindu schools and temples. The sacred temples at Kashi and Mathura have been destroyed."

Raje's eyes flashed in anger, but maintaining a calm face, he said, "Aurangzeb seems to be purposefully instigating unrest. Such persecution will never go down well with the masses. And certainly not with us!"

The men nodded in agreement. *Prataprao* caressed his moustache thoughtfully before saying, "Highness, our armies have been quiet for some time. Perhaps it is time to sharpen our blades."

"Yes, *Sirnaubat*," *Raje* agreed. "Aurangzeb has ended the peace that has existed between the Marathas and the Mughals, and has dared to destroy our temples. We embarked upon this journey to fight such opression, and so we shall. Let it be known from this day that we will fight the Mughal Empire with all our energy and resources. We will win back all the fortresses and territory we ceded to them in the Purandar treaty. And after that, we will expand our kingdom beyond that. From this day, we shall not rest till we bring the Mughal Empire down!"

The men beamed at each other as they heard their King declare war on the Mughal. Years earlier, they had been forced into quiet inactivity after their defeat at the hands of Jai Singh. They had diligently played the part of faithful vassal. But now it was time to put aside diplomatic treaties and make-believe promises and rise to the call of their motherland. If they wanted freedom, they would have to confront the Mughal Empire, and by Lord Mahadev, they would!

"*Sirnaubat*, divide our forces into mobile units. Assign these to select officers and begin reclaiming our twenty-three forts. Raid the Mughal Deccan province and throw the Mughal administration into disarray."

"It shall be done, Highness."

"Bahirji," *Raje* turned to his chief spy, "what is the state of the Mughal armed forces in the Deccan?"

"The Mughal army is spread quite thinly over the countryside. Most of their men and artillery is concentrated in the forts. Our movements should not be hampered. Besides, we should be able to take back most of the forts by night escalade."

"Aurangzeb has planned this poorly. I would have expected him to safeguard his recent gains in the Deccan more diligently."

"Highness, Aurangzeb has had to divert troops to the northern provinces where the Jats have rebelled against the Mughal administration. Aurangzeb had to march personally to put that rebellion down."

"Well, it suits us perfectly, does it not?" Shivaji *Raje* said with a laugh. "While rebellions in the north keep Aurangzeb occupied, we shall reclaim our lost forts and lands."

He rose from his seat and pulled his *Bhavani* out of its scabbard. His men unsheathed their blades as well. "By Lord Mahadev, we swore to fight these foreign rulers. It is time we keep our oath of *Swarajya*. Let our armies spread across the Deccan and liberate our people. Let this be a fight to the end, because after we are done, either we shall perish or shall the Mughals. *Har Har Mahadev*!"

A FEW DAYS LATER

The mood was effervescent as the Maratha War Council met in the Rajgad palace. The conference chamber was packed to capacity with Infantry and Cavalry Commanders heading various departments. Shivaji *Raje* sat at the head of the assembly. His *Sirnaubat, Peshwa* and other ministers were also present. The men were brimming with enthusiasm about the impending war with the Mughal.

"Your Highness, the reconquest has been planned; assault teams and Captains have been designated." *Sirnaubat Prataprao* Gujar updated the King.

"Excellent!" *Raje* beamed at him. "My men, remember what we stand for...complete freedom from foreign rule. We shall not rest till we have achieved that."

"Highness, we have not yet assigned the Kondhana mission to anyone," *Prataprao* reminded the King. *Raje* had asked him to defer the decisions on the reconquest of Kondhana till this all important War Council.

Raje looked at his men. Kondhana, the jewel of the Sahyadris, was under Mughal control. Years ago, after signing the treaty with

Jai Singh, Shivaji *Raje* had personally handed over charge of Fort Kondhana to the Mughal Commanders. That day, he had silently vowed to take it back. He only had to wait for the right moment. Since that dark day, he had often seen his mother gazing fondly at Kondhana from the Rajgad citadel. Kondhana had always been her favourite fort. It was commonly said amongst the Rajgad locals that Rajgad belonged to the King, but Kondhana belonged to the Queen Mother.

"I want Kondhana back," Jijabai had said to him many times in the past two years. Now the time had come to fulfill her wish. But it would not be easy. In fact, it would be the toughest campaign of this war. There was a reason Kondhana was called a jewel; it was one of the toughest forts to capture. In the past, Rajput Mughal troops under Jaswant Singh had toiled in vain for months to take it from the Marathas, and failed. *Raje* knew he had to appoint a Commander of exceptional qualities to take back Kondhana from the Mughals. He had a name in mind...

"Kondhana promises to be the toughest challenge we shall face in this war." *Raje* paused, looking around at the expectant faces, eager to know whom he would appoint. "Now, who is up to this challenge? Who will take Kondhana from the Mughals?"

A man stood up, "Your Highness, I shall win Kondhana for you." All eyes turned to regard the tall, well built Maratha Commander. His eyes sparkled with excitement. It was Tanhaji Malusare, *Raje*'s childhood friend and one of his most trusted men.

Raje beamed at him happily. Tanhaji was just the name he had in mind for the Kondhana campaign. But *Raje* said to him gently, "Tanhya, your son is getting married. You should be here for the marriage. I could send someone else to Kondhana!"

Tanhaji smirked. "Highness, we have set aside our families years ago and offered ourselves wholeheartedly to our cause. Kondhana shall be married off first, then my son Raiba!"

Bravo! Bravo! the men shouted, applauding loudly. *Raje* rose from his seat and approached his old friend. Placing his hands on Tanhaji's shoulders, he said, "Tanhya, may the Goddess be with you. Come back victorious and safe!"

Tanhaji bowed as his King presented him with a sword to mark his appointment to this prestigious campaign. Shivaji *Raje* watched, a prayer in his heart, as Tanhaji left the chamber to begin his preparations for the arduous assault.

In the dim flickering light of a lamp, four men poured over the map of Fort Kondhana, spread before them. They sat in a small hut, Tanhaji Malusare in the centre, flanked by his younger brother Suryaji, and his uncle Kondaji Shelar. Across from Tanhaji sat Bahirji Naik.

Kondhana sat pristinely atop the Sahyadri hills, some six *kos* north of Rajgad. The fort had two gates, one on the north face, and the other to the southeast. The paths leading to these gates were narrow and arduous. A large body of soldiers could not move up together. In any case, these approaches were closely guarded and unsuitable for assault. The fort had firm rock ramparts only in some areas, but the rest of it was unapproachable due to natural defences. Treacherous mountain slopes led up to the fort on all sides, and most of these were practically unscalable.

The fort was commanded by Udaybhan Rathore, a Rajput Mughal officer who belonged to the Rathore clan of Jodhpur. A strict disciplinarian, Udaybhan had established a rule of terror in Kondhana and in its controlled territory. His men were under strict instructions to watch all approaches to the fort, at all times, even at night. Those who failed to do so were severely punished. Anyone who strayed into the fort environs after sunset were killed outright. Udaybhan had fifteen hundred Rajput and Mughal soldiers at his disposal in the fort.

"It will be tough," Bahirji Naik summed up. "The formal approaches to the two gates are out of the question, so are most of the mountain sides. Where will you scale the mountain?"

Tanhaji scratched the stubble on his chin as he looked at the map. "What about the western face?"

"Western face?" Bahirji repeated, bewildered. "You mean the Donagiri Cliff?"

"Yes, the Donagiri Cliff!"

"Tanhaji, that cliff is a vertical rockface! How will you scale it?"

Tanhaji gave him a wry smile. "Leave that to me. Tell me about the watch on that side of the fort."

"The sentry deployment on the western side is thin, I am told." Bahirji replied. "Udaybhan probably expects no one to scale that cliff and hence does not fear an assault from the western side."

Tanhaji looked at his brother and uncle. "What do you say we give him a nasty surprise then?"

"Sounds good to me," Suryaji nodded.

The more cautious Kondaji Shelar said, "Tanha, scaling the vertical rockface in pitch darkness will be hazardous. We could lose men even before reaching the top."

"Nothing is ever achieved without taking a risk, Shelar *mama!*" Tanhaji said to his uncle. "Kondhana cannot be captured by any other means. Jaswant Singh failed in his siege, even with a large army at his disposal. In any case, I am not the kind to sit tight with an investing army for months on end. We will lead a single assault and take the fort. The Donagiri cliff seems ideal to reach the fort."

"How many men will you take along?" Bahirji asked.

"Five hundred at the most."

"There are fifteen hundred soldiers in the fort," Bahirji reminded him, looking doubtful.

"I know. But I do not think we can take any more up that slope without being discovered. In any case, I am sure each of us can bring down at least three Mughals."

"I can take down many more!" Suryaji said with a smile and the others laughed.

"Right then, the decision is made. We scale the Donagiri cliff three nights hence. We will handpick our men for the job. Surya, send for Saoji and his team of rock climbers. No one must know of this mission and the Donagiri Cliff till we actually get there."

The men looked at each other grimly. The mission was perilous, but Kondhana was worth risking their lives for.

Western face of Kondhana mountain,
night of 4/5 February 1670

The first *prahar* of the night had nearly ended. In the pitch darkness, five hundred men, having trudged through the thick undergrowth of the forest to the western face of the mountain, assembled at the base of Donagiri Cliff. Their Commander, *Subedar* Tanhaji Malusare, stared at the vertical rock that stood between him and the fort above. In the dim moonlight, one could just see the rockface. The top was lost in darkness.

"Saoji!" Tanhaji hissed. A lithe young boy jumped forward. Three other slimly built boys followed him. Each carried thick coils of rope slung over their shoulders. "Now," Tanhaji said, "scale this cliff. When you reach the top, tie the ropes to some trees and let them down for us."

The boys looked incredulously at the *Subedar*. They had been told their job that night was to scale a cliff. But they hadn't been told that it was the Donagiri! The vertical rockface of Dronagiri was daunting for even expert climbers in broad daylight. And the *Subedar* wanted them to scale it in pitch darkness!

"Well, what are you waiting for?" Tanhaji barked at Saoji. "Do you expect me to give you a royal salute and blow *shingas*?" Saoji shook his head. "Then, move it! I don't have all night!"

Saoji nodded and advanced towards the rockface, signalling his companions to follow. One by one, the boys began climbing the cliff. In the darkness, they had no visual to go by, only feel. They grabbed hold of a niche here, a crevice there and hoisted themselves up. The going was slow; one foothold at a time. Tanhaji and the others eventually lost sight of them in the darkness and could do nothing but wait for the ropes to be thrown down... or the boys themselves to drop. Tanhaji knew the perils they faced. What if they did not find adequate footholds? They were as good as blind up there. What if they slipped? What if some snake crept out of a crevice? Despite his tough stance, Tanhaji murmured a fervent prayer for help: *Let the boys reach the top, O Lord!*

Much later, a rope came slithering down the slope. The men exulted, but made no noise. Soon, another rope came down, and then another. Their first gamble had paid off. Tanhaji grabbed a rope and began hoisting himself up the slope. Suryaji followed, and then Kondaji Shelar.

Rajgad palace, the same night

Jijabai sat by the large window in her chamber and looked across the Sahyadri hills. It was the ninth night after *amavasya* and the dim moonlight just about illuminated the crests of the hills, enabling her to locate Fort Kondhana. Somewhere on that mountain, her sons were battling the enemy to wrest the fort.

Shivaji *Raje* silently entered the chamber and walked up to her. Jijabai continued to look out the window. "Do you think the battle has begun?" she asked.

"Mother, how did you know it was me? You did not even look!" *Raje* asked, surprised.

Jijabai turned to him and said, "Shivba, a mother can recognise her son's footfall without seeing."

Raje smiled and gently placed a hand on her shoulder. "The battle may have begun. If things have gone according to Tanhya's plan, he should be in the fort now."

Jijabai let out a sigh. For a lifetime she had been cursed with having to wait anxiously while her boys risked their lives on dangerous missions. Shivba was safe tonight, but Tanhaji was out there, battling, shedding blood.

"Was it necessary to send Tanha on this mission? He should have been home, preparing for Raiba's wedding."

"You know Tanhaji, Mother. No one could have stopped him from going on this mission, not even me. Besides, no one knows Kondhana better than him. If anyone has a chance to capture that fort, it is Tanhaji."

"My mind is restless, Shivba. I hope our men come back safe."

"Do not worry, Mother. The Goddess is with them."

The third *prahar* of the night had just begun. Nearly three hundred Marathas had scaled the Donagiri Cliff and now lay hidden in the bushes on top. Concealed in the foliage, Tanhaji could faintly hear the sound of voices moving in their direction. In a moment, Suryaji heard it too. Some Rajput Mughal soldiers on night guard approached their position from the north.

Several agonizing moments later, the guards were in plain view. They carried flaming torches which illuminated the surroundings. All was quiet on the western side. The guards had not spotted the ropes tied to trees and let down over the Donagiri rockface. Tanhaji fervently prayed the guards would move on before any more of his men came up the ropes.

The guards were directly in front of them now. A Mavala soldier came up a rope and scrambled to the top, panting hard. The surprised guards were momentarily speechless as another Mavala appeared, having scaled the second rope. Tanhaji knew they had been discovered. He grimaced and emerged from the bushes, followed closely by Suryaji and Kondaji. Together, they fell upon the hapless guards and cut them down. In the commotion, one of the guards escaped into the night.

"The garrison will be alerted soon," Tanhaji said to his men urgently. "Get ready to fight!"

"Only about three hundred have reached the top, *Subedar*," Suryaji said. "We are badly outnumbered."

"Then so be it!" Tanhaji growled at him. "It was three to one when we started out; now it is five to one. How does that change our agenda? We came here to fight, so we fight!"

Tanhaji quickly ordered his Captains to organize their units and the men began moving in the direction of the *Killedar*'s residence. Tanhaji knew the strength of the garrison lay not in their numbers, but in their brave Commander, Udaybhan Rathore. Cornering and killing the *Killedar* was key to capturing the fort. But that was easier said than done.

From the Rajgad palace, Shivaji *Raje* and Jijabai could now see the top of Fort Kondhana, illuminated by a faint glow. As he squinted into the distance, *Raje* saw the moving lights of the torches. *The battle has begun*, he thought, a knot forming in his stomach. *Give us victory, Mother!* he silently prayed. *Give us Kondhana! Keep Tanhya and Surya safe*. Getting control of Kondhana and its appurtunent territory was crucial to controlling Pune, the centre of the *Swarajya*. Besides, as long as Kondhana lay in enemy hands, Rajgad itself could never be safe. Shivaji *Raje* knew that to safeguard his kingdom, he had to take Kondhana. "*Jagdamb!*" he exclaimed, clutching the string of cowrie shells around his neck.

The western section of Fort Kondhana had erupted into life. A pitched battle had begun between the three hundred Marathas who had scaled the Donagiri Cliff and the Rajput Mughals garrisoning the fort. Flaming torches danced around, piercing the dark and creating moving halos of light. The previously quiet night filled with the heady din of battle as weapons clashed and men screamed. The initial Maratha assault was so fierce that the Rajputs were taken aback. Tanhaji's men bayed for blood and slaughtered the initial wave of fort defenders. Tanhaji knew they had to make haste else they would all be dead. Surprise was their biggest advantage and they had to use it to the fullest. The garrison was unprepared for an attack on the fort and that was his greatest weapon. But, battle-hardened soldiers that they were, it did not take the Rajputs long to regroup and launch a determined counter-offensive. The tide of the battle slowly turned as more Marathas fell, reducing their already paltry numbers.

Tanhaji had just disposed of two defenders when a tall, well built Rajput confronted him. The Rajput's face was contorted with rage, his clothes dishevelled. He was quite clearly hopping mad at being woken up in the middle of the night. Yet he held his sword and shield firmly, challenging Tanhaji with an unnerving yell. Though they had never met each other, Tanhaji recognized him as Udaybhan, the fort Commander. Udaybhan too, recognized the Maratha Commander. In an instant both knew that slaying the other would decisively turn the battle in his favour.

The Commanders fell upon each other with a vengeance. Udaybhan rained blow upon powerful blow on Tanhaji, who blocked his blade with his shield. But the Rajput's power and strength were undeniable and Tanhaji kept moving back trying to avoid his blows. Udaybhan sensed weakness and followed him. Tanhaji sensed his eagerness to engage and kept leading him on. Udaybhan yelled, trying to instigate Tanhaji while hammering him with more blows. The Rajput Commander, sensing reluctance in the Maratha, kept pushing on, tiring himself out in the process.

Tanhaji saw the Rajput Commander slowing and knew he had to make his move. As Udaybhan raised his sword, Tanhaji buckled, raised his shield to block Udaybhan's blow and simultaneously jabbed with his own sword at Udaybhan's abdomen in one swift motion. The Rajput was taken aback, but managed to swerve away at the crucial moment. Tanhaji's blade slashed his torso, but failed to impale him.

Udaybhan staggered back in pain. His angry eyes glared at Tanhaji, who gave him an annoying grin. "Not so tough, are you Rajput?" Tanhaji chided him.

"I am going to kill you, scum!" Udaybhan growled. "How dare you set foot in my fort?"

"Your fort is breached, Udaybhan!" Tanhaji said. "At this moment, Shivaji *Raje* stands in readiness with thousands of troops to storm it. Give up now and live."

"Give up? How dare you tell a Rajput to give up?" Udaybhan yelled and charged Tanhaji again.

The two engaged in another heated exchange and soon both had received near fatal wounds. Yet they stood their ground. But finally, fate turned against the Maratha. Udaybhan landed a telling blow which Tanhaji blocked with his shield. The Rajput's sword cleaved the shield in two. Tanhaji had lost his defence. Seriously wounded, he could see his own end as Udaybhan advanced for the final strike.

Tanhaji frantically moved back, looking for a replacement shield. In the dim light of moving torches, he could find none. Finally, in desperation, he removed his turban and tied it around his left hand and arm, hoping to use that to block Udaybhan's blows. Udaybhan knew he had his man. He had simply to land one final blow and it would be the end of the Maratha.

All over the western section of the fort, battle raged fiercely between the attackers and defenders. As more Rajputs fell, the garrison began losing heart. Suryaji and Kondaji sensed this and urged their men to press on.

Suddenly, Suryaji heard a shout from the far side: *The Subedar has lost his shield and is seriously wounded!* Suryaji's heart sank. He desperately wanted to rush to his brother's rescue, but he was cornered by two Rajput defenders. As he traded blows with them, he screamed at his uncle, "Shelar *mama*! The *Subedar* needs help. Go to him!"

Udaybhan's sword crashed into Tanhaji, who instinctively held out his left hand to defend himself. The sword went clean through his forearm, chopping off his hand. Tanhaji collapsed to the ground and lost consciousness. Udaybhan's face lit up with a smile, but only momentarily. Covered with wounds, his knees buckled and he too, fell. The two great warriors lay still, each breathing his last.

Dejected Maratha soldiers stood in line to seal the area. Kondaji Shelar arrived to find his nephew fallen. With a heart wrenching cry, he knelt beside Tanhaji and cradled his head in his lap.

Tanhaji's eyes flickered open. He parted his lips and murmured, "Take the fort...finish what we started..." Then he closed his eyes one last time.

The Subedar has fallen!

News of Tanhaji's demise spread quickly amongst the Marathas, and they began to panic. In a pitched battle, the Commander usually held the fortunes of an army together. How well a side fought often depended on how well the soldiers were marshalled, led and encouraged by the Commander. Hence, the Chief being slayed often spelled doom for his men. The Rajput Mughals realised their own Commander had killed his opposite number and their confidence soared. The resurgent defenders launched a scathing attack on the usurpers. The Marathas began withdrawing from a battle they had nearly won. They began fleeing toward the Donagiri Cliff, hoping to go down the ropes that had brought them up.

Suryaji could see the tide of the battle turning. He too, had heard the news of his brother's demise, which had wrenched his heart. But he had no time to lament. In a near fit of madness, he tore into the Rajput Mughals and rushed toward the Donagiri rockface.

The skies had begun to lighten. Suryaji physically pushed the demoralised Marathas away from the ropes and cut the ropes. The horrified men watched their last hope of escape slither down the rockface.

"How dare you flee when your *Subedar* has given his life for the *Swarajya*?" Suryaji glared at his men as he attempted to reverse the tide of defeat. "Is this what the *Subedar* taught us? Is this what Shivaji *Raje* taught us? To flee from battle? No one flees today! You either fight and win the fort or you die! Now go back and show those Mughals what Marathas are made of! Fight for our *Subedar*, our King, our land!"

Suryaji's harsh words ignited a fresh spark in the men and they turned back towards the battle with renewed vigour. The Maratha resurgence was fierce and their hot blades made the Rajput Mughal defenders pay for Tanhaji's life. By then, news of Udaybhan's death had spread too, and the garrison knew they had been done in. The surviving defenders capitulated. Kondhana was once again in Maratha hands.

Shivaji *Raje* stood impatiently by the window, gazing across at Kondhana. The skyline had brightened and he could see the hectic movement of torches had abated. As he looked closely, he saw a bonfire atop the fort. His face broke into a smile. It was Tanhaji's signal the fort had been taken!

"Mother!" he exclaimed to Jijabai, resting on a couch nearby, "Kondhana is ours! Our men have taken the fort! My Tanhya has won the fort for us!"

Jijabai rose excitedly and joined him at the window. Tears of relief escaped her eyes as she saw the flames. "Has Tanha ever failed?" she asked, laughing.

"No, he hasn't, Mother. But this was Kondhana, and Kondhana is no ordinary fort to capture. Yet Tanhya has done that too!" Shivaji *Raje* rushed off, shouting orders to ready a cavalry unit. He would ride out to Kondhana immediately and inspect his beloved fort. He could not wait to meet his victorious men...and Tanhaji.

Shivaji *Raje* alighted from his horse near the narrow path that led up to the *Kalyan Darwaza*, the southern gate to Fort Kondhana. He sprinted up the stone steps that led to the massive gate, now thrown open. *Raje* expected to be greeted by his jubiliant men, but instead saw hung heads. Suryaji, who had been waiting for him, advanced and bowed. "The fort is ours, my King. The Goddess has blessed us with victory," he said.

Raje's heart sank as he realized Tanhaji wasn't at the gate to receive him. He walked up to Suryaji and saw his crestfallen face and bloodshot eyes. "Surya," he asked, "where is Tanhya?"

Suryaji could not meet *Raje*'s eyes. He knew the news of his brother's death would deeply affect the King.

Shivaji *Raje* could not tolerate the suspense any longer. Holding Suryaji by the shoulders, he pleaded, "Where is my Tanhya?"

Suryaji broke down, sobbing, "*Raje*, the *Subedar* has fallen. My brother has fallen..."

The words fell like a sledgehammer on *Raje*'s ears. He stood still, gazing at the sobbing Suryaji, refusing to believe that his childhood friend was no more. After what seemed like an eternity, he said, "Take me to him."

Suryaji led the King to the *Killedar*'s residence, where the fallen hero lay. As Shivaji *Raje* approached, the men rose and bowed. *Raje* walked up to Tanhaji and looked down at him. In death, Tanhaji's face was calm, as if he knew his sacrifice had not been in vain. Usually bubbling with enthusiasm, Tanhaji lay quiet. A lifetime of service to his King, who now stood by his side, had come to an end.

Shivaji *Raje* could not hold back his tears. He sank down and cradled Tanhaji in his arms, not wanting to let him go, sobbing like a child. In the twenty-five years he had warred against the imperial Sultanates, *Raje* had lost countless men. He had lamented the loss of each, to the last foot soldier. But this loss ripped out his very heart. His mind refused to reconcile with the reality. Ever since they had been children, Shivaji *Raje* had taken Tanhaji's presence by his side for granted. His older mate had not just been with him through thick and thin, but had guarded him against all dangers. When *Raje* had left Pratapgad to meet Afzal Khan, Tanhaji had promised to look after the *Swarajya* and the Prince in the event of *Raje*'s death. When they had left to assault Shaista Khan, the Queen Mother had asked Tanhaji to look after his King, and Tanhaji had assured her he would. Tanhaji had been an integral part of the Maratha core group, war councils, and plans, ever since the inception of their rebellion. But now Tanhaji had left him to face the rest of his life alone. Shivaji *Raje* struggled to come to terms with his grief.

The battle hardened Maratha soldiers shed silent tears. Their hearts went out to their King, who, unlike the tyrannical Sultans, wept for his fallen men. To the Sultans only their power, their lands and their riches mattered. The deaths of their men did not. They did not hesitate to sacrifice men by the thousands to serve their political ambitions. But to Shivaji *Raje,* no riches on earth could match his real wealth, his comrades.

The Maratha King wept for a farmer's son.

RAJGAD PALACE, END FEBRUARY 1670

The pall of gloom that had enveloped Rajgad palace after Tanhaji's demise was finally lifted by the vigorous cries of a baby boy. After days of mourning, Shivaji *Raje* smiled as he held his newborn son. The infant protested angrily at being taken away from his mother.

Soyarabai laughed as she saw her husband trying in vain to quieten their son. "Your Highness is adept with a sword, yet he struggles with a baby," she teased.

Raje laughed as the boy let out another vociferous cry. Jijabai smiled and took the boy from *Raje,* cuddling him. The boy stopped bawling instantly.

Raje turned to Soyara. "Are you well?"

"It was a difficult birth," Soyara replied in a tired voice. "But the Goddess is kind. She allowed me to see your happy face while holding our son."

"We shall call him Rajaram," *Raje* said. "He shall rule like Lord Ram himself."

"The priest tells me the boy was born at an auspicious time," Jijabai said as she looked down fondly at her grandson. "He predicts this child will perform greater deeds than his father!"

Raje laughed. "Perhaps he will overthrow the throne of Delhi!"

Sirnaubat Prataprao Gujar and *Peshwa* Moro *Punt* Pingale planned an elaborate campaign of reconquest. Resurgent Maratha armies spread across the lands previously lost to the Mughal, and began reclaiming *Swarajya.* Fortresses fell to the Marathas like swatted flies and the helpless Mughal garrisons fled back north. Tanhaji and his men had begun the reconquest by capturing Kondhana. Just a month later, Nilo *Punt,* the *Muzumdar,* captured Purandar, the very fort that had been the site of the bloody war with Jai Singh and Diler Khan, years ago. Within four months, the Marathas had reconquered over twenty forts in the Sahyadris and the Konkan. The only reverse they suffered was at Fort Mahuli.

Aurangzeb was alarmed by this reigniting of the conflict with Seeva's Marathas. He immediately despatched orders to strengthen his forces in the Deccan. A number of contingents were ordered to march to the Deccan from the northern districts. But the Marathas had made headway before that could happen. Daud Khan, the Governor of Khandesh, was the only officer close enough to reach, and he did, with seven thousand cavalry. Upon his arrival, the Marathas withdrew for some time and Daud Khan marched unmolested to Fort Mahuli with reinforcements. Having done that, however, there was little else he could accomplish as all the Maratha units had moved back into the forts. So Daud Khan returned to Junnar in the north. No sooner had he withdrawn, the Marathas moved out again and resumed their acitivities.

Prince Muazzam, the *Subadar* of the Deccan, meanwhile cooled his heels in his provincial headquarters in Aurangabad, shying away from taking any decisive action against the Marathas. Emperor Aurangzeb, realizing he needed to send someone with grit to the Deccan, ordered his trusted Captain, Diler Khan, to report to Aurangabad and wait for fresh orders. Diler Khan, however, was reluctant to do so, repulsed as he was by the idea of facing Jaswant Singh, who was the Prince's confidante, and was with him at Aurangabad. Khan did not trust the Rajput at all and decided to stay put in Nagpur, a town he had newly annexed, some one hundred and fifty *kos* southwest of Aurangabad.

When he heard of this stand-off, Aurangzeb ordered Iftikar Khan to enquire into the matter. But Iftikar Khan was loathe to antagonize either the Prince or Diler Khan and so played a political game to instigate them against one another. The Prince was highly agitated when told by Iftikar, that Diler Khan was no friend of his, and began amassing troops to march against the Captain. Diler Khan, alarmed and wishing to avoid confrontation with the Prince, left the Deccan to return to Agra. Muazzam pursued him to the Tapi River on the northbound route.

This alarming news reached Aurangzeb, who immediately despatched fresh orders. Muazzam was ordered back to Aurangabad, Diler Khan was sent off to Gujarat, and Jaswant Singh received orders to march to Burhanpur. The three protagonists of the political drama of the Deccan province were thus separated, but this did not solve Aurangzeb's problems.

Rumors of a civil war amongst the Mughals were rife and Bahirji Naik's men spared no effort in fostering them. In fact, they engineered a new rumor that Prince Muazzam himself was preparing to rebel against the Emperor!

MID-1670

In the interim, Shivaji *Raje* and his Council had taken the decision to shift their capital from Fort Rajgad to Fort Raigad. Preparations for the shift had begun months earlier and had culminated in the the moving of the administration, the various offices, papers, numerous factories and stores, and finally, Shivaji *Raje*'s family.

Rajgad had been the seat of Maratha power for close to two decades and everyone was emotionally attached to the fort, especially *Raje* himself. Rajgad had been a fairly safe haven for the King. Yet they had decided to move because it was believed by many in *Raje*'s Council that Rajgad was proving insufficient to the administration in terms of space. Raigad had a much larger plateau that would provide ample space for the various offices and buildings. Besides, Raigad was further to the west in the Sahyadri range and if anything, would be a safer place.

Raigad stood atop a lone mountain close to the coastal strip of the Konkan, towering above the other peaks around it. To its east lay a strong defence line of hill forts, including Torna, Kondhana, Rajgad and Purandar. To its west lay the steep fall to the Konkan coast. The fort was not just difficult to scale and impregnable, but also difficult to invest, even with a large army. Besides, in the event of an attack, there always was the possibility of an escape westward, to the Konkan. Nearly a decade and a half ago, Shivaji *Raje* and his men had captured the fort (then called Rairi), from *Chandrarao* More, who had been eliminated. Now, this important fort would be the seat of Maratha power and witness to important years in Shivaji *Raje*'s life.

The main entrance to the fort lay on the northwest face of the mountain, flanked by two large bastions. A path led up from the village of Pachad at the foot of the mountain, to the main entrance.

Owing to its strategic importance, a large military base had been created at Pachad, with permanent offices and a standing cavalry unit of ten thousand as the fort's first line of defence.

The main citadel towered over the rest of the fort and housed the King's palace and the administrative offices. The fort also boasted of a large market place, several lakes and temples, granaries, stables and ammunition depots.

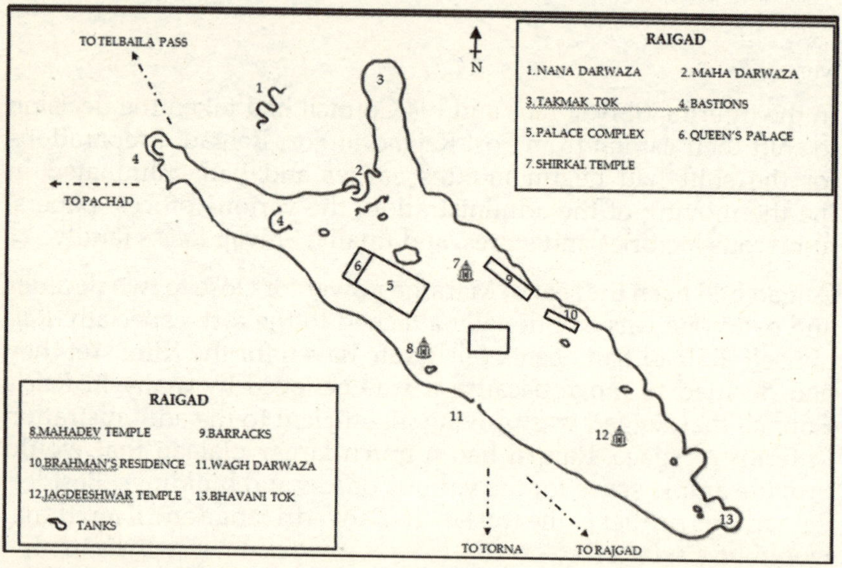

The actual shift took several weeks, but having accomplished it, Shivaji *Raje* did not have the time to reflect on the important event. He had embarked upon his final struggle with the Mughal Empire and had no respite from politics, planning and war.

Fresh alarm rose in Surat about an impending attack on the city by the Marathas. These rumors circulated for several months, worrying the rich Surat merchants. The English, Dutch and French factory owners in Surat were similarly alarmed as everyone remembered the Maratha wrath of years ago. The foreigners began making their own preparations, reinforcing their garrisons and stock piling ammunition. The common people, however, had only the Mughal administration to look to. This time, the Emperor did not disappoint them and sent Bahadur Khan the *Subadar* of Gujarat, with five thousand horsemen to safeguard the city.

Shivaji *Raje* received news of Bahadur Khan's deployment and cunningly delayed his march to Surat for several months. Bahadur Khan sat inactive in Surat for six months and begn to think Seevaji had merely been bluffing. When he became complacent, *Raje* planned a massive assault on the city.

Surat city, 3 October, 1670

Surat residents woke to the terrifying news that Shivaji *Raja* had appeared at their gates at the head of fifteen thousand cavalry and foot soldiers. Bahadur Khan made an attempt to resist the invaders, but could do no more than offer token resistance before retiring to the fort. Once again, as had happened years ago, the designated Mughal Governor left the city at the mercy of the Marathas, who plundered the city at will and gathered booty in excess of six million rupees. As had happened during the first raid, many houses were burned down. By decree of their King, the Marathas raided the town under strict discipline, sparing the poor, the women, children, the elderly, men of religion, and all those who paid up willingly.

The British and Dutch factories offered stoic resistance and refused to wilt under the many threats by the Maratha Captains. Shivaji *Raje* ordered that they be left alone, as he did not want a full scale war in Surat. He similarly left Bahadur Khan's garrison in the fort unmolested. The French were overtly friendly towards the Marathas, and even offered to provide gunpowder and shot. The British also made peace with Shivaji *Raje*, offering him gifts.

The *serais* were attacked as well. The old *serai* then housed the deposed Tartar King of Kashgar, whose men initially offered tough resistance to the Marathas, but later had to abandon the *serai* and their treasures, which fell to the raiders. The new *serai* was occupied by Turkish merchants, who firmly resisted the Maratha attacks and defended their lot.

On the fourth morning, Shivaji *Raje* ordered his men to evacuate the city with the gathered spoils.

Prince Muazzam had received news of Shivaji *Raje*'s march to Surat and had expediously ordered Daud Khan, who was at Burhanpur, to march west to intercept the Marathas. Daud Khan set out with ten thousand men, via Aurangabad and Vaijapur. After forced marches, he was within reach of the Chandwad mountain pass when he received news from his scouts that a large Maratha army was stationed in the area. He immediately declared there would be no rest and marched through the night to catch up with the fugitive army.

Chandwad mountain range, north of Nasik,
17 October 1670

The Maratha army had marched, with the loot, due southeast from Surat and had reached the Chandwad mountain range, north of Nasik, when Shivaji *Raje* received news of the arrival of a large Mughal army. The intelligent tactician that he was, he ordered his army to be divided into five units. The advance guard was despatched south with the booty, while two smaller units were sent into the hills to flank the approaching Mughals. *Raje* himself stayed put in a plain, right in the way of the marching enemy, to take them head on. A fifth unit was designated the rear guard and positioned between the expected scene of battle and the escaping booty.

Early in the morning, Daud Khan despatched his vanguard under the command of Ikhlas Khan, towards the Marathas. His job was to thwart the Maratha advance and then stay put. Ikhlas Khan could clearly see the Marathas entrenched in a plain below a mountain pass, north of Dindori village. With the zeal of youth, Ikhlas disregarded Daud Khan's orders to stay put and wait for the main body of the army. He decided to charge the Marathas. This proved disastrous for the Mughals.

As the Maratha outposts sounded the horns, alerting their men to the approaching enemy, Shivaji *Raje* donned his metal armour, breast and back plates, arm and leg guards, and helmet, readying for battle. This was what he had trained for. He was not one to stay back in his fort while his men died for him. He chose to lead his men into battle.

Ikhlas Khan's vanguard fell upon the Marathas and a pitched battle ensued. Cavalrymen charged cavalrymen, and foot soldiers engaged each other in fierce battle as the Marathas and the Mughals both attempted to disperse each other's formations. Shivaji *Raje* had spotted the Mughal Captain early on and made a beeline for his position. His personal bodyguard of armoured foot and horse soldiers surrounded him as he penetrated deep into the Mughal lines. Ikhlas Khan too, fought like a man possessed, but alas, Shivaji *Raje*'s experience and skill proved too much for him to handle. He was seriously wounded and unhorsed, and stood precariously, with a few of his men, in a sea of enemy soldiers.

Just when all seemed lost, Daud Khan arrived with the main body of the army and rescued him. The Mughal artillery was with Daud Khan's units and the Marathas had to withdraw under heavy fire from the Mughals. But *Raje* kept his units hovering around, and in a spirited attack, assaulted Mir Abdul Mabood, the Artillery Commander, thus separating him from his unit. Mabood was seriously wounded and his son killed as the Mughal artillery stood in disarray. The Mughals had suffered heavy losses by then; over three thousand of their men lay dead in the killing fields and many more were wounded. As night fell, both parties, weary from the daylong battle, withdrew.

The Marathas crossed the mountain passes and descended into the North Konkan, while Daud Khan dejectedly marched to Nasik, craving relief for his wounded. He and his men had put up a brave fight and the Marathas had suffered heavily. But in the end, Daud Khan had failed to prevent the Surat loot from reaching its destination.

November 1670

A flotilla of one hundred and sixty medium-sized and small vessels had docked at Nagaon port on the Konkan coast. Darya Sarang, Admiral of the Maratha Navy, had his hands full, organizing the massive naval exercise. Soon, they sailed north toward Daman, but once they arrived there, they turned south once again.

The Europeans along the western coast were thrown into a frenzy of activity by this massive naval movement. Bahirji Naik's sleuths adeptly circulated rumors of naval and land expeditions by the Maratha army, once again alarming Surat, as well as the English at Mumbai. Darya Sarang had his own men visit Mumbai discreetly, planting more misinformation.

While the Europeans and Mughals were thus guessing what the Marathas were up to, Shivaji *Raje* marched north with twenty thousand troops and ten thousand cavalry, and burst into the hilly

Mughal district of Baglan, north of Nasik, the very region of his recent skirmish with Daud Khan. This district had over a thousand villages and was guarded by nine hill forts, the strongest being Salher and Mulher.

Peshwa Moro *Punt* Pingale led a detachment and captured the forts of Ahiwant, Markanda and Ravala-Javala, while *Raje* himself turned to the plains east of the mountain range and swooped down upon Khandesh and Varhad. He sacked the rich trading town of Karanja late that month, and carried away over ten million rupees worth of loot.

Daud Khan, who had retired to Nasik after the bloody battle near Dindori, had moved to Ahmednagar, where he heard of the Maratha movement in Baglan. He made haste to march northwestwards and arrived in the region, doing his best to catch up with marauding Maratha divisions. However, on reaching Baglan, he learnt that Shivaji *Raje* had gone east to Khandesh and Burhanpur. So he turned to Khandesh, hot on the Maratha's heels. Alas, before he could reach Karanja, Shivaji *Raje* had already turned back west toward Baglan with the loot. The frustrated Khan turned westward again, and on the way, learnt that the Marathas had attacked Fort Salher. Every day he received new intelligence of Maratha movements spread far and wide across the Baglan and Khandesh regions. Not knowing how to counter such tactics, he entrenched himself near the Chandwad range at Kanchan-Manchan, resolving to check further Maratha depredations.

Meanwhile, Shivaji *Raje* had laid siege to Fort Salher, which sat pristinely atop the tallest mountain in the range. Siezing an opportunity in the dead of night, the Marathas attached ladders to the ramparts and scaled the fort walls to storm it. In the ensuing battle, Fathullah Khan, the fort Commander, was killed and the garrison capitulated.

Fort Salher stood in a position of tremendous strategic importance and as such awarded Shivaji *Raje* great advantages. Firstly, it gave him an admirable base for operations against the rich provinces of Gujarat to the east, and Khandesh to the west. Several important Mughal posts, including Burhanpur, the provincial capital of Khandesh and Aurangabad, the capital of the Mughal Deccan province, now lay within easy reach. Secondly, two important Mughal trade and travel routes were now flanked by the new

Maratha acquisitions in the Sahyadris – the Surat-Nasik-Junnar route, and the Surat-Srigonda route. The Marathas could thus control movement on these routes. Thirdly, the Maratha front had now advanced northward and wedged itself into Mughal territory. With the newly acquired forts and the Sahyadris to back them up, Shivaji *Raje* could now effectively keep forces at the ready and hidden from the Mughals, to check their operations.

The Mughals could neither concentrate their forces at one place, which would leave too much territory unguarded, nor spread their forces around, making them vulnerable to elimination in totality. Daud Khan had faced this dilemma while trying to stop the Maratha raids in Khandesh and Baglan. The conquests in the Baglan district, particularly Salher, had made it near impossible for the Mughals to check the Marathas.

Shivaji *Raje*'s genius in planning was plainly visible to all. While his distracting raids in the eastern district of Khandesh kept Daud Khan in continuous chase mode, his other units made important conquests and consolidated their position in the Baglan district.

Finally, as the Maratha units left the Khandesh territory they had raided, they took written undertakings from the residents that they would pay a fourth share of taxes to the Marathas. This was a direct psychological attack to undermine the prestige of the Empire. *Raje*'s logic was simple: *Destroy their trade, control their trade movements and make them pay a share of taxes to us.* The Mughals were just awakening to these ingenious moves.

November 1670 to June 1671

The Maratha raids in Khandesh, followed by the advancement of their front in Baglan, distressed the Emperor. He clearly saw how the Marathas would benefit in the future from these conquests and could not permit them to remain in Baglan. He appointed Mahabat Khan as General of the Mughal army in the Deccan and ordered him to deal with the Marathas and wrest back the lost forts from them.

Mahabat Khan landed in Aurangabad with fresh troops, bringing the Mughal cavalry numbers in the Deccan to nearly fifty thousand. He set out for Chandwad, and thence into Baglan, and systematically besieged fortresses recently lost to the Marathas. The smaller forts around Salher capitulated quickly. The monsoon arrived and

Mahabat Khan marched first to Ahmednagar, and thence to Parner, to camp during the rains.

But Baglan was not allowed to remain at peace, for Mahabat Khan left behind Bahadur Khan, *Subadar* of Gujarat, in charge of Mughal forces, with Diler Khan as his second-in-command. These determined officers laid siege to Fort Salher at the height of the monsoon. Once the siege was in place, Bahadur Khan himself departed, leaving Ikhlas Khan in command.

1671

Shivaji *Raje* had decided to simultaneously open a campaign against the Abyssinian power ruling the western coast. The Siddis had been a thorn in their flesh for decades, lording over the maritime traffic in the western seas and making a nuisance of themselves in Maratha held coastal territories. Despite his best efforts till then, this seemingly small naval power had held out against his substantial strength on land. The Siddis' supremacy at sea was difficult to challenge, even with his own naval force.

Shivaji *Raje*'s Marathas had captured the coastal territory facing the Siddi stronghold of Fort Janjira. *Raje* ordered a fresh initiative and besieged the port of Danda Rajpuri, choking off the Siddis' supplies from the coast. Simultaneously, his navy attempted to besiege Fort Janjira itself. This simultaneous land and naval siege lasted many months, driving the Abyssinians to hunger and desperation. The Siddi ruler, Fateh Khan, had exhausted his funds and now had no money to pay his men, who were on the edge of rebellion. In desperation, he turned to the Portuguese, who, despite an earlier treaty with the Marathas, decided to help Fateh Khan. But as fate would have it, even with their help, Fateh Khan got no respite.

Raigad, late June 1671

Shivaji *Raje* paced his chamber impatiently as Bahirji Naik stood with folded hands, filling him in on the latest intelligence from the Mughal front.

"Over twenty thousand Mughal troops have beseiged Salher," Bahirji said. "They have plenty of firepower, cavalry and elephants as well."

"Who is in command? Diler Khan?" *Raje* asked.

"Ikhlas Khan is in command right now," Bahirji replied.

"Where then is Diler Khan?"

Bahirji paused for effect, then said, "Diler Khan is marching south via Nasik, with over ten thousand cavalry."

"South?" *Raje* raised his eyebrows. "Where is he headed?"

"Pune," Bahirji said grimly.

Raje sighed. Another Mughal invasion directed towards the centre of his fiefdom. They had barely recovered from the wounds of the Shaista Khan and Jai Singh campaigns, and now Diler Khan was headed their way. Once again the Mughals would inflict terrible depredation on his land and people. "We must stop him!" *Raje* said, clenching his fists.

"But how? We do not have sufficient troops here. Moro *Punt* and Kudtoji are both campaigning on the Mughal front, with most of our forces."

"If we can't stop him, then we must try and divert him back north. Where are our Commanders right now?"

"Moro *Punt* has crossed the Sahyadri passes and entered the Konkan. The *Sirnaubat* is in the Ahmednagar region."

Raje considered the situation and made a decision. "Send your fastest riders to them both, immediately. Order them to join forces near Salher and attack the Mughal camp, besieging the fort. Destroy the camp. Kill as many as possible. Let it be a massacre the Mughals will remember forever."

"We are hoping that Diler Khan will turn back on hearing the news of this attack?"

Raje narrowed his eyes. "He will have no other choice. The Mughals do not have spare forces to bolster their siege at Salher."

FORT KANER, NORTH OF NASIK

A determined fort Commander looked across from the rampart of his small fort at the enemy forces massing in the distance. Thousands of Mughals systematically began laying siege to the fort, from the north and northeast. Mughal banners fluttered in the evening breeze as posts were set up and cannons readied to begin firing at the ramparts.

Ramaji Pangera, the Commander, narrowed his eyes. His fort was small, his garrison and resources limited. Most of the small forts in the surrounding hills had fallen to the Mughals. He knew there was little hope of reinforcements arriving. With such a huge Mughal force confronting him, he had two choices – surrender the fort, or die defending it. He chose the latter.

Later that night, he ordered his garrison to assemble. Including the latest stragglers and wandering units who had gathered in the fort, he had less than a thousand men at hand. The Mughal force outside was several thousand strong. "Men," Ramaji's voice thundered, "the Mughals have arrived at our door. They want our fort, but I am not ready to hand it to them." His Captains looked at their Commander with pride.

"We cannot withstand a siege for long and we will not surrender the fort. That leaves us with only one option." He paused to look at his men, trying to guage how many would be willing to go on a suicide mission with him. "We open the fort gates and attack the Mughal camp at daybreak tomorrow. We kill as many as possible and teach them a lesson they will not forget! And when we are done with that, we will die fighting. No one comes back! Now, who is with me?"

The men were momentarily stunned and looked at each other. For a few brief moments, Ramaji thought no one would come forward. Would his ambitious plan fall flat? Then one young Captain stepped forward and said, "Commander, I will go with you. I will die for my King!"

Another Maratha joined him and then more and more. Soon every man had vowed to give his life for *Swarajya*.

Dawn broke, bathing the eastern ridges of the Sahyadris around Fort Kaner in soft light. Diler Khan emerged from his tent and stretched. His attendant fetched a bowl of water. Splashing his face, he gazed across at the fort towering in front. It was a small fort, he thought. There couldn't be more than a few hundred men; should not be too difficult for his Pathans to take. They would probably need a day or two at the most, he assessed, rubbing his stubbled chin. His men were tired after a hard march and he planned to rest them for a few days before assaulting the fort.

The Mughal camp was just coming to life after a hard earned night's rest when the peace was shattered as the fort gates creaked open and Maratha soldiers poured out, shouting *Har Har Mahadev*! Diler Khan was startled as he saw hundreds of Marathas racing down the northeastern slope toward his camp, screaming for blood. He was momentarily shaken at this unexpected move by the fort garrison. His mind went back six years when he had experienced a similar attack by the brave Commander of Fort Purandar. The mayhem then had been crazy. This attack promised the same.

Diler Khan yelled to his men to get ready for battle and himself rushed into his tent to find his weapons and armour. In a short time, the front ranks of the attacking Marathas fell upon the unsuspecting Pathans and began slaughtering them at will. Hundreds were cut down before the Pathans could regroup and get ready to retaliate. Diler Khan emerged from his tent and rallied his men. Not one to stand back and watch a battle, he threw himself into the melée.

Ramaji Pangera fought like a man possessed as he tore into the Pathan ranks. His sword moved around him at such unbelievable speed that the Pathans found it difficult to get anywhere close to him. A pitched battle had started at the foothills, one that could end in only one way. Thousands of Pathans soon engulfed the seven hundred odd Marathas and began cutting them down. Having lost many men initially, the Pathans had stabilized their defence. The Marathas now began losing men. Ramaji realized his end was near, yet he fought on, not willing to stand down.

Despite being badly outnumbered, the Marathas fought till the last man perished. A *prahar* later, Diler Khan stood with a bloodied sword in his hand, staring disbelievingly at the slaughter. What kind of madness was this? What kind of men willingly sacrificed themselves thus, knowing they stood no chance? First it was the Commander of Purandar, now this one. And years earlier, the Commander of Fort Chakan had thwarted Shaista Khan's massive force for a whole night after the ramparts had been breached! Diler Khan had never experienced such warfare before. Seevaji had some special men serving him.

ENVIRONS OF FORT SALHER, BAGLAN DISTRICT, EARLY FEBRUARY 1672

A massive Maratha army had massed south of the besieged Fort Salher, concealed in the hills. Moro *Punt* Pingale, the *Peshwa,* had cut across the Sahyadri hills with his infantry and rapidly moved east by forced marches. The Maratha *Sirnaubat, Prataprao* Gujar, had similarly moved west from the Ahmednagar region, with his cavalry. Weeks earlier, they had received an urgent despatch from Raigad: *Make haste and reach Fort Salher immediately. The Sirnaubat and Peshwa should rendezvous and attack the Mughals from both sides and destroy their camp completely.*

As they now sat face to face in the makeshift camp set up in the dense woods, Moro *Punt* said, "*Sirnaubat,* we must attack at the crack of dawn. We will not remain undiscovered for long."

Prataprao nodded. "I agree. I will spread the word amongst the men to rest a while and get ready to attack before dawn."

"How do we plan the attack?"

Prataprao thought briefly. Then, picking up a dried twig, he began drawing out a small map in the soft mud. Two attendants lowered their torches to give better visibility. Moro *Punt* crouched forward, as did the other Captains. Chief amongst those present at this final war council were Anandrao Makaji, Vyankaji Datto, Sidhoji Nimbalkar and Khandoji Jagtap. Also present were Shivaji *Raje*'s old mate, Suryaji Kakade, and his trusted Captain, Godaji Jagtap.

"*Punt,*" *Prataprao* said, placing the twig at a point on the crude map, "this is what we will do..."

The council broke up late at night after each Captain and his unit had been given precise instructions.

Ikhlas Khan, the acting Commander of the Mughal forces, had just woken up and emerged from his tent when the alarm sounded from the eastern watch posts. He strained his eyes to see, but in the faint light of dawn, he could barely see the boundary of his camp. The camp was still sluggish as his men crawled out of their tents to find out what was happening. They did not have to wait for long.

Shortly, Mughal sentries could be seen running towards the camp, screaming *Ganeem! Ganeem*! Moments later, the attack was evident.

Maratha cavalry emerged in hordes from behind the rocky ledges, trees and bushes and fell upon them. Ikhlas Khan called for his weapons and his horse. He began shouting orders to his Captains. The Maratha attack was unexpected, but there was no reason for them to give up. Their own numbers were pretty strong, and their camp well stocked with artillery, ammunition and animals.

The Mughal cavalry was soon mounted and retaliated with full force under Ikhlas Khan's command.

Earlier, while it was still dark, *Prataprao* Gujar had led a ten thousand strong unit of cavalry east, circumventing the Mughal camp. He then lay concealed in the hills and finally broke cover at dawn. As the Mughal camp came into view, his men blew horns and the horses picked up pace. *Prataprao* knew he had to cause maximum damage early on, before the Mughals had a chance to organize their defences. They could cut down men at will before the Mughal cavalry was mounted and ready to strike back. He screamed *Har Har Mahadev*! and urged his men on.

In a short while they were upon the Mughal camp, running men through, slashing, killing, torching and destroying everything in front of them. The confused Mughals ran around looking for weapons and mounts as *Prataprao*'s Marathas ran amuck. The onslaught was terrible initially, but slowly the Mughals began to retaliate. As the tide of battle turned sufficiently to make it an even fight, *Prataprao* gave the signal. Once again horns were sounded. The Maratha cavalry began to withdraw and flee eastwards.

The Mughals could not understand what was happening. The Maratha horsemen who had gained so much by their surprise attack were suddenly withdrawing. They failed to recognize *Prataprao*'s ingenious plan and convinced themselves the coward *kafirs* were fleeing in fear. Ikhlas Khan gave the order to pursue the Marathas and thus walked right into *Prataprao*'s trap.

The *Peshwa* Moro *Punt* Pingale, an efficient infantry Commander, lay concealed in the forest half a *kos* south of the Mughal camp. He had divided his men into several units and placed a trusted Captain at the head of each. They heard *Prataprao*'s cavalry blaring their horns and knew the attack had begun. Moro *Punt*'s scouts soon returned to inform him of the commotion in the Mughal camp. The *Peshwa* then gave the order to advance under cover of the foliage. Half a *prahar* later, in plain sight of the camp, they waited to allow the Mughal cavalry pursuing *Prataprao* to stray further from the main camp.

Ikhlas Khan yanked on the reins, bringing his mount to a halt. The animal reared up on its hind legs and neighed loudly. The pursuing cavalry units, numbering in the thousands, pulled to a halt as well. Ikhlas Khan's Captains soon assembled around him.

"The cowards have fled!" an agitated young Captain exclaimed.

"We have taught them a dirty lesson! They will not dare to attack again," said another.

Ikhlas Khan, however, was not convinced. The Marathas could not be trusted, he thought. The present attack had been repulsed and the Marathas had retreated east towards Fort Mulher. That suited him, as Mulher was presently under Mughal occupation. The Marathas would definitely face another attack from the Mulher garrison if they strayed near that fort. But why had the Marathas attacked with a small cavalry unit in the first place?

Ikhlas' brow creased with worry as he said, "We will have to be careful. They can attack again. Retreat towards camp for now. Once we are back, order the outpost guards to be doubled."

The Mughal Commander turned back. In their zeal to catch the fleeing Marathas, his units had strayed ten *kos* from the main camp. Devoid of most of their cavalry, the camp was now vulnerable. In a moment of terrible realisation, Ikhlas wondered if the Marathas had planned another attack on the main camp. He couldn't have been more right.

Half a *prahar* had passed and Moro *Punt* thought he had given *Prataprao* enough time to draw the Mughal cavalry away from the main camp at the foot of Fort Salher. He gave the order to attack. The Maratha infantry emerged from the forest and advanced towards the Mughal camp. They divided themselves into pre-designated units. Some units turned west to circumvent the fort and attack the northwest frontier of the Mughal camp. Some units turned east. Moro *Punt*'s units headed straight into the southern camp. In a short while, the Marathas had the Mughals surrounded. Horns blared and men screamed *Har Har Mahadev!* as the horrified Mughals, recovering from their earlier ordeal, watched thousands of Marathas descend upon them from all sides. The Mughal camp was thrown into disarray once again as the ferocious Maratha attack wreaked havoc.

Godaji Jagtap stood at the head of the second cavalry unit, stationed close to Moro *Punt*'s infantry, south of the Mughal camp. He watched the infantry head north and then launch their attack. In a disciplined manner, they had divided into units and encircled the Mughal camp. Godaji smiled. The *Peshwa* was a proven military Commander. He pitied the Mughals who were about to be decimated.

Godaji raised his hand, signalling to his Captain, who ordered the battle horns to be sounded. The Marathas were about to make their final calculated move to crush the enemy. Godaji's ten thousand strong cavalry emerged from the forests and rode straight into the southeastern Mughal camp, overrunning everything in their way. Soldiers were cut down, tents destroyed and animals scattered as the hapless Mughals, still coming to terms with the earlier infantry attack, were taken by surprise for a third time that day.

Having caused sufficient pandemonium and slaughter, Godaji now ordered his units to turn east and take the route to Mulher, where *Sirnaubat Prataprao* had fled, pursued by Ikhlas Khan. If Ikhlas Khan decided to turn back to the main camp, he would get another nasty surprise.

Ikhlas Khan's cavalry cantered back to camp. Flushed with victory, the jubiliant Captains boasted of their morning deeds, calling the Marathas cowards. Ikhlas Khan, however, was quiet. He was worried, and not without reason. He had heard how Seevaji's wily men had made Daud Khan go round in circles in Baglan and Khandesh. He knew the Marathas never withdrew without a reason. Were they planning something at the camp?

A sudden commotion up front heralded the arrival of an agitated Captain. He rode hastily towards Ikhlas Khan and said, "A cavalry unit is charging from the west! It's the Marathas again!"

So this was what they had been planning...to draw his cavalry away with one unit and attack again with a second. Ikhlas drew his sword. "Get ready to fight! The battle isn't over yet!" he yelled.

At a distance, Godaji Jagtap could see the Mughal cavalry with their banners. He shouted final orders to his Captains and urged his mount to pick up speed. The Marathas swiftly broke up into three units. Two units broke ranks and moved sideways, attempting to outflank the Mughals from both sides, while Godaji's central unit rode straight into the enemy. Weapons clashed and men screamed as hungry blades sliced through hapless bodies and the air was filled with the din of battle. Godaji's unit wedged itself into the centre of the Mughal ranks, while the two flanking units began hammering the Mughals from both sides. In a short while the Mughals had suffered heavy casualties.

Ikhlas Khan fought fiercely. He knew he had been outsmarted, but was not ready to give in. He spotted the Maratha Commander and headed straight for him. Ikhlas' unit clashed with Godaji's as both sides threw caution to the winds and plunged into the thick of battle.

As the fighting became increasingly gory, the Mughal ranks at the rear could hear battle borns blaring behind them. They turned around horrified to see a massive cloud of dust kicked up by the first Maratha cavalry unit which they had chased away.

Prataprao had waited long enough to allow the Mughals to turn back and for Godaji to ride up to them from the west. He then gave the signal to ride west into the retreating Mughals. His units had now caught up with Ikhlas Khan's cavalry and attacked from the rear. The Mughal cavalry was caught in a trap with Marathas all around them.

The battle was bloody, the result a foregone conclusion. The Mughal cavalry was completely decimated. Thousands were killed, many more injured. The survivors ran eastwards toward Mulher, for shelter. Ikhlas Khan was seriously wounded and fell, only to be captured by the jubiliant Marathas.

Once the Mughal cavalry had been neutralised, Prataprao and Godaji rode back towards the main camp to join Moro *Punt*'s infantry.

Back at the main camp, the Mughal soldiers had recovered sufficiently to launch a counter offensive on the marauding Marathas. They readied their war elephants and camels, mounted their *gajnals* and *shuturnals* in the *howdahs* atop their war animals and began retaliating in earnest. As the guns spewed fire, the Marathas suffered numerous casualties.

Suryaji Kakade had made serious inroads into the Mughal camp with his unit. His attack had been so ferocious that none had survived his sword. His men had succeeded in torching most of the tents on the southwestern side of the camp. Suryaji now turned his attention to the elephants. He gathered several of his soldiers and confronted a charging beast. The elephant trumpeted loudly and ran straight at them. Suryaji balanced a spear in his right hand and threw it at the animal. The spear hit the elephant squarely on the forehead and wedged itself there. The beast staggered and swayed, throwing the soldiers in the *howdah* off balance. One fell and was promptly trampled by the elephant. Suryaji sidestepped, attempting to get close to the frenzied beast. Too close and he could get killed. But he had to risk a strike at the elephant's trunk. He finally did, wounding it fatally. The poor animal crashed to the ground spilling guns from the *howdah*.

At other places too, the war elephants were dropping fast, as were the camels. The Marathas had successfully neutralized the Mughal camp's prime weapons. It was down to a hand-to-hand fight now. As the sun climbed overhead, the Mughal camp resembled a slaughter yard. Chopped heads and butchered limbs lay everywhere, kicked around in the melée. Blood drenched the earth and the men's feet slipped in the bloody slush. For several *kos* across the killing fields, the men could no longer recognize friend from foe.

They had been fighting for over two *prahars* but Suryaji Kakade showed no signs of tiring. Determined to take the Marathas to victory, he charged another elephant. As his comrades threw spears at the animal, he attempted to slash its trunk. But this time his luck ran out. A Mughal soldier, firing from the *howdah*, found his mark. The shot hit Suryaji in the chest and he collapsed.

As the fourth *prahar* of the day began, the Mughal strength had been severely depleted. Most had given up. Battle horns blared from the east once again as *Prataprao* and Godaji rode in with their cavalry to finish the job for the Marathas.

When the sun receded beyond the western horizon, the Marathas had won a resounding victory. They had completely routed a huge, well equipped Mughal army on a plain battlefield. Their Commanders had planned the strategy immaculately and outsmarted the Mughals. The losses were heavy on both sides. The foothills of the Salher mountain and the plains around it were covered with dead soldiers and animals. Over ten thousand Mughals had perished, and seven thousand Marathas.

The six thousand horses and over a hundred elephants and camels that survived the mayhem, fell to the Marathas, as did the provisions and treasures of the Mughal camp. Several of the Mughal Captains had been taken prisoner. It had been a great victory, but one that had been won at great sacrifice.

The Maratha Commanders had assembled to chalk out plans following the battle. *Prataprao* was there, as were Moro *Punt*, Godaji Jagtap, Vyankaji and Khandoji. Suryaji Kakde was missing and Godaji was getting increasingly worried. He had heard that Suryaji had been fighting on the southwestern side and had sent some of his own men to find him. As he paced impatiently, Godaji fervently hoped his friend was safe.

As Prataprao and Moro *Punt* debated the next course of action, a small party approached, carrying someone on a makeshift stretcher. The men fell silent as Suryaji's dead body was laid down in front of them. Suryaji lay still, his body covered in caked blood, his chest shattered by the gunshot.

Godaji stared at his friend in silence. The fatigue of battle, coupled with the effect of seeing so many killed, suddenly overwhelmed him and he sank down beside Suryaji's body and sobbed. Godaji and Suryaji, with Tanhaji, had been Shivaji *Raje*'s earliest adherents. They had unflinchingly joined the fight for *Swarajya,* declaring Shivaji *Raje* their King. Tanhaji was gone, and now, so was Suryaji.

"When the King asks me, *where is Surya,* what am I to tell him?" Godaji cried. "The gunshot that pierced your chest, will certainly shatter His Highness' heart as well."

Raigad palace, mid-1672

The Maratha Council deliberated over the political developments of the past months and their own future course of action. Bahirji Naik filled them in with fresh intelligence from all quarters.

"The Siddis have wreaked havoc in our coastal regions, Highness," he said. "Ever since they defected to the Mughals, they have bolstered their fleet and now make rapid incursions into our coastal lands to loot, pillage and kill. They disappear as quickly as they come. The Mughals have put one Siddi Sambul in charge of Janjira, and the fleet."

Shivaji *Raje* frowned. "How have our land forces coped with this?" he asked.

"Not very well," replied Bahirji. "The Siddi fleet moves very fast. Our forces cannot catch up with them in time. Besides, our strength in the Konkan is quite depleted now. The majority of our forces are engaged on the Mughal and Adilshahi fronts."

Raje considered this for a moment and then asked, "What about the people?"

"Most of the inhabitants have abandoned their villages and shifted into the hills for safety. Yet, thousands have died, crops have been burnt and..." Bahirji looked away in frustration. "... scores of young women have disappeared."

Raje banged a clenched fist on his thigh. To bring him down, the foreign powers continued to target his people. "The only way to counter the Abyssinians is to have a powerful navy that can checkmate their own," he said. "Our navy is, as yet, no match."

Moro *Punt* nodded. "And we cannot allocate any new funds for building large ships."

"The problem is two-fold *Punt*," *Raje* said. "Funds are an issue. But the more sticky problem is the lack of trained ship-building personnel on our side. We have to depend upon the *firangis* for that. Not to mention the dearth of good Navy Commanders. The Abyssinian and English Navies are simply better than our own."

"The English allow Siddi Sambul to dock his ships at Mumbai, from where he moves rapidly along the coast," Bahirji added.

Raje gave him a questioning look. "I thought we had objected to that?"

"Yes, we had, Sire, but now, with Siddi Sambul being a Mughal vassal, the English are bound to help him. They dare not invite Mughal ire by refusing."

Raje thought for a while and then said to Moro *Punt*, "Send an envoy to the English to ask for help against the Siddis. Offer them a suitable place on the mainland, opposite the Mumbai island, to build their factory. Invite them to trade from our lands."

"Very well, Highness," the *Peshwa* said. "What sort of help should we ask for?"

"Mortars, big guns, ammunition," *Raje* said. Then as an afterthought, he added, "also ask for a person to operate the artillery and teach our men."

"The English may not be willing to side with us openly," Moro *Punt* cautioned.

"Then tell them we will carry out the deal surreptitiously. The Mughals will never know."

"There's more news from the Mughal Empire, Highness," Bahirji said. "The revolt in Afghanistan has proven to be a far stickier problem than Aurangzeb had anticipated. He had sent Mohammed Amin, the *Subadar* of Kabul, to crush the revolt with a large army. A few weeks ago, the Afghans routed Amin's force in the Khyber Pass. The Emperor has been forced to divert forces to the northern frontier. I hear he has summoned both Prince Muazzam and Mahabat Khan for the job."

"That is good news," *Raje* said. "Let the Afghans keep him busy for some time while we bolster our latest acquisitions in Baglan. The territory we have recently annexed is a narrow strip of land with hills. To its east lies the Empire, while to its west lie the principalities of Jawhar and Ramnagar. Further up north are the Portuguese territories." The men nodded. *Raje* turned to Bahirji, "Naik, tell us about these kingdoms."

"Both states are ruled by independent Kings. Jawhar lies some twenty-five *kos* north of Kalyan, and twenty *kos* west of Mughal occupied Nasik. It is ruled by Vikramshah, a Chieftain of the Koli tribe. Ramnagar, ruled by a Rajput Chieftain, Somshah, lies further north. The Portuguese territory of Daman lies to the northwest. As such, Jawhar and Ramnagar are in no position to get immediate help from the Mughals."

Shivaji *Raje* thought briefly before deciding on the next campaign. "I think the time is ripe for us to annex these kingdoms. Moro *Punt*, you will lead our forces. Plant our saffron standards at both places and return victorious."

Moro *Punt* led a successful military campaign and annexed both Jawhar and Ramnagar, which were added to *Swarajya*. The Koli Chieftain of Jawhar fled to Mughal-ruled Nasik, while the Ramnagar ruler fled north to seek refuge with the Portuguese. On Shivaji *Raje*'s behalf, Moro *Punt* went on to demand taxes from the Portuguese, which had been earlier paid to the Jawhar and Ramnagar rulers. With the Marathas now so close, the residents and rulers of Surat trembled in fear.

The talks between the Marathas and the English factors failed as the English stuck to their demand of reparations for the Rajapur losses, while Shivaji *Raje* insisted on artillery help against the Siddis, which the English were reluctant to provide.

To stalemate both the Siddi and English navies, Shivaji *Raje* needed a naval base between Janjira and Mumbai, where he could build a strong fortress and create a base to check maritime traffic on the western seas. He found a place suitable for just that. The island of Khanderi, south of Mumbai port and a short distance from the western mainland, was ideal for building a naval base. Shivaji *Raje* recognised its potential and gave orders to fortify the island, releasing the requisite revenue.

But the news soon reached both the English and the Mughals and these powers made conscious efforts to thwart the Maratha attempt to fortify Khanderi. The English especially, realized the potential threat to Mumbai if the Marathas established themselves on the island. Their urgent efforts paid off as the Marathas failed in this first attempt to set up a naval base on the western seas.

13
WAR ON ALL FRONTS

RAIGAD, LATE 1672

"Qutubshah Abul Hasan has removed the Persian Sayyid Muzaffar, from the Prime Minister's post," Bahirji Naik said, providing the Maratha Council with the latest intelligence from the neighbouring kingdoms. "He has made a Hindu nobleman named Madanna, his new Prime Minister."

Shivaji *Raje* smiled. "That is surprising. These Sultans rarely appoint Hindus to such high posts. Why was the Persian sacked?"

"From my man's report, I gather that Abul Hasan was tired of the Persian's autocratic demeanour. He probably feared too much power passing into his Prime Minister's hands."

"Well, with Madanna at the helm now, our earlier pact with the Qutubshah should be strengthened," *Raje* opined.

Shivaji *Raje* had received the news of Abdullah Qutubshah's death several months earlier. As he had no natural heir, his son-in-law, Abul Hasan, was placed on the throne, largely due to the political moves of the Qutubshahi Prime Minister, Sayyid Muzaffar. Abul, a spoilt hedonistic fool, had allowed Sayyid to control the government, leading to the Persian gaining a stranglehold on the administration. But Abul Hasan seemed to have now woken up to reality and removed Sayyid. With Madanna as Prime Minister at Bhaganagar, Shivaji *Raje* hoped to secure an advantageous treaty with the Qutubshah.

"There is news that Madanna has already approached the Mughals for a truce, and agreed to pay a tribute," Bahirji said. "He clearly seems more inclined to please the Mughal."

"I bet he is," *Raje* laughed. "Many years ago, when Aurangzeb invaded Qutubshahi as a Mughal Prince, he had forced Abdullah

Qutubshah to name Mohammed Sultan, Aurangzeb's son, as the heir to the Qutubshahi throne. Now, by placing Abul Hasan on the throne, the Qutubshahi Sultanate has directly defaulted on that assurance."

Bahirji nodded. "Abul Hasan must now dread the thought of a fresh invasion by Aurangzeb."

Raje stroked his bear, deep in thought. "Yet, Madanna might prove a useful ally in the future. Moro *Punt*, instruct our envoy at the Qutubshah's court to remain in Madanna's good books."

"Certainly, Sire," the *Peshwa* assured him.

"What is the latest news from the Adilshahi?" Shivaji *Raje* asked Bahirji the more pertinent question.

"Ali Adilshah died recently and his four-year-old son, Sikander, was placed on the throne." Bahirji looked around with a smile as he was sure this news would create more buzz in the Council than the earlier news from Bhaganagar.

Shivaji *Raje* raised his eyebrows and asked in mock anger, "And why have you held this news from us this long, Bahirji?"

The spy laughed. "I saved the best news for the end."

Raje grinned. "Tell us more, Bahirji."

"The administration is controlled by the *Vizier*, Khawas Khan. My men in Bijapur inform me that the Bijapur government is once again torn into factions and there is tremendous internal discord."

"There is bound to be," *Raje* mused. "From what we know of Khawas Khan, he will not be keen to share control."

"The Adilshahi is struggling with the infighting," Bahirji said.

Shivaji *Raje* nodded, saying firmly, "Sooner or later, Aurangzeb will take advantage of that. Before he does, we should expand south into the Adilshahi. The Mughals are quiet right now as they are busy with the revolts up north. They should not bother us for a while. Let us turn our attention to the Adilshah!"

The men nodded enthusiastically at the thought of another campaign.

"Where do we open hostilities, Highness?" *Sirnaubat Prataprao* Gujar asked.

"Panhala!" *Raje* declared. "Our favourite fort has been with the Adilshahi for more than ten years. It is high time we get it back!"

RAIGAD, EARLY 1673

A middle-aged, rugged looking Maratha Captain stood at attention before his King. His greying sideburns and moustache betrayed his age, but his firm jaw and stern look identified him as a soldier. Next to him stood a determined administrative officer, a few summers younger. The two had just been entrusted with the first responsibility of a fresh campaign against the Adilshahi – that of capturing Fort Panhala.

"Kondaji *Farzand*," Shivaji *Raje* said to the Captain, "you will lead our charge on Fort Panhala. Anaji Datto here will be your second-in-command." *Raje* often included his administrative officers in military campaigns, to keep them active and fit. "Anaji *Punt* will help you in getting the campaign organized."

Kondaji bowed. "This is an honour, Sire. It shall not be long before our saffron standard flutters atop the fort."

The King smiled affectionately at him. "How many men do you need, Kondaji?"

Kondaji hesitated. He was planning to assault the fort with a small party of men, but feared his King would feel he was being overconfident. Hence, he decided to demand a reasonable number of men, though he knew he would not use most of them. "One thousand handpicked foot soldiers should suffice, Highness."

Anaji *Punt*'s smile vanished as he looked incredulously at Kondaji. Was Kondaji crazy? Shivaji *Raje* himself had failed miserably in assaulting Panhala many years earlier, and he had five thousand men with him. What could they achieve with just a thousand?

Shivaji *Raje* could not hide his curiosity. "Kondaji, are you sure about this?" he asked his Captain. "Panhala is a huge fort and very tough to assault; not to mention that a garrison of two thousand defends it."

Prataprao Gujar and Moro *Punt* Pingale threw surprised glances at each other. The last thing they wanted was a disastrous beginning to the Adilshahi campaign.

"Your Highness..." Kondaji stammered, "...in reality I need very few men, but I thought that would sound inappropriate, hence I asked for a thousand."

Shivaji *Raje* laughed as he looked disbelievingly at Kondaji. He rose from his seat and walked up to the Captain. "Kondya," he said to the man gently, "what are you planning? You must remember my own defeat at Panhala years ago. That memory is like a wound on my soul that shall never heal. I do not want to repeat that debacle..."

Kondaji raised his head. "Rest easy, my King. Kondaji shall not return in defeat. Have faith in me."

Raje nodded. "I would not have appointed you to lead this campaign if I did not trust you. Yet, as your King, I must know what you plan to do."

"Merely act on the principles of *ganimikawa,* which you yourself have taught us, Sire. Defeat the enemy with the minimum of your own troops and with minimum casualties on our own side."

Shivaji *Raje* laughed heartily as he realized his Captain did not wish to reveal his plans in front of everyone. Secrecy was his *mantra* and he was glad his Captains followed it.

Kondaji and Anaji *Punt* bowed and prepared to leave on their perilious mission. On impulse, *Raje* unhooked a gold bracelet from his wrist and said, "Kondaji, extend your hand."

Kondaji held his hand out and *Raje* fastened his bracelet on Kondaji's wrist. Then, patting Kondaji's back, he said, "Go my friend, may the Goddess be with you. I shall await your return."

As they stood watching the two men walk away, a soft voice uttered what was on everyone's mind. "Your Highness, gifting a gold bracelet before the job is done, seems inappropriate."

Shivaji *Raje* looked at his *Muzumdar,* Ramchandra *Punt,* who had voiced this opinion. "I know it is, *Punt*. The accepted custom is for the King to reward his Captains after a job is concluded successfully. But so many of my comrades never returned to claim their rewards. They fell fighting for me..." Shivaji *Raje*'s eyes moistened as he thought of all those slain in battle. "Baji Prabhu *Deshpande,* Baji Pasalkar, Tanhaji Malusare, Suryaji Kakade.... the list is endless. I could never honour them for their service, for their victories. My heart is heavy with the losses, *Punt*. What if Kondaji too, fails to return to claim his rightful reward?"

Raje stopped as he realized what he had said. *O Goddess Bhavani, what have I said! Such inauspicious words at the beginning of a campaign… Forgive me Mother, and safeguard Kondaji. Raje* closed his eyes momentarily as he prayed silently for Kondaji's safe return. Then, without another word, he turned and left the assembly.

ENVIRONS OF FORT PANHALA, NIGHT OF 6 MARCH 1673

The first *prahar* of the night was more than half way through. It was pitch dark in the forest, as one thousand Marathas halted four *kos* south of Fort Panhala. The forest stood still. Nothing moved. Kondaji *Farzand* raised a hand for his men to halt. As Anaji *Punt* walked up to him, he said, "*Punt*, you wait here with the men. Give me a head start and then advance slowly towards the fort. Be sure to halt a *kos* away from the western foothill and watch for my signal. As soon as my men open the gates, we will light a fire on the rampart so you can see it. When you do, make haste to the gates. You must enter the fort without delay."

In the dim moonlight, Ananji *Punt* looked at Kondaji and fervently hoped the man would be able to carry out his audacious plan. "And you plan to assault the fort with sixty men and open the *teen darwaza*," he said doubtfully.

Kondaji nodded.

"Man, I sure hope you know what you are doing!"

"I do, *Punt*. Now take up your positions while we move forward. And lie low; do not be seen by the scouts."

Sixty Marathas halted for a breather at the foot of the western face of the mountain. Kondaji looked up at the barely visible rampart. It would be a relatively easy climb, he thought, except for the final part, which was a vertical rockface leading to the rampart itself.

Kondaji had spent the past two months in Rajapur, gathering intelligence about the fort, the garrison, the night watches, and more importantly, about the *Killedar*. He had learnt from Bahirji's men that the night watch on the western rampart was non-existent. The rampart itself was broken and dilapidated in this part of the fort. Probably, the *Killedar* did not expect an enemy assault from the western side at all. Kondaji did not take long to decide this would be the most suitable place to scale the mountain and the ramparts. He had also found the exact location of the *Killedar*'s residence.

Besides their weapons, Kondaji had brought along *shingas,* horns and trumpets to blow and create a commotion and a diversion. While in Rajapur, an incredible plan had formed in his mind, which none but he had the confidence to pull off; to sneak into the fort with a handful of men and fool a two thousand strong garrison into believing a large army had somehow gained entry into the fort. If they could achieve that, they could confuse them into surrendering without a real fight.

Kondaji embraced the mountain with purpose, and his men followed. Slowly but surely, in silence, they progressed up the slope, using whatever light the moon provided. In a short while, the expert climbers had reached the final hurdle, the vertical rockface. Two men moved forward and began scaling the rock, while Kondaji and the others waited patiently. Soon enough, the rock climbers reached the top and let down rope ladders.

The second *prahar* of the night was nearly over when Kondaji and his sixty men scaled the western rampart of Fort Panhala and regrouped. There were no sentries on watch. Silence and darkness ruled. A pre-designated unit of ten soldiers, led by a brave young man named Ganaji, slipped away into the shadows and made their way north towards the *Teen Darwaza,* the triple battlemented gates along the western rampart. This unit was responsible for opening the gates to let Anaji *Punt* and his thousand men into the fort. Kondaji and the remaining fifty began walking rapidly toward the *Killedar*'s residence. Their objective was to get as close to the fort Commander as possible before they were spotted.

Their presence was discovered soon enough and as the Adilshahi soldiers wondered who the strangers were, some of Kondaji's men began blowing their horns, trumpets and *shingas,* generally creating a commotion, while the rest began shouting *Har Har Mahadev!* It now dawned upon the surprised garrison that there were enemy soldiers in the fort! But before they could gather themselves, Kondaji and his men had drawn their swords and launched a scathing attack. The first unit of Adilshahi soldiers they encountered was mowed down. The commotion continued, as more of the garrison was aroused and the Adilshahis hastily gathered their weapons. Kondaji and his men now began shouting to them to throw down their weapons as a large Maratha army had entered the fort and would cut them down unless they surrendered.

The fort *Sabnis*, a Brahman named Nagoji Pundit, somehow got caught in the melée. He saw the rampaging Marathas and ran off shouting the Marathas had taken the fort. This created panic and more confusion amongst the garrison.

Ganaji and his men waited in the shadows close to the innermost of the three gateways, and marked their men. The night watch seemed lethargic. This should not be too dificult, thought Ganaji. He would just have to wait till the news of the attack and the commotion travelled this way.

Soon enough, there were men running toward the gates shouting that the fort had been breached and that there were enemy soldiers in the fort! The confused sentries on night watch heard that the *Killedar*'s residence was under attack. Several left their posts and hurried off to help their Commander. This was the moment Ganaji had been waiting for. He gave the signal. His ten men, expert archers, picked their targets with ease and soon most of those on guard at the innermost gate had been felled. The rest were cut down quickly. The gate had been taken.

Kondaji and his men cut their way through the Adilshahi garrison. He knew they had to make haste to accost the *Killedar* and take him down as soon as possible before the majority of the garrison was aroused and their bluff discovered. A fresh unit of Bijapuri soldiers charged at them. Kondaji launched himself into another murderous assault, beheading the first soldier within his reach and hacking a limb each off the next two. The commotion increased.

A tall, hefty soldier with a determined look on his face charged towards Kondaji. He was flanked by several others. In an instant Kondaji realised the *Killedar* had arrived on the scene. This was his chance to kill him and take the fort. Kondaji rushed at the man as his men engaged the *Killedar*'s bodyguards. A pitched fight ensued. The surprised Bijapuri soldiers, ill-prepared for battle, proved no match for the Marathas, and fell one by one. The *Killedar* was soon isolated and he too, perished under the assault of Kondaji's sword.

A fresh wave of panic spread once the Commander had fallen. The bemused Bijapuri soldiers began to succumb to the Marathas.

By now, Ganaji and his small party had overwhelmed the sentries at the *Teen Darwaza* and the last gate had been opened. Ganaji lit a large *mashaal* and stood atop the rampart, facing west.

Anaji *Punt*, hiding in the forest, spotted the fire signal and waved his men forward. In a short while, a thousand Marathas had poured into the fort and all was lost for the Bijapuri garrison.

Panhala, the stronghold between the Adilshahi and the *Swarajya*, the key fort in the south, had been taken by the Marathas.

MARCH 1673

The Adilshahi government was rudely awoken from slumber when the news of the fall of Panhala reached Bijapur. Khawas Khan took immediate steps to counter the Maratha moves and sent the Pathani nobleman, Bahlol Khan, with twelve thousand troopers, against them. Bahlol Khan marched west from Bijapur and halted at Umrani, a place thirteen *kos* west of the capital city, awaiting reinforcements. Khawas Khan had ordered Sharza Khan, Siddi Masud, Abdul Aziz, Khidir Khan and various other nobles to join him at Umrani with their contingents.

The efficient Maratha intelligence network brought the news to Shivaji *Raje*, who was at Fort Panhala. *Raje* held a war council.

"Bahlol Khan has intentions of marching right up to Panhala," he said. "He will try to wall us off in the fort as did Siddi Jauhar many years ago, but we will not let that happen. Our strength today is several times what it was then. We can attack him and finish him off before he reaches here."

Prataprao Gujar, the Maratha *Sirnaubat*, sat to *Raje*'s right. "Order us, Sire," he said firmly. "The Pathan shall not come anywhere near Panhala!" His Captains, who stood eagerly in front of their King, and Commanding Officer, nodded vigorously.

"Prataprao, I have received news that several officers are to join Bahlol Khan at Umrani," *Raje* said. "His strength currently stands at twelve thousand cavalry, but that is likely to increase once he receives the reinforcements. Attack him now, at Umrani, while his army is manageable. Crush and destroy him completely!"

Prataprao bowed and left on the mission to silence the Bijapuri army, followed by his Captains, Anandrao, Sidhoji Nimbalkar, Dipaji Raut, Vithoji Shinde and Siddi Hilal. Unknown to him, this would prove to be the last mission of his life.

UMRANI, WEST OF BIJAPUR, APRIL 1673

Prataprao Gujar reached the environs of Umrani by forced marches and stationed himself a few *kos* from the Bijapuri camp. From here, he sent his scout forward to reconnoitre and get him information. Bahlol Khan, on the other hand, had relaxed once he had reached Umrani, waiting for the other officers to join him. He had not bothered to spread his scouts and watchposts around the camp and, as a result, was completely unaware that a large Maratha army had arrived nearby.

Prataprao received news that the Bijapuri army had stationed itself on the far side of a river near Umrani village and obviously depended on it for its water supply. He decided to cut off their water. Under cover of darkness, he slipped his army between the river and the Bijapuri camp and entrenched himself there. As the sun rose the next morning, the Bijapuri soldiers began herding their animals to the river. To their horror, they found the enemy blocking their way to the the life giving water. Battle began suddenly as the Marathas began firing arrows, muskets and light cannon.

As the day grew hotter, the battle raged on, sapping the Bijapuri garrison's energy and determination. Without water, the soldiers began dropping more from the heat than the Maratha arrows and bullets. To add to their woes, some of their elephants, disturbed by the gunfire, ran amuck, killing their own men. *Prataprao* finally gave the order to charge. The armies clashed and some serious hand-to-hand fighting ensued, in which the Bijapuris in particular suffered heavy casualties.

With each passing moment, Bahlol Khan realized that his position was untenable. By mid-day, after two *prahars* of fighting and with the sun blazing overhead, he sued for peace. *Prataprao* decided to grant him safe passage provided he left behind his entire baggage, artillery, animals and money. Bahlol Khan agreed. After the loss of Panhala, this was the Adilshahi's second successive defeat.

Yet, the Maratha King would be displeased with his *Sirnaubat*.

Shivaji *Raje*'s legendary temper sparked when he received news of the battle at Umrani. He could not believe that his Commander-in-Chief had let the Adilshahi General off when he had him at his mercy. *Raje* knew Bahlol Khan only too well, and knew that he would return with a larger force to attack them again. That would mean another battle, more loss of life, money and material. Angrily, he wrote to his *Sirnaubat*, admonishing him:

On what pretext did you agree to a peace with Bahlol Khan? You call youself Sirnaubat *of the Maratha forces, yet you did what a common foot soldier would have. Your decision does not befit a Commander!*

Prataprao's mind went numb when he read the King's letter. With great foresight and ingenuity, he had planned his attack and reduced the Adilshahi forces, yet he had received humiliation from his King. With his mind in turmoil, he resolved to put an end to Bahlol Khan.

October 1673

For the past year, Maratha and English envoys had been travelling to and fro between Mumbai and Raigad, trying to conclude a peace between the two parties. The English were handicapped where it came to their confrontation with the Siddis of Janjira, compelled as they were by the Mughals to allow the Siddi fleet to winter at the Mumbai docks. This was precisely what irked Shivaji *Raje,* and he tried his utmost to distance the English from the Siddis. He fervently wished to uproot the Abyssinian power from Danda Rajpuri, but knew his naval strength was insufficient. For that reason alone, he needed the English to co-operate with him.

The President of the Mumbai English establishment had refused to grant Siddi Sambul permission to dock at Mumbai, and so Sambul had taken most of his ships to Janjira, leaving behind only a handful. The English President thought the worse was behind him. Yet, in a month's time, the Abyssinian returned and attacked the Maratha controlled mainland opposite Mumbai island. He caused significant depredation, torching villages and crops, and carrying away captives to be sold as slaves. He followed that up by blocking the rivers connecting the mainland to Mumbai, thus depriving the English of supplies.

When Shivaji *Raje* received this news, he moved three thousand of his troops to the mainland and drove the Abyssinians out.

"The Siddi is proving a nuisance, Sire," Moro *Punt* said as he sat in conference with his King. "The English are unwilling to help."

Shivaji *Raje* stroked his chin and looked at Bahirji Naik, who stood in front of him. "Bahirji, let us add a new twist to this political drama," he said. "Use your sources in Mumbai to leak news to the English that we have approached the Dutch for help, and that we plan to launch a joint initiative against the Siddis *and* the English at Mumbai."

Bahirji and Moro *Punt* smiled as they realised what their King had in mind. "That should unsettle the English," said the *Peshwa*.

"Yes, it should," said *Raje*. "The English and Dutch are at war in Europe. That has raised tensions between the two trading communities here. News of a joint mission between us and the Dutch may change the English President's mind."

Bahirji nodded and said, "It shall be done, Sire. Let us give the English a new worry"

"How is our purchase from the French progressing?" *Raje* asked.

"As scheduled, Highness," Moro *Punt* replied. "We shall soon procure one frigate of lead shots, ninety guns, and other articles."

"Good. Bahirji, see that this news reaches the English!"

October 1673 to March 1674

To intensify the campaign against the Adilshahi, Shivaji *Raje* led a full-fledged mission into Canara with twenty thousand troops. His men plundered several towns, including Bankapur and Kadra, sending plenty of loot back to Raigad. There were several skirmishes with the Bijapuri forces, with losses on both sides.

Around this time, the Mughal leadership in the Deccan province, decided to raise their head against the Marathas as well. Receiving intelligence that Shivaji *Raje* was away in the Adilshahi, Bahadur Khan, the Deccan *Subadar*, along with Diler Khan, attempted to descend into the Konkan via the passes in the Sahyadri hills. The Maratha spy network, however, unerringly delivered the news to Raigad and a force was swiftly despatched. The Maratha army accosted the Mughals in the Sahyadris and, in the ensuing battle, a thousand Mughal soldiers perished. Dejected, the Mughals turned back. Bahadur Khan, however, remained camped in the vicinity.

When he received this news, Shivaji *Raje* was upset. Mughal presence in his lands was risky and he had to send the Mughals back to their dominions as soon as possible. He plotted a special mission to teach the Mughal *Subadar* a lesson. Bahadur Khan's camp had seven thousand men. Besides, they had plenty of ammunition, provisions, and a stash of money. A battle without gaining it all would be a waste.

A party of two thousand Maratha troopers attacked Bahadur Khan's camp without any preamble, and took the camp by surprise. After a token skirmish, they fled, instigating the Mughals into pursuing them. The Mughals swallowed the bait. When a large portion of the Mughal garrison had been drawn away a few *kos* from the camp, a second, much larger Maratha army of five thousand, attacked the main camp and plundered it completely. The Mughal troopers who had pursued the advance Maratha party, returned victorious, thinking they had chased the Marathas away, only to find their own camp destroyed and looted.

March 1674

Bahlol Khan had meanwhile returned with reinforcements to become a serious bother for the Marathas during their campaign in the Canara. This greatly angered Shivaji *Raje*. If only *Prataprao* had finished him off the last time, he thought, he would not have been such a thorn in their flesh now. He summoned his scribe and dictated a harsh letter to his *Sirnaubat*:

March forth and finish Bahlol Khan once and for all. Else, do not show me your face again!

Prataprao was enraged when he read his King's stern order. He had followed Bahlol Khan north from the Canara, keeping a constant check on his movements. A short while before, he had received news from his scouts that Bahlol Khan's army was only a few *kos* away from his own position, near a place called Nesari. *Prataprao's* own man-strength at the time was far inferior to the Bijapuri army, and ordinarily he would have waited for reinforcements before making a move. But, having read the King's scathing criticism of his earlier decision, he decided to throw caution to the winds and march.

"We must not move right now, *Sirnaubat,*" cautioned his Captain. "Bahlol Khan's force is many times ours. It will be suicide."

Prataprao's stern gaze locked on his Captain's face. Eyes red and moist, he growled, "Since when do we scare of enemy numbers? Did you not hear what His Highness has to say of us? We are not to show our faces in Raigad till we finish off Bahlol Khan! So we march, right now!"

Six Captains stood up and unsheathed their swords at once. *Prataprao* ordered them to get their units ready. Together with their men, they numbered a few thousand. In fact, this was just an advance party and their main force was half a day's march behind them. Had they sent fast riders with orders, their entire army would have assembled in a few *prahars.* But *Prataprao* was in no frame of mind to wait.

The headstrong Maratha *Sirnaubat* rode hard, followed by six of his Captains and a small force of horsemen. They knew it was a one-way mission, but none would back down. They managed to accost the Mughal army in a narrow pass between the hills near Nesari, and fell upon them like blazing meteors. *Prataprao* rode into the Mughal lines like a raging bull, his sword chopping off heads and cutting down limbs. He thought neither of the unending sea of Mughal green ahead of him, nor the certain outcome of this battle. He wanted lives...enemy lives. And he wanted Bahlol Khan.

The surprised Mughals lost many men before they could regroup and retaliate. Thousands of faithful Mughal swords were unsheathed and fell upon *Prataprao* and his men. The valley echoed to the sounds of battle and the Maratha party was engulfed in scathing fire from all sides. They fought bravely, wantonly, with a complete disregard for life and limb, yet, in the end, they were singed alive in the fire. *Prataprao* Gujar, the Maratha Commander-in-Chief fell with his six Captains and the few thousands who had accompanied them. When it was all over, Bahlol Khan gazed at the scene of the massacre in disbelief.

Shivaji *Raje* was stunned when he heard the news of the debacle and of the *Sirnaubat*'s death, two days later. He closed his eyes and cradled his head in his hands. "*Jagdamb*!" *Raje's* voice trembled with emotion. "What have you done, *Prataprao*?" he wailed. "I admonished you, so you would make the right move and destroy the Khan. But your second move was even more rash than the first. Now, how will I make up this loss? Who will be the *Sirnaubat*?"

Raje rose and left the conference chamber even as his Council continued to debate this fresh calamity.

14
LORD OF THE ROYAL UMBRELLA

RAIGAD PALACE, FIRST HALF 1674

"Queen Mother, our King does not have a legitimate throne yet!" This utternace raised many eyebrows in the small assembly. The man who had said it was dressed in a simple cotton *dhoti, angarkha* and a cloth turban. He sat upright and confident, his fair clean shaven face belied his birth as a *Brahman* and his eyes sparkled with the enthusiasm of his younger days. His name was Gagabhatt, and he was a learned *pundit* from Varanasi. He had travelled hundreds of *kos* to meet the Maratha King.

The faintest of smiles appeared fleetingly across Jijabai's tired face. She looked across with pride at her son, who was seated next to her. Dressed simply, in non-ceremonial clothes, but sporting pearl and *cowrie* necklaces, bejewelled rings and his pearl and ruby adorned turban, Shivaji *Raje* listened attentively to what the learned *Brahman* had to say.

"The Mughal and Turkish Sultans have established their own Empires because they have legitimate thrones, which they ascend with formal ceremonies," Gagabhatt said. "They hold royal umbrellas over their heads and flaunt their official seals and insignia in their courts. Their governments have legitimacy because their thrones and titles are officially accepted across the land by the people, and by other rulers."

The significance of the *Brahman*'s words sank into the minds of those in the room. Amongst those present were Moro *Punt* Pingale, the *Peshwa,* Ramchandra *Punt* (son of Tryambak *Punt),* the *Dabir,* Ramchandra *Punt* (son of Nilo Sondev), the *Muzumdar,* Anaji *Punt* the *Surnis,* Niraji Raoji, the *Nyayadheesh,* Dattaji *Punt,* the *Waknis,* and Moreshwar *Punt,* the *Punditrao*. The customary place of the *Sirnaubat,* to Shivaji *Raje*'s left, was empty.

"It is a great misfortune that the man who has battled and kept four powerful Sultanates at bay, does not have a throne."

Gagabhatt had touched a raw nerve. The men began nodding in agreement. Jijabai's smile widened at the sweet thought of seeing her son on a throne with a royal umbrella of state over his head.

"*Punditji,*" Shivaji *Raje* said to Gagabhatt, "Shivaji did not embark upon this journey so he could sit on a throne and lord over his people. Our lifelong mission was conceived with very different goals and ideals. We wanted to establish a safe, just and tolerant state for our people, so they could call their ancestral homeland their own. Having done that, Shivaji has no wish to be crowned in some official ceremony."

"Your Highness," Gagabhatt explained patiently, "an official throne and insignia are a necessity. Chiefs and rulers who choose to support the Sultans, do so because they view the Sultan's government as official and legitimate, while they view you as a rebel. Your pure mission has been labelled for decades as a rebellion against foreign rulers. You, above all, deserve to sit on a throne and rule your people, Sire. Your *Swarajya* needs legitimacy in the eyes of the people, the world, and it cannot get that unless we perform a formal coronation of the King."

"I agree with *Punditji,* Highness," Moro *Punt* spoke up. "His words carry profound meaning. Our kingdom must have a formal existence, so future generations do not regard it as a rebel state."

Shivaji *Raje* was quiet. He could see the rationale behind Gagabhatt's suggestions, yet he was unwilling to project himself as a power hungry monarch. At the moment, his mind was too full of the political and military challenges at hand, the recent death of his Commander-in-Chief, the stalemate with the English and Abyssinian powers, and the unavoidable showdown with Aurangzeb. Briefly, his mind went back thirty years to an old temple atop a hill, where he and a handful of his earliest mates had taken an oath before Lord Mahadev, to free their homeland from Sultanate rule. On that day, he had been an unknown boy with a few hundred men, and nothing else. Today, however, he was known across the far reaches of Hindustan; he had nearly a hundred thousand troops under his command; scores of strong impenetrable mountain fortresses; arms and ammunition; and a naval force. He had established his free state as he had set out to do, lost two-thirds of it to the Mughals, and then systematically regained it. In fact, his kingdom was now much larger and healthier than ever before. But Gagabhatt was right. It lacked formal recognition.

"Shivba," Jijabai's trembling voice broke into his silent reflection. "*Punditji*'s suggestion merits consideration. Think about it carefully. Our people have not seen their own crowned King for over three centuries. It is true that you and your comrades have established our *Swarajya*. But how can we ever forget the sacrifices made by our people? Over three decades, they have seen repeated invasions by Mughal and Adilshahi troops. They have lost their lands, crops, animals, and even their own families. Yet they stood firmly behind you and never complained. They, more than anyone else, have a right to see you crowned. They must have their sovereign."

Heads nodded in the assembly. The men smiled. The Queen Mother had upheld Gagabhatt's thoughts. The King would have to agree now. They would see their King formally crowned.

Shivaji *Raje* looked at his mother and smiled. "I will think about it, Mother. I will let the Council know of my decision in a few days. Meanwhile, I have decided to make some changes to our administration. I will formalise the appointment of our eight ministers with new designations. Our beloved Marathi language has long been corrupted by words adopted from Persian and other foreign languages. We must remove these words from official usage and adopt Sanskrit words instead. Sanskrit is the language of our ancestors, and is also the mother of all languages. Our own Marathi was born from Sanskrit. Why do we need to use Persian words when we have such a pure treasure trove?

I shall begin this change by redesignating our Ministers with Sanskrit titles. Moro *Punt*, convene a special court. We shall confer these new designations on everyone. At a later date, we shall compile a listing, replacing Persian words with Sanskrit words and we shall discontinue the use of Persian in all our official communications."

The Ministers beamed with pride. "What a wonderful thought, Highness!" Moro *Punt* voiced their collective feelings. "Our own kingdom, our own King, our own official language… We have waited far too long to see this day."

The special court was convened and the eight full ministers of the Maratha administration were given new designations. The *Peshwa* became the *Mukhya Pradhan*; the *Muzumdar* became the *Amatya*; the *Surnis* took the new title of *Sachiv*; the *Waknis* was redesignated *Mantri'*, and the *Dabir* was now known as the *Sumant*. The sixth and seventh ministers were the *Nyayadheesh*, and the *Punditrao*. These were retained as the former was a Sanskrit term and the latter a Marathi word derived from Sanskrit.

The eighth post in the Council was still vacant and a capable man had to be found soon. During a routine inspection of troops in Chiplun, Shivaji *Raje* spotted a spirited Captain whose service in the army had been exemplary. He was Hansaji Mohite, and *Raje* chose him as the next *Sirnaubat*.

"Hansaji," *Raje* said to the Captain, "I appoint you to the supreme post in our army. In keeping with our recent language reforms, the former title of *Sirnaubat* has been changed to *Senapati*. I also confer upon you the title of *Hambirrao*. You shall be known as *Senapati Hambirrao* Mohite."

The new *Senapati* accepted the sword and robes of honour handed to him by his King and bowed.

Shivaji *Raje* had, by now, accepted Gagabhatt's idea of a formal coronation and agreed to hold the ceremony at Raigad, which would formally become his capital and the seat of Maratha power.

Meanwhile, an interim peace had been reached between the Marathas and the English. Shivaji *Raje* had agreed to offer the English a sum of ten thousand *hons* as compensation for their losses in Rajapur. This was to be paid partly as a customs waiver in Rajapur itself, and partly as goods, over three years. The English Presidency in Mumbai sent three high level officers to Raigad to meet *Raje*, formalize the treaty, and offer him gifts for the coronation. The English also asked that their coins be considered valid currency in the *Swarajya*, but *Raje* denied them this grant. He agreed to most of their other, smaller demands. In return, he demanded an assurance that the English would not help the Abyssinians, nor allow them to dock their ships in Mumbai.

Preparations for Shivaji *Raje*'s coronation were on in full swing in Raigad. The fort already had numerous buildings, offices, lakes, temples, granaries, ammunition dumps, animal stables and markets. Not only did these get a facelift, but new buildings were erected to befit the occasion. The ministers got new residences, new temples were built and a new marketplace adorned the trading area. Hiraji Indulkar, the Chief of Civil Works in Raigad, also constructed a new palace for the King, and a grand many-pillared *durbar* hall, to befit the status of the new monarchy.

The ceremony itself needed various buildings – the *havan kund* was constructed for the fire rituals; the *abhishekshaala* was built to perform the anointing ceremonies.

The clerks ran from pillar to post, stocking provisions in time for the ceremony. A hundred thousand people were expected from all corners of the *Swarajya,* to see their beloved King crowned. They would be housed and fed at the fort, at the King's expense. Over a thousand *Brahmans,* specially selected for their knowledge of the *Vedas* and their proficiency in reciting *mantras,* would be present with their families. The King was expected to give away plenty of *dakshina* in cash and kind to these officiating priests.

Preparing for such a mammoth gathering was no mean task, yet the Raigad officials geared up to see it through. The ceremony itself demanded a long list of provisions for the rituals. Amongst other things, they had to arrange for water from seven sacred rivers, including the Ganga. They also had to send men to collect earth from sacred places, to anoint their King with. A grand throne of solid gold was being created, to serve as the seat of Maratha power for all eternity.

Provision had to be made for sufficient food grains, items for the religious rituals, jewels, ornaments, ceremonial clothes, curtains and satin sheets to decorate the cermonial and durbar halls, gold and silver urns, gold *hons* for the *suvarnatula,* ceremonial umbrellas, *morchels,* royal palanquins, decorated *howdahs, shamianas,* elephants, horses, *shingas* and musical instruments and loads of money. There was a mountain of work, but it had to be completed quickly as an auspicious date for the coronation had been selected by Gagabhatt. It was a race against time for Shivaji *Raje* and his men.

During the months preceding the ceremony, while the Raigad administration worked overtime to prepare for the mother of all functions, Shivaji *Raje* was busy with his Commanders in securing the boundaries of the *Swarajya*. *Raje* saw to the administrative details, garrisons, provisions and ammunition in the forts as well as to the deployment of mobile troops to keep the kingdom safe from incursions.

The coronation rituals and celebration were to extend for nearly a month. The rituals began with a formal visit to the shrine of the Bhosale family diety, Goddess Bhavani. The main Bhavani temple was at Tuljapur, but as this town was under Adilshahi rule, going there was impossible. As an alternative, Shivaji *Raje* visited the Bhavani shrine at Pratapgad, and performed an elaborate *pooja* to the Goddess. He sought the blessings of the temple priest and gifted the shrine with a golden umbrella. After a day's halt at Pratapgad, *Raje* returned to his capital.

Gagabhatt had spent the months preceding the ceremony at Raigad, inking out the details of the coronation. He prepared a new manuscript with the detailed procedure according to *vedic* tradition, and called it *Rajabhishekprayog*. Centuries ago, when Hindu Kings ruled the land of the *Sapt Sindhus*, the holy Ganga, and the homeland of the Marathas, Kings were crowned in true *vedic* Hindu tradition and the procedures were well documented. However, with centuries of Sultanate rule, these traditional ceremonies had been forgotten and the details lost. Gagabhatt vowed to revive these traditions with the coronation of the first Maratha King, and prepared the new manuscript with that aim. The *Rajabhishekprayog* would act as a guide for the coronation of all future Kings.

The rituals were to begin a week before the auspicious day of the actual coronation. However, before that, several religious obstacles had to be surmounted. The assembled priests initially questioned the *Kshatriya* lineage of the Bhosales. Gagabhatt laid their apprehensions to rest when he traced the Bhosale lineage in an unbroken line, to the Sisodia Rajput clan of Mewar, who were the sole representatives of the solar line of Lord Ram. The true *Kshatriya* descent of the Bhosales was thus proven beyond doubt.

That done, the next question raised was whether Shivaji *Raje* himself had been the recepient of the traditional *Kshatriya* rituals since birth, which would make him deserving of a coronation ritual. As it turned out, the sacred thread ceremony, traditionally performed in adolescence, which was a formal initiation into a *vedic* school, had not yet been performed for *Raje*. As a result, his family could not be recognised as *dwija varna*, or the twice born caste. Gagabhatt removed this problem by performing the *upanayana* and investing Shivaji *Raje* with the sacred thread.

Raje was now eligible to perform the penances which would absolve him from the earlier irregularities in the observance of religious rites and from any sins committed knowingly or unknowingly. These penances were performed on the same afternoon and comprised of two ceremonies. In the first, called the *tulapurushadan*, a golden idol of Lord Vishnu was first worshipped and later donated to the priests. In the second, called the *tuladan*, Shivaji *Raje* was weighed against gold, silver, copper, iron and a host of other commodities like cloth, spices, fruits, butter and sugar. These were also donated to the assembled priests.

The next task was to formalise *Raje*'s weddings to his wives which, as per vedic custom, could only happen after the *upanayana*. Hence, Shivaji *Raje* had to remarry his Queens as per *vedic* rituals. This was concluded the next day, which also saw several other rituals like *Ganesh pooja* (worshipping of Lord Ganesh), *hom* (fire rituals), *kalashsthapan* (ritual installation of a metal pot filled with water). Following these rituals, the assembled *Brahmans* were given *dakshina* in cash and kind.

Shivaji *Raje* was required to fast that evening and night, in preparation for the next day's rituals, which was the *Aindrishanti* (offering to Goddess Indrani). This ritual, however, was concluded five days later, following which a thousand *Brahmans* were fed and paid *dakshina*.

Raigad palace, evening of 5 June 1674

These preliminary rituals having been concluded, the anointing ceremony began the evening before the auspicious coronation.

This was called the *Rajabhishek,* in which an *abhishek* or cleansing ritual was performed upon the *Raja.* The ceremony began in a special worship hall with Ganesh *pooja,* a ritual offering to Lord Ganesh. The *homa* or sacred fire was lit in the centre of the hall with mats for Shivaji *Raje,* his eldest Queen Soyarabai, Prince Sambhaji, and the priests. *Agni,* the Fire God, and the *navagraha* (nine stars), were invoked and worshipped. On the four sides of the fire were placed specially decorated pots. The one in the east was a golden pot containing ghee; a silver pot to the south contained milk; the one to the west was made of copper and contained curd, and an earthen pot sat on the northern side of the fire, with water. All the pots were decorated with vermillion, leaves and flowers. An *asandi,* or Lord Indra's seat, made of ficus wood, was also placed in the hall.

The Ganesh *pooja* and fire rituals completed, the entourage shifted to the *abhishekshala,* a special hall for the principal anointing ceremony. Here, Shivaji *Raje* was first anointed with scented oils and powders and then bathed in warm water. He was then asked to sit on a *peetha,* a decorated seat, where he was anointed with earths from sacred places. Following this, he was bathed in *panchamruta,* a preparation of milk, honey, curd, ghee and sugar. The *panchamruta snana* (bath) was repeated thrice, alternating with warm water. Such a bath is permissible under the *vedashastras* for the Gods, and by bathing Shivaji *Raje* thus, he was elevated beyond all castes and *varnas* of society, including the *Brahmans.*

Having changed into fresh white clothes, Shivaji *Raje* was then led back to the worship hall where he ascended the *Asandi* (Lord Indra's seat). *Raje* did this, as per instructions from Gagabhatt, by first placing his knees on the seat, without allowing his feet to touch the seat, in respect to Lord Indra. The Bhosale family priest then sprinkled holy water on *Raje,* thus acknowledging him as a representative of Lord Indra.

Shivaji *Raje* was led back to the *abhishekshala* for the third bath. He sat on a gold plated stool with his chief Queen, Soyarabai, to his left, and Crown Prince Sambhaji *Raje* to his right. The hem of Soyarabai's robe was tied to *Raje*'s, a sign of her being an equal partner. Amidst chanting of *vedic* mantras, the *Brahman* ministers and officers, led by the *Mukhya Pradhan* Moro *Punt* Pingale, carried the golden pot from the worship hall and poured the ghee on the King. The *Kshatriya* officers, led by the new *Senapati,* Hambirrao

Mohite, carried the silver pot and bathed the King with the milk it contained. The third copper pot, was carried by the *Vaishyas* and the King was bathed in curd. Finally, representatives of the *Shudra varna* carried the earthen pot and bathed the King with the water it contained.

Seven *Brahman* ministers from Shivaji *Raje*'s cabinet now stood around the King, carrying a pot each, containing waters from the seven sacred rivers. Amidst the chanting of mantras, the ministers bathed the King with waters from the Ganga, Yamuna, Godavari, Saraswati, Narmada, Sindhu and Kaveri rivers. This ritual confirmed Shivaji *Raje* as the King of all *varnas*.

Shivaji *Raje* now changed into fresh clothes and offered *dakshina* to the officiating priests. He was anointed with vermillion by sixteen pure robed *Brahman* wives, who also waved the sacred lamps. The *Rajabhishek* ritual thus concluded, Shivaji *Raje* left the palace to ascend a chariot. When he reached the chariot, he found Gagabhatt had already ascended it, as a representative of the Gods and the people. He graciously bowed to the King and vacated the chariot for *Raje*, thus bestowing the Kingdom of Indra upon him. *Raje* stood in the chariot with a bow in his hand. *Senapati Hambirrao* Mohite, the charioteer, drove the white horses harnessed to it. The King's coronation procession thus began with accompanying horses, elephants and soldiers.

Royal durbar hall, early morning, 6 June 1674

The grand *durbar* hall was packed to capacity for the final ceremony, the *sinhasanarohan* (throne ascension). The large pillared hall was beautifully decorated with rich carpets, curtains and tapestries. Strings of pearls hung everywhere, as did beautiful chandeliers from the ceiling. Every corner was adorned with expensive decorative objects. An awning of rich gold cloth was spread overhead. Rich embroidered cloth invested every pillar.

At the far end, right in the centre, on a large podium, stood the magnificent throne. Created by master craftsmen from thirty-two *maunds* of gold, the throne captured the attention of every person present that morning. The base, coated in gold, had a seat with velvet cushions. A tiger skin was spread over the seat. Eight gold pillars, embellished with gems and diamonds, stood around the seat at the eight corners, supporting a canopy of rich gold embroidery, from which were suspended strings of pearls in festoons. On either side of the throne were the royal emblems, hung from gilded lances. To the right stood two large gold fish-heads with big teeth, and to the left were several horse tails (the insignia of Turkish royalty) and a pair of gold scales (as an emblem of justice). At the entrance to the hall, on either side, were pitchers filled with water and covered with leaves. Two young elephants and two beautiful horses with gold bridles and rich trappings, also stood at the entrance.

At the auspicious time selected by the astrologers, Shivaji *Raje* entered the *durbar* hall to a buzz of excitement and anticipation from the crowd. He was accompanied by Soyarabai and Sambhaji *Raje*, who walked a few steps behind him. Raje was dressed in a richly embroidered light pink *angarkha* over silk trousers. A silk *dushela* was tied around his waist. His turban was adorned with pearls and gems. Raje wore gold and pearl necklaces as well as the traditional string of *cowries*. Bejewelled rings glittered on all his fingers. His *Bhavani* and a bejewelled *katyaar* were stuck in his *dushela*. In his right hand, *Raje* carried a gilded bow.

The Queen looked radiant in a bright scarlet *Paithani* saree and ceremonial gold adornments. Seventeen-year-old Prince Sambhaji was similarly dressed in fine clothes.

The royals were followed closely by the eight ministers. The entourage progressed with slow measured steps towards the podium. As they reached centerstage, the ministers moved away to occupy their designated positions on either side of the throne. The podium itself had two levels, the throne being on the higher one. On the lower level were three seats, one to the right and two to the left side.

Shivaji *Raje* halted at the podium and looked up at the throne. *The throne...* After three and a half decades of bloody struggle, the Marathi homeland had won *a throne*. No longer would his people bow to foreign rulers. Kings like him would come and go, but for generations, this throne would remain as the official, legitimate seat of power for his people.

Raje ascended the steps leading to the podium. As he set foot on the first step, he remembered his fallen comrades – Tanhaji, Suryaji, Baji Prabhu, Baji Pasalkar, Murarbaji...the list was endless. They had laid down their lives so he could live; so he could be King today. *Swarajya* could never forget their sacrifice. *He* could never forget their sacrifice. *Raje* briefly closed his eyes as his inner voice called out to his comrades.

Gagabhatt, who was on the podium, stopped *Raje* saying, "Halt, O King! Before you ascend the throne, you must take your vows."

Shivaji *Raje* nodded and turned to face the *durbar*. In a loud clear voice, he said, "I Shivaji am to be crowned sovereign King of this land today. I am bound by my vows to exterminate all evil and evil-doers from this earth. This land is my wife and the people who reside on this land are my children. I shall govern and protect my people and see to their welfare as would a father his children. My rule shall be just and impartial. I shall never allow the powers invested in me to be corrupted. If I ever fail in my duty, my ministers shall remind me of them and I shall be bound to descend from the throne. The royal priest shall then strike me down with punishment, which I shall be bound to accept. For this kingdom to exist was the will of our Gods, and hence, so it shall."

The auspicious moment was now upon them. Gagabhatt said, "O King, it is time. Pray walk up to the throne and seat yourself without touching your feet to the throne."

Shivaji *Raje* nodded and walked to stand before the throne. The *durbar* hall fell silent as everyone waited with bated breath. In that moment it seemed that the wind had stopped blowing, the birds had stopped chirping, the rivers had stopped flowing, and the sea had halted in its ebb and flow. The world had come to a standstill. Years of war, death, famine and suffering had culminated in this moment. Three hundred years of slavery were over. Sultanate rule had come to an end.

Gagabhatt counted the *ghatikas* and at the opportune moment, said, "Be seated, O King."

Shivaji *Raje* shuffled back slightly and seated himself on the throne, taking care that his feet did not touch it. Hundreds of faces lit up with smiles. Hearts beat as one. One tired old face in a balcony to the right of the throne quivered with emotion as tears of happiness ran down her face.

Gagabhatt moved forth with the royal umbrella and held it over Shivaji *Raje*'s head. In a loud voice he proclaimed: *Maharaj, Sinhasanadheeshwar, Kshatriya kulawatouns, Maharajadhiraj, Raja Shiva Chhatrapati yancha vijay aso...*

The assembly erupted into joyous victory slogans: *Vijay aso! Vijay aso!* Long live the King!

The people showered the King and the throne with rice grains and flowers. At the entrance to the hall, two *shinga* blowers raised their curved hornlike instruments to the skies and let out a sonorous sound that filled the hall. From the fort ramparts the cannons boomed, announcing to the world that the Marathi people finally had their own King. The guns boomed to the north, south, east and west, their echoes travelling to the ears of the Mughal Emperor, the Adilshah, the Qutubshah, and the European powers, letting them know that their governments no longer held sway in the land they now called *Swarajya.*

Jijabai was overcome with emotion as she saw her dreams being fulfilled. Her tears flowed as she looked at her son seated on the throne with the royal umbrella of state over his head. This was the moment she had admantly fought with her husband and the rest of the world for. This was the moment for which she had sacrificed her marital life, for which she had left her husband's home to return to Pune, with the desperate hope that her younger son would turn her burning ambition into his life's purpose and do what his father had failed to accomplish. Her son, *her Shivba,* had done what none had in over three centuries. He had overthrown the Adilshahi and Mughal claims to his homeland and become a sovereign King to his people. Jijabai's life had come full circle. She desired nothing more in this mortal world.

At a signal from Gagabhatt, three people moved forward to take their own seats beside the King. Queen Soyarabai and Prince Sambhaji *Raje* occupied the seats to the left of the throne, while *Mukhya Pradhan* Moro *Punt* Pingale occupied the lone seat to the right. Beyond them stood the other ministers and office bearers. Behind the throne stood Madari Mehtar, Shivaji *Raje*'s attendant, who was now the *Takhta firosh.*

Officers, ministers and dignitaries moved forward to offer their obeisance and gifts to the new King. Moro *Punt* offered *Raje* a gold plate filled with gold coins, which *Raje* accepted with a smile. Moro *Punt* then poured the gold coins over *Raje*'s head.

Senapati Hambirrao Mohite now moved forward to offer his obeisance and gifts. The other ministers followed suit.

Some English officers, dressed in formal red uniforms, came forward and bowed slightly. They were accompanied by their secretary and translator, Narayan Shenvi, who said, "Your Highness, may I present the officers of the Mumbai Council of the English East India Company – Mr. Henry Oxenden, Mr. George Robinson and Mr. Thomas Mitchell."

The presents brought by the English officers were offered, among them a diamond ring. Shivaji *Raje* beckoned them nearer and accepted the gifts by placing a hand on them.

The people could not get enough of the glittering ceremony. They jostled others for a view of the magnificent throne, which paled in comparison to their illustrious and beloved King. Generations had waited for this glorious day, and freedom; the day that would wipe away the painful memories of centuries of suppression.

Maharaj Shivaji *Raje* Bhosale looked at the bustling assembly in Raigad's ceremonial hall. Amidst the rituals, the formal obesiances, the official dignitaries with their presents, and his adoring subjects, *Raje* was fully aware of the enormous significance of this ceremony and the huge responsibility it placed on his shoulders. His state was now an official state with boundaries. He would not just have to defend it, but see to its prosperity, to law and order, to trade, to relations with the neighbouring states, and above all, to the happiness and safety of his people. Yet he felt strangely calm. It was as if he had been born to be the King he was today.

He was Master of a hundred thousand troops.

He was Master of a hundred forts.

He was Master of a powerful naval force.

He was the Protector of his people and their culture.

He was their Sovereign ruler.

He was the first *Chhatrapati, Lord of the Royal Umbrella.*

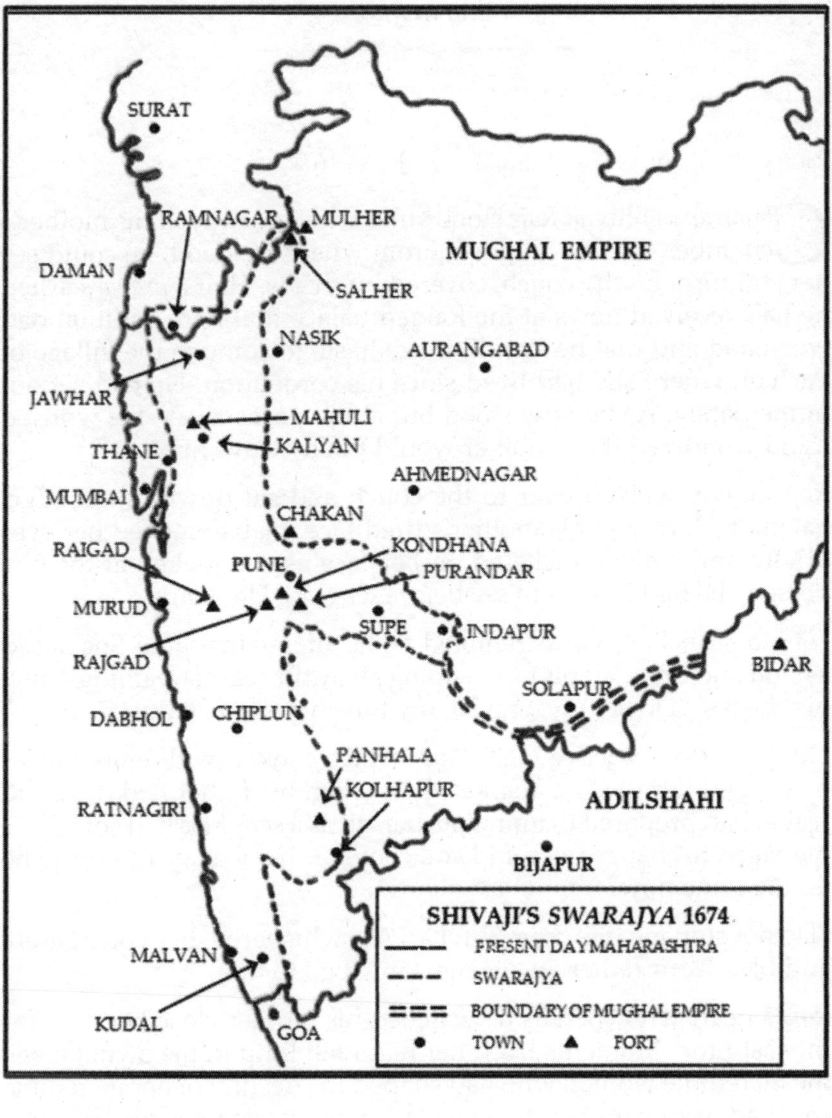
SURAT
RAMNAGAR
MULHER
MUGHAL EMPIRE
DAMAN
SALHER
NASIK
AURANGABAD
JAWHAR
MAHULI
KALYAN
THANE
AHMEDNAGAR
MUMBAI
CHAKAN
RAIGAD
KONDHANA
PUNE
PURANDAR
MURUD
SUPE
INDAPUR
RAJGAD
BIDAR
SOLAPUR
DABHOL
CHIPLUN
PANHALA
KOLHAPUR
RATNAGIRI
ADILSHAHI
BIJAPUR
SHIVAJI'S SWARAJYA 1674
PRESENT DAY MAHARASHTRA
SWARAJYA
BOUNDARY OF MUGHAL EMPIRE
TOWN
FORT
MALVAN
KUDAL
GOA

Epilogue

Pachad, foothills of Raigad, 17 June 1674

Chhatrapati Shivaji *Raje* stood still in the doorway of his mother's chamber, unable to move. From where he stood, he could see her still form on the couch, covered by sheets. Half a *prahar* earlier, he had received news at the Raigad palace that her condition had worsened and that he should make haste to come to the village of Pachad, where she had lived since his coronation. He had set out immediately. As he now stood but a few paces away, his worried mind wondered if his mother would finally leave him.

Raje slowly walked over to the couch and sat down on its edge, gazing forlornly at his mother's tired face. Jijabai opened her eyes briefly and a smile flickered on her face as she looked at the one person she had longed to see before leaving. Her son.

"Shivba," Jijabai's voice trembled as she uttered his name. She raised a hand and caressed his face, wiping away the tears streaming down his cheeks. "Do not cry, Shivba, my time has come. I must go now."

"Mother, do not leave me!" *Raje*'s voice choked with emotions as he begged her to stay. Years earlier, when his father had died and Jijabai had prepared to immolate herself as a *sati*, *Raje* had somehow managed to change her mind and convince her to stay. But could he do the same now?

"Do not stop me this time, Shivba," she whispered, her voice barely audible. "Your father awaits me. I must go to him."

Raje's heart wrenched as he watched his mother close her eyes for the last time. Moments later, her hand fell limp in his own. Jijabai, the incredible woman who had shaped the destiny of her incredible son, had passed away into memory. In many ways she was as much responsible for the *Swarajya* they lived in today, as the man they called *Chhatrapati*.

The Royal Mughal Court, Agra, June 1674

The *Wazir* Jafar Khan shifted uneasily as he glanced at the despatch from the Deccan. He was unsure how his sovereign would react to the news. Aurangzeb raised his hand, instructing him to read the despatch as he turned the beads in his hand.

"The *kafir* Maratha Seeva has been crowned King in an official ceremony in Raigad. He has assumed the title of *Chhatrapati,* has an umbrella of state over his head, and flaunts his royal insignia in court."

The turning of beads stopped. Aurangzeb's eyes glittered with anger and hatred. "*Takhliya,*" he announced abruptly in an emotionless voice, and pulled the curtain in front of his throne. Rising, he walked back slowly to his own chambers and locked himself in. Removing his adorned turban, he spread a mat on the floor and knelt down upon it. Lifting his upturned palms towards Mecca, he murmured, "*Allah*...you have taken away our throne and given it to the Maratha..."

A *tantrik* named Nischalpuri sat in front of *Chhatrapati* Shivaji *Raje,* in his private audience chamber. The man had been in Raigad for several weeks and had attended the coronation ceremony. He had objected to several of the rituals conducted by Gagabhatt, and warned the King that great misfortune would befall him if he persisted with Gagabhatt's method of coronation. The *Chhatrapati* had chosen to ignore him then, but now, after the hubbub of the coronation had died down, he began having doubts.

Barely three months before the coronation, his *Sirnaubat,* Prataprao, had been killed in battle. Days before the auspicious event, Kashibai, one of his Queens, had died at Raigad. And now, his mother too, had passed away, eleven days after the event. He had also received news of a lightning strike on Fort Pratapgad that had incinerated the stables. Alarmed by these events, the *Chhatrapati* had summoned Nischalpuri, to request him to perform the additional rites to appease the Gods.

"A few rites will not be enough, O King," Nischalpuri said. "We will have to conduct the entire coronation again according to *tantrik* rites."

"Perform another coronation?" the *Chhatrapati* was taken aback. He had no inclination to go through the entire process again, not to mention the expense involved. But his mind was depressed following his mother's death, nor did he wish to slight the *tantrik*.

"Yes, Sire," Nischalpuri said as he sat erect, looking at the prominent ministers and advisors of the *Swarajya, who* were also present. "The entire procedure of the coronation was wrong. We must repeat it. Only then can evil events be warded off."

Moro *Punt* sighed. He knew the King would probably give in to the ascetic's demands. They could ill afford another massive expense. But the *Chhatrapati*'s state of mind was of paramount importance right now.

"The Maratha Empire must survive long after the first *Chhatrapati*," persisted Nischalpuri. "The King's heirs must rule for generations to come. For that to happen, we dare not begin in an inauspicious manner. Believe me, Sire, we must do this."

Chhatrapati Shivaji Raje finally agreed to Nischalpuri's demands, much to the displeasure of his Council. And so, three months after the first coronation, Shivaji *Raje* was crowned again, this time according to *tantrik* rites, dictated by Nischalpuri.

Author's Note

During this second phase of Shivaji's life, spanning some fourteen years from 1661 to 1674, his struggle was principally against the Mughal Empire. By 1661, two major Adilshahi campaigns against Shivaji had ended in disaster for Bijapur. Afzal Khan had suffered a humiliating defeat at Pratapgad, while the Panhala campaign under Siddi Jauhar, had fizzled out without any major gains. Though Shivaji later surrendered Fort Panhala, the Adilshah's chief objective of apprehending or killing Shivaji himself, remained unfulfilled. These campaigns no doubt caused a serious dent in the Bijapur treasury and the Adilshah appears to have been reluctant to open a major new offensive against the Marathas. Shivaji was thus relieved on the Adilshahi front.

Aurangzeb had stabilized his hold on the Mughal administration by 1660, and now decided to turn his attention to matters in the Deccan. Aurangzeb had probably realized early in his reign that Shivaji was likely to be the major hurdle to his plans of expansion in the south. He probably also realized that if the Marathas were allowed to grow in power, they could become a serious threat to the Empire itself. This view is validated by the enormous size of the armies he sent out against Shivaji, who at the time, despite his achievements against Bijapur, was a relatively small force compared to the Mughal might. Aurangzeb's plans for Shivaji were thwarted both by the incompetence of the General he chose and by the brilliance of Shivaji's tactics.

Shaista Khan's first major move was his campaign on the fort of Chakan. This fort, though small and defended by only a handful of Marathas under Firangoji Narsala, resisted defeat and capture for two and a half months. This long drawn battle and the heroic stand of Firangoji's men, even after the fort rampart was breached, seems to have made an impression on Shaista Khan, as he changed his strategy soon after. He desisted from besieging any hill fort and began occupying Shivaji's territory instead. The description of the battle in this book has been created mainly from the account in *Alamgir-nama* (Extracts in Ref 25), *Shivbharat* (Ref 32), and an account by the French traveller, Tavernier (Extract in Ref 25).

The incident regarding the harsh punishment meted out by Shivaji to Khandoji Khopade, is mentioned in the *Jedhe Chronicle* (Ref 16).

Shaista Khan's decision to launch a campaign in the Konkan was a good one, but he made a fatal error in choosing his Commander. From most accounts of the Battle of Umbarkhind, Kartalab Khan comes across as someone who was ignorant of the terrain, the Sahyadri hills with its passes and forests, and the dangers they held. Either that, or his spy and reconnoitering teams failed him completely, allowing Shivaji's men to make a complete fool of the Mughals. Once again, Shivaji's ingenious mind and flawless planning is plainly apparent. He used the topography to his full advantage and reduced a huge Mughal army in less than a day of battle. The details of the battle in this book have been adapted principally from *Shivabharat* (Ref 32).

Contemporaneous sources are silent on the question of why Shivaji allowed Kartalab Khan safe passage. Shivaji was probably trying to effect some kind of truce with the Mughals at this time, as is evident from an entry in the *Jedhe Chronicle* (Ref 16), which says that Sono *Punt*, Shivaji's minister, visited Shaista Khan in the last quarter of 1660. Probably, Shivaji may have felt that a chance at some truce with Shaista Khan would be jeopardized if he either slaughtered Kartalab Khan and his men or took them prisoner. In any case, whatever political plot he was trying to hatch with Sono *Punt* does not seem to have worked.

At this point of time, the Adilshah seems to have been caught in a dilemma regarding his approach to the Maratha problem. While he no doubt wanted to check Shivaji's growing strength and reclaim the Adilshahi's lands usurped by him, he also seems to have realized Shivaji's utility as a bulwark against the Mughals. This might be the reason for his choice of tactics against Shivaji thereafter. Whenever Shivaji was at war with the Mughals, the Adilshah either remained neutral or restricted himself to minor operations, rather than opening an all out offensive. However, when Shivaji's war with the Mughals languished, the Adilshah intensified his own acitivities against the Marathas (Ref 25).

Shivaji's Konkan campaign in April 1661, has been reconstructed mostly from details mentioned in *Shivbharat* (Ref 32) and from contemporary scholarly accounts (Ref 25, 45). Shivaji no doubt sought retribution against Suryarao Surve of Shringarpur, and Jaswantrao Dalvi of Palavni, who had participated in Siddi Jauhar's campaign and blocked Shivaji's retreat to Vishalgad. Surve initially agreed to join Shivaji, but when the latter moved north, changed his mind and attacked the Maratha troops stationed at Sangameshwar. Shivaji was probably half expecting Surve's double-cross and his march northward may in fact have been a deliberate move to take Surve off guard. With startling speed, Shivaji then doubled back from Palavni and invaded Shringarpur, wiping out Surve's stronghold.

With Shaista Khan and the massive Mughal army firmly entrenched in his dominion, Shivaji seems to have realized that in comparison, his own strength was too limited to force a result in his favour through a single decisive battle. Hence, he seems to have adopted the policy of 'war of attrition' in which he tried to exhaust the Mughals by multiple small raids and by cutting off their supplies. The Mughals thus found themselves in constant danger of such Maratha attacks and Shaista Khan was forced to spread his forces over wide areas. For Shivaji, the main drawback of this strategy was that his people suffered the most as Mughal wrath fell upon them and they had to conduct mass evacuations of villages. That Shivaji had issued orders to move people to the hills is evident from his letter dated 23 October 1662, to Sarjerao Jedhe, the Deshmukh of Rohid Khore (Extract in Ref 25)

Shivaji's daring night raid on Shaista Khan's camp is a masterstroke of guerilla warfare and ingenious planning. As with most of his campaigns, the actual manner in which the raid was carried out is shrouded in mystery. The description of the raid in my book is adapted from accounts by contemporary historians, with a few bits added from chronicles. It is generally believed that some four hundred men accompanied Shivaji into the Mughal camp and presumably into Lal Mahal itself. Amongst the Captains who accompanied him, the names of Babaji and Chimnaji Deshpande, who were sons of a former Lal Mahal office bearer, and who had spent a significant part of their boyhood in Lal Mahal with a young Shivaji, have come up consistently.

Why Shivaji chose to go personally on such a perilious mission is a question one cannot reasonably answer. While studying Shivaji's life, he always comes across as a shrewd, calculating and careful person, who planned each campaign meticulously, no doubt taking his own security seriously. Yet, we find he did, on occasion, put his own life on the line. Following his decision to give the dangerous Afzal Khan a personal interview, from which he barely escaped alive, his decision to go on this raid seems a tad reckless. Think about it...sneaking into a massive enemy military camp, attempting to kill the Mughal General, and then escaping...the mission was fraught with real danger and risks at each step. One slip and the entire Maratha party would have been slaughtered. Yet, Shivaji chose to go himself. I have tried hard to reason out this decision of his. For the mission to be successful they needed a person familiar with Lal Mahal, who could move around in complete darkness. Shivaji probably felt he was the only person who could do that. Only he had a realistic chance of finding Shaista Khan in the dark. Also, Shivaji was a person who believed in leading his men by example. Time and again he seems to have engaged in missions, probably to prove to his men that he had the guts and the willingness to risk his own life to carry out his audacious plans.

No authentic source tells us how Shivaji and his men entered Shaista Khan's camp. Plausible stories of a marriage party which entered with pre-arranged permits, and some men having entered with an excuse that they were on outpost duties, have been taken from Khafi Khan's *Muntakhab-ul-Lubab* (Extract in Ref 25) and the *Sabhasad Chronicle* (Ref 36) respectively. A brief but accurate account of the raid itself can be found in Philip Giffard's letter from Rajapur to Surat, dated 12 April 1663 (Ref 3). This letter also gives an account of the men and women killed in the raid. Giffard also suggests there may have been some arrangement between the Marathas and Jaswant Singh.

The story of torches being tied to the horns of oxen in Katraj Pass, to divert pursuing Mughal troops, is mentioned in the *Jedhe Chronicle* (Ref 16).

Shaista Khan was apparently completely mortified by the raid and retreated to Aurangabad after handing over charge of the Pune camp to Jaswant Singh. He was later sacked from the *Subadari* of Deccan and transferred to Bengal, which in those days was viewed amongst the Mughal nobility as a demotion.

A Persian letter incorporated into two Persian books, *Durj-ul-gawahir* and *Khutut-i-Shivaji*, is attributed to Shivaji, and is said to have been sent to officers of Emperor Aurangzeb (Ref 25). Whether this letter was really written at Shivaji's behest or is pure fiction, cannot be confirmed. In the two Persian works, the letter is undated. The original letter has not survived. I have included this letter at the beginning of Chapter 4.

Dates of Shivaji's first raid on Surat are obtained from the *Jedhe Chronicle* (Ref 16) and *Shivapur Chronicle* (Ref 18). Details of the raid in this book have been compiled mainly from English factory records (Ref 3), Dutch records (Extracts in Ref 25), and from accounts of modern historians (Ref 25, 30, 45). Brief accounts of English, French and Dutch travellers are also found in these references.

The efficient manner in which the raid was carried out is testimony to the fact that Shivaji had detailed information not only about the city itself but also about its richest inhabitants. The Marathas seemed to know exactly where to hit and how. It is popularly believed that his Chief of Intelligence, Bahirji Naik, was primarily responsible for the spy work (Ref 36).

The incident of an assasination attempt on Shivaji's life at the behest of Inayat Khan was witnessed by Anthony Smith, a servant of the East India Company, who was captured by the Marathas and taken to Shivaji's camp outside Surat. The incident was related by him to others after he was released by the Marathas and is mentioned in a letter by Rev. L'Escaliot to Sir Thomas Browne, dated 28 January 1664 (Ref 3). Smith's account is, however, not corroborated by any other source and Smith himself appears to be an untrustworthy source.

In any case, it does appear from various sources that the raid, which was reasonably peaceful up to a point, did turn suddenly ugly and most of the torching of dwellings seems to have occured later. It is quite likely that some incident triggered anger amongst the Maratha troops. It is quite clear from the accounts of Bernier (Ref 5), and Thevenot (Ref 46), that Father Ambrose, the Capuchin missionary, was treated with great respect by Shivaji. This adds credence to the popularly held view that Shivaji had in fact given instructions not to harm priests and padres, which would mean indirectly that the loot of Surat was not a free for all plundering but was carried out in a disciplined manner, at least initially.

The fact that the East India Company President, Sir George Oxenden, made a show of courage and defiance by marching through the streets of Surat, is mentioned in a Surat Council letter dated 28 January 1664 (Ref 3). Aurangzeb did recognize the efforts of the English and Dutch, by granting them exemption from customs duty (Ref 3).

Shivaji's objective in the Surat raid appears to go beyond procuring valuable funds for his *Swarajya* and striking terror in the Mughal administration. Surat was one of the chief sources of revenue for the Mughals and destruction of the city would have meant cessation of the flow of money, at least for some time. His raid was thus clearly aimed at crippling the Mughal economy.

Atrocities were no doubt committed on Surat residents during the raid, but before blaming Shivaji for this, one must consider the background of this raid. For the previous three years, Shaista Khan's army had despoiled Shivaji's dominions and caused great harm not just to his people but also to his economy. It was natural that Shivaji would try to get some compensation for these losses and that he would have to necessarily do it by force. His newly formed kingdom had, as yet, no robust state economy to sustain his army. Shivaji would have been forced to make war pay for war. In all fairness, Aurangzeb's administration and armed forces were responsible for the safety of Surat, as that of the entire Empire. That they completely failed in their duty was the primary cause of the loot. Shivaji simply made the most of their incompetence. After all, it was an established military custom in those days to plunder enemy territories to collect much needed revenue. Thus, considering the background of Shaista Khan's campaign, Shivaji delivered in Surat the proverbial tit-for-tat.

Shivaji's campaign against Khawas Khan in 1664, has been reconstructed from details in the *Sabhasad Chronicle* (Ref 36) and letters of the Dutch Resident at Vengurle (Ref 4). That Shivaji attacked Baji Ghorpade and eliminated his clan is mentioned in *Sabhasad* (Ref 36).

The *tula* ceremony at Mahabaleshwar is mentioned in the *Jedhe Chronicle* (Ref 16).

The naval expedition to Basrur in 1665, is mentioned in the *Jedhe Chronicle* (Ref 16), the *Shivapur Chronicle* (Ref 18), and in an English factory letter from Karwar to Surat dated 14 March 1665 (Ref 3).

Aurangzeb probably realized his own folly in appointing Shaista Khan to the Deccan campaign, for he then chose his ablest and most experienced Commander, Jai Singh, to head his Deccan army. In Jai Singh, Shivaji finally found a match for his own guile and shrewdness. The Rajput King of Amer (now Jaipur), planned his campaign meticulously and carried out his plans relentlessly. Wisely, he chose Fort Purandar not just as his first attack point, but also as a place to land the majority of his troops. By doing so, he wedged himself between Shivaji and the Adilshah, thus preventing a possible coalition between the two, which could have proved disastrous for him. From this central camp, he spread his armed forces into Shivaji's fief, thus effectively preventing Shivaji's troops and Commanders stationed at various forts, from joining hands to form a large body. At one point, Shivaji, stationed at Rajgad, further to the west, seems to have been isolated from the rest of his forces.

Jai Singh seems to have judged Shivaji's strengths and weaknesses astutely, because, in just over three months, Shivaji was forced to accept a humiliating treaty of surrender. Why Shivaji capitulated to Jai Singh in such a short period of time is a question I haven't been able to answer fully. Perhaps the answer lies more in what had already happened prior to Jai Singh's arrival in the Deccan.

Being at war with the Mughals for several years had been hard not just on Shivaji and his troops, but also on the country itself, and more importantly, on the common people. At some point, Shivaji seems to have seen the futility of continuing the war when his lands were devastated, people exhausted and the economy in ruins. Why else would a man, a King to his people, who had stoically refused to give up in the face of grave dangers in the past, suddenly fold up and surrender in such a short time? The defeat at Purandar, with the death of Murarbaji and scores of his troops, only seems to have been a trigger for his decision.

Similarly, why Jai Singh suddenly chose to discuss a peace treaty while he had Shivaji on the mat is equally baffling. Jai Singh was under explicit instructions from Aurangzeb to finish Shivaji and his rebellion. Three months into his campaign, he was in a favourable position to do just that. Yet he suddenly decides to negotiate peace. Probably, the constant threat that Shivaji would join with the Adilshah if pushed too hard, may have had something to do with his decision. It is entirely my surmise that Shivaji, through his spies, fed him the information that he was negotiating with the Adilshah. Some of these facts can be found in Sarkar's English translation of Jai Singh's letters to Aurangzeb (Ref 42). The incident in which Shivaji appeals to Jai Singh to join hands with him to fight the Mughal is entirely fictional.

The defeat to Jai Singh was the worst in Shivaji's entire life, for he had to give up not only twenty-three of his forts, but also nearly two-thirds of his fief to the Mughals. The forts ceded by Shivaji have been mentioned in the *Alamgir Nama* (Extracts in Ref 25) and *Haft Anjuman* (Extracts in Ref 42), but the lists are not identical. The list of forts retained by Shivaji is mentioned in Sarkar's English translation of Aurangzeb's *firmaan* dated 5 Sept 1665 (Ref 42). The terms of the treaty itself are mentioned in Sarkar's English translation of Jai Singh's letters to Aurangzeb (Ref 42).

I have reconstructed Jai Singh's campaign, the battle of Purandar and the terms of the subsequent treaty, from Sarkar's works (Ref 40, 42, 45), which contain numerous translated passages from original Persian sources and Jai Singh's letters, Sarkar's translation of the *Maasir-i-Alamgiri* (Ref 43), from other works by modern historians (Ref 25, 30), and some Marathi works (Ref 35, 37).

The epic battle between Murarbaji Deshpande and Diler Khan has been described in the *Sabhasad Chronicle* (Ref 36).

After this dazzling success against Shivaji, Jai Singh's colossal defeat against the Adilshah seems to have been due to a combination of poor planning and poor intelligence. Since Jai Singh comes across as an astute Commander during his war with Shivaji, the former seems a less likely cause. I feel, his spies and reconnoitering units failed him. He completely misjudged the topographical conditions his army was marching into. He was also mis-informed about the Adilshah's preparredness for the war. This can be gauged from Jai Singh's letters to Aurangzeb in which he writes that the Bijapur's army is disunited, its officers are quarelling amongst themselves, the castle has no provisions and that most Bijapuri nobles and officers would defect to the Mughals once they reached Bijapur. Nothing could have been further from the truth.

Despite his own shortcomings, Ali Adilshah had managed to rally his Commanders and Captains under his banner, well in time. The Adilshahi army offered stiff resistance to the Mughal advance and adopted a policy of harassing them without directly engaging in full battle. Thus, the Mughals could not force a result in their favour by a decisive battle and remained in constant danger of attack. The Bijapuris also resorted to a 'scorched earth policy', relocating villages, filling up wells with earth and chopping trees, so that the advancing Mughal army suffered great hardships on account of lack of water and shade. The description of this war between Jai

Singh and the Adilshah has been recreated mainly from Sarkar's work (Ref 40, 42, 45).

The fact that Diler Khan may have hatched a plot to kill Shivaji while he was in the Mughal camp, is mentioned in English factory records (Ref 3), and by Manucci (Ref 24). The incident of Shivaji's defeat at Panhala in January 1666, and the resultant distancing of Netoji Palkar, is mentioned in *Haft Anjuman* (Extract in Ref 40). Sabhasad (Ref 36) narrates the meeting of an angry Shivaji with his Commander-in-Chief, in which he asks "Why did you not reach in time?" Sabhasad further mentions that Shivaji sacked Netoji and appointed Kudtoji Gujar in his place as *Sirnaubat*. He, however, places this incident after the Siddi Jauhar campaign (circa 1660). This, we now know to be incorrect. Sabhasad may have confused the two incidents as both took place after a battle at Panhala (Argument in Ref 25).

The cause of Netoji's disaffection is, however, not clear. Did Shivaji really sack him (as Sabhasad says), or did Netoji defect first to the Adilshahi and then to the Mughals, of his own accord? This is open to debate. There seems to have been ample reason for Shivaji to sack Netoji, as the Commander had, in the past, committed errors on more than one occasion (reported late to Wai after the Pratapgad war against Afzal Khan, and failed to rescue Shivaji from Siddi Jauhar's siege of Panhala). His reporting late to Panhala in January of 1666, must have been the final straw which sparked Shivaji's temper enough for him to sack the man. The second view, that Netoji himself may have defected, also appears probable. Netoji was considerably senior to Shivaji in age and there may have been at least some insubordination in his behaviour. Thus, the presumably hot-headed Commander may have left service after being admonished angrily by Shivaji. There is no documentary evidence for the preceding argument.

Another baffling question is why Shivaji decided to visit Agra, despite knowing the inherent risks involved. He knew for sure that once in Agra, he would be completely at Aurangzeb's mercy. Yet he took this grave risk, and that too, with his nine-year-old son in tow. Sabhasad says that Shivaji had offered to conquer the Adilshahi and Qutubshahi for the Mughal Emperor (Ref 36). Perhaps Shivaji may have held a belief that Aurangzeb would appoint him Head of the Mughal army in the Deccan, and he could then utilize the vast Mughal resources to annex the two southern Sultanates. At a later date, he could then cast off Mughal overlordship and usurp the lands for himself.

There is no doubt that Jai Singh used every means at his disposal to persuade Shivaji to visit Agra. In his letters to Aurangzeb, he writes that he used 'a thousand devices' to persuade Shivaji (Ref 45). It is not entirely unlikely that amongst the various enticements used, was a possibility that Shivaji would be appointed to the *Subadari* of the Deccan province. This has been mentioned in Marathi chronicles (Ref 7, 36 50). However, Persian histories and Jai Singh's own letters do not mention anything to that effect. Sarkar accepts it as a possibility (Ref 45), while Pagadi rejects it (Ref 30). To me, it seems plausible that Jai Singh may have made some unrealistic promises to convince Shivaji. I also feel that Jai Singh must have used pressure and force.

The incident involving Saf Shikan Khan at Aurangabad is narrated by Bhimsen Saxena in *Tarikh-i-Dilkasha* (Ref 19). Shivaji's entourage and his appearance is described in great detail by Parkaldas, one of Jai Singh's officers, in his letter to the Amber office dated 29 May 1666 (Ref 44).

Shivaji's visit to Agra has been recreated mainly from Sarkar's work (Ref 40, 42, 44, 45), which includes material from Rajasthani letters and records, as well as Haft Anjuman; from Marathi chronicles (Ref 7, 36, 50), *Maasir-i-Alamgiri* (Ref 43), and from works of modern scholars (Ref 25, 30, 35).

What went wrong with Shivaji's audience with Aurangzeb? According to Sarkar, Shivaji's historic visit to Agra began as a 'comedy of errors due to Rajput incompetence' (Ref 45). The royal retinue which should have been sent by the Mughal administration for Shivaji, who was a state guest, never materialised. Shivaji was forced to spend a night in a *serai* meant for common travellers, which itself would have irked him. Ram Singh, who was supposed to receive Shivaji, failed to do so the next morning as well. Shivaji would no doubt have felt insulted by this breach of protocol. We do not know why Ram Singh did not reach the *serai* on time. Probably the fact that Aurangzeb had posted him on guard duty at his own palace may have had something to do with it (Ref 35).

Thus, it was in an irritated, probably even angry frame of mind, that Shivaji entered Aurangzeb's *durbar.* Not to mention the fact that he had been riding for several hours in the summer heat, before reaching Agra Fort. Shivaji had probably expected to be treated with respect at court, but Aurangzeb slighted him further. Far from being welcomed, the Emperor refused to even acknowledge his presence. He was then made to stand behind several rows of *mansabdars*. The final insult was when Jaswant Singh, standing in front of Shivaji, was awarded a robe of honour. This final rebuke proved too much for the proud King of the Marathas and his temper flared uncontrollably. Thus, it does appear that a perceived difference between his own expectations and the reality of the Mughal *durbar*, combined with the cumulative effect of repeated insults, were the reasons behind Shivaji's loss of self-control at court. As a direct result of the drama in the *durbar*, Shivaji no doubt lost a golden chance of securing political favours from Aurangzeb, but more importantly, the Emperor too, lost the only chance he had to turn Shivaji's mind in the Empire's favour.

Having studied Shivaji's life in detail, I do not have a shred of doubt in my mind that *Shivaji never intended to surrender his political ambitions to Aurangzeb*. I am convinced that Shivaji never wished to become a servant of the Empire. He had fostered a burning ambition to establish his own free state in Maharashtra for two decades and he wasn't about to give up on that, no matter what favours Aurangzeb conferred upon him. So, I feel, even if Aurangzeb had treated him with the utmost (albiet forced) respect, it would not have changed the final outcome of Shivaji's career or of the Maratha Empire. At the very most it would have avoided the embarassing scene at court and probably some of the events in Agra after that.

Why did Aurangzeb put up with Shivaji's humiliating demeanor? Why did he not order his execution right away or even later, while Shivaji was in Agra for three months? Shivaji, after all, was at his mercy. There are no easy answers to these questions. Aurangzeb may have been hampered in his own decision by Jai Singh's pledge about Shivaji's safety. No doubt Ram Singh too, would have played an important role in thwarting the Emperor's moves. Aurangzeb was probably reluctant to hurt the Rajputs, either by slighting an officer of Jai Singh's stature, or by forcibly removing Ram Singh from the scene. Even after he had ordered Fulad Khan to stand guard around Shivaji's camp, Ram Singh had placed his trustworthy men inside Fulad Khan's ring of soldiers, to secure Shivaji's safety. This would no doubt have sent a message to the

Emperor that the Rajput's were willing to die to keep the promise they had made to Shivaji. This intense politics bought Shivaji precious time.

There is no doubt too, that Shivaji had heavily bribed Mughal officers in Agra to speak to the Emperor in his favour. Most importantly, he had bribed the *Wazir*, Jafar Khan, who interceded with Aurangzeb and secured a pardon for Shivaji. Shivaji's sharp political brain and shrewd diplomacy is there for all to see as he hatched a counter plot to every plot of the Emperor, thus delaying his own death, and in the time he thus bought himself, planning his escape.

Shivaji's escape past Fulad Khan, from his Agra camp, is the stuff of legend. I have reconstructed the escape chiefly from the *Sabhasad Chronicle* (Ref 36), and from Sarkar's works (Ref 40, 42, 44, 45), which contain extracts from Rajasthani letters. Some details are also obtained from the *Jedhe Chronicle* (Ref 16) and some English letters (Ref 3). Sabhasad mentions that Shivaji was momentarily overcome by tremendous grief when Fulad Khan besieged his camp on the Emperor's orders. There is general agreement that Shivaji and Sambhaji fled in large boxes (Ref 16, 36). Sabhasad mentions that it was Hiroji *Farzand* who lay in Shivaji's bed after Shivaji fled from the camp. The drama after his escape has been recreated partly from extracts of Aurangzeb's court history (Ref 15).

Though we know a lot about Shivaji's Agra visit, we know precious little of the actual route of his return journey, which is shrouded in mystery. Sabhasad clearly mentions that after leaving Agra, Shivaji decided to go to Mathura to throw Mughal pursuers off his track. That Shivaji left his son Sambhaji behind at Mathura, with the brothers-in-law of Moro *Punt* Pingale, is mentioned in the *Sabhasad Chronicle* and the *Jedhe Chronicle* (Refs 16, 36). Sabhasad further says that Shivaji returned via Bhaganagar (Hyderabad). Thus it may be surmised that Shivaji took a circuitous route home, avoiding the regular roads, to confuse his pursuers. The *Jedhe Chronicle* states that Shivaji and Sambhaji escaped on 17 August 1666, while a Rajasthani letter from Delhi states that Shivaji reached his fort in twenty-five days, which would peg his return date as 12 September 1666 (Ref 25). If these dates are to be believed then one could also argue that Shivaji must have taken the shortest route back home (rather than a circuitous one). Even in the former case, he would have had to travel some sixty kilometers a day.

The *Jedhe Chronicle* mentions that Raghunath *Punt* and Tryambak *Punt* were arrested and detained in Agra. The same source also mentions that they later returned to Shivaji (Ref 16).

A Rajasthani letter dated 19 Nov 1666, from Delhi, states that 'Shivaji's son died on the way (Ref 44). Since we know that Sambhaji survived the Agra visit, we may surmise that the rumour of his death had reached Delhi and that Shivaji's spy network may have had something to do with it.

The letter from Jai Singh to Jafar Khan, quoted in Chapter 11, in which he mentions *...though Shivaji's pedigree is so low that men like me do not even eat food touched by him...* can be found in the *Haft Anjuman* (Extracts in Ref 45).

That peace was finally concluded between Shivaji and Aurangzeb can be gauged from Prince Muazzam's letter to Shivaji dated 9 March 1668 (Ref 42), in which he says: 'His gracious Majesty has elevated your head by granting you the title of *Raja*.'

That Aurangzeb had given orders to destroy Hindu temples and schools is mentioned in the *Maasir-i-Almagiri* (Ref 43) and *Jedhe Chronicle* (Ref 16). The former reference also states that idols 'were brought to Agra and were buried under the steps of the mosque'.

The main cause for the rupture of the Maratha-Mughal peace in 1670, is unclear. Sabhasad (Ref 36) states that Aurangzeb ordered Prince Muazzam to arrest *Prataprao* Gujar and Niraji Raoji, who were stationed in Sambhaji's *jagir* in Varhad region. But the Prince received this news from his own court agents, even before the Emperor's *firmaan* and hence, on the sly, told Niraji to leave at once. This, according to Sabhasad, was interpreted as betrayal by Shivaji and caused him to end the peace treaty. The *Tarikh-i-dilkasha* states that the Emperor confiscated Sambhaji's *jagir* against repayment of rupees one lakh, which was provided to Shivaji for his Agra visit, and this was why Shivaji recalled *Prataprao* (Ref 19). A third possible, though less likely cause, may have been the unrest caused by the desecration of temples and religious persecution, around Agra. An English letter from Henry Gray, dated 23 January 1670, corroborates these facts (Ref 3).

The unrest on the north-western frontier of the Empire had forced Aurangzeb to move a large part of his Deccan forces away. As a result, the Mughal army in Deccan was significantly depleted, spread over a vast area, and limited mostly to garrisoning troops.

The Mughal Emperor was thus unable to efficiently hold and control the territory gained in the Purandar treaty, and this seems to be the prime reason for the spectacular success of Shivaji's troops in regaining lost fortresses.

The historic battle to regain Fort Kondhana, between a small Maratha contingent led by Tanhaji Malusare, and the defending Rajput-Mughal garrison, has been recreated mainly from the description in the *Sabhasad Chronicle* (Ref 36). The dates are mentioned in the *Jedhe Chronicle* (Ref 16) and *Shivapur Chronicle* (Ref 18). The view held by some that Kondhana was renamed 'Sinhagad' after this battle, is incorrect, since the name Sinhagad appears in a letter from Shivaji to Moro *Punt* Pingale dated 2 April 1663, much before this battle (Ref 25). The belief that a reptile (*ghorpad*) was used to scale the Dronagiri Cliff is nothing but fiction, as no source makes mention of it. Sabhasad clearly mentions that Tanhaji used expert rock-climbers to scale the cliff and let down ropes for his men (Ref 36).

Sabhasad's claim that twenty-seven forts were captured in four months (Ref 36), may not be entirely accurate, but is not imaginary either. An English letter from Mumbai to Surat dated 28 June 1670, clearly states that 'Shivaji had recovered all his castles and strongholds upon the hills except Karnala' (Ref 3).

That Shivaji shifted his capital from Rajgad to Rairi (which was renamed Raigad), around this time (1670), is mentioned in the *Jedhe Chronicle* (Ref 16), some English letters (Ref 3), and the *Sabhasad Chronicle* (Ref 36).

The 1670 drama between Diler Khan, Prince Muazzam and Iftikar Khan, has been recreated from details mentioned in *Tarikh-i-dilkash*a (Ref 19), *Maasir-i-Alamgiri* (Ref 43) and English records (Ref 3).

Details of the second sack of Surat (1670), are obtained mainly from English and Dutch letters (Ref 3, 4), the *Sabhasad Chronicle* (Ref 36), and Mughal court newsletters (Ref 15).

The battle of Vani-Dindori (1670), has been recreated mainly from details in *Tarikh-i-dilkasha* (Ref 19), the *Sabhasad Chronicle* (Ref 36), and the *Jedhe Chronicle* (Ref 16).

The entire Maratha campaign in Baglan and Karanja, as well as the gory battle of Salher, have been recreated from details in English records (Ref 3), the *Jedhe Chronicle* (Ref 16), the *Sabhasad Chronicle*

(Ref 36), Mughal court newsletters (Ref 15), *Tarikh-i-dilkasha* (Ref 19), and *Shiva Charitra Pradeep* (Ref 12).

Ramaji Pangera's suicidal attack on Diler Khan's forces (1671), is described by Sabhasad (Ref 36).

Shivaji's interactions with the Siddi of Janjira, the English factors and the Portuguese, are recreated mainly from details in the English records (Ref 3), Pisurlekar's work (Ref 33), and Mehendale (Ref 25). No contemporaneous account of the Jawhar and Ramnagar campaign is found, though some details appear in Abbe Carre's description (Ref 46).

The ingenious capture of Panhala by Kondaji *Farzand* has been recreated from details in *Parnal Parvat Grahanakhyam* (Ref 34), and the *Jedhe* and *Shivapur Chronicles* (Ref 16, 18).

The battle of Umrani between *Prataprao* and Bahlol Khan (1673), the events after it, and the battle at Nesari, which resulted in *Prataprao*'s death (1674), have been recreated from *Parnal* (Ref 34), the *Jedhe* and *Shivapur Chronicles* (Refs 16, 18), Sabhasad (Ref 36), and English records (Ref 3). The famous sentences attributed to letters from Shivaji to *Prataprao* ('On what pretext did you agree to a peace with Bahlol Khan?' and 'Finish Bahlol Khan, else do not show me your face again') are from the *Sabhasad Chronicle* (Ref 36). The actual letters with these words, however, are not extant and hence it is not possible to comment whether Shivaji really wrote them or these are the imagination of the chronicler. A famous folk tale (and ballad based on it), describe the battle of Nesari thus: 'Having read the scathing letter of his King, Prataprao's face turned red with anger and he mounted a horse and rode off alone toward Bahlol Khan's camp. Seeing his mad charge, six of his loyal Captains rode off after him. The brave seven, maddened by anger and revenge, fell upon the enemy camp and slaughtered many before they were mercilessly cut down.' There is no evidence to support this romantic tale, though some historians have included it in their works (Ref 45). However, it does appear likely that Prataprao was either surprised by Bahlol Khan's army when he had insufficient troops with him, or may have led a charge with a small force without waiting for reinforcements.

The incident of the plunder of Bahadur Khan's camp in 1674, has been recreated from an account in the Surat despatch of 1 August 1674 (Ref 3), and another account by Cosme de Guarda (Ref 46).

I have recreated the events around the coronation and the ceremony itself mainly from *Shri Shivrajyabhishekprayog* (Ref 13), the *Jedhe Chronicle* (Ref 16), the *Shivapur Chronicle* (Ref 18), Henry Oxenden's narrative (Ref 3), and from some modern works (Ref 25, 30, 35, 45). The rationale for the coronation has been discussed in detail by Mehendale, Pagadi and Sarkar. Of all the reasons mentioned by the scholars, I feel a formal 'on paper' recognition of his fief as an independent kingdom, must have been foremost.

Whatever may have been the true reasons, Shivaji's coronation as an independent ruler with the title of *Chhatrapati,* was an event of tremendous significance not just for the Marathi people, but for all Indians. As Sabhasad writes in his chronicle, 'It was an event of no ordinary importance' (Ref 36). It is not possible to reliably state what may have been Aurangzeb's thoughts on the event, as Persian sources make no mention of the coronation. Sabhasad's dramatic description of Aurangzeb's laments on hearing of the coronation, may be exaggerated or even imaginary (Ref 36).

Jijabai's death at Pachad, is recorded in both the *Jedhe Chronicle* and the *Shivapur Chronicle* (Refs 16, 18).

Glossary

A listing of the Marathi, Hindi, Sanskrit, Urdu and Persian words with their approximate meanings in English

A

Aai: Marathi term for 'mother'

Abhiskek: Hindu offering to God in the form of a ceremonial ablution (eg: pouring water/milk over an idol or Shivling). Also used for a anointing ceremony performed on a King

Abhishekshala: A special hall to perform an '*abhishek*'

Agni: Fire God / fire

Aindrishanti: A ritual performed to Goddess Indrani

Alamgir: Siezer of the Universe

Alampanaah: Protector of the Universe

Allahu-Akbar: God is greatest

Amatya: Finance minister

Amavasya: New moon night

Ameen: Exclamatory expression meaning 'By the grace of God!' or 'God willing!'

Amir: Noble/*mansabdar* ranked higher than 1000 dhat (see below)

Amir-ul-Umrao: Amir of Amirs, a high title awarded to select nobles

Angarkha: Knee-length, full-sleeved coat

Asandi: Lord Indra's seat

Aukshavantha wha: Marathi blessing meaning 'Be long-lived'

Ayushyamaan bhava: Sanskrit blessing for longevity

B

Ba-adab ba-mulahizah hoshiyaar: *Ba-adab*: with respect, *ba-mulahizah:* stand facing, *hoshiyaar:* alert

Baba: Father

Badi Begum: Eldest wife

Badshah: Corruption of *Padishah*, which means 'Emperor'.

Bael: A plant, the leaves of which are offered to Lord Shiva

Baithak: A seat, traditionally made with matresses and cushions

Bala-i-qilla: Fortified citadel within a fort

Banjaras: Nomads, gypsies

Begum: Wife

Bhai/Bhaiji: Brother

Bhavani: A Hindu Goddess; the titular Goddess of the Bhosales. Shivaji's personal sword is also called 'Bhavani'

Bhumia: Landlord

Bhumipoojan: offering to mother earth, a ceremony performed before laying the foundation of a building

Brahman: One of the higher Hindu castes; traditionally, Brahman men worked as priests or in administerial positions in the medieval kingdoms of India

Burqa: a long, loose garment covering the whole body from head to feet, worn by Muslim women

Buruj: Bastion of a fort

C/D

Chaitra shuddha ashtami: Chaitra (lunar month corresponding to March 22nd to April 20th), shuddha ashtami (8th day of the waxing phase of the moon)

Chhatrapati: A title; literally means: Lord of the Royal Umbrella

Chhoti: Younger

Chitnis: Secretary of correspondence

Cowrie: A type of sea shell

Dabir: Minister for external affairs

Dakshina: Gift in cash or kind to a priest or teacher in lieu of services provided

Damdama: Raised wooden platform

Darwaza: Door

Deen: a war cry; means 'For our religion'. 'Deen' means 'religion' or 'faith' in Urdu

Desai: The head of a *pargana* (district).

Deshmukh: Hereditary Chieftain holding a fiefdom granted by the ruling monarch

Deshmukhi: A hereditary post; also used to refer to the fief itself

Deshpande: Hereditary post of Accountant and Records-Keeper, who worked under either the *Patil* of a village or the *Deshmukh* of the district

Devghar: Means 'House of God'; used to refer to the designated place of worship inside the home

Dhat: Arabic word which means 'person' or 'self', used to indicate a Mughal *mansabdar's* rank in the military hierarchy; the greater the number, the higher the rank; Mansabdars with ranks higher than 1000 dhat were called Amirs

Dharkari: A warrior, soldier with special training and special rank, superior to a common foot soldier

Dhoti: A long unstitched cloth draped around the lower body; ethnic Indian men's wear

Diva: Ritual lamp

Divan: Traditional sofa

Diwan: Chief administrative officer

Diwan-e-Aam: Hall of public audience; diwan meaning 'court/ office' and aam meaning 'common'

Diwan-e-Khaas: Hall of private audience; *khaas* means 'special', to denote the hall was for special diginitaries

Du-aspa sih-aspa: a number used to increase a *mansabdar's* (noble's) contingent without promoting him in rank

Durbar: Royal court; the grand hall of audience where the monarch conducted official matters of State

Dushela: A waistband made from a long and narrow piece of cloth; weapons like swords and daggers were stuck into it

Dwija varna: twice born caste.

F/G

Faqir: Sufi Muslim ascetic

Farzand: Son

Fauzdar: Administrative head of a district

Firangi: foreigner; a term used by the Marathas to refer mainly to the Portuguese

Firmaan: A royal communication from the ruling Muslim Emperor/ Sultan, with the monarch's seal/palm-thumb print; *fir* is pronounced 'fur' and *maan* has an extended 'a' as in 'bath'

Firmaanbadi: A tall open canopy erected for the purpose of a ceremony to hand over an imperial *firmaan*

Gajnal: Light cannon carried on and fired from elephant back

Ganeem: Urdu word for 'enemy'

Ganeshpooja: Ritual offering to Lord Ganesh

Ganga: One of the longest rivers in India, and considered the most holy; 'Ganges' in western literature

Ganimikawa: Guerilla warfare; from ganeem (enemy) and kawa ('crafty scheme' in Marathi)

Ghat: Mountain pass; Western Ghats is an alternative term for the Sahyadri mountain range

Ghatika: A unit of time, roughly twenty-four minutes

Ghee: Clarified butter

Ghusalkhana: Antechamber

Gondhali: A person belonging to a caste of singers and musicians who perform during the festival consecrated to the Goddess

Guz: A unit of length, still used in some parts of India; its exact length varied from region to region, but was roughtly equivalent to twenty-eight inches

H/I/J

Hakim: Urdu term for a doctor or physician

Haraamjadya: Abuse; means a bastard

Hasham: Urdu term for a foot soldier or servitor

Havaldar: An Adilshahi administrative officer of a Suba

Havan: Ritual burning of offerings in a fire

Havankund: A place to light a ritual fire

Hom / Homagni: Ritual fire used by Hindus

Hon: Gold coin used in medieval India

Hookah: An instrument used to smoke tobacco

Howdah: A carrier tied to the backs of elephants, meant for seating people

Hundi: A bill of exchange, similar to a cheque

Huzoor: A word used to address a superior officer with respect, similar to the usage of the word 'Sir'

Jagir: Fiefdom gifted by a sovereign, usually to a court noble

Jagirdar: Baron or Chieftain of a *jagir*, usually a court noble; overlord of all officers of the district, including the *Deshmukh*

Jahanpanah: One who gives shelter to the world

Jai: Victory; the cry Jai Bhavani means 'Victory to Bhavani'

Jali: A fenestrated screen behind which Muslim women sat to converse with men or observe proceedings

K

Kafir: Urdu term for non-believer; used by Muslims in medieval India to refer to the Hindus

Kala Buruj: Literally means 'Black bastion'

Kameena: Abuse; means rascal

Katyaar: A triangular bladed dagger with a peculiar grip

Kayastha: One of the higher Hindu castes

Khilat: Robes of honour gifted by a sovereign

Khind: Narrow pass between mountains

Killedar: Commander of a fort

Kos: An ancient unit used to measure distance; used in India for over 3000 years; a *kos* was 2.25 miles

Kothi: Building, house

Kotwal: Chief police officer of a village or district

Kshatriya: Sanskrit term meaning 'rule' or 'authority'; one of the four varnas (social strata) of ancient vedic Hindu society

Kshudra: One of the four varnas (social strata) of ancient vedic Hindu society (see *varna*)

Kulawatouns: The ornament of a tribe or a family

Kunwar: Prince

Kurnisaad: A form of salutation offered to a sovereign or one of high rank, usually by bowing low and bringing the right hand forward towards one's forehead

Kurta: Traditional Indian wear for the top half of the body

L/M

Lal Mahal: Literally means 'Red Palace'

Lota: A round metal tumbler used to store water or drink from

Machi: Marathi word for a level outcrop of land on a mountain

Mahabaleshwar: Maha means 'great' and Baleshwar is the name of a Hindu deity, a form of Lord Shiva

Mahadev: Name for Lord Shiva (literal meaning 'great God'), one of the holy trinity in Hinduism

Maharaj/Maharaja: A title, means 'Great King'

Mahout: Elephant handler

Malik-i-Maidan: 'Monarch of the Plains'

Mandap: Pavilion, porch, raised platform

Mansab: Arabic word meaning 'rank'; a military post at the Mughal court specified by the number of mounted soldiers the person was allowed to be maintain (ie: a 5000 or 10,000 mansab)

Mansabdar: A person (usually a court noble), holding a *mansab*

Mantra: A holy chant in homage of some Hindu God

Mantri: Minister; also used as a new term for the *'Waknis'*, who was the minister for Internal and external intelligence

Maund: A unit of weight; varies in different regions and different time periods (from twenty five to one hundred sixty pounds)

Mavala/Mavale: Inhabitants of the Maval region of the Sahyadris

Mehtar: Sweeper in Persian

Meherbaan: Kind

Mir Bakshi: High ranking military officer, in charge of nobility, intelligence and information agencies

Mirza: A high court title, awarded to select nobles

Mlechha: A term used in medieval India to refer to a non-Hindu and foreigner; someone not bound by the usual Hindu codes

Morchel: A brush made from peacock feathers to be waved over idols and Kings; a sign of royalty

Mubarik: Good wishes

Mukhya Pradhan: Prime Minister (same as '*Peshwa*')

Munshi: Secretary

Muzumdar: Finance Minister

N

Nagarkhana: The place near (usually above) the entrance to a palace or fort, from where the musicians would sound the horns and play the drums (*nagara*) on the arrival of dignitaries or during festivals or celebrations

Naik: General Marathi term meaning 'Chief' or 'Headman' of a body of men/soldiers/labourers, usually denoting *Deshmukhs*

Namaste / Namaskaar: The act of offering a salute or respectful greeting to another or to God, by joining the palms

Navagraha: Nine planets

Nishan: A sign or seal; used in the Muslim Sultanates/Empires of medieval India (especially the Mughal), to denote a letter or royal order from an imperial Prince

Nyayadheesh: Chief Justice

P

Padishah: Persian for Emperor/Sovereign, originally applied to the Shah of Iran and the Sultan of Turkey

Padishah-e-Gazi: Emperor who fights for his faith

Paithani: Beautiful silk saree made in Paithan, Maharashtra, with intricately embroidered gold or silver borders

Panchamrut: A preparation of cow's milk, yogurt, honey, sugar and ghee, used by Hindus as an offering to God

Pandit/ Pandita: A learned person

Pathan: Used to refer to Pashtun people, the largest ethnic group in Afghanistan and the second largest in Pakistan

Peshwa: Prime Minister; head of the Cabinet of Ministers

Peetha: Decorated seat

Pooja / poojan: Hindu worship rituals in which prayers and offerings are made to God

Powada: Marathi ballad composed and sung in a characteristic way

Prahar: A unit of time used in India from the Puranic Age; one prahar was approximately three hours

Pralay: Dissolution, annihilation

Prasad: Food offered first to God in Hindu religious rituals and later consumed by worshippers as a gift from God

Prataprao: A title; *Pratap* is 'act of bravery'; *Rao* is an honorific

Punditrao: Head of religious affairs

Punkah: Fan

Punt: A suffix denoting a person's administrative function; usually Brahman or Kayastha

Q/R

Quorchi: Personal attendant

Rai Baghan: An honorific meaning 'Royal Tigress'

Raja: King

Rajabhishek: An '*abhishek*' (anointment ceremony) performed on a '*Raja*' (King)

Rajabhishekprayog: Procedure for a '*Rajabhishek*'

Raje: Marathi word used to refer to a King or Chieftain; also used as a suffix after the name of a King/Prince, eg: Shivaji *Raje*

Rajgad: Means 'King of Forts' or alternatively 'the King's fort'

Ramzan: (Ramadan) Ninth month of the Islamic calender, observed as the month of fasting.

Rupee: Indian currency used since medieval times

S

Sabnis: Attendance Keeper of the troops; also Head Clerk in charge of paying the troops and government servants

Sadara: Ethnic Indian men's wear for the upper torso

Safed buruj: Literally means 'White bastion'

Sahib/a (Hindi)/*Saheb/a* (Marathi): Boss, employer, Sir, superior officer, respected person; also used as a respectful suffix, eg: Afzal Khan *sahib*

Saree: An unstitched length of cloth, 6 yards long (9 yards for Maharashtrian sarees), worn by Indian women in various ways

Sarjerao: A Marathi title/honorific meaning valiant or brave

Sar-o-pa: A robe of honour

Sanyasi: Hindu ascetic

Sapt Sindhu: The seven sacred rivers in Indian mythology

Sati: Ancient Hindu custom in which a widow would self-immolate on the burning pyre of her husband

Sawar: Literally 'mounted person/soldier', hence a cavalryman. The sawar number indicated the rank of a military officer, specifying the number of mounted soldiers under his command, eg: 5000 sawar

Senapati: From *sena* (Army) and *pati* (Lord); Commander-in-Chief of the armed forces

Ser: A unit of weight; slightly less than a kilogram

Serai: A halting place/tavern for travellers

Shamiana: A pavilion; a grand tent usually built for a military Commander, a Prince, or a person of consequence

Shastras: Sacred Hindu scriptures

Shawl: A woollen drape worn by both men and women

Shehzaada: Prince

Shiledar: A mounted soldier who possessed his own mounts and weapons, usually having better military training than a common foot soldier; as opposed to a *bargir*, a soldier provided with a mount and weapons by the state

Shinga: A wind instrument shaped like a large horn

Shivling: Symbolic representation of Lord Shiva in stone

Shuturnal: Light cannon, carried on and fired from camel back

Sijda: The act of offering obeisance by kneeling and touching the forehead to the ground

Sinhasanadheeshwar: One who sits on a throne

Sinhasanarohan: The act of ascending the throne

Sirdeshmukhi: Additional tax levied on districts already taxed

Sirnaubat: Literally 'Master of the Drum' or Commander-in-Chief of the armed forces

Snana: Bath

Suba: An administrative district

Subadar: The presiding officer of a suba, appointed by the sovereign and supreme in his suba but for the Emperor

Subedar: This Marathi term was distinct from *Subadar* and denoted a captain in the Maratha army, with a platoon under his command

Subhan Allah: Meaning 'Allah is pure' or 'Allah is great', in Urdu; also used as an exclamation like 'Wow!' or 'Great!'

Sultan dhawa: A sudden attack by concentrating all forces at hand

Sumant: Minister for external affairs (same as *Dabir*)

Surma bahaddar: Brave person

Surnis: Minister for land revenue

Suvarnatula: A ceremony in which one (usually a King or sovereign) is weighed against gold

Swarajya: 'Self-ruled state'; in the context of Shivaji's struggle, the term Swarajya meant a state ruled by a son of the soil; here, self-rule should not be confused with democracy

T/U

Takhliya: Solitude; used as a command by Sovereigns when they wanted to be left alone

Takhta firosh: One who takes care of the royal throne

Tathastu: A blessing which means 'So be it'

Teen Darwaza: 'Three Doors'

Thali: A large metal plate used to serve/eat food, or carry items

Tilak: A prominent mark on the forehead, made with either vermillion or coloured powder/paste

Tula: The act of weighing or comparing

Tuladan: Weighing one (usually a King), against gold and other material and then donating the same

Tulapurushadan: Ritual of donating a gold idol of Lord Vishnu

Umrao: High ranking noble

Umr darraz rahe: May you live long

Upanayana: Traditional Hindu ritual (Thread ceremony) which starts a boy's education

Uparna: A long folded cloth worn over the shoulder

V/W

Vaishya: One of the four *'varnas'* (social strata) of ancient vedic Hindu society (see *'varna'*)

Varna: Ancient Indian Vedic society was divided into four divisions called *'varna'*. The *Brahmans* were the priests, teachers and preachers; the *Kshatriyas* were the soldiers, warriors, governors and rulers; the *Vaishyas* were the herders, agriculturists, businessmen, merchants and artisans; the *Kshudras* were the labourers and service providers. Each *varna* was further sub-divided into sub-castes.

Vedas/vedashastras: Ancient Indian (Hindu) scriptures in Sanskrit

Vijay aso: A cry/slogan which means 'Victory to him/her'

Vizier: The Prime Minister at the court of a Muslim Sultan; the most powerful person after the Sultan himself; would often be Regent after the Sultan's death

Waknis: Minister for internal and external intelligence

Watan: Arabic term, literally means 'homeland/ motherland'. In the context of 16th-17th century Maharashtra, the term denoted the hereditary office or post granted by the Sultan (Patil, Deshpande, Deshmukh, Kulkarni, Havaldar, Killedar etc) and held by a person; these offices were often passed to son/s on the demise of the original awardee, unless the Sultan/Emperor decided to cancel or confiscate the *watan*

Wazir: Head of revenue department in Mughal Empire; usually the highest ranking officer at court (similar to a Prime Minister)

Y/Z

Yavans: A term used in medieval India to refer to a non-Hindu and foreigner; someone not bound by the usual Hindu codes

Zamindar: Landlord

Zenana: Literally 'of the women' or 'pertaining to women' in Urdu; used to denote the inner apartments where the ladies resided (as opposed to the outer apartments or mardana, for the males and guests); also used in medieval society to refer to the ladies of the principal male of a Muslim family

Bibliography

1. Ahmed, Laiq. The Prime Ministers of Aurangzib (A Thesis submitted for the Degree of Doctor of Philosophy): History Department, University of Allahabad 1971.
2. Amatya, Ramchandrapant. Ed. Kulkarni, Dr. A.R. Ajnapatra (Modi-Marathi-English): Diamond Publication 2007.
3. Anon. English Records on Shivaji: Shiva Charitra Karyalaya 1931.
4. Bal Krishna. Shivaji the Great (Vol I, Parts I & II): D.B. Taraporevala Sons & Co. 1932.
5. Bernier, Francois. Ed: Smith, Vincent A. Translated by Archibald Constable. Travels in the Mogul Empire, AD 1656-1668: Low Price Publications 1994.
6. Chile, Bhagwan. Famous Forts in Maharshtra: Shiva Sparsh Prakashan 2011.
7. Chitnis, Malhar Ramrao. Ed: R.V. Herwadkar. Shri Shiva Chhatrapatinche Saptaprakarnatmak Charitra (Marathi): Venus Prakashan 2000.
8. Cooper, Randolf G.S. The Anglo-Maratha Campaigns and the Contest for India: The Press Syndicate of the University of Cambridge 2003.
9. Cousens, Henry. Bijapur - The Old Capital of the Adil Shahi Kings (A guide to its ruins with historical outline): Archeological Survey of Western India 1889.
10. Eaton, Richard M. Temple Desecration in Pre-Modern India (Article): Frontline Dec 22, 2000.
11. Eaton, Richard M. Temple Desecration and Indo-Muslim States (Article): Frontline Dec 23, 2000.
12. Eds: Apte, D.V. Divekar, S.M. Shiva Charitra Pradip (Marathi): Bharat Itihas Samshodhak Mandal 1931.
13. Ed: Bendrey, V.S. Coronation of Shivaji the Great (Gagabhatt Krut: Shri Shiva Rajyabhishek Prayog): Jayant S. Bhatt, P.P.H. Book Stall 1960.
14. Ed: Foster William. The Embassy of Sir Thomas Roe to the Court of the Great Mogul 1615-1619 (As narrated in his Journal and Correspondence): Hakluyt Society London 1899.

15. Eds: Khare, G.H., Kulkarni, Govind Tryambak. Aitihasik Farsi Sahitya: Aurangzebchya Durbarche Akhbar (Persian Original with Marathi Translation): Bharat Itihas Samshodhak Mandal 1976.
16. Ed: Kulkarni, Dr. A.R. Jedhe Shakavali-Karina: Diamond Publication 2007.
17. Eds: Majumdar, R.C. Chaudhari, J.N. Chaudhari, S. The History and Culture of the Indian People: The Mughul Empire. Bharatiya Vidya Bhavan 2007.
18. Ed: Sovani, Avinash. Aitihasik Shakavalya (Marathi): Shabdavedh Prakashan 1998.
19. Ed: V.G. Khobrekar. English translation of Tarikh-i-Dilkasha (Memoirs of Bhimsen relating to Aurangzib's Deccan Campaigns): Government of India 1972.
20. Eraly, Abraham. Emperors of the Peacock Throne: Penguin Books 1997.
21. Eraly, Abraham. The Mughal World: Penguin Books 2007.
22. Gribble, J.D.B. The History of the Deccan Vol I & II, Rupa and Co 2002.
23. Kincaid, Dennis. Shivaji The Grand Rebel (An Impression of Shivaji. Founder of Maratha Empire): Rupa Publications India Pvt. Ltd. 2015.
24. Manucci, Niccolao. Translated by Irvine, William. Storia Do Mogor or Mogul India. John Murray for the Govt. Of India 1907.
25. Mehendale, Gajanan Bhaskar. Shivaji: His Life and Times: Param Mitra Publications 2011.
26. Mehendale, Gajanan Bhaskar. Shri Raja Shiv Chhatrapati Parts I & II (Marathi): Diamond Publications 1999.
27. Mehendale, Gajanan Bhaskar and Shintre Santosh. Shiva Chhatrapatinche Armaar (Marathi): Param Mitra Publication 2010.
28. NCERT. Themes in Indian History Part II: NCERT 2007.
29. Oak, P.N. Agra Red Fort is a Hindu Building: Hindi Sahitya Sadan 2000.
30. Pagadi, Setumadhavrao. Chhatrapati Shivaji: Continental Prakashan 2014.
31. Palsokar, Col. R.D. Shivaji the Great Guerilla: Nataraj Publishers 2003.
32. Parmanand, Kavindra. Ed: Sadashiv Mahadev Divekar. Shri Shivbharat (Sanskrit original, Marathi translation): Shabdavedh Prakashan 1998.
33. Pissurlencar, P.S. Translated from Marathi by Parvate, T.V. Portuguese-Mahratta Relations. Maharashtra State Board for Literature and Culture 1983.

34. Pindye Jayram. Translation by Desai, Rajaram Damodar. Parnal-Parvat-Grahanakhyam (Sanskrit text with Marathi translation): Sadashiv Mahadev Divekar 1923.
35. Purandare, Babasaheb. Raja Shiv Chhatrapati (Marathi): Purandare Prakashan 2008.
36. Sabhasad, Krishnaji Anant. Ed: Dr. Y.M. Pathan. Sabhasad Bakhar (Marathi): Snehvardhan Publishing House 2007.
37. Samant, Dr. Shrinivas. Vedh Mahamanavacha (Marathi): Deshmukh and Co. 2012.
38. Sarkar, Sir Jadunath. Anecdotes of Aurangzib (English translation of Akham-i-Alamgiri with A life of Aurangzib and historical notes): M.C. Sarkar and Sons 1949.
39. Sarkar, Sir Jadunath. History of Aurangzib Vol III: M.C. Sarkar and Sons 1921.
40. Sarkar, Sir Jadunath. History of Aurangzib Vol IV: M.C. Sarkar and Sons 1930.
41. Sarkar, Sir Jadunath. History of Aurangzib Vol V: M.C. Sarkar and Sons 1924.
42. Sarkar, Sir Jadunath. House of Shivaji: S.N. Sarkar 1940.
43. Sarkar, Sir Jadunath. Maasir-i-Alamgiri (A History of the Emperor Aurangzib-Alamgir by Saqi Mustaid Khan translated into English and annotated): Royal Asiatic Society of Bengal 1942.
44. Sarkar, Sir Jadunath, Sinh Raghubir. Rajasthani records: Shivaji's visit to Aurangzib at Agra (A Collection of Contemporary Rajasthani Letters from the Jaipur State Archives): Dr. S.P. Sen, Department of History, University of Calcutta 1963.
45. Sarkar, Sir Jadunath. Shivaji and His Times: Orient Longman 1973.
46. Sen, Surendra Nath. Foreign Biographies of Shivaji (Extracts and Documents relating to Maratha History Vol II): Kegan Paul Trench Trubner & Co. Ltd.
47. Sen, Surendranath. Siva Chhatrapati (Extracts and Documents relating to Maratha History Vol I): University of Calcutta 1920.
48. Shivde Sadashiv. Jwaljwalantejas Sambhaji Raja (Marathi): Diamond Publications 2001.
49. Truschke, Audrey. Aurangzeb: The Man and the Myth: Penguin Random House 2017.
50. Vakeniwis, Dattaji Trimal. Ed: V.S. Vakaskar. Shri Shiva Chhatrapatinchi 91 Kalmi Bakhar (Marathi): Venus Prakashan 1962.

Acknowledgements

I wish to thank the people who have continued to help me in my journey. My family comes first: my wife Dipali, my children Aditya and Aryaa, my mother Vijaya, elder sister Meera, niece Nupur, in-laws Anil and Neela Gupte... they continue to be my strongest pillars of support.

I am ever grateful to Leadstart Publishing Pvt. Ltd. for continuing their association with me, and publishing the second book in the series.

Senior historian Shri Gajanan B. Mehendale continues to be my guide and I extend my heartfelt gratitude to him. I could never thank him enough for the help he has given me in the past few years. Suffice it to say that my books would not have materialised without him.

I must also thank my friends and family, who have encouraged and helped me, offering invaluable advice and criticism that helped me improve my work.

Finally, I must make special mention of the chief inspirations behind my work:

Shri Babasaheb Purandare, through his numerous books and lectures.

Shri Ranjit Desai through his book, *Shrimaan Yogi,* a dramatized novel on *Chhatrapati* Shivaji in Marathi.

Alex Rutherford, through his historical fiction series, *Empire of the Moghul*. I must also thank Alex for reading a chapter of my book and sending me an encouraging mail.

The Marathi teleserial, *Raja Shiva Chhatrapati,* produced by Chandrakant Productions Pvt. Ltd and aired on the Star Pravah channel on TV.

300 BRAVE MEN

BOOK I: 1641—1660

The incredible story of *Chhatrapati* Shivaji *Raje* Bhosale, legendary warrior-king, guerrilla fighter, brilliant tactician and clever diplomat. But above all, a remarkable human being.

The Indian sub-continent is ruled by three tyrannical Sultanates – the powerful Mughals in the North, and the Shia Adilshah and Qutubshah in the South. The very idea of freedom has been wiped from the minds of the native population, suppressed for centuries. As incessant battles rage between the Sultanates, Maharashtra, once a prosperous and peaceful land, has been reduced to a wasteland.

In this dark era, the sixteen-year-old son of an Adilshahi *jagirdar* rises up to declare: *I shall not serve, and neither shall my people*! With the dream of a free State and an identity for his people burning in his heart, he dares to rebel against the powerful Sultan, Adilshah. He begins with nothing...no army, no weapons and an empty treasury. Yet he achieves what no soldier, chieftain or king has ever achieved in defiance of imperial rulers.